NONE SO BLIND

NONE SO BLIND

Alis Hawkins

THE
DOME
PRESS

Published by The Dome Press, 2018

Map of Teifi Valley by Meredith Lloyd James

A CIP catalogue record for this book is available from the British Library

ISBN 9781912534036

The Dome Press
23 Cecil Court
London WC2N 4EZ

www.thedomepress.com

Printed and bound in Great Britain by Clays Ltd, Elcograf S.p.A.

Typeset in Garamond by Elaine Sharples

MIX
Paper from
responsible sources
FSC
www.fsc.org
FSC® C110794

For my mum and dad
with much love

Contents

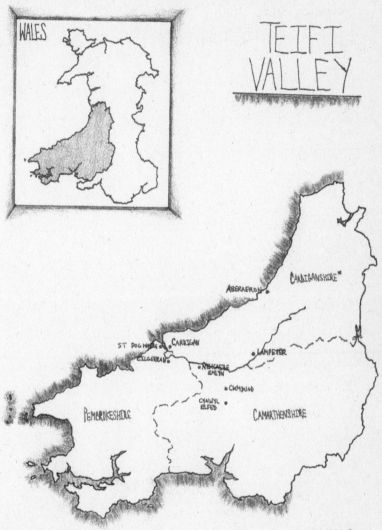

WALES

TEIFI VALLEY

CARDIGANSHIRE *

ABERAERON

ST DOG MAELS • CARDIGAN
CILGERRAN •
• LAMPETER
• NEWCASTLE
EMLYN
• CWMDUAD

CYNWYL
ELFED •

PEMBROKESHIRE

CAMARTHENSHIRE

* NOW CEREDIGION

A brief historical note on law and order in nineteenth-century West Wales

Police forces

Home Secretary, Sir Robert Peel, established the Metropolitan Police Force in 1829. Typically, the rest of the country lagged behind the capital in taking up new ideas and it wasn't until a decade later that the County Police Act was passed enabling provincial forces to be established. Somewhat surprisingly, Cardiganshire and Carmarthenshire were relatively early adopters, Carmarthenshire establishing its force in 1843, and Cardiganshire in 1844. Of the three counties which comprise the Teifi Valley, only Pembrokeshire waited until the 1856 County and Borough Police Act made establishing a police force compulsory.

These early police forces did not have the same remit for detective work that today's police have; Peel's principles of policing made it quite clear that their role was far more as keepers of the peace than as investigators. The purpose of the county constabularies was to prevent crime as much as possible by keeping undesirables off the streets and to suppress public disorder swiftly and effectively. It's quite clear why Cardiganshire and Carmarthenshire were keen to establish police forces: the Rebecca Riots (1839 and 1842-3) which feature as the backdrop to *None So Blind*, probably represent the most concerted campaign of civil disobedience and public disturbances that Wales has ever seen.

Rural police officers were appointed by county magistrates (also known, tellingly, as Justices of the Peace) and police forces were, effectively, at the disposal of these local politicians. In *None So Blind* the police force is conspicuous by its absence as no senior officer would have dreamed of going against the wishes of the local Justices. Even had the bench of magistrates not made its feelings known, however, no police force in 1850 would have seen it as its business to investigate the discovery of unidentified bones.

Coroners and inquests

Until 1888, county coroners were elected by male property freeholders. As they were unpaid until 1860, it was essential that coroners had an independent income which meant that they came from the professional or landed classes. Unlike modern coroners who must hold legal or medical qualifications, there were no such requirements in the 1850s.

Nineteenth-century inquests were conducted by a coroner and a jury of at least twelve and no more than twenty-four men. Jurymen were required to view the body as soon after death as practicable in order to see its condition, assess the seriousness of any visible injuries and to form an opinion as to cause of death. This viewing, along with evidence heard during the inquest, formed the basis of the jury's verdict which had to be agreed by at least twelve of its members. Though the coroner could offer guidance, as we see in *None So Blind*, juries were not obliged to heed it.

Glossary of Welsh terms

Ceffyl pren: wooden horse

Gwyn (as in Harry Gwyn): white or fair

Betgwn: the outer garment of most Cardiganshire working women in the nineteenth century. It featured a tight, low-cut bodice, worn over a blouse, with a long back, sometimes gathered up into a 'tail', worn over petticoats and an apron.

Plwyfwas: literally 'parish servant'. The English equivalent might be 'beadle'.

Clom: a building material comprising clay, straw, subsoil and small stones. Considered superior to turf but inferior to stone.

Prynhawn da, boneddigion: Good afternoon, gentlemen

Gwas bach: literally 'little servant'. A term reserved for the youngest or most junior servants

Siment: a crushed-stone-based floor surface

Crachach: gentry or upper classes.

Prologue

You know the one thing I wish about that night?

I wish I'd seen my father.

I just wish I'd known – without so much as a scholar's doubt – that he was there. Because all through the weeks and months afterwards – all through watching that girl die in the rain and being terrified that I'd be next if I said a word – the thought that Dada was one of them made it all right.

If Dada was part of it, it had to be.

Mind, that's not what I thought when I first saw them. Didn't think much, to be honest, just felt a half-terrified excitement go through me – you know, that scalding thrill that makes you scared you're going to piss yourself.

Shots'd slapped me awake. Ear-clapping powder shots. And the smell of smoke. And noise.

I was halfway towards the loft ladder before I was properly awake. Heart hammering, breath catching in my throat.

Fire!

Scrabbling, hands and knees over the hay – get out, *get out!*

But then sense caught up. Fire didn't make that noise.

I stopped. Listened. Moved back, towards the window. Footsteps. That's what the noise was. Footsteps outside.

I didn't have to lift the shutter, it was warped enough to see around. And there was my fire, going by on the road down below. Rag-and-pitch torches. The reek of them was black and tarry in the freezing air.

I watched the lights bob down the road and my heart followed the clump and clack of boots and clogs on the wet road. Men marching. Not just walking by, like they'd have done if it'd just been one or two of them. Marching.

Clump, clump, clack, clack. They weren't in perfect time. They were a bit ragged, as if they could see themselves doing it and thought – *look at us, marching like soldiers!* But still, marching they were.

I pulled the shutter further open and stared down. Their faces were black and gold in the flames and the smoke from their torches hung in the air after they'd walked by, as if it was trying to hide them.

Dozens of men, there were. Maybe a hundred. Not easy to count a mob in the dark, even with a bright moon.

I pulled the shutter right up so I could see down the road to the tollgate. And that's when the piss-pressing excitement grabbed hold of me. *It was happening.* Here. In front of my eyes. Because there he was, on a tall horse, huge in the moonlight. Sitting there, his face so black he almost disappeared clear into the night. Only the white nightgown on him showed he was there.

Rebecca!

My father'd been wishing The Lady here for months. *Rebecca from Efailwen*, he'd said. *That's who we need.*

But wishful thinking was all it'd been. He hadn't really, honestly thought she'd come. Not in the flesh. Not for us.

I shivered. Needed my blanket, now I wasn't going to be burned to death.

All that last summer the newspaper at chapel'd been full of a new word. *Unrest.* The paper'd gone from hand to hand between service and Sunday school until the print was just dark grey smudges. Men who could read recited the words to those who couldn't. And we'd listened, us boys. Quiet for once, pretending we weren't there. Listened with our ears out on stalks. Working men were taking up weapons in England and walking away from manufacturing machines. The militia was putting down Chartism – whatever kind of violence that was – in Merthyr Tydfil. In our *own country!* Workers were trying to force a bit of fairness for themselves and their families.

Unrest.

Then, after the newspapers, it was the Bible. And we listened again. More than we'd ever listened to scripture before. Suddenly, it was speaking to us, the way the minister'd always said it would, one day. Only we'd never believed him.

They that be slain with the sword are better than they that be slain with hunger. That was the one we kept saying to each other. Hunger wasn't killing us yet, but we knew it was crouching nearby, teeth bared. We'd heard our fathers dreading it. And we wanted to fight. *They that be slain by the sword...* of course, we turned that round. In our minds, it'd be us with a sword in our hand. We'd be the ones doing the slaying, thank you very much.

And it wasn't just us boys, either. We watched the men looking at each other from under their eyebrows. Nodding and muttering. Finding words to give voice to a defiance that didn't sit easily with them. *We're men, not cattle. If it's one or the other, better to die with a sword in your hand, isn't it, than with the cramps of hunger in your belly? Got to do something, haven't we?*

We'd thought it was just words. When had we ever seen our fathers lift a finger against their betters? Never. *We'd* do something when we were men, of course we would. But not our fathers. Not the men who touched their caps and scraped up their bits of English for the squires and their stewards. Not our fathers who paid over every ancient farthing in the house for rents and rates and tolls and got nothing but tired, bony land in return.

But then Rebecca'd come down from the hills and it wasn't just words any more.

And now the Lady was here. Not up in the Preselis. Not in gossip and tales. Here, right in front of me.

Was my father in the crowd? The other men from our chapel? I strained the marchers with my eyes but black faces were all I could see. Was he there? I looked and looked but I couldn't see him. Couldn't see anybody I recognised, not for definite. Every man-jack I knew in the world might've been there and I couldn't've put a name to one of them. I stared as hard as I could but even moonlight and firelight added together couldn't show me what I wanted to see. My father with a sword in his hand.

Truth to tell, I couldn't see many real weapons. Everyday tools, the men had. Axes, hammers, saws, billhooks. Heavy, sharp tools for hacking and smashing.

I shivered. My teeth were chattering from excitement and cold.

Heads and shoulders were still going by beneath me. They were as noisy as you like, didn't care who heard them. Shouting, laughing. Even singing a bit of a hymn. And all of it had a shrill edge to it. It wasn't everyday laughing and singing and shouting – it was like that moment in an argument when words suddenly turn weak on you and fists finish things.

Some of the men had nightgowns on, like Rebecca. But most just had an apron or a shawl. There was the odd tall Sunday hat but not many. I didn't bother looking under the hats for Dada. My mother'd never lend him her best hat to go gatebreaking, I knew that for a certainty. She'd be afraid of never getting it back.

I raked my eyes through the crowd pushing up to the tollgate. Was he here? We were half an hour's walk from home and that was nothing to Dada. He'd walk that far to give you an egg.

He was desperate enough to risk the militia and come here, I knew that.

He'd told me straight – we didn't have the money for lime-tolls in the spring. And if we couldn't spread lime, our land wouldn't yield. Caught in the old farmers' trap, weren't we? Penniless now if we did pay out, penniless later if we didn't. That was why Dada'd hired me out. If Uncle Price fed and clothed me for a year, Dada could put lime on our ground. If I stayed home, he couldn't.

I wiped a nose-drip with the side of my finger and pulled the blanket up around me. Was Uncle Price watching from the inn next door? Or was he snoring after the skinful he'd had with the farmer he'd come to buy a bull from? I didn't care. He'd brought me with him and I was going to see Rebecca.

The air bit at my nose and cheeks. Stragglers hurried not to be last at the tollgate. Bootnail sparks came off the road in the dark with the haste of them.

A sudden bang made me jump so hard my teeth rattled. A powder shot like the one that'd woken me up. Then another bang came and I saw an axe handle beating against the tollhouse door.

The man holding the axe was shouting. 'Out. Get out here, now!' Bang, bang, bang.

The gatekeeper came out quick enough. Quicker than I'd've come for a mob. Passed himself round the edge of the door and shut it behind him, as if he was just keeping the cold out.

Shouting turned to jeering, then, and a big man in a shawl stepped forward and started pushing him. Perhaps he was crooked, the gatekeeper – took more than the proper toll off people who couldn't read the notices.

I pulled the blanket up round my face. The cold was making my face bones ache.

The big man was still going at the gatekeeper. Pushing him with the haft of his axe. Holding it at both ends, like a staff.

Push, push.

The keeper stumbled backwards and went down.

There was some ragged cheering and my heart started banging at my ribs again. What was going to happen now? Crooked or not, I didn't want them to kill him.

No. That wouldn't happen. Beca didn't kill people. It was the gate they'd come for. And maybe the tollhouse as well. Easy enough to put a gate back up, isn't it? Not so easy to get a gatekeeper to stay and take tolls if he's got no house.

A sound came from somewhere to my right. I whipped round and hit my head on the window frame.

I tried to rub the pain away, staring and staring back up the road until my eyes burned and I could see a thousand pinpricks in the dark. But there was nobody there. Nothing.

Then a latch clicked shut on the street below. It must've been a door opening I'd heard. Somebody wanting a look.

I turned back. The gatekeeper had an axe in his hands now and the crowd were shouting and jostling. 'Break it' a voice shouted. 'Break it!'

Then they were all shouting: *Break it! Break it!*

The gatekeeper didn't move. My heart was thumping against my ribs. *Break it,* I wanted to shout. Don't make them beat you into it.

I stared into the crowd, desperate to see my father. He wouldn't let anything bad happen. The gatekeeper might get a hiding but my father wouldn't let them kill him.

Black face after black face I looked at, and any one of fifty of them might've been him. *Dada, are you there?*

Break it, break it!

A man in a tall hat stepped forward and pushed the gatekeeper towards the gate.

Break it, break it!

Whatever was holding the gatekeeper back suddenly gave way. He turned, swung the axe over his head and brought it down, hard, on the top bar of the gate. Must've jarred every inch of him from fingernails to backbone.

Something like a cheer went up, then, and filled the night. A terrible, savage sound it was – full of hate and fear and triumph and bloodlust. Made me shake at the thought of what might happen next. The mob rushed forwards like weaners at a trough, pushing and shoving, all wanting to be at the front. I couldn't see the gate or the keeper any more, only axes and hammers swinging.

The sound of it was tremendous, even from fifty yards away. Like a whole wood being cut down. A hundred axes biting into a hundred trees. Bits of gate splintering and getting thrown onto the road. A hollow, ringing sound. Good, solid timber on frost-hard ground.

Two men were standing, one on each side of the gate, holding all the torches. Two or three in each hand, they had, and the flames were running together, like bonfires that've caught at the trash, twisting in the cold air, pitch smoke pouring up into the black sky. But the night bore down on them and all the flames lit up were the soot-blacked faces of those two men.

When the smashing was finished, the Rebeccas gathered the splintered wood into a pile and pushed the torches into the middle of it, one by one. Stabbed the flames in as deep as they'd go.

I thought Rebecca'd stay till the end. Till the gate'd burned to ash. But he didn't. As soon as the flames were high enough and hot enough to stop anybody trying to kick them out, he turned his horse and walked it back through the middle of them. And every man turned and fell into step behind him.

Within a minute there was nobody watching the gate burn but its keeper. Rebecca was gone. And so was my last chance to see my father.

I never saw him again. In less than two months, he was dead.

And, the next time I had anything to do with the Lady, it would damn' nearly kill me, too.

PART 1: DISCOVERY

Harry

Cardiganshire, November 1850

There is never a convenient moment to discover that you are going progressively blind. I think I can say that without fear of intelligent contradiction. But life has an odd way of evening things up. If my sight had permitted me to continue harassing witnesses in the dock for a living, I would not have been at my father's house on the day Ianto Harris came banging on the door and the course of my life would have been utterly different.

Moments before the door-hammering demanded our attention, I had been introducing my friend Gus to the antique delights of shuffleboard. And he, not entirely unpredictably, had been mocking my enthusiasm.

'Honestly P-L, is this what you've been bleating about? This pastime for rustics? I mean to say, shoving a filed-off ha' penny down a table?'

I fixed him in my peripheral vision. 'What did you expect from a game called shuffleboard?'

'I expected it to be a name, not an exact description of the whole enterprise!' He turned his head to the door. 'Dear God what is that battering? No, don't tell me – it's a horde of natives eager to shuffle your ancient coinage.'

I ignored him and moved towards the library door which stood slightly ajar. A housemaid's footsteps scurried across the entrance hall, indoor shoes pattering on the tiles. Then I heard another, more measured, set of footsteps and the brook-no-argument tones of our butler.

'I'm aware of the commotion, Ann. Go about your business.'

I knew I should allow Moyle to deal with whoever was standing on the doorstep but, with the front door now open, I could hear the heavy-fisted messenger stumbling over the English phrases he had been forced into and I knew exactly what expression the butler would have on his face while he failed to help the poor man.

'Won't be a moment, Gus.'

I pulled the door fully open and stepped into the hall, leaving my friend a clearer view of the man on the threshold than I had. 'Is there some difficulty, Moyle?'

The butler half-turned, as if he was trying to keep one mistrustful eye on the visitor. 'This… person… wishes to see Mr Probert-Lloyd. At least, I think that's what he's trying to say.'

I moved towards the doorway and addressed the visitor in his own language. Moyle would not like it but that could not be helped. 'Mr Probert-Lloyd is sitting in the magistrates' court today. He won't be back until tomorrow.'

The figure on the doorstep raised a forearm to blot the sweat from his face, as if my speaking Welsh had given him permission to behave like a man.

'I've come from Waungilfach,' he began, as fluent now as he had been halting in English, 'Mr William Williams's place along by the—'

I held up a hand to stop him, hoping that he had seen no change in my face when he mentioned the name of the farm. 'I know it. Why has Mr Williams sent you?'

'We were cutting an old fallen tree in the Alltddu – me and Dai Penlan, we work for Mr Williams – and when we pulled the roots out – mind, to be honest, we weren't supposed to do that, Mr Williams said to leave the roots where they were because—'

Dear God, we would be here till Sunday if I allowed him to carry on. 'What's your name, friend?'

'Ianto. John. John Harris.'

John, his baptismal name, the name I would use if I appeared for him in court, or wrote him a contract; the English name nobody ever addressed him by. 'Right, Ianto. Tell me what happened when you pulled the roots out.'

His hat-twisting hands dropped to his sides. He had probably been sent to Glanteifi with no more than a 'Go and ask Mr Probert-Lloyd to come.' I was the wrong Mr Probert-Lloyd but I was making myself available, so I would have to do.

'We found somebody buried. That is, bones. We found bones.' Somebody buried. At Waungilfach. The news was like a kick in the stomach.

Gus's curiosity was palpable as we stood in the stableyard waiting for the horses. Only his wariness of listening ears was saving me from an interrogation. Having told him that human remains had been found, I had avoided any questions he might have asked by fleeing upstairs, ostensibly to change but, in actual fact, to quell the shaking that had taken hold of me.

Bones confirmed what I had always feared. She was dead. But *buried?*

Buried implied a second party. It implied – no, surely it was *evidence* of – murder.

A stable boy led the horses out and held them while we mounted up. 'How far is it?' Gus asked, nodding to the boy and taking up the reins.

'Five minutes or so.' In fact, had we set out to walk instead of changing and waiting for the horses, we would almost have been there by now. But it would not have done to arrive on foot. Williams of Waungilfach would have felt slighted and it was altogether too soon to allow my father to begin finding fault with me.

In two minutes we were trotting through the gates at the end of the drive. I urged my little mare up the hill towards Treforgan and we passed the hamlet's open-fronted forge, made our way down the steep little hill past the silent, weekday chapel and the mill with its rhythmically thumping wheel, and found ourselves on the edge of the river meadows where the flat pasture was bounded by the wooded slope of the Alltddu.

Eyes averted so as to give me an impression of the path ahead, I was aware of the stiff, leafless cages of last summer's brambles lining the edge of the path and my mind's eye conjured up memories of an exuberance of black-spattered bushes rambling up the slope. Blackberries and wild strawberries and damsons – we had picked them all. My mouth puckered at the memory of the sharp sweetness of those damsons, those days.

A sudden greeting snatched me back to the present. 'Henry Probert-Lloyd!'

William Williams. The sound of his voice brought a slew of unpleasant recollections and I fought down an old anger.

'Good day to you, Mr Williams.' I dismounted and found my reins being taken by Ianto Harris.

'I barely recognised you,' Williams sounded somewhat resentful. 'You look quite different!'

My hand rose involuntarily to my beard; even I was not used to it, yet, but its novelty did not excuse his tone. I gave what I hoped was a sufficiently forced smile to act as a dignified rebuke and proceeded to introduce Gus before clarifying why I had come instead of my father.

'Yes, I see,' Williams said. 'It's good of you to come yourself, of course, but I think I would rather wait until your father can attend to this himself.'

I stiffened. I might have been little more than a boy the last time Williams and I had had dealings with each other but I was a barrister now and more than competent to deputise for a magistrate.

'Is it not,' I suggested, 'simply a case of confirming that these remains are human and sending for the coroner?' Both of which Williams might have done already, had he not been so afraid of being seen to overreach himself.

'Your father is a county magistrate—'

'That's hardly a necessary qualification, surely?'

'No but, I think we should wait—'

'And I am quite sure that he would wish us to act like sensible men' – let him take that as a compliment if he felt so inclined – 'and deal with this ourselves.'

Unable to look Williams in the eye and utterly unwilling to tell him why, I turned my head towards the wooded slope beside us. She was up there. That was where she had been for the last seven years. Despite all my desperate hopes and wild imaginings, she had been here all along. Dead, as I had feared. But murder... I had not, for a second, entertained that thought.

'Now that the remains have been exposed,' I said, cutting across some vague further protestation, 'we cannot leave them to be dispersed by scavengers. They must be exhumed to await due process.' Let him put that bit of legalism into his pipe and smoke it.

7

I started up the wooded slope and was relieved to hear not only Gus but Williams following. Excellent. First round to me.

The steep bank was treacherous with rotting leaves and badger scrapes and we slipped more than once on the way up. My pulse was racing but I chose to see that as the result of unaccustomed exertion and ignored the churning in my stomach.

After a minute or two of panting, bank gave way abruptly to beaten track. No wider than a sheep path, I remembered it as a shortcut from Williams's farmyard to the edge of the hamlet. My feet knew this path and memories seemed to pass directly from the soles of my boots to my mind's eye, memories of walking this way almost daily in that summer between boyhood and manhood. The summer when I had first felt the terrible doubts and delirium of love.

Further up the slope, I could just make out the figure of a man sitting on the ground, half obscured by the confusion of branches and twigs that pushed down the slope from the crown of the fallen tree. Dai Penlan, the second root-digger, I assumed.

I turned to Williams who was labouring up behind us. 'When exactly did this tree fall down, can you remember?'

'Four, five years ago, maybe?'

I was sure he was wrong. She had disappeared seven years ago.

As I scrambled up to where he sat, Dai Penlan got to his feet and pulled his hat off his head. I nodded a greeting and walked around the upended roots to the pile of disturbed earth.

'Can you see?' Gus murmured, at my side.

'Enough.' I knelt on the damp ground. In truth, my remaining sight was inadequate to identify what I was looking at and, without forewarning, I would have dismissed the pale shape at the edge of my vision as a rock. Only because I was expecting it was I able to make out the dome of a human skull.

I reached towards it but found my fingers reluctant to touch the bone. It was not squeamishness; not exactly. It was simply that she should not be dead. These bones should be covered in flesh, muscle, warm skin, bright auburn hair. I swallowed, almost undone by my last memory of her. There had been nothing bright about her then.

Nothing.

Was this really her?

I turned to Gus, motioned at the skull. 'Could you get it out? Carefully.'

He took my place and, as well as I could, I watched him patiently loosening earth from bone before lifting it free with a grunt.

'Here.' He did not release the skull's weight until he was sure that I had a secure hold and, when he did so, I realised why; it was far heavier than I had been expecting. A gentle exploration revealed cold earth impacted into every orifice.

I set it on the ground in front of me. Then, cautiously, because I had no idea how easily skeletal teeth might be dislodged, I began rubbing soil away, picking off dryish chunks with my fingernails, forcing myself to scrub at the surfaces of the front teeth.

Keeping my voice barely above a murmur so that Dai would not hear, I asked, 'Is there a gap between the two front teeth? A bigger gap than usual?'

Gus leaned forward. 'Yes, there is. It's quite pronounced.'

I could see those teeth in my mind's eye: the two big front ones she used to call coach-house doors because of their shape. The gap between them had given her an endearingly child-like smile.

But she had not been a child. Seven years ago, when somebody put her beneath this tree, she had been twenty-two years old.

Gus stirred at my side. 'Do you know who this is?'

Instead of answering his question, I laid the skull gently back down and rose to my feet. I was aware of William Williams waiting on the footpath below and I knew that decisiveness was called for if I was to carry the day.

Taking care not to slide on the wet leaves, I made my way back down to him determined to engage in no discussion, simply to act as if I had the right to organise affairs as I saw fit.

'Mr Williams, will you send Ianto back to the house for something to carry the remains in, please? An old sheet, perhaps, or some kind of cloth?' I could not bear the thought of a sack being produced and her bones being bundled up like so much firewood. 'They must be taken to the mortuary at the workhouse until the proper course can be decided.'

'You should make sure to take the surrounding soil as well,' Gus chipped in, reducing the likelihood that Williams would object. 'To be sure of collecting all the bones.' He half-turned towards me. 'Don't frown like that P-L, I've seen antiquarians do it. It's how you ensure thoroughness.'

'I beg your pardon, Mr Gelyot, who did you say did that?'

'Antiquarians, Mr Williams. They go about looking for evidence of our ancestors – trying to put flesh on the bones of myth, so to speak.' Gus tailed off, clearly regretting his choice of phrase.

'You think this is somebody from long ago? Is that what you're saying?'

The hope in Williams's voice was naked, embarrassing, and I was not going to allow him to harbour it for a second longer. 'No, Mr

Williams,' I said, before Gus could respond. 'Unlike Mr Gelyot, I think we both know very well who these remains belong to.'

I could feel Williams's eyes on me. 'No,' he said. 'No, that's not right. She left. She ran away in the night.'

But if she had run away I would have found her.

I had always known, in my heart of hearts, that she was dead. And now William Williams would have to face his share of the guilt that had tormented me for the last seven years.

Harry

I wanted there to be no confusion about what should be done with the remains when they arrived at the workhouse so I decided to ride out there with Gus.

'Don't you think we should inform the proper authorities first?' Gus asked, once we'd left Williams and the labourers behind.

I half-turned. 'The coroner, you mean?'

'The police? Or isn't there a force here yet?'

'We do have a county constabulary, as it happens so you can stop thinking we're quite so medieval. But it's not like London. The magistrates still hold the reins.'

'So shouldn't we find a magistrate?'

'My father will need to be first to know.' I did not dare think of taking this to anybody else. 'It'll wait until tomorrow.'

I knew I would be rehearsing a dozen different ways to break the news from now until my father's return. He would be unwilling to take my identification of the bones at face value.

Teeth – what are you talking about, boy? Is no other person in the history of South Cardiganshire to be allowed to have had teeth with a gap in the middle? You can't be sure of these bones. Best to have them decently buried and make an end of it.

Just as he had wanted me decently tidied away to Oxford and an end to my association with the young woman whose remains we had just seen.

'How far is it to this workhouse?' Gus asked, clearly trying to change the subject.

'About another mile.'

'It's odd' he ruminated, 'half the people one sees in court live in absolute fear of the workhouse but I've never been near one.'

'You'll find this one quiet. Small by London standards. Beyond the master and matron – Mr and Mrs Davies – the only other official is a clerk. That used to be a Mr Thomas but I don't know if he still holds the position.'

I almost heard Gus's mouth fall open. 'You're *acquainted* with these people?'

Out of the corner of my eye I could see that his face was turned towards me but I could not make out any expression. That sort of detail was beyond me, now. 'We've been introduced,' I said. It felt expedient to admit that; goodness only knew how Davies was going to greet a visit from me on this particular errand. The last time I had visited the workhouse it had been in search of the woman whose remains I was now having delivered to Davies's door.

'P-L, how on *earth* did you come to be introduced to a workhouse master and his wife?'

I sighed. Gus and I might both be the sons of gentlemen but our upbringing had differed in almost every respect. Whilst I had grown up in the damp, green country where the three counties of Cardigan, Carmarthen and Pembroke meet in a tangle of wooded river valleys, Gus had seen out his childhood in one of the newer, smarter garden squares in London. My father was a landowner and a magistrate, his a second-generation manufacturer whose wealth came from northern mill towns. And, though my father might command respect on the bench and in polite Welsh drawing rooms, his enjoyed friends in government.

'I used to ride over with my father while the workhouse was being built,' I told him. 'He was chairman of the board of Guardians. Still is.' Because nobody else would take on that particularly thankless task.

'Your father is a Poor Law Guardian?' He tried to keep his astonishment to himself but did not quite succeed.

'Gentlemen who live on their estates have duties.' *Unlike the absentees who use them only for entertaining in the summer,* I might have added, had I not felt a degree of affection for Gus's father.

'And have you been there since?' Gus was gabbling, trying to make amends. 'To learn the trade? Will you succeed him as a Guardian when you inherit the estate?'

'As it happens, I've not been to the workhouse since the riots.' I was trying to avoid his second question as much as to answer the first and I was taken aback by a yelp of astonishment.

'*Riots?* Here?'

'Yes, here! You think we're so bucolic that rioting is beyond us?'

'What riots? When?'

'The *Rebecca* Riots! Come on, Gus – Welsh farmers daring to defy the authorities, questions asked in parliament, pretty well daily reports in *The Times*—'

'Not *recently?*'

'During my first year up at Oxford. Just before we met, I suppose.' I saw his hand wave as if it were swatting a moribund fly.

'Oh, there you are then. I never so much as looked at a newspaper while I was an undergraduate. Who does?'

I could not help but smile; I had been far from a daily reader of the papers at Oxford myself. Had I known then that in a few short years I would be unable to read at all, I might have been a more avid consumer of newsprint.

'Bread riots, I suppose?' When I did not answer straight away, Gus's tone changed. 'What? Is it a deep, dark secret?'

He meant it in jest but, in truth, the riots *had* assumed the status of communal secret; as if the collective shame of three counties had taken physical form and hidden people's past from their own view.

'Tollgates,' I said.

'What? People rioted at the notion of having to pay to use a decent road?'

I hesitated. Short of a lecture on post-war economics I could not possibly make Gus understand why the farmers of West Wales had cast off their characteristic docility and defied their betters over three counties for the best part of twelve months. 'Yes,' I conceded. 'More or less.'

'And Rebecca? Who was she?'

'She wasn't anybody. It's from the Bible. Something about Rebecca being the mother of thousands and possessing the gates of those that hate her.'

'Quaint.'

I did not correct him but, as anybody who has lived through a period of insurrection knows, once people unaccustomed to power have felt its potency, they are apt to begin wielding it indiscriminately, with results that are usually far from quaint.

'Rebecca wasn't a person' I said. 'There wasn't a leader who went by that name. Rebecca was… an idea.' An idea, I might have added, that persuaded men to do things they would never have done without its imprimatur; an idea that had swept through the three counties like a contagion, leading to a widespread rash of violence and unrest.

I urged Sara, my little mare, into a canter. 'Come on. I'd like to get this done while it's still light.'

John

The news from Waungilfach spread like summer rain.

It was as if it'd rushed about everywhere of its own accord. As if it wanted to be told.

The air in the Drovers' Arms was thick with it when I walked in after work that evening.

'You remember that servant girl of William Williams's? The one from before? The one with the red hair?'

'What one?'

'The one from years ago. The one that just went off.'

'What about her?'

'They've found her.'

'Where?'

'Didn't go off, did she? Somebody killed her.'

'Killed?'

'That's right. And put her in the ground. Under a tree. On Williams's land.'

And so it went on. But it was that one phrase that stuck in my mind. Like a boot stuck in mud, it held me fast.

The one from years ago.

Years ago it might be, but the night she died was like yesterday to me. Wet. The sound of rain on dead leaves. The smell of damp earth. Drops from the trees cold on the hot skin at the back of my neck.

I could still feel the terror. Terror that I'd be seen, that I'd lose my own life because of her.

Seven years. You'd think the dreams would've faded.

16

Every time I woke, panting and sweating, I told myself the same thing. *You couldn't have done any different.*

Rebecca was to blame. Beca. She ordered it. And Beca must've had good reason. The Lady always had good reason. It wasn't for me to question it.

But the dreams had never left me alone. And now, somebody had found her.

I just had to hope they wouldn't find me.

Harry

When my father arrived home, I was standing at the shuffleboard with Gus, about to win for the third time. Gus might scoff, but at least my long familiarity with the game allowed me to compete on almost equal terms; unlike billiards or cards, neither of which I would ever play again.

'I hear you've been to Waungilfach on my behalf.'

Having forgotten the uncanny speed with which Cardiganshire news travels, I found myself on the back foot. 'I didn't really have a choice in the matter. Williams sent a man over here at the gallop – I didn't think it would be right to wait for you.'

My father put an unaccustomed hand on my shoulder. 'You mistake me, Harry. I wasn't finding fault. You did exactly as I would have wished. You lifted the burden of responsibility from Williams and made rational provision for the disposal of the remains.'

I watched him out of the corner of my eye as he turned away, embarrassed, perhaps, by his own demonstrativeness. 'I'm glad you approve.'

'Now, we must take care that they are interred with the minimum of fuss. Gossip will undoubtedly be rife and we need to discourage further speculation.' I saw his hand reach out to pick up one of the shuffleboard pennies. 'I assume you asked Davies to have a grave dug?'

'No. She can't be buried until—'

'She?' The frown in his voice was unmistakable and I realised that he did not know whose bones had been discovered. Of course; the gossip would have been judiciously edited when it reached my father's ears.

'Margaret Jones.'

I am sure I did not imagine the fraught quality of his silence. 'You think this is—' he hesitated. Was he looking at Gus, wondering how much I had told him? 'You think it's Williams's dairy maid?'

'I'm quite sure of it.'

His hand reached out into my field of vision and placed the gaming penny on the end of the table. 'And am I to understand that you object to a discreet burial?'

I moved my head slightly. His figure, outlined against the long windows behind him, seemed smaller than my memory of him and I wondered whether this was yet another optical effect of encroaching blindness. 'I would like to give her a decent burial,' I said, emphasising my own choice of adjective. 'But first there will have to be an inquest, obviously.'

'Obviously?'

I should have known he would not allow himself to be swayed by rhetorical tricks. 'Of course. I know the death isn't recent but it's certainly unexplained and quite obviously suspicious.'

My father moved towards the fire, speaking as he went, his face turned away from me. A wasted effort if he was trying to hide his expression but he could not know that. 'Have you informed the coroner?'

The county magistrates controlled the public purse and, if they did not approve an inquest, nobody would be paid – not the coroner, not the jurors, not the parish officer who would be expected to find witnesses and empanel the jury. Given that my father was both a senior magistrate and the one whose land lay closest to Waungilfach, any decision to involve the coroner would, effectively, be his.

'No,' I said. 'I thought you would wish to do that.'

When he did not reply, I picked up the penny he had put down and pretended to look at it. 'Don't you think it would give rise to comment if we fail to hold an inquest?'

'Given your opinion on the identity of the deceased, it will cause a damn' sight more comment if we do!' His tone took me by surprise. My father rarely blasphemed and it was an indication of his agitation that he would do so in front of a guest.

'You think we should disclaim all knowledge and simply bury her anonymously?'

He hesitated. 'Will her family *want* an inquest?'

As far as I knew, Margaret had had no family to speak of. 'Whether they do or not,' I said, 'shouldn't justice be done? Are we just going to ignore the fact that somebody murdered her?'

My father made his way towards the cabinet in the corner and I turned my head in Gus's direction in a kind of apology for his exclusion from the conversation.

The cabinet's ill-fitting door opened with its familiar whine, a sound followed by the scrape and clink of decanter and glasses and the liquid sound of brandy being poured.

I walked over and picked up two glasses. My father acknowledged the service with a small grunt of thanks and moved to the winged chair nearest the fire. As he lowered himself into it, I realised that, between my increasingly sporadic visits, he had become an old man.

'Why don't you tell me exactly what you saw at Waungilfach and what Williams has told you.'

As succinctly as I was able, I did as he asked. When I had finished, he sat, his chin lowered to his chest, eyes apparently on the rug at his feet.

The quality of his silence was such that I found myself wondering whether he was thinking of happier times before my mother died; times when, every week, the rug would have been hung on a line in the garden and beaten to rid it of every speck of dust. It had still been taken out regularly when I was a little boy, when neighbours still called on my father but, in recent years, his widower's demeanour had deterred all but the most determined callers, causing Glanteifi's servants to sink into a kind of deferential negligence.

Finally, he roused himself. 'You must concede that there is little or no prospect of bringing anybody to justice for this crime. We have no information as to when this young woman died, or indeed by what method—'

'But we do! We *do* know when she died.'

'I beg your pardon?' His tone suggested that I might be eight years old again and guilty of some shocking linguistic *faux pas*.

'At least...' I tried not to stammer, 'we know *when* she disappeared. It was May eighteen forty-three. The May of the riots.'

Harry

I had first got wind of the riots in a letter from home which arrived at my college in April a little more than seven years earlier.

> *Dear Harry*
> *I trust this finds you well.*

I remember grinning at my friend's salutation. It was the style I had been taught in my first term at school – *You will begin your letters home, gentlemen, with these words* – and, lacking any other model, he had copied it.

> *I am sorry to write with unwelcome news but you are needed at Glanteifi. You have probably heard about the riots. Rebecca who broke the Efailwen gate three years ago is riding again. And she is here now. The farmers are meeting by night to break tollgates down. The trusts put them up again but they are down again the next night.*
>
> *The magistrates have made more specials and they are supposed to be out at night but they know what is good for them and they look the other way. The millisias* – I stumbled over the misspelled word before realising he meant militias – *have been called out but they are useless. Rebecca has been and gone before the soldiers can get on their horses.*
>
> *The magistrates have offered rewards but nobody is willing to speak against the Lady.*
>
> *Your father has put up notices ordering his tenants to have nothing to do with Rebecca and he has sent Ormiston round to all the farms on the*

estate to warn men not to ride out at night. Not even if they are threatened. But the farmers take no notice. They are afraid of Rebecca's threats even if he is not. They know why Rebecca wants all of them to ride out. So nobody can think of informing on his neighbours.

Beca won't stand for your father's pig-headedness. She has already sent him two letters telling him to show her more respect. The second one warned him if he did not keep his opinions to himself, his house would be burned down.

And Beca will do it. She has power. The magistrates are going to have to learn that. They think that now the illegal gates are down, the Lady will go away. But they are wrong.

Your father will not keep quiet. You know that. You know what he is like. You need to come home, Harry, and talk sense into him. I do not want us all to burn in our beds.

He will not want you to know what is happening. I am sure he has not written to tell you about any of this.

He had not. My father wrote, punctiliously, every Sunday, detailing events on the estate. He always filled exactly one sheet. Just one solitary page. I was not in the least surprised that he had mentioned neither riots nor threats.

As you can see, it is urgent that you must come home.
Your friend,
David Thomas.

David Thomas. Davy. Though he had not said it, I did not doubt for a second that he rode out on these nocturnal gatebreakings himself. Despite the fact that tollgates were no concern of his, he would be unable to keep away.

I could readily imagine my father's outrage at these 'Rebecca' riots; and I knew that there was not a threatening letter in the world that would persuade him to withdraw his opposition to them. He was a magistrate; he would see nothing here but a clear duty to uphold the rule of law.

So, as swiftly as I was able to organise matters, I returned to Glanteifi, defying my father's specific instruction to remain in Oxford until the end of my first year.

In coming home, I had ensured that I was at Glanteifi when Margaret Jones most needed my help. But, for reasons which now seemed petty and ungenerous, I had failed her.

No matter who had murdered her, I was partly responsible for her death.

John

'Mr Probert-Lloyd, the magistrate, has summoned the coroner.'

My employer announced it like a royal proclamation. Loved to know things, Mr Schofield did.

He wanted me to be agog, I could tell. I tried to look eager for him. 'Does that mean there's going to be an inquest?'

He nodded. 'In all probability, yes.'

An inquest. I swallowed a mouthful of panic. Calm down. Nobody knows. Nobody's going to call you to answer questions.

But who *would* the coroner call?

William Williams, Waungilfach, obviously.

What would he say? Anything to get his own neck out of the noose if he had any sense.

Nobody in town was talking about the bones any more. Not since people remembered when she'd disappeared.

It had only taken a whisper. *'She went missing in Beca's time.'*
Beca.

The name still made men look over their shoulders. Power can be like a shadow, sometimes. Longer and darker with the passing of time.

Beca was a name to silence tongues. To make people forget things. It was a name to force obedience. And in that way, it was just like the *ceffyl pren* – the wooden horse, as Mr Schofield always had it. As if he could tame it with its English name, with the Greek myth sound of it. But our horse was nothing like the Greeks'. The *ceffyl* wasn't a sly trick, it was a warning. A punishment.

25

Nobody'd carried the *ceffyl pren* in Newcastle Emlyn for years. Not since the riots. Not since *before* the riots.

They still carried it in Cardigan. That was the main reason why the county magistrates had decided to go for a police force – to try and stamp it out. The magistrates hated the *ceffyl pren*. An *arrogation of the law into the hands of people unfit to wield it* – that's what Mr Schofield said it was. I had to ask him what arrogation meant. I never liked asking him the meaning of words – he always gave me that 'good boy you want to learn' smile of his. You'd swear he'd invented me from his own designs.

If you listened to Mr Schofield, the *ceffyl pren* was illegal. Carrying it was illegal and going out with it was illegal. Even if you were at the back of the procession with three hundred other people in front of you, being there was illegal. A breach of the peace. Hard labour if you were caught.

The magistrates wanted people to take notice of the Queen's law, didn't they? But the *ceffyl* was our law. The old law. The punishment for adulterers and seducers and wife-beaters. For cheaters and beer-waterers. And magistrates' informers.

My parents took me out with the *ceffyl pren* once, when I was a tiny boy. Dada wore Mam's everyday shawl and apron. Mam wore his jacket inside out and tied her Sunday shawl around her head like a heathen. Then Dada blacked our faces with soot from the chimney. Blacked up, he was a stranger, and his eyes terrified me – white and staring.

Just like all the black faces I'd seen at the Nantyclawdd gatebreaking when I was with Uncle Price. I still wondered whether my father had been there.

But – God! – the noise we made as we followed the *ceffyl pren* through the dark! The righteous din of people seeing justice done.

Mind you, all I could think, as a little child, was how wrong it seemed, men and women being in each other's clothes. It worried me, adults being so naughty. Made me afraid of what might happen. The men at the front of the procession pulled the man we'd come for out of his house and forced him onto his knees at his own threshold.

The *cantwr* recited his sins and the man shrank and shriveled in front of us. Fear'll do that to you. Believe me, I know.

After the accusation came the shouting and spitting. Our leader just sat on his horse, silent, waiting for all that to finish.

One by one, every soul in the procession fell quiet. Dada put me on his shoulders for me to see the man begging for forgiveness. Hoping to escape a beating, I suppose. But they beat him and tarred him anyway. Then, they put him on the pole of the *ceffyl pren* and paraded him around the village. Everybody knew what he'd done now. He'd better mend his ways.

It took weeks for the tar to come off his skin. And nobody from the procession spoke a word to him in all that time.

I never knew what he'd done. I was too little to understand. But I understood the look on his face when he was pushed down onto his knees.

The *ceffyl pren* struck fear into men's hearts. And Rebecca was the *ceffyl pren* by another name.

Harry

Not only did Sir Leighton Bowen, coroner for the Teifi Valley, decline my father's offer to stay with us while the inquest was being conducted but he failed to present himself at Glanteifi for breakfast, as invited, on the morning after his arrival. Instead, a note was delivered requesting a rendezvous at the workhouse.

'Is he always so uncivil?' I asked.

My father placed his cutlery on his plate. 'I don't believe he intends it as incivility. It's just Bowen's general way of going on. He prefers not to sit down with people while he's conducting an investigation.'

'Meticulous,' Gus observed.

'He is that.' My father agreed as he rose from the table. 'Now, do you still wish to examine the bones before he arrives?'

Our route to the mortuary took us through the workhouse complex and, as Mr Davies led us through the central yard, I vividly recalled looking at the plans for the workhouse with my father, just after he had received them. The memory of being able to see each detail clearly filled my throat with a hard lump of frustration.

'It's a plan drawn up for the government's Poor Law commissioners throughout the country,' my father had told me, unrolling the stiff paper. 'Here, here, here and here,' he pointed to four squares set on each side of a large quadrangle, 'there will be blocks for different categories of inmate.'

I looked at the symmetrical diagram. 'What categories?'

'Women and babies here,' his finger descended on a square. 'The older children, here, the able-bodied men, here, and those unable to work, here.'

'So families will be separated?'

My father's expression told me that, in his view, I had too many opinions and too little knowledge. 'With limited space, it's only proper to keep the men and women separate. The safety of young, unmarried women is the guardians' responsibility.'

'I don't understand why the system has to change,' I said, 'what's wrong with going on the parish like people do now?'

My father rolled up the plans and tied them again. As usual, I had disappointed him. 'The parishes can't afford to keep paupers in that fashion any more. Nobody will tolerate a poor rate that increases every year. People are already complaining that the industrious work to keep the indolent. Banding parishes together into unions and giving each union a workhouse will save money.'

But all the stableyard talk I had heard about the new law had left me with the conviction that it was a terrible, godless act on the part of the government. My father must have seen it because he sighed. 'Being on the parish isn't such a humane system as you seem to think, Harry. For people who've lost their homes, parish provision is little better than slavery.'

'And won't the workhouse be slavery? People are saying there'll be hard labour.'

'The inmates will have to work, of course. That's only right if they're fit and able. But the old and the infirm will only be given light work – and not even that if they're truly incapable.'

I looked at him. What he was saying seemed eminently reasonable but all the servants at Glanteifi, not to mention the labourers out on the estate, were dead set against the whole notion of the workhouse.

Once you're in you'll never get out again was the general consensus. *It's a prison for people who've done nothing wrong but fall on hard times.*

'Isn't it like punishing people for being poor?' I asked.

'It's not a prison, Harry. People are free to leave whenever they like.'

'Then why would they go there in the first place?'

'Because they're starving.' The look he gave me was equal parts frustration and regret. 'Believe me, if it's a choice between dying of starvation and going into the workhouse, then the workhouse will seem a welcome haven.'

I looked around me, now. A haven for the destitute it might be but the workhouse was an uninviting place. High, whitewashed walls pierced by small windows, yards paved in sluiced-down slate; it might not be a prison but it felt like one.

'What's that?'

Though I could not see him, I still turned at Gus's question. 'That sound,' he clarified.

A slow thudding was coming from one of the yards behind the high walls, repetitive but ragged, as if many people were engaged on an enterprise to which nobody cared to bring any kind of method.

'The able bodied men break stone,' Davies said. 'For the roads.'

Davies left us at the dead-house, a low, slate-roofed building, with a single window let into each long wall. As Gus and I passed into the chill, gloomy interior, I was struck by how much the building resembled the dairy at Waungilfach where Margaret had worked. It had the same flat, cold light as the north-facing dairy and the walls were similarly plastered and whitewashed for cleanliness. Even the position of the door, at one end of the building, was the same. In the dairy, its position had been designed to stop the wind blowing dust into the skimming trough; here, I was at a loss to account for it.

'Well,' Gus said, 'this lacks a certain welcoming air.'

I made my way to the trestle table that stood under the window on the far wall.

Evidently, Ianto Harries had been given an old blanket to transport the bones in. As I put my hand out to where the bundle lay, I felt how the thin, well-worn fabric had been gathered and grasped in the middle like a tinker's bundle. Having carried the remains here, probably unwillingly, Ianto had simply dumped the blanket and its contents and made good his escape.

'How did you come to know her?' The kindness of Gus's tone almost unmanned me. Until now, he had refrained from asking me any questions about Margaret Jones or her remains and I had repaid his delicacy by giving him no information whatsoever.

I saw her and lost my head, I wanted to tell him, *if not my heart. She filled my mind, my senses. I couldn't sleep for thinking of her.*

I kept such gaze as was left to me fixed on the blanket. 'My father and I were paying a social call at Waungilfach,' I said. 'I seem to recall there was a bull that Williams wanted my father to see.'

I will carry my first sight of Margaret to the grave with me as the moment that separated boyhood from manhood. Bored by talk of bovine husbandry, I was standing a little aside from William Williams and my father and I saw her as she came into the yard, a cloth-draped pail of milk in each hand. Her auburn hair had been gathered up beneath an ancient felt hat but one curling strand had escaped to bounce against her cheek as she strode across to the dairy.

I stared and, as the eyes of young people will, ours met. She might have been expected to look away – any Glanteifi servant certainly would have done – but she held my gaze and raised an eyebrow, causing a heat to rise not only in my face but, somewhat disconcertingly, in another area too.

How lightly I took the gift of sight in those days – the gift of being able to catch the eye of a young woman and see interest there. I would have valued it so much more had I known that it was soon to be denied me. I would have gazed and gazed.

But I was ignorant of so much, then. At the beginning of that summer, I had a head full of learning but no experience of female company. Before our encounter in the yard at Waungilfach, I had nurtured no expectations of the months before I began my studies at Oxford beyond helping with haymaking and harvest – if my father would still allow me those boyhood pleasures – and indulging in whatever idle pursuits came my way. But Margaret Jones's unabashed gaze, her simple lift of an eyebrow, turned my head completely and, from that moment, any day on which I did not see her was a wasted day.

I do not know whether William Williams saw that first look pass between me and Margaret or whether he simply wanted to flaunt the productiveness of his farm in front of my father but, whatever his reason, he barked a question as she walked away from my blush.

'Margaret Jones – a moment!'

She turned quickly towards him causing the milk to slop in the pails, catching at the covering cloths and soaking them. Later, when we exchanged memories of our first meeting, Margaret told me that she hated getting the covering cloths wet because rinsing milk from them took such a lot of water. 'If I don't rinse them properly, she knows,' Margaret told me, referring to her employer's wife, 'she sniffs them every day to see if they're clean.'

'How much butter is there to take to market tomorrow?' Williams asked.

'I don't know, Uncle,' Margaret said. 'Do you want me to go and count?'

She called Williams 'Uncle' in accordance with local custom, just as she would call his wife 'Aunty'. At that moment, my gaze still full of her flirtatiously raised eyebrow, the nomenclature seemed a silly infantilisation.

'No,' Williams said. 'Leave it. I thought you'd know, that's all.'

Just then, the dogs started barking and, a few moments later, a man strode into the yard carrying a long staff tied with brightly coloured ribbons. He banged it on the ground three times, swept his similarly beribboned hat from his head and began declaiming.

It was Shoni Penglais, the local *Gwahoddwr*, and I listened as he recited verses of his own composition, inviting friends and neighbours to the wedding of Hepzibah Jones of Henllain and Thomas Roberts of Pantyrefail.

My father, knowing what was happening but unable to understand anything beyond the names and farms of his tenants, turned to me.

'The wedding's a week on Saturday,' I told him. 'Bidding the day before, obviously.'

He nodded. 'We must send something.'

Williams took his cue. 'I expect I shall have to give all my servants leave to go or there will be grumbling.' He smiled indulgently but the look he gave Margaret was sharper than his tone.

'It would be kind of you to let us go, Uncle.'

'Of course you'll go. And I'll send something for the young couple with you.'

And I would be there. From that moment on, nothing would have stopped me.

I looked at Gus as best I could. 'Margaret caught my eye,' I told him, 'and I' – my own youthful audacity seemed amazing to me, now – 'contrived a meeting.'

'And then?'

And then I had fallen in love. I had made a fool of myself, or been made a fool of. But I did not want to have to explain any of that to Gus. With both hands, I began opening the blanket so that its edges trailed over the sides of the trestle table, leaving the contents in a mounded-up heap in the middle. Though the light from the window above fell directly onto the table, I was unable to distinguish bone from stone and earth. All was a jumble of darker and paler browns in what Figges, the eye doctor at Moorfields hospital, called my peripheral vision.

'I'm going to need your help, Gus.'

'You don't say.'

I stifled an impulse to punch him. How dare he make a joke of my failing sight? I obviously failed to hide my feelings because he made an inarticulate noise of contrition. 'Sorry, P-L. Nerves. Never been in the company of the dead before. How can I assist?'

I took a hard breath. My chest felt tight, as if somebody had put a fist beneath my diaphragm. 'We need to separate the bones from the earth and lay them out decently.'

'Then we'll need a second table.' As he spoke, Gus moved away from me and I made out several boards stacked against the wall, trestles beside them.

With a second table set up at right angles to the first, I stood, suddenly reluctant to begin. Though it had to be done if I was to be certain that this was Margaret, separating bones from grave-soil suddenly seemed horribly intrusive.

Gus must have sensed my reluctance.

'Right, P-L, you stand here,' he manoeuvred me to one end of the debris-covered table, 'and I shall stand here,' he shuffled himself into the right angle formed by the two boards. 'We shall be methodical and go through the soil picking out the bones as we find them. If you pass whatever you find to me, I shall attempt to lay them out in some kind of skeletal order.'

'Gray would be proud of you,' I said, referring to a medical friend.

'For once, I'm grateful for all his endless droning about bones,' Gus said. 'Now. Let's see if we can remember anything he's forced us to listen to.'

Invoking Gray and his meticulous approach had the effect of steadying both of us and we set to.

Our first task was to spread the contents of the blanket evenly along the trestle board so that the bones might more easily be seen, at least by Gus. We had hardly begun to do so when I became aware of something anomalous beneath my fingers. I picked up a small clot of something lighter than earth and rubbed off the worst of the clinging soil. As much by feel as by sight, I discerned that it was a knot of fabric. I held it out to Gus.

'Can you see whether this has a pattern to it?' He took it from me.

'Chequers. Red and blue.'

In what remained of my vision, colours were muted, though I had been fairly sure that I was seeing something other than brown.

Taking the knot of fabric from him, I turned it over in my fingers. Even though I was unable to look at it properly, I knew what it was. 'It's the fastening knot of a shawl,' I told Gus.

The chequered shawl she wore to chapel on Sundays had been Margaret's most treasured possession. It had been her one bit of finery, the only item of clothing she possessed that said she was not a drudge, that she had hopes and dreams.

'Have you told your father yet?' Gus broke into my thoughts. 'About your sight?'

'No.'

'Do you think he knows?'

How could my father have failed to notice that I could not look him in the eye, that I was constantly averting my gaze, that I failed to greet servants I had known all my life until they spoke?

'I don't know, Gus.'

'Has he broached the subject of your turning up here out of the blue?'

I shook my head and Gus said no more. What more was there to say? We both knew that, when I told my father about the dramatic deterioration in my sight, he would understand that my legal career was over, that I had no choice but to do what I had promised myself I never would – come home and learn to be squire.

A few minutes later, Gus picked up something and held it to the light.

'What do you think this is?'

I took the object from him and positioned it at the edge of the central blur that dominated my eyesight, so that I could form an impression of its shape. Detail I could perceive only by touch and inference.

Weighted at the bottom, Gus's find had a slim, corroded shaft topped by sprung jaws. I tried to pull the little, flared lever which would compress the spring and open the jaws but rust had taken hold and the joint was stuck.

'It's a rushlight holder.'

'What's a rushlight?'

I blinked. 'It's what it says – a light made out of a rush. A kind of small reed that grows in damp ground,' I added. Rushes were unlikely to have figured much in Gus's London childhood.

'I see.' There was a pause during which I was aware of him staring at the holder in my hand. 'How do you make a light out of a reed?'

I took in a breath. As a boy, I had been proud to know how to make a rushlight; now, with Gus waiting for an explanation, I was forced to acknowledge that it was an incongruous accomplishment for a gentleman. I put the holder down. 'You take your rush,' I said, miming the action of holding the delicate shaft with my left hand. 'And you peel off half of the outer skin until you have the soft inside of the rush on display. The remaining skin supports it and acts as a wick. Then you dip the rush in whatever animal fat you have to hand, and let it soak into the pith. When it's dry, you trap it in the rushlight holder like so.' My fingers pinched at my imaginary rushlight. 'You light the end of the rush like a taper and it burns for about twenty minutes.'

'Why would you use that rather than a candle?'

'Because you can't afford a candle, Gus! Because you're so poor you're lucky if you've got the fat to make rushlights.'

'I see.'

But I knew that he did not see, not really. He had never encountered poverty in the flesh, it was as foreign to him as the Ottoman Empire. I turned the rushlight holder over in my hand, remembering its place in the loft where Margaret had slept. It was just as well for me that Gus could not see my memories; I did not want to explain myself to him. No doubt the inquest would furnish him with all the details he could wish.

With both of us working steadily, after an hour or so, Gus had assigned most of the major bones to torso or limbs and my searching fingertips had found another of Margaret's few possessions: a flat little tin in which she had kept her needles and some thread. Already dented and scratched before it had been interred under a fallen tree, it was now so stained and corroded that Gus was unable to see that it had originally been made in the shape of a tiny book. Margaret had told me that it had once held snuff though she had had no idea where it came from.

'Somebody must have brought it back from the war, I suppose,' she had said, taking the little tin from me and putting it on the wall-top that served her as a shelf.

Why had she been carrying her rushlight holder and her sewing things when she was murdered? And why had she been wearing her best shawl?

Could Williams have been right – had she been in the process of running away?

When I had gone to Waungilfach looking for her, I had found the other servants thin-lipped. Nobody knew where she was. With the onset of blindness still two or three years away, the disapproval on their faces had been obvious: they all blamed me, in one way or another, for her disappearance.

Guilt had sent me on a fruitless search. She had still been at Waungilfach, even as I rode over half the county looking for her. Murdered and buried less than half a mile from the loft that had been her home.

Gus held something up to the window. 'Pity Gray's not here,' he said, 'he could tell us what's a finger bone and what's a toe bone.'

Sidelong, I scanned the mass of drying earth and stones on the table. 'Gus, can we put up a third table? I want to be able to sift all this and get rid of some of the earth.'

Gus looked at me. 'Are you going to look for every tiny bone?' His tone told me that he thought I was being over-assiduous.

'No. I'm looking for something specific.'

'What?'

I swallowed. 'Little bones.'

'What kind of little bones?'

'Little ribs, little arm bones, little leg bones—'

'A *child?*'

'She was pregnant.' I moved over to the pile of trestles before he could ask the obvious question and picked one up, willing him to follow my lead; instead he stood his ground behind me.

'P-L… this unborn child…'

Concentrating on the trestle, I stretched out the legs as wide as the stretcher rope would allow. 'It wasn't mine. But that was my mistake. It would have been far better for Margaret if it had been.'

My father had announced that, while he was waiting for Bowen, he would conduct an impromptu inspection of the workhouse with the matron, Mrs Davies. Now, however, he appeared in the doorway of the mortuary in the company of a tallish man in boots and a long riding coat.

'Gentlemen,' my father addressed us, 'may I present Mr Leighton Bowen, the coroner for the Teifi Valley. Bowen, this is my son, Henry. And his friend, Mr Augustus Gelyot.'

There were only two occasions on which my father called me Henry: when he was introducing me and when I had displeased him. On being presented to his peers, therefore, I could never quite shake off the suspicion that I was a disappointment.

Polite bows exchanged, the coroner approached the tables. 'These are the remains in question?'

'Yes.' I moved to his side.

'And who was given the task of extracting bones from soil? Whoever it was has done an excellent job of work – there can be no doubt as to what we have here.'

'I'm glad you think so. Mr Gelyot and I are responsible.'

Bowen swung around. 'Indeed?' I was certain that he was looking into my face and I felt, for the thousandth time, the disadvantage of being unable to look a man steadily in the eye. 'Your father tells me that you have a personal interest in this discovery?'

'I knew her, yes.'

'Let us say, rather, that you knew the person we *presume* to be the deceased, Mr Probert-Lloyd. No inquest has yet determined identity.'

I inclined my head, irritated at being corrected.

'And these?' The skeleton was incomplete but Gus had confirmed that the remains were obviously those of a human infant.

'She – the *presumed deceased* – was carrying a child at the time of her death.'

'Indeed?' Bowen imbued the word with even more significance than he had given it the first time. He turned to my father. 'May I ask why you didn't see fit to tell me this?'

'I was not aware of it.' My father's voice gave little indication as to his emotions and I knew that his face would give away no more.

Bowen turned back to me. 'I understand you feel there should be an inquest? What exactly is it that you hope to gain from investigating the provenance of these remains, Mr Probert-Lloyd? Who would benefit from it?'

I would. I would know who had murdered her and I would know

exactly how much blame to ascribe to myself and my own actions. Or failure to act.

'Does there have to be a beneficiary?' Gus asked, filling the silence.

'I understand that you are a barrister, sir, in London?' At the edge of my vision, Gus bowed slightly.

'Then, surely, you must understand the sheer expense to which an inquest puts local ratepayers?'

I saw Bowen's hands come together behind his back as he turned away from Gus and put a question to my father. 'The owner of the farm, this William Williams – has *he* requested that an inquest be conducted? In his position, he might find it expedient to ensure that no suspicion clings to him.'

Did my father glance across at me? 'No. As far as I'm aware, he has not.'

'So, Mr Probert-Lloyd,' the coroner turned back to me, 'let us say, for the sake of argument, that an inquest *is* held. The identity of the deceased is established to everybody's satisfaction and a cause of death is decided upon by the jury. What then does the ratepayer get for his money, so long after the event?'

I fixed my gaze where I estimated his face would be. 'He sees the murderer brought to trial.'

'Can you be so confident that an inquest would reveal the culprit?'

'If the right witnesses are brought forward and the truth is told then, yes, I am confident.'

'In my experience, Mr Probert-Lloyd,' the coroner said, 'the truth is rarely told where a suspicious death is concerned. And certainly not the *whole* truth.'

Harry

As I told Gus, as soon as I had met Margaret Jones, I knew I had to see her again so I had contrived to meet her at the bidding day advertised by the *Gwahoddwr*, Shoni Penglais.

It may be that the folk custom of 'bidding' was unique to our western counties for I have never heard of it being practised anywhere else but it was essential to young couples in the Teifi valley, as few of them could have afforded to set up home without it.

In essence, bidding was the giving of wedding gifts in the expectation of repayment in kind: the friends and relations of bride and groom gave presents of goods or money on the understanding that, when they or their offspring came to be married, the gifts would be reciprocated. In a way, it could be seen as a system of lending and borrowing, on which couples drew at need and repaid on demand.

Naturally, a family as wealthy as ours was in no need of repayment but, had Glanteifi not sent a contribution to the purse of a young couple on the estate, it would have been seen as a gross discourtesy.

As a general rule, my father sent his gifts and compliments with a servant but, as I had received the invitation in person, I managed to persuade him that I should take Glanteifi's gift myself.

'You might take Ormiston with you,' my father said. 'Jones at Henllain has one of the biggest tenancies – only right we should wish his family well on the day.'

But turning up in the company of the estate's steward would not advance my plan at all. How could I speak to Margaret with Ormiston in attendance? I might as well have outlined my hopes in a brief note and left it on my father's breakfast plate.

I tried for nonchalance. 'Actually, some of the young men from the home farm are going – I thought I'd go with them. If you wouldn't mind.'

'Harry, I hope you're not going to fall back into your old ways – spend all your time with those beneath you? You need to cultivate some friends of your own class.'

I knew there was nothing to be gained by arguing. Best to agree, then he might concede the point this once. So I nodded, my father reluctantly acquiesced and I was free to go to the bidding in whatever company I chose. In fact, I intended to take only one companion. Davy Thomas.

'Hepzibah and Tom's bidding?' Davy said when I asked. 'Might go. Why?'

'I'd feel odd, going by myself. I've been away at school such a lot. Not sure they'd know me.'

He continued working oil into a long rein. 'Need a chaperone, do you, Harry Gwyn?'

Harry Gwyn. He and his mother had always called me that on account of my hair which, as a small child, had been so fair as to be almost white. Was it that early nickname that had established my preference for Harry over Henry?

'No,' I said. 'Just an excuse.'

'Oh yes?' He looked up, grinning. 'Some little girl caught your eye has she?'

I tried to will myself not to blush. 'Well? Are you coming or not?'

'Maybe I should. Might be entertaining.'

The Henllain holding was hidden away in the rolling countryside between the Teifi and the sea and our way took us up from the river valley onto the higher ground where the wind bent smaller trees into a permanent stoop.

As we walked under a sky like soaked linen, I reflected that this was an odd time for a farmer's daughter to be married. Hepzibah Jones's father could not have known, weeks ago when the wedding was arranged, that early July would turn out to be so damp and unpromising. In the ordinary way of things, he would have been bringing in hay this week, not attending to the endless preliminaries of his daughter's marriage.

'Hepzibah Jones…' I said.

'What about her?'

'Having to get married, is she? Before it shows?' I sketched a swollen belly in front of my own waistcoat.

'Hah!' Davy cuffed my arm. 'What do you know about any of that?'

'Enough, thank you. So? Is she? It's haymaking time, isn't it? Not exactly convenient.'

'Haven't heard anything. Mind you, her and Tom have been courting long enough – wouldn't surprise me. But then, Jonah Jones is a tight-fisted bastard – most likely he was hoping everybody'd be busy on the hay – hoping that they'd come, offer congratulations, slap their gift down and rush off again without eating or drinking anything.' He spat at a towering thistle at the side of the road. 'Serves him right that the weather's turned against him.'

At the cloth-draped trestle tables set up outside the Jones's house, I presented the estate's gift to Hepzibah and wished her well. Though her mother was entirely flustered at my arrival, Hepzibah accepted my coming as no more than her due; this was the one occasion in her life when the complimentary attentions of the whole community were hers by right and she was obviously intent on making the most of it.

Taking the bag of shillings from me, Hepzibah looked me in the eye and gave a regal dip of her head. 'Thank you, Mr Henry. It's very kind of you to come. Please have some wedding ale and cheese.'

If the money paid over for the ale had been destined for Jonah Jones's pocket, doubtless there would have been a great deal less consumed but, as the proceeds would go to the newlyweds, there was much good-natured slapping of pennies into the hand of the bride's sister who was acting as tapstress for the day.

As I took my ale, the assembly broke out in greetings to another new arrival and I turned to see Margaret standing there, looking around the busy crowd as if in search of somebody in particular. Initially, her gaze passed over me but, then, as if she had only belatedly realised who I was, her eyes shifted back to my face and she smiled. My stomach, already fluttering at the sight of her, contracted with a combination of apprehension and high excitement.

It took me several minutes to make my way towards her, obliged as I was, with every forward step, to exchange increasingly forced pleasantries about the delayed haymaking or the wedding tomorrow; but Margaret had obviously been aware of my approach. When, finally, I found myself standing in front of her, she touched her companion's arm and inclined her head slightly in my direction. The girl reciprocated the hand-on-arm gesture and moved away, flicking her eyes towards me as she went.

Our mutual good-days out of the way, I delivered the line I had been honing into nonchalence for a week.

'So, Mr Williams was as good as his word, then?'

If she was surprised at my continuing to speak to her in Welsh she showed no sign of it and responded in kind. 'Not really – he just sent me with his present. I think he's giving everybody an hour or two for the wedding tomorrow but it's only me today.'

'So you'll be at the wedding?'

She hesitated. 'For some of it. I don't really know Hepzibah so I don't expect I'll come to the house after.' She looked at me steadily. 'Nobody's going to do my work while I'm not there and I don't want to have to give up my Sunday to scrub in the dairy.'

'Will you be here to see the groom's men come for her?'

'It's a long way to walk for somebody I hardly know. Most likely I'll just go to the chapel.'

'Oh. She's not getting married in the church, then?'

'We are *allowed* to get married in chapel now, you know.' Her smile was all dimples and mockery.

'Yes, I know, but I thought, with the expense of having to get the registrar in…'

'You thought Jonah Jones wouldn't bother.'

I grinned. 'I would've thought he'd want his money's worth out of the church, that's all. I know he grumbles enough about paying his tithes.'

She put her head on one side. 'Know him well, do you?'

I shrugged, embarrassed at being caught out. 'Oh, you know… as much as I know all my father's tenants.' I cast a quick glance at Jones himself, standing to one side of his front door. 'My father sends me out with his steward at least once a year.'

'That's good. You can get to know your tenants. I mean the people who *will* be your tenants.'

46

I made a non-committal grunt and raised my almost empty cup to my lips.

'What? You *are* the heir to Glanteifi, aren't you?'

Previously, though I had been using the familiar Welsh form '*ti*' for 'you', she had addressed me formally as '*chi*' but, now, in her teasing question I was '*ti*' and the implied intimacy excited me into indiscretion.

'Yes, but it shouldn't *be* me inheriting. Glanteifi's the Proberts' estate and I haven't got a drop of Probert blood in me.' I upended my mug and tipped out the thick end of the ale. 'My father had another son – from his first marriage. George. He should be squire. He had the blood.'

'So where is he?'

'Dead. Before I was born. And his mother. She was the real Probert.'

Margaret looked at me, a little smile on her lips and her dimple just suggesting itself. 'Seems to me you're just lucky then. Instead of being the little brother with no prospects, you can be squire. You should be celebrating.' She raised her ale cup to me.

I shook my head. 'It's not just blood – I don't want to be one of them – a squire, a magistrate. My mother was a solicitor's daughter,' I finished, lamely, as if that explained everything.

She stared appraisingly into my face and, before her gaze, I felt like nothing more than the little brother with no prospects. No prospect of ever interesting a girl like her. 'You should come and talk to our minister,' she said. 'He'd be delighted to hear you don't want to be one of *them*. He's a great boy for all men being equal in the sight of God.' She adopted a cultured voice and intoned, 'There is no Greek nor Jew, male nor female, slave nor free in God's kingdom.'

'Perhaps I *should* come to your chapel,' I laughed. 'If I didn't like what the minister was saying, I could just look at you, instead.'

I could hardly believe I'd said it. It must have been the ale: especially brewed for the day, and potent enough to make people part with more pennies than was wise.

Margaret smiled again and this time the dimples were in full view. 'Silly boy,' she said. 'You must know plenty of pretty girls – and in proper dresses too, not an old *betgwn* like this!'

I was a silly boy; much too silly to know that she was fishing for a compliment.

'No – I don't know any pretty girls. In fact the only girls I know at all are the housemaids at Glanteifi.'

'Poor Harry.'

Her eyes met mine then slid away. My heart set up an animated tattoo; my moment had arrived. I knew Davy was watching from his position amongst a group of young men at the ale table and his scrutiny made me even more nervous.

'Would you… I mean… I'd like to… if you're walking back to Waungilfach – I'm walking too – we could walk together. If you like?'

'Unchaperoned?' She smiled but looked as if she was trying not to.

Was she laughing at me? I was suddenly consumed with the feeling that I had made a complete fool of myself. 'Oh, of course, if there's a friend who's going that way—'

She put a hand on my arm. 'I'm teasing you. I'll take my chances. If you're prepared to risk your reputation being seen with somebody like me?'

I stammered something, unsure whether she was still teasing.

'But let's not start any gossip, shall we?' she said. 'You go and give your compliments to Hepzibah and her parents and I'll follow you in about five minutes. Wait for me at the end of the lane.'

Despite everything that happened that summer and the next, that walk home remains one of the most glorious hours of my life.

Most of our conversation I barely remembered later – trivialities about the weather, her work, my pleasure at being home – but one brief, audacious exchange I did not forget.

'So,' I summoned the courage to ask, 'will we be seeing you holding court at a bidding in your own father's house sometime soon?'

'If you mean am I courting,' she answered, plainly, 'then the answer is no.' We walked on in silence for a few seconds, and spots of rain began to appear on her apron. 'But, even if I was, there'd be no bidding for me. I have no parents alive. Nobody to make a wedding ale or cheese for me.'

She looked at me, our eyes meeting easily as I was scarcely taller than she was. 'I must make my own way in the world.'

Harry

'Harry? A moment?'

Gus had announced that he would turn in if a candle could be put in his hand and Fred, the footman, was in the act of lighting one for each of us when my father spoke. As Fred left the room, I stood with my candle in my hand, Gus at my side.

My father made his wishes clear. 'Goodnight, Mr Gelyot.'

The library door closed and I perched myself on the edge of the table.

'This inquest,' my father began. 'It's important that you understand the conditions under which I am allowing it to take place.'

'Conditions?' I kept my tone even but a small spark of something – perhaps resentment, perhaps anger – had burst into life.

'Whilst I understand your desire to see justice done, I can neither approve nor applaud a public airing of your association with this young woman. I will not see this family's name publicly pilloried, Harry. Therefore, I am stipulating that you do not give evidence at the inquest.'

'I beg your pardon?' There was no doubt now, the emotion was anger and it propelled me back on to my feet.

My father remained seated. 'I want you to give me your word that you will not interfere with proceedings. I have discussed it with Bowen and he has agreed that there will be no need to call you as a witness as long as I can satisfy him on two points.' He put down his brandy glass. 'Firstly, that you do not know who committed this crime and, secondly, that you are not the father of the unborn child.'

His tone told me how much it had cost him even to ask the question.

Despite my outrage, I could not deny him an answer. 'No. I did not father Margaret's child. And neither do I know who killed her. God help me, until three days ago, I wasn't even sure she was dead. But, if I am not allowed to testify—'

I saw him hold up a hand. 'There is no "if". You *will not* testify. If I do not have your word that you will keep silent during proceedings, there will be no inquest. Do I make myself clear?'

There was nothing I could do but acquiesce.

John

An inquest. Everybody in Newcastle Emlyn was talking about it. And the *plwyfwas* – the *parish functionary* as Mr Schofield would've called him – was out trying to find a jury.

I was glad it wasn't my job. The men who usually filled the jury bench like pigs in the sun weren't going to want to touch this one. Not with Beca's name being muttered over the inquest like a curse. It's one thing to let people know you're well off enough to pay somebody else to carry on your business while you suck your teeth at a dead body and sit listening to the coroner's witnesses. It's another thing altogether to defy Rebecca.

I knew, better than anybody, what the Lady would do to protect her own.

Old Schofield didn't know what to think about this inquest. The lawyer in him wanted to see the law upheld and the law said that murderers should be hanged by the neck till they were dead. But the pragmatist in him – and *pragmatist* was one of his favourite words – thought Probert-Lloyd the magistrate should've left well alone.

'It'll be the son who's behind this,' he told me. 'You watch and see if I'm not right.'

'The son?' I knew I wouldn't have to work too hard to find out what he was talking about. Old Schofield was bursting to flaunt his familiarity with the *crachach*. The gentry.

'Yes. Young Henry. George Probert's son. Probert-*Lloyd*, I should say.' Mr Schofield tapped the end of his pen on his writing board. Going to start teaching me, he was. He always tapped his pen when he was going to *impart knowledge*. 'Mr Justice Probert-Lloyd was just plain George Young when he came here to be married, did you know that?'

I shook my head.

'Yes. Had to take the Probert name as a condition of the match.

His wife was the only heir to the Glanteifi estate and her father didn't want the name dying out.' Mr Schofield pursed his mouth like a cat's arse and I thought he'd stop there. But, no, on he went. 'George was a second or third son of some big family in England – Worcestershire, I think. The Proberts wanted the prestige of the association and, obviously, young George,' he sniggered at his own weak little pun, 'wanted the fortune. An inheritance for a name, not a bad bargain.'

I took advantage of his confiding mood. 'If she was Probert and he was Young,' I asked, 'where did Lloyd come from?'

He gave me the beady eye. *So sharp you'll cut yourself.* 'That was his second wife. He didn't need money once he had the estate so they say he married Jemima Lloyd for love.' His face got a pinched, mean look, then. 'Well, what man of nearly fifty wouldn't love a girl of twenty-one?'

He wasn't looking for a reply.

'Miss Lloyd married him, produced an heir, and was dead. All within a year.' He snapped his mouth shut, as if there was more but he wasn't going to tell me.

'Didn't he have any children from his first wife?'

Schofield sucked a breath in through his thin nostrils. 'I forget how young you are. Mr Probert-Lloyd *did* have a son from his first marriage – George, after his father – but he was killed. In a hunting accident. Before he came of age.' He did some more lip-arsing as if he was shutting himself up.

53

'So Mr Probert-Lloyd married again because he needed an heir?'

Old Schofield gave me a single nod, as if somebody'd pushed his head forward against his will. 'Took her name when they married, just like he had the first time. Of course, it was his choice, on that occasion, rather than her family's. Not that he would ever say as much, naturally.'

Always careful not to *misattribute*, Mr Schofield. You'd think the world was holding its breath, waiting for an excuse to sue him.

'Mr Henry Probert-Lloyd.' He looked over my shoulder, as if the man himself might walk in through the door. 'His mother died giving birth to him. And, now, here he is, insisting on an inquest for a young woman who's been dead the best part of a decade. A dairymaid.'

I let the silence reel out. I knew he'd have to tell me.

'The boy always had the common touch. Worked in the fields with his father's men. Went hare-coursing with stable boys.' Mr Schofield checked to see if I was suitably agog. 'And took a fancy to this girl. The one he's called the coroner for. If it is her.'

'Henry Probert-Lloyd was courting the dead girl?' I couldn't believe I'd asked the question. Mind, it was even more unbelievable when I got an answer instead of a thick ear.

'Yes. Well. Not courting exactly, I dare say. But, whatever it was, it was sufficient to make his father send him away.'

'Probert-Lloyd the magistrate won't let all that come out at the inquest.'

Mr Schofield turned and looked at me as if he'd just remembered who I was. 'I don't think it's your place, John Davies, to speculate on what Mr Probert-Lloyd will or will not do.'

'No. Of course. I'm sorry, Mr Schofield.' I looked at the floor, all repentant.

Peter'd been following all this from the other clerk's desk, mouth open like a dead trout. Saw his chance to suck up, now. 'Will you be going to the inquest, Mr Schofield?'

Old Schofield went over to the window and I hung my tongue out at Peter. *Arse-licker.*

'We'll all go,' Mr Schofield pulled his waistcoat down like he always did when he wanted to be definite. 'You and John and I. We'll all go.'

I sat and stared down at my work.

I couldn't go to that inquest. No. I couldn't.

How could I sit there, watching, as if it was just a spectacle? I couldn't go.

The trouble was, I knew I'd have to.

PART 2: DEFIANCE

Harry

The inquest was held at the Salutation Hotel. It was the only establishment in Newcastle Emlyn with an assembly room large enough to accommodate the anticipated level of public interest.

'Now that an inquest is decided upon, there is nothing to be gained by attempting to hide what we are about,' Coroner Bowen had declared when my father queried his choice of venue. 'This is a suspicious death. A death, moreover, in which your family is not uninterested and which occurred at a time of notorious disturbance. Any attempt to hide the inquest away in a public house that struggles to hold twenty souls would generate gossip, if not outright speculation. We must not allow the populace to claim that they were prevented from hearing the evidence.'

I was encouraged by Bowen's attitude. Given that he had questioned the value of an inquest, I had assumed that he agreed with my father and would cede all decisions to him. But, possessed of the necessary authority to act, Bowen was evidently his own man.

On the assumption that the hotel's stables would quickly fill up, we were driven to Newcastle Emlyn in my father's carriage. I found it an uncomfortable journey. Though I knew that Gus would not dream of pointing out such a thing, I was acutely aware that, in contrast with his own father's carriage, ours was lumbering, dark and aged. Like shuffleboard, it placed us in a bygone era and I hoped that the conduct of the inquest would not further convince Gus that Cardiganshire was stuck somewhere in the reign of the first King George.

Still, at least the carriage kept off the rain and we arrived at the inquest a good deal drier than most of the people stamping mud off their boots as they filed in.

Alive with chatter, the air in the ballroom was a fug of damp wool, tobacco smoke and the sharp smell of beer which was being sold to spectators as they came in.

Knots of people moved aside for us and, as we walked through the crowd, I became aware of a silence spreading on either side. Though I would like to have interpreted it as nothing more than an indication of respect, I feared that the sudden breaking off of animated conversations meant that my presence was not simply being noticed but appraised for what it might mean.

My suspicions were soon confirmed. A voice, evidently confident that I would not understand if it spoke in Welsh, muttered, 'I don't know how he can show his hypocritical face. If he gets up there and tells the truth about what he did I'll eat a toad.'

It was on the tip of my tongue to retort, but I could not. I did not doubt for a second that my father would make good his threat if I uttered a word that he had not already approved.

I kept moving. 'Is *everybody* staring at me?' I asked Gus in an undertone, hoping that at least a few of those who had gathered for the inquest might be indifferent to my appearance.

'Not everybody, no. But some, I must admit, are agog.' He did not append the codicil which, knowing him as well as I did, I could hear in his voice: *What on earth have you done, P-L, to excite such disapprobation from the citizenry?*

Head held unwisely high, I strode forwards. I risked missing my step for the boards underfoot were already slick with tramped-in filth but I was damned if I was going to appear cowed. To distract myself from the glances I could not see and the murmured words I could not quite hear, I tried to calculate how much the magistrates might be obliged to pay the Salutation's owner to compensate him for ruining his dancing-floor. Doubtless he would double the actual cost, knowing full well that they would never pay what he asked.

Gus took my elbow, briefly. 'Over here.'

We wove our way through the ranks of benches to the chairs waiting at the front of the room for the favoured amongst us. Latecomers of whatever station would be obliged to lean, damply, against the walls.

Gus and I took our seats with my father and sundry other magistrates. I felt sweat trickling down my back. Blind to the general gaze, I imagined every eye in the place on me, judging me, finding me wanting.

'Where's Bowen?' Gus asked. I looked up; even I could see that the table set up before us for the coroner was, as yet, unoccupied.

'He'll be instructing the jury on their duties during the inquest,' my father said. 'I gather half of them have never sat before.'

'Chief of those duties,' Gus murmured in my ear, 'will be not running away if they hear the name "Rebecca" mentioned.'

I put a grin on my face, grateful for his attempt at humour, but it was hardly a laughing matter. The inquest had been postponed twice while sufficient men willing to serve on the jury were sought.

'Are the men of the parish always so miserly with their time?' Bowen had asked after a frustrating conference with the parish officer responsible for assisting him in the conduct of the inquest. But, as murmurs of a possible connection between Rebecca and Margaret's death became ever louder, I knew that it was not meanness that was keeping men from doing their duty but the fear of what they might hear, what they might be called upon to decide. And I began to fear that my blithe assumption that the truth would present itself once an inquest was convened had been naïve.

Eventually, a jury of fourteen men had been assembled and Bowen had gathered its members at the workhouse earlier that morning, for the obligatory viewing of the remains.

Gus put a hand on my arm. 'Here they come.'

Once he had alerted me to the movement, I was able to make out figures filing in through the service door at the end of the long room. Silence was called for in Welsh and then, more politely, in English.

After a moment or two of increased noise as folk commented on the coroner's appearance – *so thin and grey,* I heard behind us – the hubbub quieted and I felt some of the tension go out of me, glad that I had been replaced as the focus of interest.

Bowen formally opened proceedings and began his introduction, his dry voice pitched to carry clearly to the corners of the crowded room.

'Though I dislike being obliged to begin on a note of doubt, it is not clear, as matters stand, whether this is an inquest to determine the identity and manner of death of one person or of two.' A susurration passed lightly around the room as people wondered what he meant but Bowen carried on as if the silence had not been disturbed. 'The jury has recently viewed two sets of remains in the mortuary of the Emlyn Union workhouse. One is that of an adult, the other of an infant child.'

This time, the crowd's stirring could not be ignored as those whose English was better than their neighbours' leaned mouth-to-ear to translate Bowen's words. Were accusatory glances being darted at me, eyebrows raised as heads were cocked in my direction? Agonising as it would have been to see people's censure, it was almost worse to be forced to imagine it.

'It is yet to be determined,' Bowen raised his voice, 'whether the child was born or unborn at the time of its mother's death. It is my hope that this will be clarified during the course of these proceedings.'

He fell silent as the noise of the crowd increased, and Ianto Harris was called as the first witness.

'Poor man looks terrified,' Gus muttered as Ianto moved to the chair indicated by the coroner's officer.

Having heard the interpreter confirm his name, Bowen asked the labourer to explain how he had come upon the remains and the room listened to the same details that Ianto had given me on the Glanteifi doorstep.

'Mr Harris,' Bowen said, 'did Mr Williams *instruct* you to pull the roots of the fallen tree from the bank?'

Ianto had made the mistake of gabbling revealing details to me. If I was not to be allowed to give evidence then I was going to make damn' sure that Bowen had all the information I could give him as to the discovery of Margaret's remains. Williams had given specific instructions to the labourers not to dig up the roots and I wanted the inquest to notice that fact. I did not, in all conscience, think that Williams had killed Margaret but I was quite sure that he bore as much responsibility for her death as I did.

'No, sir,' Ianto admitted, 'he didn't. He told us to cut it off at the roots and leave them in the bank.'

'But you thought you could take the roots for yourselves – you and David Davies, for firewood?' Bowen was parroting my own guess; I could see no other reason why Ianto and Dai would have disobeyed an explicit instruction.

Once Ianto had admitted as much, Bowen paused. 'You were asked to dig the bones out and take them to the workhouse mortuary, were you not?'

'Yes, sir. Mr Probert-Lloyd – the son, that is, Mr Henry – said we must dig till the spade came up ten times with no bones in so we could be sure of having them all.'

Again, I felt the discomfort of scores of invisible eyes on me. Had people been unaware, until now, that it was I who had overseen the recovery of Margaret's bones? No. This was simple prurience; I would be stared at every time my name was mentioned or my involvement implied.

'I see. Mr Harris, did you see whether the bones of the child were lying within the skeleton of the woman?' Bowen asked.

Once Bowen's question had been translated, Ianto's response was immediate and I imagined him shaking his head for good measure. 'No, sir. The bones were all mixed up. I didn't even know there *was* a baby till I came here today and that's the truth, sir.'

Bowen then asked about the objects found with the bones but Ianto said he had not noticed any of them. He and David Davies had just done what they were told – they had dug up all the bones and he had taken them to the workhouse in the box cart and that's all he knew.

'And,' Gus murmured, 'quite evidently, all he wants to know.'

Dai Penlan was called next but, when his testimony simply confirmed Ianto's, the crowd began to get restive.

'The next witness,' the inquest's officer raised his voice to silence the conversations that had sprung up all over the room, 'is Rachel Ellis.'

'Who's she?' Gus asked as I heard a woman's hesitant footsteps coming through the crowd. I shook my head, but, as soon as Rachel Ellis spoke to confirm her name, I knew her. A hare lip and cleft palate meant that her speech was difficult to understand and, in order to make herself more readily understood, she pinched her nostrils with the fingers of one hand as she spoke.

'She worked with Margaret at Williams's place,' I told Gus as Mrs Ellis was invited to sit. I had known her as Rachel Evans; she had obviously found a husband in the intervening years.

Through the interpreter, Bowen quickly established that Rachel Ellis had worked for Williams and his wife for a total of ten and a half years, from the time she was twelve until she had left to marry her husband, Aaron Ellis.

'And while you worked there, Margaret Jones was also employed there, as a dairymaid?' Bowen asked.

'Yes, that's right.'

It was odd, this three-way question and answer. Rachel addressed all her responses to the interpreter, whom she obviously knew as she did not address him with the formality she would have used had she been speaking directly to the coroner. Even so, as the questions turned to Margaret, Rachel's voice had become querulous.

I moved my gaze about the front of the room until I found the spot, between the coroner and his witness, where I was able to form an impression of the movements of both. Though I could not see their expressions, sometimes I was able to infer what people might be feeling from discernible movements or changes in posture.

'Mrs Ellis, could you examine the things that Mr Evans is going to show you and tell me whether you recognise them?'

The parish officer's footsteps as he approached Rachel were loud in the silence and I imagined the spectators leaning forward to see the objects he showed her. Again, I felt the relief of knowing that people's eyes were no longer on me.

'The material is the same as a shawl she had,' Rachel said.

'And the other things?' Bowen asked.

A long silence followed. It was clear that Rachel Ellis did not want to commit herself.

'They might be hers.'

'Did Margaret Jones possess anything else that you might expect to be in a bundle of her things?' Bowen asked. 'Anything at all?'

I could have answered that question for him; I had seen her possessions often enough, laid out neatly on the wall in her corner of the loft. If she had been wearing her Sunday shawl then her bundle would have been tied in her work shawl and would have comprised underlinen, a Sunday petticoat and apron, her tin, her rushlight holder and the thick woollen stockings she wore when it was very cold.

'No, sir,' Rachel answered. 'Well, only some clothes.'

'So,' Bowen pushed on, 'there was nothing found with the bones that Margaret Jones did not own and everything that she did, is that right?'

I tried to conjure up Rachel Ellis's fearful expression as she listened to the interpreter untangling the nothings and everythings of the coroner's question. I remembered her as having a plain, flat face, as if the bones had been pushed backwards when they were baby-soft.

'Yes,' she said eventually, 'that's right.'

'Very well, then, do you know why Margaret would leave Waungilfach with all her belongings?'

'No.' It was hardly more than a whisper.

'Are you sure? She'd been with Mr and Mrs Williams for some time. Didn't you think it was strange that she should leave so suddenly?' The room held its breath. 'Mrs Ellis?'

She raised a hand to pinch her nose. 'I thought it was a man.'

I swallowed, shifted my position on the hard chair, hoped nobody had been watching my face while she spoke.

'You thought she had left with a man?' Bowen asked. I heard nothing but she must have nodded because he prompted, 'The father of her child?'

There was no reply. Gus leaned towards me. 'She's not answering. And she's not looking at him.'

'Mrs Ellis,' I heard Bowen insist, 'do you know who the father of Margaret Jones's child was?'

Her 'No' was barely audible. But it was not only her reluctance that made me suspect she was lying. Though Margaret and Rachel had not been the best of friends, they had shared a sleeping space and had, of necessity, found a way of rubbing along together. If anybody knew the identity of the baby's father it would be her.

'Very well.' Bowen appeared to be making a note. 'Now, Mrs Ellis, I'd like to talk about how it was discovered that Margaret Jones had gone missing. Can you tell me what happened?'

'She just wasn't there in the morning when I woke up.'

'Perhaps we might start a little while earlier. Can you tell the hearing what you and Margaret did from the time you finished work the previous day, please?'

The room listened to the interpreter rendering the coroner's polite request and Gus leaned towards me again. 'She's looking happier now we're off the subject of the child's father.'

'It was May,' Rachel began, 'so there was light to do more work after milking. I'd just finished bringing the hens in and finding all the eggs when the bell rang for supper.'

'And where did you eat supper?'

'In the servants' kitchen.'

Rachel, thrown from her narrative path by the question, said nothing more until Bowen asked 'And did Margaret Jones come in for supper?'

'Yes, she did. But she didn't eat very much. She said she was tired. It's hard, working all day when you're near your time, so she went to bed early.'

I wondered if Bowen mistrusted this sudden loquacity as much as I did; I had seen this tactic on numerous occasions. A witness, wishing to appear helpful without actually telling the barrister what he wanted to know, would prattle on, supplying any amount of superfluous information. I wondered what Rachel was hiding behind this sudden urge to oblige but Bowen seemed to feel that he had finally learned something new. 'Margaret Jones left the kitchen while everybody else was still eating – is that correct?'

'Yes.'

'And did you see her after that?'

'Only lying in bed. Or what I thought was her. When she went out of supper, she told me not to wake her when I came up to the loft because she was tired. So, when I went up, I kept to my place and didn't go near her.'

'Can you explain what you mean by "your place", Mrs Ellis?'

I pictured the loft that Rachel had shared with Margaret. It stood over the larger of the two cowsheds where Williams's milk cows were tied during the winter. Rachel, having worked at the farm longer, had occupied the corner furthest away from the door and, therefore, from draughts.

'In the loft – she had her place and I had mine. Because there was no hay there in May, there was only a pile of sacks and things between us so I thought I could see her when I went in, even though it was getting dark. She always curled up with her back to the door, you see, with the blanket pulled up over her head to keep her warm. I thought it was her lying there when I went in. Because she'd said to be quiet, I didn't speak to her. It wasn't till the next day I saw it was only a few rolled-up sacks under the blanket, not her.'

'But didn't you see that her possessions had gone?' Bowen asked.

'No. It was getting dark.'

'So you believe that Margaret Jones had already left before you went to the loft after supper?'

The question interpreted for her, Rachel hesitated. 'I don't know. She might have. All I know is, when I went to wake her in the morning, it was sacks under the blanket, not her.'

Bowen did not respond and, as his silence lengthened, I leaned towards Gus. 'Is he writing notes?'

'Apparently. Might be a ploy to make her nervous so that she'll let something slip.'

I watched Bowen as well as I was able to. His tall frame was largely hidden by his seated posture behind the table but it seemed to me that his economy of movement had something painful in it, as if anything more might cause him to cry out.

'When you left the kitchen,' I heard him say a few moments later, 'and went across the yard to the loft, did you see any strangers, anything out of place?'

'No. I didn't see anybody.'

'Mrs Ellis,' Bowen asked, apparently still bent over his pen, 'do you know when Margaret Jones's baby was due to be born?'

'No. Not really.' Even with her nostrils pinched, Rachel Ellis's answer was difficult to hear, her voice barely audible.

But I knew. Margaret's baby had been due in the middle of June. 'She was quite near her time, I think you said?'

'I suppose so.'

'Is it possible, do you think, that Margaret Jones felt the baby coming and didn't know what to do?'

'I don't know. I was asleep.' It could not have been more obvious that Rachel Ellis was giving her evidence with the greatest reluctance. But was she reluctant to tell the truth or to hide it?

'Do you think she might have gone in search of help?' Bowen persevered. 'Gone to the midwife?'

'The midwife comes to you, not the other way around.'

'Mrs Ellis,' I could hear Bowen's frustration, 'I'm going to ask you again – do you know who the father of Margaret Jones's child was?'

Rachel's head was bowed; she wished to look neither Bowen nor his translator in the eye. 'No.'

'Do you know who might have wanted to harm her?' the coroner asked.

'No. No, I don't.' It was a whisper. And I could tell, even if Bowen couldn't, that it was a lie.

As if the crowd had been holding its breath, once Rachel Ellis was dismissed, a great exhalation of comment and speculation broke out. Behind us, I could hear people rising from the benches, pushing them backwards on the ravaged floor. Looking out for late-coming friends, I assumed, or possibly trying to see who else was waiting to give evidence.

Above the rising level of conjecture, I heard Bowen's voice. 'Ask Mr Williams to come forward, would you?'

Evidently the bench-sitters had heard, too, because the noise around us suddenly fell away as people looked about for William

Williams. His being called as a witness could hardly be a surprise – the remains had been found on his farm, after all – but, nonetheless, his appearance was bound to stimulate gossip.

Gus leaned closer to me. 'Do I get the impression that there's no great respect locally for our friend Williams?'

'He doesn't really fit.' I kept my voice low, acutely aware of the listening ears all around. 'He's not a tenant, like most farmers, but he's not a gentleman either.'

In fact, William Williams owned just enough land to make the larger tenants envious but by no means sufficient to qualify as one of the gentry. As a boundary-neighbour, my father treated him with a nicely calculated civility but most of the other local landowners found Williams presumptuous. 'Jumped up' was the general opinion and Williams knew it. It was for this reason that my father had advised Bowen to address Williams as if he were a *bona fide* member of the gentry. 'I know it goes against the grain,' I had heard him say, 'but you'll get nothing but an irritable standing on his dignity if you don't treat him as one of us. He is not an astute man. If he thinks you're giving him the respect he thinks he deserves, you'll be able to induce him to tell you more than he intends.'

The coroner's officer called for order, silencing the rumble of voices. After suitably courteous preliminaries, Bowen asked Williams whether he could positively identify the objects found with the bones as belonging to Margaret Jones.

Williams took his time in answering. 'Well, as far as I can be expected to remember the garments of my servants, the scrap of material does resemble a shawl I seem to recall her possessing. But, as to the other things, I couldn't say. As private possessions there would be no reason for me to have seen them.'

A few suppressed snorts and murmurs around the room took issue with this but, if Bowen did anything but ignore them, I could not tell. 'I see. Yes. Thank you.' The coroner moved on to his next question and I caught a subtle change of tone. 'Mr Williams, just to be clear and to silence any malicious gossip that might seek an alternative explanation, could you tell this inquest why you asked your labourers not to pull up the roots of the tree they were cutting? I understand that the more common practice would be to remove the whole thing – root and branch, so to speak.'

It was a question I should have asked Williams myself but here, in the context of an official hearing, it seemed less impertinent.

'That *would* be the common practice, Mr Bowen,' Williams agreed, ponderously, 'but not on such a steep bank. The soil there is very unstable, you see. Apt to slide. I wanted to protect the slope whilst removing the wood for use.'

'So your instruction was simply a precaution against the bank slipping?'

'Yes. Exactly so.'

'Thank you, Mr Williams. Now, if you'd be kind enough, it would be helpful for the jury to hear how Margaret Jones's disappearance, seven years ago, came to your notice?'

There was a pause, then the farmer cleared his throat. 'Well, it was some time ago, obviously. I'm not sure that all the details are clear in my mind.'

'Just as much as you can remember. If you'd be so good.' Bowen's tone suggested a forced smile.

'Very well. I went out that morning to see that the milking was well underway, as I did every morning, only to find that Margaret wasn't there. Rachel Evans – I beg your pardon, Mrs Ellis – was doing the milking alone.' He cleared his throat again: a nervous gesture, I realised, rather than a necessary one. 'I asked her where Margaret was and I was told that she wasn't there. Mrs Ellis said that she'd woken up to find Margaret and all her things gone.'

'I see. And what did you think it meant – that she had taken all her possessions with her?'

'That she wasn't intending to come back, obviously.'

There was a pause while Bowen waited for a brief burst of laughter occasioned by an inaudible comment to subside. Then he asked, 'When had you last seen Margaret Jones, Mr Williams, prior to that morning?'

'It would have been the previous afternoon. I always go out to the dairy to make sure that everything is as it should be before the servants go in for their supper.'

'And did she seem as usual? Was she agitated in any way?'

'Mrs Williams and I asked ourselves that when we realised that she'd left us. But we could think of nothing that would have warned us that she was about to do such a thing.'

'Running away from *you*, wasn't she?' a voice called out from the back corner of the room, followed by laughter from the same quarter.

'Drunks,' Gus dismissed them. I nodded without comment. Drunk they might be, but these men knew Williams's reputation and they were not wary of letting him know it.

Bowen, inured to extempore contributions from the floor, simply waited for the laughter to die away, then continued. 'Had anybody come to speak to her that day? Anybody at all?'

'No. I would have been aware of it if they had.'

I did not doubt that. Williams had always kept an alarmingly close eye on his female servants.

73

'And nobody who didn't have business on your farm was there the previous evening?'

Williams hesitated then said, 'No. No, there wasn't anybody.'

What was the significance of that hesitation – Bowen's double negative? Williams just trying to cast his mind back? Or something else? Unable to scrutinise the farmer's face, it was infuriatingly difficult to tell.

'And during the night? Did the dogs bark at all?'

'No. I would have heard them if they had – my wife was up most of the night with our youngest child. He had colic and was crying so much that none of us slept for very long.'

'So, when you went out the following morning to be told that Margaret Jones had gone, what did you think?'

'To tell you the truth, Mr Bowen, I was astonished.'

'Astonished?' I caught a movement from Bowen which might have been the removal of spectacles. 'Why is that? Surely, in her condition, it was only to be expected that she would leave before the child was born? That she would go back to her family?'

A silence developed. I could feel every eye in the place on Williams. 'I don't believe she had any family. None that would take her in, at any rate.'

'Did she tell you that?'

'In a manner of speaking.'

In the silence that followed, I wondered whether Bowen raised an eyebrow and fixed Williams with a questioning look. From the muttered hubbub around the room other eyebrows were certainly being raised at Williams's imprecise answer.

'One day…' I could almost see Williams swallowing, sucking his lips to moisten them, 'one day I asked her what she was going to do.'

'When the time came for the baby to be born?'

'Yes.' Bowen's failure to ask another question forced more from Williams. 'She said she hadn't decided.'

A spasm of guilt gripped me; Margaret had not decided what she should do because she was waiting to see whether someone would rescue her. Whether *I* would rescue her.

'And what was your reply?'

Again, Williams produced that uneasy cough. 'I can't really remember.'

'Liar! You'd've thrown her out!' the drunk again. And, again, I knew he spoke nothing but the truth.

Bowen ignored him and addressed Williams. 'You didn't make it clear to her that she would have to leave?' A gentleman would see that as the only course open to an employer. Allowing a girl in Margaret's condition to stay would imply that he condoned immorality, not to mention the fact that it would encourage all the other female servants to think that they, too, could presume on his liberality.

'No.' Williams tried clearing his throat, as if he could summon up phlegm as an excuse. 'No, I didn't.'

'May I ask why?' Bowen sounded genuinely surprised; unremarkably so, given my father's emphasis on Williams's desire to be seen, in every way, as a gentleman. As he waited for a response, people turned to their neighbours wondering, behind their hands, how Williams was going to explain himself.

'Things were… there is… that is, there *was* a lot of feeling locally,' he began, 'about girls who got themselves into trouble.'

'Feeling? What do you mean by that?' Bowen was evidently tiring of the need to treat Williams with kid gloves.

'Well,' Williams's voice strengthened as the topic veered away from events at Waungilfach and into a more public arena, 'when Margaret Jones disappeared, the old system had only recently been replaced by the workhouse unions. People still hadn't quite got used to the idea that girls couldn't just go to the minister anymore and say that so-and-so had got them with child and expect the father to provide. There was a lot of resentment against the new law at that time.'

At that time. A frisson went through the room. Rebecca had been violently against the new Poor Law. During the riots the militia had been billeted at Newcastle Emlyn's workhouse to protect it.

'And I was conscious of that feeling. I didn't want to outrage opinion by throwing Margaret out of house and home.'

For a few seconds, Bowen said nothing and a murmuring became audible here and there. It was too low for me to catch any words but I could have made a good guess at the substance. Then the inebriate in the corner gave voice to it. 'You liar! You never kept her on to save her from the workhouse!'

Try as the coroner's officer might to stem the onrush of corroboration unleashed by the accusation, I knew it to be true; Williams had had no compunction about throwing young girls onto the tender mercies of the Board of Guardians. I also knew that his neighbours had taken it upon themselves to mend his ways.

I knew, because I had been there.

Harry

Waungilfach, 1841

It was August. Margaret and I were courting in her corner of the loft, our voices discreet so as not to disturb Rachel, sleeping on the other side of the loft's freight of hay.

As anyone who has been in a hayloft knows, they are ill-lit enough places by day; at night, the dark is almost absolute. And the dark has its own laws; I did and said things in the warm blackness of that loft that I would never have dared venture in the bright light of day.

That night, as had quickly become the habit between us, Margaret was trying to seduce me and I was resisting.

'Why not? We both want to.' I felt her fingers on my face in the dark. 'Or don't you want me, Harry?'

'You know I do. But I'm not going to dishonour you.'

'*Dishonour* me?'

'You know what I mean.'

'What then?' She was getting impatient. 'Going to marry me, are you?'

'Why not?'

'*Why not?*' In her exasperation, Margaret pushed me away and sat up. 'Because I'm not a lady, that's why. Because everybody would laugh at you. And at me.'

I propped myself up on one elbow and looked at the pale shape of her face in the dark. I did not need a candle to see that she was cross with me. 'But what does it *matter* whether you're a lady or not?' I asked, desperate for her to take me seriously. 'The world is changing.' It was fifty years since French aristocrats had been dragged to the guillotines by working men in pursuit of liberty and equality, surely we could allow ourselves the gentler route down the aisle?

'Don't be stupid, Harry!' She caught herself and moderated her tone. She did not want to have to explain my foolishness to Rachel. 'We could never be man and wife.'

'You're wrong, Mags. I'll talk to my father.'

'Yes, and he'll tell you I can be your mistress but never your wife!'

She sighed and put a hand on my face. 'Harry, even if you carried me away and married me secretly, it wouldn't work. I could never be a true wife to you. I'd be like the bearded lady at the fair – something to gawp at. Let's just take things as they are and make the best of them.' I took her hand and she lay down beside me again. Some minutes later, her hand found the front of my breeches and who knows what a different course both our lives would have taken had I not heard a shot at that moment.

Margaret tensed in my arms. 'What was that?'

Unsteady with desire, I got up and staggered to the door. Open, it let in enough moonlight to allow me to make my way down the stone steps without missing my footing. 'Stay there,' I hissed back up to Margaret, 'I'll be back when I've seen what's going on.'

The byre stood on the main yard, facing the back of Williams's house. Ignoring the dogs who fawned on me to the ends of their chains, I crossed the yard in the direction of the house, its whitewashed bulk looming huge in front of me. As I made my way cautiously around the side, another shot rang out and I became aware of laughter and a scattered clatter as if boys were hitting things with sticks.

Something clawed at my shirt and a thrill of pure terror pierced me from head to toe. I stood, rooted to the spot for several seconds, unable to move until reason reasserted itself and told me that I had simply caught a tendril from the rambler rose that climbed the side of the house. Weak with relief, I unhooked the barbs and moved forward.

What I saw when I peered around the side of the house forced words out of me as a thump on the back forces breath.

'Oh my God!'

A great mass of people was streaming down the lane towards the front of the house, the way lit by torches and lanterns in the hands of a few at the front while those behind carried sticks and pots and horns and fiddles with which they were making a cacophonous uproar. As I watched, another shot was loosed off to great guffaws of excited laughter.

I jumped as I felt a hand on my back.

'The *ceffyl pren,*' Margaret murmured.

'I said to wait in the loft.' My pulse was racing from her unexpected touch.

'You said you'd be back, too.'

I forbore to point out that I had been gone less than a minute and we both turned our attention to the people gathering in front of the house. Men draped in nightdresses, women with their menfolk's coats fastened at the back, some with their shawls about their heads in the fashion of an Indian turban, children held by the hand and seated on their fathers' shoulders. And every face – the face of every man, woman and child – was blacked so as to be almost invisible in the surrounding night.

A man stepped forward, a lantern in his hand, a grotesquely large wig on his head. Two other men followed him. Between them, on their shoulders, they carried a sheet-draped pole fixed, at one end, with the long skull of a horse.

The straw-wigged man strode towards the farmhouse door and hammered on it with the knob of his staff.

'William Williams,' he called into the cool summer air, 'come out.'

I looked around at Margaret, 'What are they doing here?'

She shrugged. 'You know what he's like.'

I certainly knew what she had told me: of Williams's inability to keep his hands to himself, his obvious assumption that his female servants were there for his pleasure. So far, Margaret had not suffered his attentions but his pursuit of one of the housemaids, Hannah Rees, was relentless and Margaret feared that she would be next. 'If he finds out you're coming here to see me at night, he'll be after me like a terrier down a rabbit hole,' she had said.

The cool, night-furled petals of a rose brushed my cheek as I turned back to the crowd and I lifted my hand to break it off and give it to Margaret.

Quickly, she put her hand over mine. 'Don't. I can't have it – they'll say I stole it and I'll be in trouble.'

A shout turned our attention to the front of the house. 'William Williams!' one of the men carrying the *ceffyl pren* shouted, 'Come out! Or we'll break your windows and come in!'

The crowd roared its approval of this threat and I felt a prickle of apprehension raise the hairs on my scalp.

'That's Elias Jenkins from our chapel doing the shouting,' Margaret whispered, 'I recognise his voice. The leader – the one in the straw wig – that's our minister, Nathaniel Howell.'

Nathaniel Howell. That night, with Margaret, I could not know that I would be confronted by the minister, myself, in the months to come, Howell once more blacked and bewigged.

The sound of bolts being drawn back carried to where we were standing and the front door opened. The lantern in his hand showed that Williams was fully dressed. The *ceffyl pren* might be here to chasten him but he was not going to connive at his own humiliation by appearing in his nightclothes.

'What is the meaning of this?'

It was bluster, nothing more; Williams knew perfectly well what was standing in front of him. And he must have known that they intended to offer him none of the privileges of gentry. He could protest all he liked in outraged English but both Nathaniel Howell and Elias Jenkins had called him out in Welsh, as their equal.

I waited for the *cantwr* to step forward and lay out the charges. If Williams was lucky, accusation would be leavened with amusement and the crowd would vent some of its anger in mocking and ridiculing him. Were they going to make him ride the *ceffyl pren?* Quite apart from the indignity of it, being forced to sit astride the wooden pole was, by all accounts, a physically painful experience.

Suddenly, I felt warm lips on my neck. 'Let's go back to the loft,' Margaret whispered in my ear.

I turned to her in surprise. 'Don't you want to watch?'

'I'd rather go back to the loft with you. Leave him to them.'

But I could not. Whether it was because I could not divorce the mob's judgement on Williams from my own behaviour or because I could not countenance taking my pleasure with her while Williams was vilified and manhandled, I do not know. But I stood and watched till the end, till Margaret had left my side and gone back to her warm blankets, till Nathaniel Howell had issued his final threat.

'Do not forget what we have said this night, William Williams. Your wife is watching at that window,' he pointed to a spot above the farmer's head, 'and she has seen that you are known for a fornicator and deflowerer of young women. You and she are Uncle and Aunty to your servants – you are responsible for their welfare. Make sure that, in future, you look after them better. Or we shall be back.'

I waited until the last of them had disappeared before moving from my place at the side of the house. As I crossed the yard, intending to rejoin Margaret in the loft, a light appeared at a first-floor window in the farmhouse. Somebody, lantern in hand, was looking out over the moonlit yard.

Whoever it was could not have failed to see me.

John

For years, I wouldn't let myself think about that night in the Alltddu. Not ever. If a memory came into my head, I slammed a door on it. Bang. I wasn't going to give it houseroom.

I couldn't help my dreams. Nobody can. And sometimes my body jumped me awake, my skin slick with terror. But a man's waking thoughts are his own and I wasn't going to think about it. It was past. Done. Nothing I could do about it.

Then the inquest was announced, and the memories seemed to grow a will of their own. They *wanted* me to remember. Dozens of times a day they came. Scores. Hundreds. Hundreds of times a day, a picture of that dark wood slid in front of my eyes. I couldn't keep the memories out. I couldn't work properly. I couldn't sleep. *Dared not* sleep.

And the questions. They came with the memories. They were in my head all the time. Asking, asking.

Who gave the order?

What had she done to offend Beca? Why did she have to die?

Until then, I'd never asked myself *why*. That was Beca's business, not mine.

Until then, I'd never wanted to know her name or who she was. There was nothing I could do for her. I didn't want to know.

Now it was everywhere. Margaret Jones. Margaret Jones. Margaret Jones.

And I couldn't keep any of it in the back of my mind any more.

Because the questions I'd slammed the door on were going to be asked in court.

Who? Why?

I was terrified of what I knew. Terrified of the new dreams that started. Dreams where I stood up in front of the coroner and said *I can answer your questions.*

I was terrified of going to the inquest. Terrified I'd see *him*. That I'd give myself away. That something I did or said would tell the coroner that I knew the truth.

Stand up, John Davies, and give testimony!

I could do Margaret Jones no good. She was dead and gone. But I could do myself a world of harm.

So I sat there in the Salutation's assembly room, stiff with fear, Mr Schofield on one side of me, Peter on the other. Old Schofield probably thought I was being respectful, sitting up and taking notice of every single word. Especially when Peter was sprawled in the chair next to me, legs wide as if he was waiting for a dog to rush up and sniff his crotch. The only way he could've looked as if he cared less was if he'd started picking his nose and eating it.

I envied his couldn't-careness so much I could've punched him. My heart'd been banging my ribs so hard when we walked in that I kept expecting Mr Schofield to ask what the noise was. I looked about, casual-like, as if I was searching for a friend.

I saw plenty of people I knew, but nobody that looked like him.

Perhaps he'd keep away. Or perhaps he just wasn't there yet.

I was glad when Mr Schofield took us to sit on the chairs near the front. Most people'd only see the back of my head.

William Williams's wife was called to give evidence straight after him. I could only hope, for her sake, that the drunks'd already had their fun shouting at her husband from the back of the room. Still, the way they were putting the Salutation's ale away, the hecklers soon wouldn't be able to speak, never mind shout.

Good thing for Esme Williams.

People in Newcastle Emlyn still called her Esme Owens sometimes – not to her face, mind, only when they were talking about her. She'd married above herself – married into land – and she tried to play the lady. Did her no good. Not in Newcastle Emlyn where everybody knew she was Owens the grocer's daughter.

I don't think the coroner knew, mind. Gave her almost the same respect he'd given her husband, he did. Except, thinking about it, I didn't think he'd've asked a real lady to give evidence at all. Especially not in front of the rough crowd who'd come in out of the rain that day. 'Mrs Williams,' he said 'can you tell us what kind of young woman Margaret Jones was?'

The crowd got in before Esme could open her mouth.

'A slut!'

'No better than she should be!'

If Mr Schofield was right and Henry Probert-Lloyd was behind this inquest, then he was doing Margaret Jones's memory no favours at all. People were remembering her, now, and nothing they remembered was to her credit. Always the way, isn't it? Do ten good things and one bad, and the one bad deed is what you'll be remembered for. Guaranteed.

'Isn't it obvious what sort of young woman she was?' Esme asked Mr Bowen when Matthew Evans, the *plwyfwas*, had shut the crowd up. 'She was carrying a child out of wedlock.'

'Quite so.' Mr Bowen nodded. Then he took his little pinch-nose specs off and looked over at her. 'Mrs Williams, I hardly like to ask the question I'm going to put to you next, but circumstances dictate that I must.'

Esme smoothed her skirt down as if she'd just seen a crease in the silk.

'Mrs Ellis has stated that she did not know who the father of Margaret Jones's child was – do *you* have any suspicion or knowledge in that regard?'

'In other words,' a voice called out, in English, 'was this another of your husband's bastards?'

Half the crowd rocked with laughter and the other half turned to ask its neighbour what he'd said. I looked around to see if I could spot who'd spoken and saw a group of men at the back, all slapping the shoulder of one man or trying to shake his hand.

That man! His expression almost made me retch with fear. The look of him as he stared over at William Williams was savage. Like the face in my nightmares. The face of the killer.

I'll kill you boy!

No. It wasn't him. Too old. Nobody aged that much in seven years. But that look! Hatred – that's what it was.

Eyes on Esme, I put my hands on my knees, gripped tight to keep them from shaking.

'No, Mr Bowen,' Esme raised her voice above the heckling, 'I do not know who the child's father was. But I do know, from speaking to *respectable* people, that young men gathered around Margaret Jones at the chapel like wasps around a windfall.'

'She was popular with the young men?'

'So I've been told.'

'But you can't recall one young man in particular who made a nuisance of himself at your farm?'

That made her stop and think. She wouldn't want to give people the idea that she couldn't control her servants.

'No,' she said, when she'd finished thinking, 'we wouldn't have allowed that.'

Bowen made some more notes and Esme went back to smoothing her skirts. Probably trying to draw attention to the fact that in a roomful of *betgwns* and aprons she was wearing something expensive and fashionable. And yellow. It was very showy, but it didn't suit her complexion. Made her look peevish.

I took a breath, sat back in my chair, folded my arms. Didn't want Peter asking what I was so strung-up about. But the look on that man's face had scared me to my bones.

'Mrs Williams, your husband stated that he would have known if anybody had come to Waungilfach on the night Margaret disappeared because the whole family was wakeful. Is that your belief, too?'

'Oh yes, no doubt. The dogs would have barked if somebody came onto the yard. They always do.'

Some clown at the back started barking. Beer. Always makes men think they're funny.

Mr Bowen ignored the dog noises and checked his notes. 'But my understanding,' he said, 'is that the house was hardly silent. Your husband told this inquest that your youngest child was crying so much that nobody slept that night.'

Their youngest child. Hah! Her *husband's* youngest he might've been. But not hers. Little Samuel, born the wrong side of the blanket. Hidden behind the pretence of charity so Williams could hold on to his respectability.

'Yes. He cried all night with the colic.'

'So, if the dogs *had* barked, you might not have heard them over the child crying?'

'Well… *I* might not – because I was in the nursery at the front of the house. But the big bedroom is at the back overlooking the yard. Mr Williams would hear the dogs from there.'

The 'big bedroom'. Hers and Williams's. No gentleman's dressing room for William Williams, Waungilfach. Was that why Esme tolerated his behaviour with the maids? Why she was prepared to treat his bastard son like her own – because she was sick of having to share the 'big bedroom' with him?

'And you're quite sure that Mr Williams was in the bedroom at the back of the house all night? He didn't come into the nursery to see the child?'

'No. He leaves the children to me.'

He'd have to, wouldn't he? The Williamses might have a 'nursery' but they couldn't've afforded a nursemaid. Not if gossip was to be believed.

'Mrs Williams, was it not somewhat unusual for female servants to be sleeping in a hayloft? Would it not be more customary for them to have a place in the house?'

It was a good question and a few in the crowd whooped and clapped at it. *Yes, Esme, why were they sleeping out?* Margaret Jones wouldn't've been able to leave the house as easily as she'd slipped away from the loft.

For the first time since she'd come up to give evidence, Esme Williams looked uncomfortable. 'To speak plainly, Mr Bowen, our house is a good size, but, by the time we've found space for all the indoor servants there's nowhere for the outdoor ones to sleep. Better for the dairymaids to be in the loft than on the kitchen floor.' In other words our house might not be the size of a gentry house but, by God, we employ a lot of servants!

Something that might have been a sly smile fought with the lines on Bowen's grey face but the tone of his voice didn't change. 'You weren't worried that the young women in your employment might not be safe, sleeping in the loft?'

'No. The dogs are chained up outside that byre. Nobody could get in.'

Nobody the dogs didn't know, at any rate.

'It's your belief, then, that Margaret Jones must have left of her own free will, taking her possessions with her?'

'Yes, I'm quite sure of it.'

'But you don't know why she might have done that?'

Esme looked at him as if he was a fool. 'I can only hope it was from shame, Mr Bowen.'

The coroner nodded as if he was agreeing with her. But the longer the pause went on, the more it looked like he was just letting her comment sit in the air between them. Because it wasn't only Margaret Jones who had reason to be ashamed.

'Mrs Williams,' he said finally, 'one of the things this inquest must determine is whether the jury is required to bring in a verdict on the deaths of one person or two. Do you think it's possible that Margaret Jones might have given birth before leaving the loft? That she might have been taking her child somewhere?'

I kept my eyes down, then. I knew the answer to that question and I didn't want anybody to see it written on my face.

Esme pursed her lips. 'No, I don't believe it *is* possible. The girl showed no signs of being uncomfortable at servant supper and she would if she was in the early stages of labour.' Esme Williams, mother of three daughters, seemed quite sure of herself. 'I don't think it would be possible for her to give birth and get away before the morning.'

You don't think it *would have been* possible, I corrected in my head. Who did she think she was fooling, acting the lady?

'Do you think she might have gone to the midwife?'

'Possibly. First children usually take their time coming, so she might.'

What did Esme know about midwives? Williams would've made sure that he had a doctor at the birth of his children.

'Mrs Williams, as you were awake the whole night with your little boy, do you happen to remember what the weather was like?'

'Yes. It rained most of the night. Not much wind, just rain and more rain.'

Rain and more rain. I could still feel it dripping down the back of my neck. If it hadn't been for that rain, I'd never've seen what I'd seen.

'So, wherever she was going,' Bowen suggested, 'Margaret Jones must have been determined about her journey – it wasn't the kind of night on which a young woman would choose to go tramping about.'

'No.' Esme agreed with him. 'The clouds made it very dark. And Margaret didn't have a lantern.'

Bowen took his specs off and smiled at her. 'Mrs Williams, thank you. You've been most generous in coming to give testimony here. I'm going to release you, now, unless you have anything to add which would help this hearing determine whether or not these remains *are* those of Margaret Jones and, if so, how she came to be buried beneath a tree in your woods?'

For the first time, Esme didn't seem to know how to answer him.

But she wanted to say *something*, you could tell.

Then, about half a second before the layabouts got bored and started heckling her, she spoke. 'It's my belief that this *is* Margaret Jones. I don't know how she died, but I do know how she lived. She was a young woman who had her eye on the main chance. And perhaps that's what caused her downfall.'

Harry

I was glad when Bowen ordered a break at midday. Both Mrs Williams's testimony and the drunken spectators' comments about Margaret had made me feel profoundly uncomfortable.

'We have a meal waiting for us,' my father declared as soon as we had made our way out of the ballroom. 'I asked James to arrange it before he took the carriage back.'

'You have a more reliable coachman than my father does if you can trust him to do that,' Gus said.

'That,' I managed, 'is because you treat your servants as if they hadn't the wit they were born with and they behave accordingly so as not to embarrass you.'

Gus aimed a cuff at my shoulder which, not having seen it coming, I failed to avoid; a further indication, if my father had noticed it, that I could not see as well as I pretended.

More evidence to that effect accumulated over lunch as local society presented itself at our table to pay its respects. Meeting a speaker's eye guided solely by the location of their voice is a hit-and-miss affair and I knew that I must, often, be directing my gaze at necks and ears and hairlines. I would soon have a reputation as a shifty-eyed fellow.

Morosely, I wondered how many of the people I had met over the years who had seemed unwilling or unable to meet my eye had, in fact, been suffering from a similar loss of sight. My eye-doctor, Figges, had told me that my condition was far from unique, though it was more often seen in those of advancing years. 'It *does* occur in the young,' he said, 'though far less frequently. Do you have siblings? I only ask because it tends to run in families.'

I had always wished that I were not my father's only living child, that there might have been a brother or a sister to share the burden of comparison with the dead and deeply lamented George; but now I felt my aloneness still more acutely. 'If only I had,' I said, 'it would be a comfort to discuss this blindness with somebody who understood it.'

But Figges had taken exception to this. 'No, no, Mr Probert-Lloyd – your condition is not to be thought of as true blindness. If it follows the usual path you will always retain your peripheral vision – vision outside the central area.'

Very well. I would continue to need lanterns and candles and I would, by constantly looking askance at the world, be able to see where I was going. But if I could not read, or see a person's face, or scrutinise an object, was I not blind?

I was oppressed by the knowledge that soon I would have to tell my father why I had come home, why I was not hurrying back to my practice at the bar. And then he would have the upper hand.

Bowen had wanted to call Nathaniel Howell to give evidence. Not as leader of the *ceffyl pren* band who had visited Williams to warn him to mend his ways – Bowen knew nothing of that – but as the minister of Treforgan Unitarian chapel and Margaret Jones's pastor. However, as the Reverend Howell had left, at the height of the riots, to take up a post somewhere in the east of England and could not, therefore, easily be recalled, the only witness left to examine was the local midwife.

Unlike Rachel Ellis, the midwife gave not the slightest indication of being intimidated by Bowen or his proceedings.

'You are Ann Davies and you act as a midwife, is that correct?'

Though she waited for the interpreter to finish before she replied in Welsh, I wondered whether, in fact, Ann Davies understood English perfectly well.

'I am.'

I eyed her in my peripheral vision. She was not tall, but the way she held herself gave the impression of self-assurance.

'Mrs Davies, were you acquainted with Margaret Jones?'

'Not well, but I knew her to speak to.'

'How did you come to know her?'

'Sometimes the congregation from her chapel and the one I attend would meet to sing together.'

Gus leaned closer. 'Interesting. Both the labourers and Rachel Ellis directed their comments to the interpreter but she's listening to the question then looking at Bowen to give her answer even though she gives it in Welsh.'

My impression of self-assurance had not been wrong, then.

'Did Margaret Jones consult you about the birth of her child?'

'No.'

'Did you know she was carrying a child?'

'Yes. Mrs Williams, Waungilfach, sent a message to me that the girl might need help.'

'What do you mean by that?' The sudden curtness of Bowen's tone told me his suspicions had been aroused – as had mine – by her use of the word 'help'; not to mention the disclosure of Esme Williams's involvement.

'The message said that the girl had no family near,' came the unperturbed reply. 'So she would need help to deliver the child.'

'Just to be clear, since we have a dead infant to consider in this inquest,' Bowen said, his tone only slightly less pointed, 'did Margaret

Jones – or any other person – procure your aid in delivering and then doing away with her baby?'

Ann Davies did not wait for the interpreter this time. 'I am a midwife, Mr Bowen,' she shot back, in English. 'It is my job to bring children into the world not take them out of it.'

But Bowen was not going to be fobbed off with stiff-backed outrage, however surprised he might be at her expression of it. 'Answer the question, please.'

'The poor translator's trying to catch her eye to see what to do,' Gus whispered. 'But La Davies has fixed Bowen with a gimlet eye.'

'Very well,' I heard Ann Davies say. 'No, Margaret Jones did not ask me to kill her baby. Nobody asked me to kill Margaret Jones's baby. I did not kill Margaret Jones's baby.'

I had always wondered exactly what kind of pin's drop was supposed to be audible in such silences. Now I knew. The very finest muslin-holding pin would have clanged to the ground in the hush left by Ann Davies's vehemence.

Bowen might have been expected to reprimand her insolence but he chose to take the midwife's words at face value and to put her tone aside. 'Thank you,' he said, mildly, before pausing to make a note. I applauded the strategy: in not taking offence when he might easily have done so, he had given the midwife a reason to be conciliatory and, perhaps, give him more information than she might have intended. 'Now,' he continued, 'you have said that Margaret Jones did not consult you, but did you seek her out, offer your services?'

'As it happens, I did.'

'And what was her response?'

'She thanked me.'

'And you left it at that?'

'No. I asked her when her baby was due, so that I would be ready.'

'And did she tell you?'

'Yes. She said the baby was expected in the middle of May.'

No. That was not right. Margaret had told me that her baby was due to be born in June.

'When she disappeared, therefore, her baby was due within two weeks or so?'

'Yes.'

The confusion and disquiet that I felt at this news was clearly not shared by the crowd; there was scarcely a murmur as Bowen paused to write something. Had Margaret been confused about when the baby would be born, or had she lied? And, if she had lied, who had she been trying to deceive – me or Ann Davies?

'You have said,' Bowen continued, 'that a young woman with no family would need your help in giving birth to her child. Could Margaret Jones have delivered the child on her own, with no help?'

For the first time, Ann Davies hesitated. 'It does happen,' she said, guardedly. 'Young women who don't know – or don't want to know – that they are with child do sometimes deliver their babies alone.'

'And are children delivered successfully under such circumstances? I ask merely to form an idea of whether this child could have been born before its mother's death.'

'Some are. Some are not.'

I could not see Ann Davies's mouth, but I would have been prepared to bet that it was shut tight, a line drawn across her face. There cannot have been many people in that crowded, muttering ballroom who were ignorant of the fate of infants born in those circumstances. As Ann Davies had intimated, many did not survive and there were no witnesses, save the mother, to say why.

Was that why Mrs Williams had procured the midwife's help before the event? So that Rebecca could not level accusations in Waungilfach's direction? Letting the midwife know of Margaret's need for help was the last thing I would have expected of Williams's wife.

Suddenly, I was aware of one of the jurors standing up. 'Mr Bowen, may I ask Mrs Davies a question?'

'Of course. That's your right.' It was notable, in fact, that the jury had addressed none of the previous witnesses.

'Mrs Davies, I'll ask the question the coroner is too delicate to ask. In your honest opinion, do you think it's possible that Margaret Jones gave birth to her child and then killed it?'

Did Ann Davies ask herself why the juror had requested her *honest* opinion? Was he reminding her that she was under oath to tell the truth?

'As I said, I hardly knew Margaret Jones. I can't say what she might or might not have done.'

'You weren't in the room when Mr Williams gave his testimony,' her interrogator continued, 'but he said that because of the way people felt about the workhouse, he and Mrs Williams wouldn't have dared to send Margaret Jones away. Do you believe that?'

The room waited.

'I can't say,' the midwife said, finally. 'Yes, people were angry about young women and their babies going into the workhouse, but I can't say whether that would have stopped the Williamses of Waungilfach from throwing her out. And,' she added before he asked, 'I can't say what Margaret Jones believed either.'

'Thank you.' The questioner sat down.

'Would any other juror like to ask a question?' Bowen asked. Nobody spoke.

'Then I will resume. Mrs Davies, I have one last question.' The coroner paused. 'Is it possible that Margaret Jones, feeling the onset of her labour pains, would have been able to pack up her belongings and leave Waungilfach farm without anybody being any the wiser?'

'I can't say whether anybody would know she'd gone, but I can say that if she was only in the early stages then she would've been able to pack up and leave. I don't suppose she had very much to carry.'

She seemed to have finished, but then added, 'But, if she did that, where was she going? If she was looking for help with the baby, why would she take all her things with her?'

The room broke out in a hum of rapid translation and muttered agreement.

Bowen, allowing the crowd to chatter, thanked the midwife, dismissed her and proceeded to address the jury.

'I am going to ask you, now, to go out and decide whether you have heard enough to say whether the remains you viewed this morning at the workhouse do, in fact, belong to Margaret Jones and, if they do, whether you have sufficient evidence to say what caused her death. I have heard no evidence to convince me that the child had been born at the time of its mother's death, so I am not going to ask you to give a cause in that case.

'As to a verdict in the case of the mother, you know the options open to you. Logic would dictate that some of these are ruled out by the situation in which the body was found but it is up to you, gentlemen, to provide a verdict in this case.'

Each man, whether he was farmer, butcher, shopkeeper or teacher would be getting the going rate for jury service – a shilling a day. Given the circumstances, most people would have considered it onerous work for a pound.

I waited for Bowen to conclude his remarks, wondering whether he would make specific reference to Rebecca.

'Thank you gentlemen. If you would be so good as to let Mr Evans know when a decision has been reached, I will return to hear it.'

And with that, he stood and left the room, as did the jurors, to an immediate upwelling of excitement from the spectators. The sound of benches scraping beneath the rising posteriors of the crowd was barely audible over the babble of voices.

Gus took my arm. 'Come on,' he said, 'let's leave the populace to its speculation for a while.'

As the rain had stopped, we walked onto the bridge and stood overlooking the brown and turbid Teifi.

'When I was a boy,' I said before Gus could start asking questions, 'the head ostler at the other hotel over there' – I indicated the Emlyn Arms – 'used to take the horses out of the traces when a coach arrived and bring them down here. He'd make them jump in the river on a long line and swim to the other bank and back. Then the stable lads would rub them down. Said he never lost a horse to overheating.'

Gus snorted. 'No, just to drowning I imagine.'

I was aware of him looking at me as I kept my face turned to the river. He was not going to be diverted by local anecdotes. 'You're convinced it's her?' he asked.

I let out a breath I had been unaware of holding. 'Unless somebody with an identical gap in their teeth and who was also carrying a child stole all her things and was murdered on the farm from which she went missing, then yes, I'm convinced.'

'What about the jury?'

I shrugged. 'I wasn't allowed to testify as to the physical resemblance so they only have the possessions and the timing to go on. And Rachel Ellis and the Williamses were both a bit lacklustre about whether the rushlight holder and tin were definitely hers.'

'You think nobody wants to be the one who says definitively 'This was Margaret Jones'?'

'That's exactly what I think.'

'But if your father hadn't forbidden it, you'd have stood there and said it – you'd have said that, beyond a shadow of a doubt, this was her?'

I stared at the river, his face frustratingly indistinct in my peripheral vision. 'Why are you asking, Gus?'

'Because I think there's a significant chance that the jury will find that the body can't be positively identified. And I'm concerned as to what you'll do then.'

'Is that what you'd find – that there wasn't enough for a positive identification?'

'No. I'm persuaded. But I'm not intimidated by Rebecca of the Gates.'

'And manner of death?'

'Well, since she didn't bury herself, it's hard to come to any conclusion other than murder or manslaughter, isn't it? And I have to say, I'd be looking pretty hard in the direction of William Williams.'

I could not help myself, I looked around at him in surprise and he vanished into the central blur that I thought of as The Whirlpool. 'You think *Williams* killed her?'

'If that clod in the crowd is to be believed he was free enough with his dairymaids to give him a motive and he certainly had the opportunity – the wailing brat kept his wife busy all night. He could easily have slipped out.'

'He'd have had to be out for at least half an hour, if not more. How would he account for that to his wife?'

'He wouldn't have to if she was as preoccupied as she said.'

I heard running footsteps and a figure skidded on the greasy cobbles of the bridge. 'Mr Probert-Lloyd!' a boy's voice cried. 'The jury's coming back.'

The noise in the assembly room was, if anything, more clamorous than when we had left. From the snippets of conversation I heard as we made our way back to our seats, it seemed that the crowd was divided into those who felt, like Gus, that William Williams would be committed for trial at the assizes and those who declared that Beca would not allow a murder verdict.

'What are they all saying?' Gus asked.

I was not going to tell him they agreed with him. 'They're talking about Rebecca intimidation.'

We sat down.

'Where are your father and his cronies?' Gus asked.

'Wherever they are, I expect Bowen's with them.'

'The jury look as if they can't get all this over quickly enough.'

'All of them?'

Gus considered. 'No. Two of them look as if they want to knock some heads together.'

'Is one of them the foreman?'

'No. One's a carroty-haired fellow with an Adam's apple you could slice fruit with and the other's... oldish, white hair, well-dressed. Wearing spectacles.'

With regard to the second man, Gus's description brought nobody particular to mind, but I had a feeling that the red-haired man would turn out to be Dic the saddler. As a child, I had always been slightly afraid of that Adam's apple of his, fearing that, one day, it would bob right up out of his mouth.

A wave of silence pushed its way into the room. Bowen was back. After seeing him to his table, my father and the other magistrates took up their seats once more.

'Gentlemen,' Bowen addressed the jury, 'I apologise for my tardiness. You took me somewhat by surprise with your swift decision. Are you agreed upon a verdict?'

The foreman rose. 'No, sir,' he said, 'we are not agreed. That is to say, we are agreed about who the bones belong to, but not how she died.'

A murmur of question and translation rose in the crowd.

'Then why have you returned so soon?' Bowen asked. 'Did you not feel you should spend longer in deliberation so as to reach a consensus?'

The foreman's head turned and I heard the interpreter say 'agreement amongst you all'. The foreman had not understood the word 'consensus'.

'I beg your pardon, sir, but we knew that we would not be coming to an agreement,' he said.

Bowen said nothing for a few moments and I could sense the discomfort of the jury under his gaze. From the frenzied murmuring all around the ballroom, the crowd could scarcely contain itself.

'Are twelve of you agreed on the cause of death?'

'Yes, sir.'

So, a legal quorum then. At least there would be no question of empanelling another jury.

'Very well. You say that you are unanimous as to identity. Whose remains have you determined these to be?'

'Those of Margaret Jones, formerly employed at Waungilfach farm.'

The murmuring of the crowd grew louder but Bowen raised his voice above it, apparently unperturbed. 'And how does the majority find that she died?'

So keen was the foreman to rid himself of the unwanted words that Bowen had barely articulated his question before he got the answer.

'Accidental death.'

I felt a surge of anger so powerful I had to press down on my thighs to keep myself seated. *Accidental death?*

'How—'

As close as we were to him, Bowen's question was lost in the sudden outbreak of anger, disbelief or I-told-you-so from the crowd and one of the magistrates leapt to his feet. 'Silence! Silence!' he bellowed. 'The coroner wishes to speak!'

Bowen did not wait for absolute quiet but spoke over a residual hum. 'How on earth did you arrive at that verdict?'

'If he had a pistol to his head,' Gus said into my ear, 'the foreman couldn't look any less happy.'

'We determined, sir, that she had smothered the child and was trying to bury it beneath the tree when it collapsed on her, burying them both.'

No! That could not be true.

'Silence!' the magistrate roared again as the crowd threw off all restraint and voiced its various opinions.

Bowen was forced to raise his voice as he spoke to the jurors. 'Despite my explicit instructions not to bring in a verdict on the child's cause of death, you have decided that Margaret Jones gave birth to a live infant, smothered it, and then died in the act of attempting to hide its body. Is that what you are telling this inquest?'

'Yes, sir.'

'Carrot-top and spectacles look as if they're trying to dissociate themselves from the verdict.' Gus's voice was barely audible above the general outcry despite the fact that his face was close to mine.

'And the rest?'

'Look mulish, but glad it's over.'

But it was not over. I would not let it be over. To allow this travesty of a verdict to stand was unthinkable.

I would have to act.

Harry

The following morning, Moyle came into the dining room while Gus and I were lingering over the remains of breakfast to inform me that Mrs William Williams had asked to see me and that he had shown her into the morning room.

'Bit early for social calls isn't it?' Gus asked once the butler had left.

I stood, filled with a sudden apprehension. 'I don't suppose it *is* a social call.'

As soon as I opened the morning room door, Mrs Williams moved away from the long, east-facing windows and came towards us.

I made the introductions without asking whether she objected to Gus being present; if she wanted to speak to me in private she would have to say so. However, far from voicing reservations about speaking in front of a stranger, Mrs Williams came immediately to the point.

'Mr Probert-Lloyd, I know that you and your father must be as unhappy as Mr Williams and me about that ridiculous verdict yesterday.' Unlike her husband, who had been schooled to speak English with very little trace of an accent, Esme's somewhat less-than-perfect English had a strongly Welsh flavour, so much so that I wondered what language she and Williams spoke at home. Then again, on the basis of her current forthrightness, perhaps she did not converse with her husband so much as fling pronouncements in his direction.

I nodded. 'It was certainly a surprising verdict.'

'Scandalous is what it was, Mr Probert-Lloyd! Scandalous!'

I motioned at the furniture. 'Do take a seat.' The three of us sat within warming range of the newly-lit fire. 'Would you like a cup of tea?'

'No. Thank you. I mustn't stay long. Mr Williams doesn't know I'm here and I must be back before him. There wasn't time to send a servant to ask you to call on me at Waungilfach so I came myself.'

Presumably, she had come in her husband's impractical gig.

Fashionable, my father had said when he'd first seen her being driven about in it *but it's only a matter of time before it tips over on these roads and she comes to harm.*

'So, how may I be of service to you?' I asked, matching her own directness.

'That inquest was a sham,' she said, flatly. 'Everybody knows Beca told the jury to bring in that verdict. There's not a person from here to Cardigan who actually *believes* that Margaret Jones died by accident. It's quite obvious the girl was done away with. And where is suspicion going to fall? On us. On Williams and me. And I thought Bowen' – I winced inwardly at her familiar use of the coroner's name – 'made it plain by his questions that he suspected my husband.' She stopped, presumably looking to me for some kind of response.

'Are you sure,' Gus asked, 'that Mr Bowen wasn't simply being thorough, Mrs Williams?'

'Yes, Mr Gelyot, I am quite sure, thank you very much.'

'Even so' – Gus was courteous, conciliatory – 'people will surely not suppose for a single moment that you and your husband—'

'Excuse me, Mr Gelyot.' Mrs Williams's tone was in no way apologetic. 'But you don't know people here – they don't want an excuse to suspect people – it's enough for them that we were called to answer questions. Nobody will want to be associated with Waungilfach. We'll be ruined.'

I heard a note of desperation under the stridency and, to my shame, felt a grim satisfaction. 'Mrs Williams,' I forced myself to match Gus's civility, 'you can be assured of the continued friendship of Glanteifi—'

'Thank you Mr Probert-Lloyd, but that's not why I'm here.' I waited, taken aback.

'I'm here to ask you to clear my husband's name.'

Her eyes were on me, now. I could feel the heat of their challenge. And challenge it was; she could not be ignorant of the ill will I owed her husband.

Gus broke the silence. 'Surely it's the job of the magistrates to order any further investigations?'

She turned to him. 'But they *won't*, you see, Mr Gelyot! They won't want the expense. And then there's Beca. The magistrates'll be hoping she'll go away again now the jury's done what she wanted.'

Much as I did not wish to find myself on the same side of any argument as Mrs Williams, I suspected that she was right. 'Be that as it may, Mrs Williams,' I said, 'I'm not sure what you think I can do.'

'You know them. Those Rebeccas.'

I glanced involuntarily at Gus. 'Mrs Williams—'

'You *know* them,' she insisted. 'We both know that.'

An image flashed, unbidden, on my mind's eye. Myself, seven years ago, holding the infant she now referred to as her youngest child in my arms; arms clad in the long sleeves of a woman's gown.

'I wouldn't ask you,' she said, sidestepping from threat to entreaty, 'except that I have nobody to turn to. You know we're not respected as we should be – we'll be cut off from local society entirely if nobody clears Williams's name.'

I said nothing. Unquiet as my conscience was, outraged as I was at the verdict, I had absolutely no wish to undertake an investigation into Margaret's death as a favour to William Williams and his wife.

'You can find out who did this,' she insisted. 'I know you can.'

'Mrs Williams,' I leaned forwards in my chair, 'I may once have been... *accepted*... into certain kinds of company – but that was years ago. I haven't spent any length of time here to speak of since that summer. I was a boy then—'

'But you're a *lawyer* now. A barrister. And you're Henry Probert-Lloyd of Glanteifi. People respect you.'

I stared into the blind whirlpool that obscured her face.

'If not for us, won't you do it for Margaret?'

My jaw clenched in silent fury. How dare she mention Margaret's name to me?

'You were fond of the girl,' she pressed. 'Don't you want to know what happened to her?'

Try as I might to summon the necessary indifference to thwart her, I could not. At that moment, I wanted to find out what had happened to Margaret Jones more than I wanted anything else in the world.

John

Were you there? At the inquest?

Did William Williams really say he kept her on out of charity? Is it true the coroner told the jury they were cowards and liars?

The day after the verdict. The public houses of Newcastle Emlyn were crammed to the walls. Rumour and speculation spilled out into the street every time somebody opened the door. And then more walked in.

'Accidental death' had gone from house to house, farm to farm. The rain hadn't stopped it, nor the state of the November roads. It went as quickly as a mouth could carry it. Men who hadn't been off their own land in weeks made the journey into town to see if it was true.

Is this Beca?

Is she back? Up to her old tricks?

Beca's tricks. Intimidation. Deciding what was right and making the rest of us go along with it.

I sometimes wondered if Dada had been carried along with things after the gate breakings. Whether he'd found himself dragging English clergymen out of their houses and taking illegal tithes back. Or setting fire to the haystacks of squires and magistrates to stop them speaking out against Beca. I didn't want to think he had. But then a lot of men had done things they didn't want to think about.

'Who was there?' a man shouted, swinging his head from side to side. 'Who was at the inquest?' Barely through the door and already shouting. Drunk from another public house more than likely.

But it was what people'd come into town for – eye-witness testimony. Men stood in their shirt sleeves, coat dripping in one hand, cap in the other, looking around for somebody who could tell them what they wanted to know.

Is it true the jury didn't even go out?

No! So scared of Beca they said accidental death straight away!

You saying you wouldn't be scared if you'd been warned?

But not everybody was willing to see Beca's hand in the verdict.

Or, come to that, in Margaret Jones's death.

What's Beca got to do with it? Everybody knows those banks in the Alltddu come down for a sneeze. If the girl dug under that tree to bury her bastard, it's more likely than not the tree would come down on top of her.

Don't talk nonsense! It wouldn't bury her whole body – you'd still see some of it.

Not for long. Not after the foxes and badgers and crows had got at it.

No. That's not right. The jury saw a whole skeleton – if animals had been at the body there'd be bones missing.

Then the arguing parties would look about for a juror. Or somebody who knew a juror. Or said he did.

I sat in a corner, keeping myself to myself.

Beca. I didn't want to remember that, once upon a time, that name had excited me beyond anything. I could still feel a prickle of it, that old thrill of half-scared defiance I'd felt in that loft. The thrill of hearing about tollgates going down night after night for weeks after. The thrill of knowing that men were travelling miles to say 'No more!' And the thrill of thinking – hoping desperately – that my own father might've been one of them.

But then it had gone. It had died in front of my eyes. With

Margaret Jones. And, for the last seven years, Rebecca'd been a name that I'd hidden from. A name that had ordered a killing and brought terror into my life. *I'll find you boy! I'll kill you.*

So I sat in a corner, quietly. Just listening.

And, as well as what I did hear, there was something I didn't. A question even the men who spoke up for murder weren't asking.

Who did it?

That was a question with a dangerous answer.

Harry

Gus and I were sitting in the library warming our limbs in front of the fire after an afternoon's wet riding when my father returned home. 'I gather that Mrs Williams paid an early call on you today?'

Damn Moyle. I had planned to discuss the implications of the inquest's outcome with my father before mentioning the morning's visit; Mrs Williams's feeling that she and her husband had been slighted could only muddy the waters.

And so it proved. I had barely finished outlining the reason for her visit before my father was dismissing her request.

'Out of the question! I shall go to Waungilfach myself, tomorrow, and explain that any further action must be left to the discretion of the magistrates.'

My father had been swept up by his fellow justices of the peace after the inquest and had not returned home the previous evening; I had hoped that they were giving serious consideration to an appropriate response to the jury's nonsensical verdict and this seemed to confirm it. 'The bench intends to order some kind of investigation, then?'

'Nothing has been decided.'

Hope vanished like a pricked bubble. 'In other words,' I said, 'you can't agree.'

'On the contrary. We are unanimous in feeling that it would be unwise to make any hasty decisions. These are unusual circumstances, they need careful consideration.'

'Mrs Williams isn't interested in careful consideration! She simply wants her husband's name cleared and the blot on Waungilfach's reputation removed.'

My father drew in a long breath, as if he were inhaling patience as well as air. 'If that is the case, we must be unequivocal in our support – have some kind of occasion here to which everybody, including Williams and his wife, is invited. That will make it clear that we have no doubt of his innocence.'

His willingness to throw his house open to guests in some grand social gesture indicated the extent of my father's aversion to my becoming involved in any attempt to investigate the circumstances of Margaret's death, and I found that I did not know how to respond. Whilst I had no desire at all to participate in the clearing of Williams's name, I could not simply allow Margaret's murder to be ignored.

'Not my place to comment, of course,' Gus chipped in when the silence seemed about to become unbroachable. 'But I'm afraid Harry did attempt to assure the lady that she and her husband would always enjoy your full support, only to be brushed aside. She seemed to feel that only the conviction and hanging of some other fellow would prevent gossip and ostracism.'

I heard the rueful half-smile in Gus's voice, saw, in my mind's eye, the expression that went with it and suddenly realised that I would still be imagining the same expression on his face when he was seventy and no longer bore any resemblance to the young man I remembered. I would never again be able to look into the face of my friend. Never.

Shaken by the thought, I perched on the edge of the shuffleboard table and forced myself to speak.

'Albeit unintentionally, Bowen has exacerbated the situation. Mrs Williams feels her husband was questioned as if Bowen suspected him of Margaret's murder.' I held up a forestalling hand as my father began to protest. 'She also said – and it's hard to contradict her – that they were the only people of any standing who were called as witnesses.'

'As I'm sure I don't need to remind you, the remains were found on their farm.'

Remains. All that remained of a life.

I rose and poked the fire into throwing up some grudging flames. 'I'm well aware of that. But to be so insistent about what they did or didn't hear on the night she disappeared—' I pulled myself up, took a breath. 'Surely if Rachel Ellis heard nothing when she slept in the same loft as Margaret, then the Williamses, in their house, couldn't possibly be expected to have heard anything?'

I was well aware that only Gus's presence was preventing my father from openly disliking my reference to Margaret's sleeping arrangements.

'A servant might have had reason to conceal what she knew,' he said, stiffly. 'Bowen was *obliged* to ask Williams whether he had heard anything out of the ordinary.'

'And was he not also obliged to quell the suggestive remarks coming from the crowd?' I asked. 'That they were allowed to stand made a laughing stock out of Williams and his wife.'

'Bowen claimed not to have heard exactly what was said.'

'Then he's so deaf that he shouldn't be presiding at inquests!'

My father crossed the library to stand at the long windows. 'What answer did you give Mrs Williams?' he asked, his face to the afternoon darkness of approaching midwinter.

'I told her I'd consider her request overnight.'

'Very well. Then you will be able to let her down gently.'

Was he trying to provoke me? 'I haven't yet decided what answer I'm going to give her. First, I need to know what action the magistrates are going to take – it's quite clear that the verdict can't be allowed to stand—'

He turned, suddenly. 'And what, exactly, makes it so clear?'

'The jury didn't do its duty! An inquest is supposed to find cause of death without fear or favour—'

'You speak very glibly of *duties* considering you've shown no interest whatsoever in coming home and applying yourself to your own!'

Outraged that he would say such a thing in front of Gus but unable to produce an apt reply, I stood, jaw clenched, as he moved towards the corner cabinet and the brandy.

'Does Williams know his wife was here?' he demanded. 'Did he send her here to beg on his behalf?'

'I have no reason to think that Williams asked his wife to beg,' I said. 'In fact, she gave me the distinct impression that he mustn't know she'd been here.'

'Good.'

He spoke as if something had been decided. I could feel my breath coming quickly. 'Tell me truthfully, father – what are the magistrates going to do?'

I watched him as he appeared to stare into his brandy glass. Was he trying to decide whether to tell me the truth?

'For the last seven years,' he began, 'Rebecca has been silent. Since the turnpike trusts were brought to heel, people have found nothing to complain of. There have been no carryings of the *ceffyl pren*. People are satisfied with the law we give them.' He stopped and raised his head, presumably to try and get me to look him in the eye. 'So, if you – a gentleman – now choose to dislike a verdict brought in by a legally constituted jury, if you imply that you know better, that you will not be bound by the law, what do you imagine the response will be?'

I was not going to be turned aside by this spurious argument. 'You haven't answered my question,' I said. 'What are the magistrates going to do?'

He drew in a heavy breath and moved to a chair at the fireside. 'Ask yourself what the world would be like if, every time the bench disliked the verdict of an inquest jury, they pronounced that it was clearly in error and a new inquest must be held.'

'It happens! If it can be *proved* that the jurors were intimidated there'd be grounds to open a new inquest, surely?'

'Harry, nobody wants a resurgence of Rebeccaism. If you take it upon yourself to go about saying that the jury was incompetent, that it was not fit to stand in judgement but *you are*, do you imagine that it won't cause resentment – even a call to arms? That was one of Rebecca's charges against us, was it not? That the squires and the magistrates were over-mighty, that they used the law for their own purposes?'

'So because the gentry misused their power in the past, are we going to allow the Rebeccas to misuse theirs now? Surely they *must* be challenged if they think they can dictate that murder is to be called accidental death – or where will it end?'

I saw my father shake his head. 'It *has* ended. I will not discuss this with you any further. And I forbid you to mount any kind of investigation into the jury's verdict.'

Incredulity forced me to my feet and I stared down at him, unseeing. 'You *forbid me?* I'm of age! I'm not a schoolboy you can order about any more.'

'No. You are heir to Glanteifi and some decisions are, therefore, not yours to make. How on earth do you imagine you will command respect in future if people see you grubbing about in the affairs of the lower orders?'

'May I make a suggestion?'

Gus's question startled me. I had almost forgotten that he was there.

'Perhaps all concerned should sleep on it and see how the morning finds us?'

I did not want to sleep on it. I wanted this argument thrashed out now. But my father spoke before I could marshall a coherent response. 'Thank you, Mr Gelyot. Let us, by all means, draw this distasteful conversation to a close. But, before we do so, you must hear this, Henry. If you are determined on this course of action, then you must leave this house. I cannot and will not have my authority called into question or my support for my fellow magistrates thrown into doubt. You will not conduct any investigation while you are living under my roof.'

I was dumbstruck.

'And there is one further consideration,' he said. 'How do you imagine your chambers will greet a request for an extended leave of absence?'

I could feel Gus's gaze. *The moment has arrived, P-L.*

But I could not do it. Not now. 'You don't need to concern yourself,' I said, 'that will be for me to negotiate once I have found alternative accommodation.'

Harry

I lay awake and ill at ease most of the night. I could not reconcile what had taken place in the library with what I knew of my father as a magistrate. That he would allow murder and jury-intimidation to go unpunished, in the hope that the previously dormant forces of Rebecca would fall into quiescence once more, was beyond belief. Surely it was manifestly obvious that, on the heels of this demonstration of her continuing power to intimidate, Rebecca might decide that there were other matters she wished to take an interest in?

However, lest I seem to be presenting myself as a pure and impartial seeker after justice, I was not proposing to endure banishment from Glanteifi simply in order to prevent a resurgence of Rebecca activity. If the bones discovered at Waungilfach had not belonged to Margaret, I might have been content to let the magistrates make what mistakes they chose. But I knew that I was not guiltless in the matter of Margaret's death, and I could not allow her to be branded an infanticide who deserved the fate that had befallen her.

If only it had not been Mrs Williams who had asked me to intervene. The thought of benefiting her and her husband in any way stuck in my throat. Without Williams's jealous malice I would not have been sent away to Oxford and Margaret would not have been left defenceless. Could Mrs Williams be unaware of that? Or had she simply forgotten that, on the day after the *ceffyl pren* had visited her husband, he had paid a visit to Glanteifi?

I had walked into the house that morning, seven years before, all ease and contentment from a walk in the late summer sun, to find myself summoned to my father's study. When I opened the door, I found him standing there with William Williams.

The abruptness with which my father came to the point was an indication of how greatly I had embarrassed and disappointed him.

'Williams tells me you have been making a nuisance of yourself with one of his female servants. That you have been leading her on.'

I turned to Williams. The look on his face suggested that he was not unhappy with my father's abruptness. 'Margaret is an impressionable girl,' he told me. 'She will think you're offering more than you can give. I know you're young, Harry, but it's not kind.'

His calling me Harry, as if he were an intimate, infuriated me. His appearance at Glanteifi could mean only one thing – that he had seen me in the yard the night before and blamed me for the humiliating visitation of the *ceffyl pren*. And, now, he was taking steps to ensure that I was granted none of the privileges I had – apparently – taken pains to deny him.

If my father had set out to design the most exquisite torture for me, he could not have done better than to censure my involvement with Margaret under Williams's gaze. In the acute disappointment he expressed, in the coldness of his tone as he told me I must never see 'this unfortunate girl' again, in his demanding of my word that I would do as he wished, all the warm, hopeful notions that I had treasured about a future with Margaret had withered and died.

Just as a grand world of make-believe is dispelled when the nursery door is opened, revealing the table cloth tied about your gallant neck and the schoolroom ruler in your hand, my father's dismissal of my love for Margaret had left me feeling both bereft and foolish.

But worse had been yet to come. Once the stiffly triumphant Williams had been shown out, my father had turned to me.

'You will go and pack. Immediately. You will leave for Oxford tomorrow. If rooms cannot be found for you in college you can lodge in the town until term starts. You will not return for Christmas. Find a friend prepared to invite you or stay in your rooms. I will not have you at Glanteifi until you are cured of this infatuation.'

I had not seen Margaret again until Davy Thomas's letter had called me home the following spring.

Was I now going to clear William Williams's name because his wife requested it? The thought of Williams preening himself at the news that I had agreed to help him made my skin crawl, but I could not let pride stand in my way; it would be foolish to spurn such a ready excuse for conducting an investigation. *Following the inquest's verdict, I have been asked by an interested party to look into the matter of Margaret Jones's death*, I would say to anyone who challenged my right to ask questions. Erroneous conclusions would, no doubt, be drawn as to who had asked me but I could not help that.

However, if I was to accede to Mrs Williams's request, I determined that it must be on the strict understanding that she would not tell her husband.

And, as I consoled myself with the thought of my investigating without Williams's knowledge or consent, it occurred to me that it was not out of the question that his wife's recruitment of me would backfire.

There was always the possibility that Gus's suspicions were correct and William Williams had murdered Margaret.

PART 3: INVESTIGATION

John

Three days after the inquest, Newcastle Emlyn got something else to gossip about. Young Harry Probert-Lloyd had moved into the Salutation Hotel with his London friend and it was all over town that he'd had a falling-out with his father.

'This will be about the inquest,' Mr Schofield said. 'The magistrates have failed to call the verdict into question – young Henry was bound to dislike it given his... *association* with the girl.'

And he wasn't the only one to think that. All the gossip had jogged people's memories. Hadn't they heard something about Harry Probert-Lloyd being involved with the dead girl?

Heard something *back then*.

Why didn't he give evidence? they wanted to know. *What does he know about her and her baby?*

More to the point, far as I could see, was what he was going to do next. He was still here. There had to be a reason for that.

I knew a man who worked at the Salutation. A few drinks did the trick.

There they were, he said, *young Harry Glanteifi and Mr Gelyot, eating their steak and kidney pudding. And Harry says, quite casual, as if he already knows the answer, 'Of course, I'm counting on you to stay and help me with all this, Gus.' But 'Gus' shook his head, didn't he? 'P-L,' he said, 'you know I can't. I've got to get back to London for next week. And anyway...' he said, 'I'm not the man you need. You need somebody who knows the people here. Somebody who can be your eyes.'*

'Be your eyes?' '

'That's what he said.'

So, when Harry Probert-Lloyd walked in to Mr Schofield's office the next morning, it felt as though I'd summoned him with my thoughts. As if he'd come to say *Why is John Davies thinking about me all the time? Instruct him to stop, Mr Schofield!*

The way he looked at me when he came through the door made it worse. Came in and turned his eyes straight on me, even though he was saying good morning to Mr Schofield at the same time.

Why was he looking at me?

Old Schofield slid out from behind his desk to do the Good-days and the How-are-yous. He always sat in the front office. Said it was good for business if people could see him hard at work. He had a room behind where he took people for private meetings.

'Come through to my office, Mr Probert-Lloyd. My clerks can be about their business without distraction then.'

I glanced up at Peter as they went through the inner door. He raised an eyebrow and I shrugged. I didn't know any more than he did. But I was pretty sure his heart wasn't beating fit to burst out of his body.

I didn't have long to wait, thank God. It can't have been five minutes before Mr Schofield put his head round the door. 'John? Come into my office, would you?'

Years of working for Mr Schofield had taught me what he liked. He liked us to be waiting for him outside the office door at eight o'clock. He liked the lines on his paper to be ruled exactly a third of an inch apart. He liked to see us using a particular brand of boot black. What he didn't like was surprises. Put him at a disadvantage, surprises did. His lips'd go thin, then.

That's how they were now. Thin. *Compressed.* What had Harry Probert-Lloyd told him?

Did he *know?* He couldn't. Could he?

No.

But if he'd been involved with the girl…

I stood just inside the door, trying not to let anything show on my face.

Harry Probert-Lloyd spoke up. 'Have a seat, John.'

I glanced quickly at Mr Schofield. He nodded, just once. It felt strange, sitting down with him and another gentleman as if we were equals. Could they hear my heart beating? Or see it? I was sure I was shaking with each thump of blood.

'Mr Probert-Lloyd has a proposal for you, John.' Not an accusation. A proposal.

Well, whatever it was, I'd be saying yes, wouldn't I? If old Schofield had called me in to his office, he must've approved this proposal already. I looked over at Harry Probert-Lloyd but he was looking down at the desk. Apparently, a brass blotter was more interesting than me.

'As I've been explaining to Mr Schofield,' he said, 'following the inquest earlier in the week, I've been asked to look more fully into the circumstances surrounding Margaret Jones's death. To find possible grounds for reopening the inquest.'

Asked? Who'd asked him? Must be his father and the bench. Perhaps there hadn't been a falling-out, then. But, if not, why had he moved into the Salutation?

He looked up from the blotter but didn't get as far as looking me in the eye. His gaze settled somewhere about my chin. Thank God I'd stopped cutting myself whenever I shaved. 'I need somebody to assist me in my investigations,' he said. 'I can't go to Jervis and Evans because they're solicitors to Glanteifi and the estate can't be seen to be involved. So, Mr Schofield has very kindly agreed to help.' Hah! Very kindly agreed to let me do the helping was what he meant. 'He's agreed – if you're willing, John – to allow you to work with me.'

'It will mean a lot more work for Peter,' Old Schofield piped up, 'so I'll expect you to be here if, at any time, Mr Probert-Lloyd doesn't need you.'

'We're assuming, Mr Schofield, that John is happy to do this.' Harry Probert-Lloyd looked into the air somewhere around my ear. 'Would you be so kind as to be my assistant for a week or two, John?'

Help him investigate her death? How could I do that?

But then, didn't have a choice, did I? If I embarrassed Mr Schofield, he'd make my life miserable. Sack me, even.

So I said, 'Yes. Thank you, Mr Probert-Lloyd.'

'You should thank your employer, too. He speaks very highly of you.'

I glanced at old Schofield. Pinched smile. He didn't like Harry Probert-Lloyd telling me that. 'If you work hard, John Davies, this is a great opportunity for you.'

'Yes, Mr Schofield. Thank you.'

It *was* a great opportunity, but not in the way Schofield meant. And only if I could manage it carefully.

Harry

Of course, I had known from the moment John Davies sat down in Schofield's office and agreed to my request that I would have to tell him the real reason why I needed an assistant. But, now that the time had arrived, I realised just how loath I was to do so.

For months I had been taking steps to prevent my loss of sight being noticed, in the hope that Figges was wrong and my affliction would prove to be temporary. Alone in my rooms, I had become practised at fastening neckties without the benefit of a mirror image and finding button-holes without being able to see what I was doing. Now, with my sight stubbornly refusing to improve, I was glad of my proficiency. But, though I might be able to arrange my clothing neatly, there were other aspects of my appearance that were more problematic.

A few weeks prior to leaving my lodgings in London, I had discontinued my daily barbershop shave and gone about with a scarf around my face, eating from a pie-shop like a working man instead of dining out, waiting for stubble to become beard. I had never had a valet and I was not about to ask for one at Glanteifi. If I could not see well enough to shave myself then I would be bearded.

Now, as I waited for John Davies to arrive, I nerved myself to say the words. *I am going blind.* I had not yet been able to bring myself to tell anyone. Gus knew, of course. It had been his uncharacteristically bald 'You're having trouble seeing aren't you?' that had first sent me to Figges.

Wanting distraction, I forced my deficient sight around the room.

I had been assured that it was the best the Salutation had to offer and, as well as all I could reasonably want in the way of wardrobes, drawers and desks, I had been mightily relieved when the maid showed off the enclosed night table. I had had a horror of being forced to endure the presence of a pot under my bed.

But, despite its comforts, the room's outlook was considerably less pleasant than the view from my bedroom at Glanteifi. The prospect of the Teifi and its meadows from my bedroom window remained clear in my mind's eye. Swans nested on an island in the middle of the river's wide loop beneath the house and otters played with their pups when they thought nobody was there to see them. It was a source of great sadness to me that, for the rest of my life, I would catch only sidelong glimpses of that view. But at least I had the recollection of its full glory. How much worse to be born blind and never to understand the beauty of the world around you, never to know the expressiveness of a human face, the comic antics of a hound pup, the seductiveness of a raised eyebrow.

I walked over to the window and stood, trying to spot a break in the clouds. Since Gus's return to London, I had been fighting the demon despondency and trying hard not to question the course I had set. I had even wondered, briefly, whether I should go back to Glanteifi and tell my father everything that had happened that summer. Perhaps, then, he would understand why I could not let the jury's verdict rest.

A knock at the door spun me around. John Davies had arrived.

He was a quiet young man. It was not simply that he did not speak until spoken to, he was quiet in his movements, too; he sat still, not obtruding himself upon one's notice. He would be easy to overlook and that would make him an excellent observer.

John's only experience of me, thus far, had been in English as Charles Schofield did not speak Welsh. But I was in need of a companion as much as an assistant and English would only serve to emphasise the differences between us.

'You may have got the impression from Mr Schofield that I needed a translator,' I told him. 'But, as you can see, my Welsh is perfect and I'd much rather we spoke Welsh together.'

'If that's what you'd prefer.'

'It is.' I sat down on the old-fashioned silk-covered chaise under the window. I was trembling. 'Have you noticed anything odd about me?' I asked. I wanted to know whether he would say what he thought or maintain some kind of deferential ignorance.

'It's not really my place to say…'

'Yes it is. I've just asked you.'

Silence. I sighed. Since he had walked through the door, I had done nothing but wrongfoot the poor fellow. 'Listen, John, I don't want a servant. I don't want "yes sir, no sir". I want somebody I can talk to, somebody who'll give me their true opinion. Do you understand?'

'I *understand*, Mr Probert-Lloyd…'

'But you don't think I mean it. You think that the first time you offer an opinion I don't like you'll get a mouthful of "how dare you?" Am I right?'

'Well—' I could hear a wary smile in his voice, 'I wouldn't have put it exactly like that.'

'I won't do that. You have my word. So, let me ask you again. When we met yesterday, did you notice anything odd about me? Or have you noticed anything since being in this room?'

It was more than just a test of his mettle; I had to know how obvious my loss of sight was to those around me.

'Alright then,' John said, audibly bracing himself. 'Yesterday, at Mr Schofield's office, I thought you were deliberately not looking at me. Now… from the way you touched the chair before you sat down – as if you were reassuring yourself where it was – well, I wonder if… if you can't see very well?'

Could he tell that my smile was two parts relief, one part ruefulness? I now knew that he was both observant and capable of parting with unpalatable opinions; but if he had spotted my difficulties so easily, how many others had suspected something but been too polite to say? Perhaps my father had already guessed and hoped that banishing me from Glanteifi and the ministrations of its servants would bring me to heel. I put that thought aside.

'You're quite right,' I said. 'I can't see your face. In fact, from here, if I look straight at you I can't see you at all. I can see the window,' I indicated with my right hand, 'and the bed over there. But nothing here.' I sketched a circle in the air to indicate the extent of the whirlpool at the centre of my vision.

'So I'm going to need you to tell me what you see. And, whatever you think, it *is* your place to speak your mind. That's what I want from you and if you're not prepared to do it I'll find somebody else.'

There was a moment of silence as he digested this. 'Right.'

'Move your chair closer, will you – about six feet away?'

He did so.

'Now, your face is a blur but I can see your legs. If I look down at your feet, they disappear and your face pops into view but I can't see it in any detail. I can see you've got dark hair and spectacles but unless you were to move right next to me, I wouldn't be able to see any expression on your face.'

I caught him nodding. 'I need you to speak, John. I *might* see you nodding but I probably won't and I don't always want to be asking whether you agree with me.'

'I'm sorry.'

'No need to apologise.' Now it was my turn to hesitate. 'I'm not going to insult you by asking if you can keep your mouth shut, but nobody here knows about my sight yet. Or, at least, they may have guessed, but I haven't let it be known. You're the first person I've told.' Perhaps that would assure him that I meant us to be more than employer and servant.

'Nobody will hear it from me.'

'Thank you.' I took a breath and tried to strike a matter-of-fact tone as I ground on with my own humiliation. 'Obviously, because I can't see detail, I can't see to read – I can write when I need to but not easily and, anyway, I can't read what I've written, so I'll need you to make notes for me. Any questions?'

A considering silence, then: 'Can I ask how you manage to write?' I got up and went to the bureau in the corner. After some fumbling, I managed to open my writing box and take my frame out. I unfolded it then beckoned for him to come and see.

'I had a cabinet maker construct it for me,' I told him as he bent over the desk. 'Each turn of the small cogwheel on the left moves the ruler down a line. As long as I keep my wrist on the ruler I can write relatively legibly. So I'm told, anyway.' Sidelong, I watched him. Something in his stance suggested that he wanted to pick the frame up – see how it felt, how it was made. 'Once it's positioned correctly, as long as I take care not to move the paper, it works relatively easily.' I kept to myself the long evenings of practice: how best to hold the paper still, how to keep my left thumb on the paper at the exact spot where I had left off in order to dip the pen.

I thought I detected a small smile. 'Ingenious.'

I folded the frame and closed the bureau once more. 'Mr Schofield told me that you were with him at the inquest.'

He nodded, but also remembered to speak. 'Yes.'

'Tell me your impressions, will you?'

'Impressions of the inquest?'

'Yes. Anything about it that struck you.'

Charles Schofield had spoken of John as a young man with acute powers of observation and analysis so I assumed that the ensuing silence meant that he was marshalling his thoughts rather than simply stuck for anything to say.

'I think,' he said, finally, 'that everybody was very careful in what they said. They answered the coroner's questions but they didn't tell him much.' He stopped and I waited to see if he would say anything more. Unlike most people, however, he did not succumb to the urge to fill a silence.

'What did you think of Mr Williams, Waungilfach?' I asked.

'He looked very ill at ease.'

'And his wife?'

'Cross.'

I found myself smiling. 'Yes. She was. Do you think Williams had anything to do with the death?'

When he didn't reply immediately, I added, 'I'm not asking whether you think he killed her. I'm just asking whether you think he knows more than he said.'

'I think every one of those witnesses knew more than they said.'

I nodded. 'They were all afraid of something. And I think that something was Rebecca.'

John did not reply. What was he thinking? He must have heard the gossip but he was young, he would not have experienced Rebecca and her methods at first hand. Still, time would tell. 'There were two jurors who didn't agree with the majority,' I said. 'Was one of them Dic the Saddler?'

'Yes.'

'And the other?'

'Pridham, the chemist from this end of town.'

There was no point speaking to those jury members who had successfully been intimidated; we were far more likely to get useful information out of the two who had refused to be swayed.

I stood and took my overcoat from the hook on the door. 'Right,' I shrugged my way into the heavy wool, 'we'll go and see Dic, first.'

We did not have far to walk – the saddler's shop was mere yards away from the hotel.

A familiar apprehension rose in me as I approached the door. In order to see where people were, I needed to scan a room quickly and the need to let my eyes roam in my head made me self-conscious. But John stepped forward. 'Let me' he said, thumbing the latch and pushing the door into the shop. 'Behind the bench, to your right,' he murmured as I went through.

I had half a second to be grateful for his quickness of understanding as the dry smell of newly tanned leather filled my head with childhood memories.

'Mr Jones!' I greeted the saddler 'I don't suppose you remember me.'

Dic had made my first saddle – *one made especially*, he had told me, *for a fat little grey pony* – and I had loved it. It had been the first thing I owned that belonged to the world beyond the nursery and I had insisted on cleaning it myself.

'Good grief, Mr Probert-Lloyd, of course I remember you!' Dic's voice was high, reedy. 'Not looking for a new saddle are you, sir? I'm sure there are far more fashionable saddlers than me, up there in London.'

'More fashionable, Mr Jones, but not more skillful.'

Dic had always spoken English to my father and, not wanting to disconcert him, that was how I had addressed him. However, I could see, now, that English would confine us to conventional platitudes so I switched to Welsh. 'Dic, I need to ask you about the inquest.'

He hesitated, then responded in kind. 'What about it?'

I fixed the whirlpool on the workbench between us and, above it, saw his red hair, his pale face turned towards me. Was his Adam's apple bobbing anxiously?

'I've been asked to look into the verdict. And, more generally, into the death of Margaret Jones.' I paused for a second, trying to gauge his reaction but I could detect maddeningly little. 'You and Mr Pridham were the jurors who didn't agree with the accidental death verdict.'

'We were, yes.' His voice was non-committal.

'Apparently,' I was feeling my way, acutely aware that I had no professional standing here, that Dic was not obliged to tell me anything, 'everybody's been saying that the jury members were given instructions to bring in the accidental death verdict. That threats were made.'

Dic said nothing. Then I heard John speak, behind me. 'You don't have to worry about me, Mr Jones. I'm working for Mr Probert-Lloyd so I won't be blabbing any gossip about.' He had obviously caught a worried glance in his direction.

'John is assisting me,' I said. 'He will treat everything he hears in the strictest confidence. So… were *you* threatened?'

Dic hesitated. 'No. Nobody came near me.'

I heard his subtle implication. 'But some jury members *were* intimidated?' Silence. Was he nodding?

'How?' John's voice again. He had grasped my failure to see Dic's response. 'How were people threatened?'

When Dic didn't answer straight away, I rested a hand on the workbench between us and leaned towards him. 'Dic, this isn't just about Margaret Jones's death. It's about Beca coming back.'

'You don't have to tell me that, Mr Probert-Lloyd,' the saddler said. 'The thought of Beca's what made me sit on the jury.'

During the riots, some businesses in town had received Rebecca's unwanted attentions and I wondered whether Dic had been on the rioters' list. He frequently did work for Glanteifi and his loyalties might, therefore, have been regarded as suspect. I tried my best to look at his face. 'So?' I asked. 'Who *was* threatened?'

'Stephen Parry,' he said, at last. 'The printer. He got a letter.'

'What did it say?'

'That he'd better persuade the jury to vote for accidental death,' Dic said, 'or his shop'd be burned down.'

With all the supplies Parry kept in his printing and stationer's shop it would be like living on top of a powder keg. 'Was it just a letter?' I asked.

Dic did not reply. In my peripheral vision, John moved forward. 'Mr Jones?'

'Parry's got a yard at the back of his shop,' Dic said, eventually. 'The morning after he got the letter, he found a half-burned *ceffyl pren* out there.'

The implication was clear. If somebody could get into his yard they could fire his shop, with Parry and his family asleep upstairs.

'So,' I said, 'Parry persuaded everybody else for his sake?'

'Not for his sake. For their own. I gather the letter said that anybody on the jury who didn't find for accidental death would be in danger of their life. Parry was passing it around when we went out to the workhouse for the viewing.'

'How did he manage that without the coroner seeing it?'

'The coroner *did* see it. But he didn't ask what it was and we didn't tell him.'

I could imagine Bowen ignoring any conversation in Welsh. He would see it as beneath his dignity to ask the jurors what they were talking about.

'When you say "I gather" – does that mean you didn't see the letter yourself?' John asked. I was impressed; the question showed close attention to what Dic had said.

'I told Parry I didn't want to see it. Told him I wasn't going to be threatened.'

'Does Parry have any idea who sent the letter – who put the *ceffyl pren* in his yard?' I asked.

'If he does, he's not saying.'

I nodded. 'Do *you* know who did it, Dic?'

'No, Mr Probert-Lloyd, I don't.'

I hesitated, turning the question I was about to ask him over in my mind. 'Why didn't you go along with the majority? About the accidental death verdict.'

Dic didn't reply immediately and, when he did, he spoke deliberately, weighing his words out. 'The *ceffyl pren* had its place,' he said. 'Years ago, I mean. And Beca had her place – for a while, anyway. Something had to be done about the tollgates, didn't it? But time's moved on. This is the modern world. We've got families from

136

Newcastle Emlyn living in America, now. We've got a police force. The railway's coming soon and then we'll be joined to the rest of the empire – we can't go on behaving like we did a hundred years ago.'

'You're not afraid of Beca, then?' John asked.

'I *am* afraid, John Davies. I'm not ashamed to admit it. Any sensible man would be afraid – we all saw what Beca was capable of, didn't we? It wasn't wise to cross people who used that name. But, like I said, this is the modern world – I want my sons to understand that we can't go about doing what we're told by letters – anonymous letters, mind you – put under people's doors at night.'

I could feel Dic's eyes on me and I nodded, fixing my gaze in apparent contemplation on his workbench. But he had not finished.

'And, just in case you're wondering, John Davies, I don't have friends in Beca who are going protect me. I never rode with Beca – not for tollgates and not for anything else. And I didn't belong to Nathaniel Howell's chapel either.'

Even after all that time, I felt a frisson of something like alarm at the sound of Howell's name. If the minister had given testimony at the inquest, as Bowen had wished, my father might have had an apoplexy when he heard what Howell had to say about me.

'Nathaniel Howell?'

I looked around to answer John's question. 'He was the minister at Treforgan – the chapel Margaret Jones attended.' I pushed myself away from the saddle horse and stood up. 'I haven't asked after your family, Dic – how are your boys?'

Dic's voice softened and the stridency with which he had addressed John's unspoken challenge was gone. 'Both doing very well, thank you for asking. Huw's working with me, now, and Joseph is in Mr Davies's school. Wants to go for the law. Like your young assistant here.'

If he shared his father's progressive views then Joseph Jones was probably looking to go further than the life of a lawyer's clerk. Times were changing.

I could only hope that they were changing enough to allow others to follow Dic's lead and speak to me about what had happened seven years ago.

John

As I closed the door of Dic's shop behind us, Harry Probert-Lloyd turned without a word and began to walk up the hill. Was I in trouble already? He'd told me to ask questions but perhaps he'd just meant to ask him, not witnesses.

I followed him quickly up the street towards the middle of town.

Where was he off to – Pridham's house or Parry's shop?

The rain'd stopped but the high street was all running water and mud and horseshit. It was quiet and some of the shops had lamps lit to try and tempt people in out of the gloom.

I glanced over to see how Harry was coping – I'd already started to think of him as Harry, even before his little 'I don't want us to be master and man' speech, and I was going to have to make sure I called him Mr Probert-Lloyd to his face. He wasn't stepping in anything so he knew where to put his feet. It was going to take me a while to work out exactly what he could and couldn't see.

Every now and then we'd get a greeting from passers-by. Each time, Harry bowed and smiled. Benevolent, Mr Schofield would have called it.

Ladies, he'd say, or, *Good morning*, or, if the weather'd been mentioned, *Yes, terrible, isn't it, I hope it doesn't mean we're going to have a wet winter.* But he didn't stop, just carried on walking. It was a handy enough trick, but it wasn't the same as being able to look people in the eye.

'What did you make of what Dic had to say?' he asked suddenly, eyes straight ahead. For a second, I was afraid he couldn't look at me for being cross. Then I remembered – sideways was the only way he could see me.

'Well, now we know that Beca definitely *is* involved. It's not just a rumour.'

'Yes. A Rebecca note and a *ceffyl pren* left as a threat doesn't leave much room for doubt.' Harry skirted around a trail of what looked like pig shit. We were almost at the top of town now.

'Are we going to see Stephen Parry?' I asked.

'Yes. I want to know more about that threatening letter before we talk to Pridham.'

I didn't fancy his chances. If Parry'd got a letter from Beca, his best bet was to keep his mouth sewn up. Especially to Probert-Lloyd the magistrate's son.

I looked up at the sky. It was going to rain again any second, I could tell. 'If we hurry,' I said, 'we can get there before it rains.'

Even if Parry didn't want to speak to us, at least we'd be out of the wet.

Harry

I was acquainted only slightly with Stephen Parry, but what I knew of him suggested that he was a weak and easily influenced man. Here, I needed to be Mr Henry Probert-Lloyd, London barrister, not little Harry Glanteifi as I had chosen to be at Dic's.

Parry was a large man and I remembered him as being soft around the edges, as if he might be easy to squeeze into a blancmange mould. His voice, when he returned my greeting, was aquiver with apprehension.

'We're here to ask you about the threatening letter you received from Rebecca,' I told him, without preamble.

Parry reared back as if I had brandished a pistol in his face. 'What letter? I never had a letter.'

'Mr Parry, I understand that this is difficult for you but I need to know about the contents of that letter.'

'There wasn't a letter!' His voice had a hand-wringing tone.

'Other jury members say differently. They say that you were passing a letter around – in full view of the coroner – on the morning of the inquest.'

'They're lying!'

'And,' I continued, determined to be implacable, 'that Beca made threats to you and your business. We know that you were told to persuade the rest of the jury to bring in a verdict of accidental death. We also know that somebody burned a *ceffyl pren* in your yard the night before the inquest.'

'No. No! I'm telling you – there was no letter! It's all lies!' Parry's hands were waving his desperation.

'Perhaps we should speak to your wife—'

His tone dulled. 'I haven't got a wife. She died five years ago.'

Damn! I had completely wrongfooted myself. 'I'm sorry.'

Parry made no audible response. Was there reproach in his face? Resentment? Inwardly, I berated myself; I should have checked with John about Parry's current family circumstances.

I tried to regain momentum. 'What did you do with the letter, Mr Parry?'

He did not reply. Perhaps he thought that my *faux pas* gave him licence to defy me. 'Whatever the verdict was,' I said, 'you and I both know – *everybody* knows – that Margaret Jones was murdered. We can't just leave it.'

'You can.' It was barely more than a whisper. 'You should.'

Just then, I became aware of something at the very edge of my eyeline; something I might not have noticed in the days when I was able to focus on what was in front of my nose. There was a figure standing in the doorway to the next room. Standing, in fact, just behind the doorjamb; almost, but not quite, out of sight.

'You can make me go away,' I told the printer, 'but I'll keep coming back until you tell me what I want to know.' I allowed him to think about that; about my continuing to appear on his doorstep, in full view of those who might have threatened him. Then, more gently, I asked, 'What did you do with the letter, Mr Parry?'

The answer, when it finally came, was defiant. 'I burned it.'

'Why?'

'Because it was like having Beca herself in the house! I didn't want it here.'

'You shouldn't have destroyed it. It was evidence.' Evidence that Rebecca had roused herself; that there was something about Margaret

Jones's death that those who had ridden under the Lady's name did not want discovered.

I angled my head just slightly to one side; the figure was still there. A barely-moving shoulder, a grey, apron-covered hip. 'Do you know who sent the letter, Mr Parry? Who put the *ceffyl pren* in the yard?'

'No. And I don't want to.'

'Back then,' I began, treading carefully, 'did you ride out... with Beca—'

'No!' A hand slapped down on the counter. 'No I did not!'

I ignored his denial. 'Did the letter threaten more than your shop – did it threaten to inform on you, inform the magistrates?'

'No! I'm telling you,' he dropped his voice, obviously afraid that whoever was in the house would overhear us. 'I never rode with Beca – *never!*'

The light in the shop had dimmed noticeably since we came in and a sudden downpour began to hiss onto the sodden ground outside. Water, I thought, must be almost as inimical to a shop full of paper as fire. Damp customers and their dripping boots would bring a humidity into the air that could not fail to damage the ledgers whose smell of glue and new cloth was as distinct on the air as their blue covers were on the shelves. How many days' rain had to fall before the ledgers' corners began to fox, before the cut-edged post papers and folded writing sheets that Parry kept in the drawers beneath his countertop lost their perfect smoothness and began to bloom and soften?

'I'm told the letter was written in Welsh' I said. 'Was it well-written – as if the person was educated? Did it look as if the person who wrote it was used to writing or as if it was something they did rarely?' Knowing whether the hand was that of a literate person or someone barely schooled would help. It was unfortunate that Dic had refused to read the letter. 'Mr Parry?'

'Can you protect me if I tell you what you want to know, Mr Probert-Lloyd? Can you guarantee that my shop won't be burned down? That my children will be safe?'

At the edge of my vision, the grey woman had disappeared. I imagined her slipping away, made apprehensive by Parry's combative tone. 'No, Mr Parry, I can't. But I think it's reasonable to promise you that if we don't find out who brought that letter, Rebecca won't let it end here. She'll get worried about who'll say what.' I turned and looked theatrically out of the window, as if I could see witnesses gathering in front of Parry's shop. 'Somebody might get a conscience and go to the magistrates. Do you really think threatening letters are going to be the end of it? When there's a murderer to hide?'

'There *was* no murder.' His voice was low but there was defiance there. 'It was accidental death. That's what we said. And that's what it was.'

I heard John take a breath. 'I was wondering, Mr Parry, why you agreed to be on the jury in the first place? Plenty of men refused.'

'And who are you, John Davies, to be questioning me?' Parry vented on him all the anger he'd had to keep from his tone in speaking to me.

'Mr Parry, John is acting as my assistant in these investigations. There's an expectation that we will discover sufficient new information to have the inquest reopened.'

'And you think that's a good idea, do you? You, of all people?'

I spun around. 'I want to see justice done!'

'Justice?' He let the word hang in the air. 'Are you sure?'

I could feel his eyes boring into me, defying me. Was this how it

144

was going to be? Magistrate's son or not, had my own youthful indiscretions compromised anything I attempted, now, to make amends?

'You'll never find out who did this.' Parry sounded as if he would like to put the matter beyond doubt himself. 'You should let it go, before they come after you.' He moved, suddenly disappearing from my sight. 'I'm shutting the shop, now, so you'll have to leave if you don't mind.'

He hurried past me towards the door and opened it. The sound of the rain immediately intensified, a hissing counterpoint to the redundant ringing of the shop's bell.

'Mr Parry—'

'Please. I'm not feeling well. You'll have to go.'

Seconds later, we were out in the downpour, listening to the sound of a bolt being rammed home behind us.

John

I opened the door of The Lamb, and we ducked in out of the rain. The taproom was quiet but I still put a hand on Harry's arm to stop him marching in.

'Best if we scrape the mud off our boots first.' Nelly James had standards. She'd throw you out if you trailed mud and shit through her rooms.

'John Davies,' Nelly frowned at me as we walked in. 'What are you doing here in the middle of the day?'

'Working, Mrs James. For Mr Probert-Lloyd here.'

That changed her tune. Sweet and English now. 'Good grief it is too! I beg your pardon, Mr Probert-Lloyd, I didn't recognise you.'

'I hope you don't think I'm leading John astray, Mrs James. We just had to get out of the rain and find somewhere dry to discuss our business.'

'Well, you sit over there – never mind your boots, I'll clean it up after. Sit down and I'll get you something to drink.'

We sat down next to the window and Nelly drew pots of beer for us. Harry smiled. 'You never see barrels tapped in London any more. They've set pumps up everywhere now – fixed to a counter with the barrel beneath.'

'Mrs James wouldn't like that. She's not one to stand behind a counter like a shopkeeper. She likes to be amongst her customers.' So she could take them by the scruff of the neck if she needed to throw them out.

Once Nelly had given us our beer and gone discreetly through into the back room, Harry turned to me.

'What did you make of Parry?'

I tried to gulp a mouthful of beer, so I could answer him quick-smart. But I choked and almost coughed beer over him. This business of having to speak so he knew I wasn't ignoring him was going to drive me mad.

'He's scared,' I croaked.

Harry nodded. 'He won't want whoever threatened him to know that he's been talking to us.'

I put my beer down. I didn't want him to think I was a gossip, but I knew things about Parry that might be useful. I needed to think.

'Do you think they threatened his children?' Harry asked. 'What did he say? "Can you keep my children safe?" Something like that.'

'Possibly' I said, taking care to sound cautious.

'Go on.'

'Well... a fire wouldn't just threaten his family, would it?'

'His business, then?'

I had to be careful now. I knew that Parry was being sued for bad debts but I couldn't tell Harry that. Didn't want him to think I couldn't keep a discreet tongue in my head.

'I don't think the business is doing as well as it used to,' I said.

'What makes you think that?'

There'd been clues in the shop. Especially if you already knew. 'I go to Parry's shop pretty often,' I said, 'for Mr Schofield, you know.' Harry nodded. 'Well, until recently, there was always a fire burning in the grate. To keep the stock dry. And he used to like to sit his well-off customers down next to it.'

'And there was no fire today.'

It was a statement, not a question. Parry's shop'd been as cold as a miser's charity.

'Then there's his stock,' I said. 'Most of it's out the back but he used to keep more in the shop – you know, to catch people's eye. It's gone down a lot recently.'

'You think he's in debt?'

I *knew* he was in bad, bad debt. If Beca burned even a fraction of his stock, Stephen Parry'd be in deep trouble. No way to fulfil orders. Out of business.

'He might be,' I said. 'Common knowledge that he's doing a lot less printing than he used to. What I hear' – I'd heard this in town, so I could pass it on – 'is that he's got unreliable. His work's shoddy sometimes, late other times. And whatever he earns, he's drinking half of it.' To drown his sorrows and put the workhouse out of his mind. 'He's in the Drovers' more than he's in his shop.'

Harry's face went still, as if he was seeing something I couldn't. 'Do you know if he's got a maid living in?'

'Must have. Somebody's got to do all the women's stuff.'

'But you don't know who it is?'

'No.' I set my sights a bit higher than maids-of-all-work, thank you.

He sighed. Then he changed the subject. 'That question you asked Parry – about why he'd agreed to be on the jury?'

The one he'd avoided by turning on me. 'Yes?'

'It was obviously a tender subject for him – how did you know?'

'Because I was there when Matthew Evans – you know, the *plwyfwas*, lives at Tregorlais farm? I was there when he came in to talk to Parry about being on the jury.'

'Came in? Where was this?'

'The Drovers' Arms.'

'So what did Evans say?'

148

I cleared my throat. Clear and concise, Mr Schofield would have instructed. Clear and concise.

'Matthew came in and said he'd like a word with Parry outside. Well, Parry refused.' He'd been with his drinking cronies; told Matthew he wasn't going outside with anybody, thank you very much. 'So Matthew told him, in front of everybody, that he had to be on the jury for this inquest—'

Harry pounced. '*Had* to be – that's what he said?'

Matt Tregorlais had stood over Parry. *Right then,* he'd told him *if that's how you want it. Here's the message. You've got to be on the jury for this inquest into Waungilfach's servant.*

'Yes,' I said. 'Had to be.'

'Then what?'

'Parry objected.' *Who are you to tell me what I've got to do, Matthew Tregorlais?*

'And, presumably, the *plwyfwas* whipped him into line?'

I took a mouthful of beer, slowed myself down. I had to make sure I got this right. Kept his suspicions on Beca where they belonged. And I needed him to trust me when it came to details. I was going to have to watch my step if I wanted to steer Harry in the right direction. 'Well,' I said, 'Parry was drunk – and loud – but Matthew wasn't. He kept his voice down so I couldn't hear what he said. But, whatever it was, it shocked Parry. He looked'– what was the polite way to say he'd looked like a ram lamb who'd just had his balls nipped off? 'Stunned,' I said. 'And frightened, too.'

'What d'you think Matthew'd told him?'

I shrugged, then remembered to speak. 'I don't know.'

Harry drank some of his beer, then asked, 'Did you hear anything else Matthew Evans said to him?'

'Yes. You know that minister Dic the saddler was talking about – Howell was it?' I knew it was. Dic's mention of the minister's name'd had Harry changing the subject as if his life depended on it.

He nodded. 'Yes, Nathaniel Howell.' His face gave nothing away.

'Well, his name came up. Parry said something like "Nathaniel Howell's long gone!"'

As it happened, that was exactly what he'd said. *Nathaniel Howell's long gone*. 'What do you think he meant by that?' I asked.

Harry shook his head, eyes on the table. 'I don't know. Howell moved away, years ago. Did either of them say anything else?'

'Not that I heard. They went outside, then, and didn't come back.'

The Reverend Howell might have moved away years ago but his name meant something to Harry. Was it to do with his involvement with the girl, or was it possible that Harry Glanteifi had ridden out with Beca?

Either way, I needed to know. I couldn't afford to make any mistakes. Not if I wanted to keep myself safe.

Harry

Nathaniel Howell. Dic had brought his name up and, now, it seemed that Matthew Evans the *plwyfwas* had mentioned him, too.

On the face of it, what Dic had said made little sense, an apparent non sequitur: *I never rode with Beca. And I didn't belong to Nathaniel Howell's chapel either.* But I had discovered the minister's association with Rebecca soon after my return from Oxford at Davy Thomas's behest.

Beca won't stand for your father's pig-headedness Davy's letter had said. *She has already sent him two letters telling him to show her more respect. The second one warned him if he did not keep his opinions to himself, his house would be burned down.*

My father – the supposed beneficiary of my homecoming – had been less than enthusiastic to see me; not only had I defied the year-long order of banishment that was supposed to cure me of my feelings for Margaret, I had also come back to a disturbed and disturbing situation.

'What can you possibly hope to achieve by abandoning your studies and coming home?' he had demanded.

'I was given to understand' – I did not mention Davy's name as my father would bitterly have resented any intervention on his part – 'that life and limb, not to mention hearth and home, were at risk from your response to the Rebeccas.'

'My *response*?'

'You constantly denounce the actions to remove illegal tollgates—'

'Because it's not the farmers' place to remove them! They presume to take the law into their own hands.'

'Only because the law fails them and does nothing! Prior to Rebecca's actions, had the magistrates prosecuted a single tollgate keeper for overcharging? A single trust for placing illegal gates?' I had never confronted my father before. Always, when challenged, I had retreated into compliant obedience. But he had removed me to Oxford and instructed me to change my ways; so change them I damn well would.

'Do you *defend* these Rebeccas?'

'I defend their right to take action if nobody else will uphold the law!'

'To take action? They're *rioting*, boy!'

'Riot is in the eye of the beholder.'

'Do not bandy words with me, Henry! What do you know about any of this? Nothing!'

'No, because you *sent me away*—'

'For your own good! You presume to return home, without my permission, and cast yourself in the role of saviour of the estate when these sympathies of yours would very soon bring us to ruin! You will oblige me by returning to Oxford and allowing me to run Glanteifi as I see fit.'

Was our argument overheard? Glanteifi was not an exceptionally large house and servants were apt to be here and there around it, outside doors, under windows. But whether our disagreement was relayed to Nathaniel Howell from within or Margaret Jones had mentioned me to her minister, the preacher of Treforgan soon knew both that I was home and that I had some sympathy with the Rebecca movement. So it was that I received my summons.

Prosaically, it was sent in the mail and handed to me by Moyle after the daily collection from Newcastle Emlyn. Neatly folded and sealed, the stamp's edges cut with scissors, not torn, the letter seemed carefully done, even genteel. Baffled at who could be writing to me at my father's house when few knew I was there, I opened it.

The hand was even and literate and addressed me in Welsh, showing that its author knew more about me than simply my name and place of residence.

As it has come to our attention that you are sympathetic to our cause, you are bid to help us in a pressing matter. Be in the lane outside Treforgan chapel tomorrow night at half past ten o'clock. Come in a carriage, arrayed in every particular as a lady. In this you will show your sympathy to the unjustly treated amongst us. You will see how you may be of service when you come.

    Signed,

    Rebecca and her children.

John

As we left The Lamb for Pridham the chemist's, I had to tell Harry that I didn't have a notebook. Good memory I might have but I knew I was going to need to write some things down. I should've told him straight away, when we met in his room but, to be honest, I'd been embarrassed. Somebody like him would always have a notebook. He wouldn't even think about it. But I couldn't afford to buy one for myself.

'We don't use them in Mr Schofield's office,' I told him. 'If we need to make notes, there're always off-cut pieces of paper lying about.'

So, back we went – not a word of complaint from Harry, fair play – and he pulled a large portmanteau from under the bed. Very deft, he was. Undid the buckle on the heavy lid in a second.

'There'll be something suitable in here, I'm sure. It's full of things I threw in from my digs in London and haven't had need of since.'

Piles of shirts and underlinen and neckties came out onto the bed. I gave a quick glance into the case's blue-and-white-striped lining. Didn't want him to see me looking. Then I remembered – I could look all I liked. He wasn't going to know. So, I watched as carefully as if I'd been taking an inventory for Mr Schofield.

Item: one rectangular silver flask, filigree-engraved.

Item: one letter opener, porcelain-handled.

Item: one pocket watch, gold.

He dangled the watch by its chain. 'I've no use for this, now. But we may need to know the time while we're out and about. Carry it, will you?'

I took it from him. It was a handsome thing, pretty new by the look of it. It'd stopped so I'd have to set it by my landlady's long case clock.

'I'll take good care of it, Mr Probert-Lloyd. I promise.' He gave me a small smile and went back to his search.

Item: two long wooden bcxes – probably pen holders.

Item: one small chess board.

Item: one inlaid wooden box – containing chess pieces if the similarity of the wood was anything to go by.

All of those things would be useless to him, now. He couldn't check the time, make a note, play a game of chess with a friend. But at least he had the Probert-Lloyd fortune to fall back on. If I lost my sight I'd lose my position with it. I'd be in the workhouse.

'Here we are.'

Item: one notebook, covers marbled.

With the book in his side-vision, he flicked through the first few pages. Making sure he hadn't written in it, I supposed. Then he passed it to me. 'Obviously you'll need a pencil as well.' He tossed something small at me. 'You can use that one until we can get you one of your own.'

I looked at what he'd given me. A tiny silver model of a pistol, about two and a half inches long. I was embarrassed for him.

'Mr Probert- Lloyd, I'm sorry but this isn't a pencil.'

He took it from me, twisted the barrel and handed it back. The twist had released more of the silver tube, with a pencil lead at the end. He smiled. 'I didn't know what it was when it was given to me, either.' I looked at the pencil. Even opened up, it was still only about as long as my palm, it'd easily fit into my pocket with the book. A name was engraved along the side of the barrel: S. MORDAN. Who was that? I wondered. Carefully, I held the pencil point-up and twisted.

The extra length disappeared back into the barrel.

'It's a beautiful thing,' I said. 'I can't take it out and about in my pocket.'

'I'm afraid, for obvious reasons, I don't have a lot of pencils. I only keep that one for sentimental reasons – it's one of a pair I was given as a coming-of-age present. You'll see the date and my initials engraved on it.'

I opened the pencil again and looked. S. MORDAN on one side, the initials HGPL and a date, 26 June 1845, on the other.

I counted backwards. When Margaret Jones died, Harry'd been not yet nineteen years old. But he'd had some kind of romantic association with the girl before that. I looked at him. Fair, curling hair, small, slight build – it was only his beard that stopped him looking girlish himself.

There was more to Harry Probert-Lloyd than met the eye.

Edward Pridham didn't run his chemist's shop any more, he'd given that over to his son. But he still thought it was his job to tell Newcastle Emlyn what to do. It wouldn't've surprised me if he'd summoned Matthew Evans and announced that he was going to sit on the inquest jury instead of waiting to be asked. Gave himself airs.

On the Pridhams' handsome double-fronted doorstep, Harry turned to me. 'Will you knock and announce us?'

So, he was going to treat me like a servant, whatever he said. I banged the heavy brass knocker and told myself I shouldn't be surprised. He was the squire's son. But then another explanation put its hand up. He'd've been embarrassed, wouldn't he, if he couldn't recognise the person who opened the door? Easier for me to be the one they saw first.

He needn't have worried, as it happened. A maid appeared. And local gossip was right. The Pridhams'd put their servants in uniform. No young woman hereabouts wore a black skirt and a white apron and, to my mind, she looked out of place on a Newcastle Emlyn doorstep. I wondered what Harry thought, fresh from London.

'Good morning. How can I help you?'

We explained our business and she showed us in to the front room. 'I'll see if Mr Pridham's available.'

She'd been well trained. Her English was as good as her manners.

Once the door had closed on her, I looked around what Pridham probably called the drawing room.

Money. Everything in that room shouted it. The striped wallpaper was fresh and bright, not a trace of lamp– or candle-smoke. The cut weave of the carpets was thick and the velvet chairs looked new – no worn patches in the fabric, no scuffs or scratches on the legs.

And the room was warm. Good-sized chunks of anthracite burned in the grate, not like the culm and blankets of dusty small-coal my landlady used. A fire burning in a room nobody was in. That was what having money meant.

The door opened and in he came. Edward Pridham.

'Probert-Lloyd the younger! I saw you at the inquest looking very solemn-faced. Back for good, now, are you?'

He didn't ask us to sit down. Either Harry didn't notice or he knew how to keep his feelings to himself. Time would tell.

'Good day to you, Pridham. May I present John Davies, currently acting as my assistant.'

I sketched a bow. Mr Pridham stared. The words 'organ-grinder's monkey' might as well have been floating over his head, like in a newspaper illustration.

'Assistant? And with what is he *assisting*, may I ask?' The way he asked the question, I was pretty sure he already knew the answer. Had Old Schofield been bragging about Harry recruiting me?

'I've been asked to make enquiries into the circumstances surrounding the death of Margaret Jones,' Harry said. 'And into the rumours that the jury's verdict was procured by threats of violence.'

It was a good *addendum*. The chemist wouldn't care two farthings about a dead farm servant but he'd've been furious to be outvoted by cowards on the jury. But Harry didn't give him time to answer, just waded straight in, so I knew he *had* noticed Pridham's rudeness and was paying him back.

'I understand that you were one of the two jury members who refused to bring in a verdict of accidental death?'

'And from whom do you *understand* that?'

It was a challenge and Harry wasn't having it. Just stood and waited with his eyes somewhere near Pridham's face.

'Jones the saddler being indiscreet, I suppose. I shall have words with him.'

'I would rather you said nothing to Dic, if you don't mind.' Harry sounded pleasant enough but it wasn't a request. 'He couldn't very well refuse to answer my questions.'

If Harry was going to take that tone with people like Pridham, in front of me, we weren't going to get far. The chemist was looking at me as if he'd like to see me struck dead on the spot.

'I think perhaps you've forgotten that you're not in London, now, Probert-Lloyd. The Metropolitan police and associated magistrates may choose to ride roughshod over the ancient customs of our democracy but, *here*, we respect the verdict of a properly constituted jury.'

Harry didn't turn a hair. 'You consider it to be a legitimate verdict, then? Despite the intimidation of jurors?'

'I know of no such intimidation.'

'Others have borne witness to it.'

'I cannot comment on what *others* have seen fit to tell you.' Pridham narrowed his eyes at Harry. 'But I can assure you that nobody attempted to suborn *me* in any way.'

I was shaking, waiting for Edward Pridham to turn on me, doing my best to pretend I wasn't there. Harry was as calm as a Sunday afternoon.

'May I remind you of Burke's maxim, Pridham? When bad men combine, the good must associate.'

'Bad men?'

'You don't consider an attempt to cover up a murder to be bad?'

'I see no evidence of such a thing! I may not have agreed with the jury's verdict at the time but, on mature reflection, those who voted in favour of accidental death can be allowed to have a greater experience of the lives and motives of girls like that.'

No. That wasn't right. Men like Pridham didn't change their minds. Not so they agreed with working men at any rate. Somebody'd been talking to him. Not Beca, I didn't think. Not in his case. More likely the magistrates. They'd changed his mind for him.

'You'd do well to pay more heed to your father, Probert-Lloyd. He understands these matters. Go home. Be reconciled. Don't make a fool of yourself – and him – over this.'

I was looking at the carpet so as not to catch Pridham's eye, so I couldn't see whether Harry's expression changed. But, when he spoke, something in his voice was stretched very thin. Like a rope that's holding a weight too heavy for it. You're just waiting for the snap to whip it into your face.

'One last question, if I may. Did you receive a letter instructing you to bring in a verdict of accidental death?'

I couldn't help myself then. Had to look up and see how Mr Pridham took that. But I had a surprise. He was laughing.

'You see? This is what I'm trying to tell you. You don't understand our ways here. Nobody would attempt to threaten a man of my standing. They'd be all too aware that I would go immediately to the magistrates and insist that whoever had done such a thing be found and prosecuted.'

A brisk clop, clop of horses trotted a carriage past the window. It felt like advice – *hurry on to the next thing, down the road and away.* Harry didn't heed it, of course. 'And yet,' he said, 'you didn't go to the magistrates when you saw Stephen Parry's letter.'

I watched Mr Pridham from under my eyelashes.

'Probert-Lloyd, I am beginning to find your persistence somewhat insulting. I know my duty before the law. If I had seen such a letter I would have reported it. I did not. Now, if you will excuse me, I have business to attend to.'

The maid was rung for, and we were back out on the street quick-smart. A small rain was falling again, fine and clinging. I was all a-jitter but Harry looked as if he'd just had tea with his grandmother.

'So,' he said, 'do we believe him? Did he not get a letter?'

Was he really asking for my opinion or just thinking out loud?

'John?'

Real question then.

I stepped over a puddle. 'Beca probably wouldn't've bothered

160

sending him a letter. More likely to threaten people she knew she could frighten.'

We walked past the baker's shopfront and the smell of bread made my head turn. The baker's boy, Iorri, was just coming out with his baskets full and covered against the rain. A bit late to be delivering bread. Must've been a special delivery – cakes or something. Iorri caught my eye and nodded a greeting. He didn't speak because I was with Harry but I nodded back at his raised eyebrow and he trotted off ahead of us up the high street. He'd be asking about this next time he saw me, that's what his raised eyebrow'd said.

Harry hadn't seen any of that, of course. His mind was still on threatening letters. 'Dic didn't get a letter, either,' he said. 'Which makes me wonder whether Parry's was the only one.'

I buttoned my jacket up. It was cold out, after the warmth of Pridham's house. 'Dic Jones would've said, I think, if anybody else on the jury'd had one.'

'You think people would've spoken up – admitted to getting a letter themselves?'

'No reason not to once Parry'd shown his about.'

'So,' Harry's face said he was thinking as he spoke, 'assuming there *was* just Parry's, why? Whoever sent it was taking a risk in assuming that Parry'd be able to persuade the rest of the jury.'

The eaves above us dropped fat drops of water on our heads. We were both bareheaded. My old cap was too worn to wear for best but goodness knows why Harry wasn't wearing anything. Perhaps he thought he'd be too *London* for people if he wore a tall hat in Newcastle Emlyn.

'Maybe Parry was just the one who *received* the letter,' I said. 'Nothing to say it wasn't addressed to all the jurors, not just him.'

Harry looked over at me. I knew he couldn't see me properly but I still made my face look respectful. Habit.

'What?' he asked. 'Something along the lines of "we know who you all are, we know where you all live and we can burn your houses down if you don't say what we want?"'

A face appeared in my mind's eye. A face I hadn't seen, outside my dreams, since that rainy night seven years before. *Say nothing boy or I'll kill you!* I shivered. Was *he* behind the threats, the intimidation? What if Harry's investigation brought me face to face with him? What would I say? If I said what I knew, would anybody believe me?

No. Too much time had passed. *Why didn't you speak up then*, people'd ask. *Very convenient that you're remembering these things, now, when you're working for Harry Glanteifi.*

I had to put my faith in Harry. And in my own wit to steer him. 'It'd be safer to only write one letter,' I said. 'Most people don't have much use for writing paper, do they? They don't keep it at home. It'd look very suspicious if somebody who doesn't usually buy paper went into Parry's shop and asked for fourteen lettersheets. *And* Stephen Parry'd know exactly who'd bought it when he got the letter.'

Harry nodded. 'True enough. Come on, we need something to eat before we go any further.'

Thank God for that. I'd begun to think he wasn't going to stop all day.

I'd never been in the Salutation's dining room before, never mind eaten my dinner there. The food wasn't anything special if I'm honest, but there was a lot of it and just being in that dining room made me feel as if I was going up in the world.

Just before he put a forkful of beef into his mouth, Harry asked, 'Does your family have a connection with Mr Schofield?'

I knew what he was asking. Who are you, where are you from, what's your family like? Maybe Edward Pridham's sneer at me had made Harry think twice about who he was associating himself with.

'No. Mr Davies at the grammar school found a place for me with Mr Schofield.'

'You were at Mr Davies's school? I hadn't realised.'

Now I'd gone up in his estimation again. Mr Davies's academy was famous. Boys came from miles to him. 'Yes. He took me in when I was eleven years old.'

'Took you in?' Harry wiped his lips with a pocket handkerchief. Used to napkins, obviously. 'You're an orphan, then?'

'Yes. Both my parents died when I was young.'

His eyes were on his food. But he couldn't see it, could he? He was trying to look at me. 'I'm sorry,' he said. 'It must be hard to lose your parents when you're a child.'

I remembered what Mr Schofield had said about his mother dying in childbirth. 'Harder never to have had them, perhaps.' I held my breath. Was I allowed to mention his family?

He half-smiled. 'I've got nothing to complain of. My early life was less conventional than it might have been with a mother on hand but none the worse for that.'

Alright then, I *was* allowed to mention them. But I wasn't going to push my luck. Curious I might be about that 'less conventional' start but I couldn't ask. Not yet.

Still, the way Harry spoke Welsh was an oddity. When he'd asked if we could use the language between ourselves, I thought he'd use that old, formal Welsh some of the gentry take it into their heads to learn.

But no, he spoke the local dialect, same as I did. Who'd he learned it from? Or, as Mr Schofield would insist, from whom had he learned it?

Whoever it was, Harry Probert-Lloyd's Welsh made him feel less like the squire's son and more like one of the clever older boys I'd known at Mr Davies's school.

I pushed my scraped-clean plate away. 'Can I ask you something, Mr Probert-Lloyd?'

'Of course.'

'Do you think the *plwyfwas*, Matthew Evans, is one of them – a Rebecca?'

Sometimes, when Harry's eyes fixed in one position, you didn't know whether he was thinking or trying to see you. It was uncomfortable. 'I've been asking myself the same thing. I don't know him, personally, but he was friendly with somebody I knew, years ago.' Harry hesitated, thinking. 'He's old enough to have ridden with Rebecca.'

'D'you think he knows who killed Margaret Jones?' I asked. I knew it wasn't him who'd killed her, but if Harry was going to have a hope of finding out *why* Beca had Margaret Jones murdered, we needed to talk to the men who'd ridden with her.

He pulled in a big breath, eyes on the table. 'I don't know. As *plwyfwas*, obviously, he'd have been in a position to hand-pick the jury—'

'Not really,' I interrupted before I could help myself. 'Sorry,' I muttered.

'No – what were you going to say?'

I had to feel my way carefully, here. Didn't want to sound like Pridham, with his *you have no idea how things work here*.

'Well, there are men who generally sit on juries, aren't there? Men who *expect* to be asked. You know, shows they're well-off enough not to mind a day away from their business.' I was watching his face.

Waiting for any little sign that I'd said the wrong thing. So far, so good. 'If Matthew went to *other* men for his jury,' I went on, 'men he knew he could intimidate – there'd be talk, wouldn't there?'

Eyes on the table. I was pretty sure he was thinking. Chewing the inside of his bottom lip, he was. Peter in the office did the same thing. Sometimes he chewed the end of his pen, too. Old Schofield hated that.

'It depends how clever he is, I suppose,' Harry said. 'Perhaps he was able to put the usual jurors off, subtly. You know –"I know you're usually the man for the job, I'm just more loath to ask you this time because of all the rumours" – that kind of thing. Then whoever it is asks what rumours and Matthew makes up some blood-curdling tale about what Rebecca's threatened. Then he says he'd quite understand if, on this particular occasion, whoever it is would prefer not to sit…'

I nodded. 'Yes. I can see Matt Tregorlais doing that.'

'Right then.' He looked up, almost meeting my eye. 'We'd better go and see him, hadn't we?'

But it wasn't to be. We hired livery horses to get up to Tregorlais farm but, when we got there, Matthew's father told us that he was elsewhere, on parish business.

'Gone down to see to some vagrant who's been making a nuisance of himself by the church,' the old man complained. 'Of course, he had to do it *today*, didn't he – when the rest of us are stone-picking? That damn vagabond's been there more than a week, but Matthew had to go today. He'd barely put in half an hour with the stones when a boy turned up with a note and he was off.'

As we turned away, it started to rain again.

'A boy with a note,' Harry said. 'Sounds as if somebody took the trouble to warn Matthew Evans that we were coming.'

Harry

Rebecca came for me that night. It was to be expected, of course; how could she leave me alone when I had chosen to start turning over her most concealing stones? She came to me in the Salutation Inn, while I was lying in my bed, shutters closed, fire banked.

Black faces, the whites of their eyes horribly vivid in the light of the lanterns and torches they carried; shawls and aprons and nightgowns pale in the darkness. They stood around me, silent and menacing. I saw a wig on one head, a huge straw wig. Beneath was an implacable face. One I had not seen for seven years.

And then another appeared, as if from the air. A huge face, soot black streaked with sweat and matted into his thick, dark beard. When he opened his mouth, a dark-lit hole in the moonless night, words emerged between bared teeth.

> *You are judged and found wanting, Glanteifi's son*
> *In the bones of the Alltddu, In what you have done.*
> *You claim kinship with us, Glanteifi's son,*
> *But you have betrayed us*
> *In what you have done.*

I was terrified; all the more so as the voice that came from that terrible mouth, that huge, blackened face, was the voice of a woman. The *cantwr* sang my sins, charged me and accused me, so that Rebecca's children could judge and find me guilty before meting out whatever punishment they saw fit.

A mouth opened behind the *cantwr*, a great red mouth of condemnation and fearfulness.

You shall be done to death and buried beneath a tree.

Then a great crashing thud came as every man standing around my bed raised his staff vertically before him and brought it down on the floorboards. Again and again; thud, thud, thud – a rhythmic threat.

'Mr Probert-Lloyd!'

More thudding. But now it was coming from the door. 'Mr Probert-Lloyd, please open the door.'

I opened my eyes. The faces around me were gone, the tails of the dream whipping away and, with them, the clear sight that was always restored to me in sleep.

I lay, motionless, for a moment, unsure whether the fear coursing through me was caused by the dream or the beating at the door; unsure, indeed, whether the beating at the door was part of the dream.

'Mr Probert-Lloyd!'

My knees trembling, I pulled myself out of bed, shrugged into my overcoat for warmth and decency and headed towards the knocking. After a few moments' frustrated fumbling with the key, I managed to unlock the door and was able to make out two people in the early morning gloom.

'Mr Probert-Lloyd.' The man's tone, an uneasy combination of embarrassment and irritation, told me that he had been the one shouting. 'I'm sorry to wake you so early but something has occurred which cannot wait.'

Cultured Welsh accent, excellent English, average-sized man; the Salutation's major domo, Mr Roberts.

I was thankful for the need to blink sleep from my eyes. 'What is it, Mr Roberts?'

'This.' Roberts stood aside. The man behind him was clearly holding something swathed in what might have been a sheet or a tablecloth.

I made a show of rubbing my eyes. 'I'm sorry Mr Roberts, it's dim and I'm afraid I'm still a little blurry – what is it?'

Roberts moved back to his previous position. 'It's a *ceffyl pren*, Mr Probert-Lloyd. With a rotting sheep's head on the end.'

I swallowed, having become aware of the sickly smell as he spoke.

It was left outside your door, sometime in the night. The boot boy found it.

'I see. Was there a note attached to it?'

'A note?'

'A letter, then. A threatening letter or something of that sort.'

Roberts turned to his employee. 'No,' he said, facing me again after a moment or two, 'nothing like that.' Turning again he snapped, 'Get rid of it. Bury the head and chop the rest up for the kitchen fire.'

The man clumped along the landing towards the stairs while Roberts moved forward, forcing me to allow him into the room.

'Mr Probert-Lloyd,' his tone was not conciliatory, 'I understand that you're here in trying circumstances—' He faltered and my lawyerly instinct was to go on the attack, ask him what trying circumstances he was referring to, in the hope that I might find out what rumour was currently explaining my presence here; but I could not afford to offend him.

He regrouped. 'I cannot have this kind of thing happening. Some criminal has invaded my hotel after dark. I cannot have the other guests put to fright by such grotesque appearances.'

He was not, I noted, overly concerned that *I* might be put to fright, despite the fact that – presumably – that had been the purpose of the *ceffyl pren*.

'I'm sorry that you've been inconvenienced, Mr Roberts—'

'I'm afraid *sorry* isn't good enough, Mr Probert-Lloyd. I need your assurance that this will not happen again.'

Hardly the way to speak to a gentleman, even one who has been reduced to paying for his bed and board. I had to reassert my position before the whole town was looking down on me. 'I'm afraid I'm unable to give you any such assurance, Mr Roberts, as *I*,' a distinct emphasis on the pronoun left him in no doubt as to my meaning, 'am not the person responsible for ensuring that nobody without lawful business enters these premises. Though I sincerely hope *not* to have my person threatened in this manner again, you and your staff are the only people able to ensure it. This time it was a *ceffyl pren* – who knows what an intruder might do if allowed into the premises a second time.' I paused, fractionally. 'I would not wish to have to give a less than complimentary report of my stay here to anyone who asked.' I allowed him to digest this for a moment or two. 'And, now, if you'd be so good, perhaps you could have some hot water sent up. I have a long and trying day in prospect.'

John was incredulous.

'A place like this – I'd've expected Mr Roberts to have had that sheep's head *ceffyl* destroyed before you even thought of getting up. I mean, letting a gentleman be embarrassed like that? You could ruin him.'

I locked the door behind me and we made our way along the gloomy landing.

'It's this investigation, isn't it? It's not *proper*.' I turned at the head of the stairs and grinned at him, hoping that he was grinning back. 'Leaving that aside,' I said, 'I wonder whether this answers your question about whether Matthew Evans was involved?'

'You think he's responsible for this?' John sounded dubious.

'We've only seen Dic Jones, Parry and Edward Pridham. And failed to see Matthew Evans whose father no doubt alerted him to the fact that he'd missed us. One of them has to be involved, surely? Unless we're going to suspect the magistrates or Bowen.'

John snorted a polite laugh at the thought.

'I was suspicious when Evans wasn't at home, yesterday,' I told him as we made our way down the first flight of stairs. 'Now, after this, I'm convinced that he'd been warned we were coming. Parry's the most likely informant. He must have gone straight out and found a boy to take a message when he threw us out of his shop yesterday.'

John made a non-committal noise and I stopped at the window-lit turn of the stairs. 'You don't agree?'

'I don't know.'

'But if not Parry, then who?' I kept my voice low, following his lead. 'We didn't see anybody else all day.'

'Well, nobody except the servant at Pridham's and Nelly James in The Lamb. But I suppose neither of them were in the room when we were talking.'

Something caught at me when he mentioned the servant but it was dislodged by a stab of apprehension at the thought of quick-witted Nelly James overhearing our conversation. 'Where was Nelly while we were talking?' I asked.

John came to a halt at the bottom of the stairs and I caught a movement of his head as he looked to and fro; he was nervous about being overheard. 'Out the back.'

'Outside, or in the scullery?'

'Scullery, I think.'

'With the door open or closed?'

'Open – she always leaves it open so she can hear if anybody calls for her.'

So she could have heard us. John and I had not been keeping our voices down.

'Can we go outside?' he asked. All this talk of being overheard was obviously making him nervous.

Once we had left the hotel, John walked onto the bridge, then turned to me again. 'You don't think Nelly James told Matt that we were coming for him?' he asked, his voice still low. 'She can't have been involved with Beca.'

'Why – because she's a woman?'

He obviously heard the edge to my question, and made no reply. Deliberately, choosing my words with a care that he could not fail to notice, I said, 'There were women – women in a certain situation – who had reason to be very grateful to Rebecca.'

I hoped he would know what I was talking about, but he said nothing. We both looked down into the winter-swollen waters of the Teifi beneath us and I felt John shiver beside me; the day was damp and grey with the kind of wind that seems nothing when you are first out in it but which soon seems to be following you around, pummeling at you.

'Rebecca was against the workhouse,' I began, 'I'm sure you know that?' Even as a small boy, he would have been aware that dragoons had been garrisoned at the Emlyn Union workhouse to protect it from the Rebeccaites.

'William Williams said something about it at the inquest – that Rebecca was against sending girls in trouble to the workhouse.'

I swallowed, my mouth suddenly dry. 'Yes. Rebecca – or I should say, one Rebecca band – took it upon themselves to take over where the law had left off. Or, rather, to uphold the spirit of the old law.'

A cart clattered by and we exchanged cheery Good-days with its owner.

'You mean Rebecca made men marry girls they'd got pregnant?' John said, once he could make himself heard again.

I nodded, pleased at his quickness of understanding. 'That, or, at the very least, made them provide for their illegitimate children.'

'And you think Mrs James might be grateful to Rebecca for that reason?'

I tried to look upriver out of the corner of my eye, towards the walls of the castle mill. Like so much else in the world, now, I knew it was there but I could not see it. 'It's possible,' I said. 'Not necessarily for herself, of course. A daughter, maybe. A niece or a friend.'

'Are you going to talk to her?'

'Not yet.' I turned and faced the town. 'But we need to remember to be careful.'

As we began to walk up Bridge Street towards the livery stable, an image appeared in my mind's eye: Nelly James standing just out of sight behind the open door of her back room. And then I grasped what had eluded me earlier – a grey-clad woman's figure behind the doorjamb at Parry's, listening.

John

I was dreading getting back in the saddle. For one thing, my arse was still sore from the previous day's wasted visit to Tregorlais. And then there was the horse. Sooner or later it was going to realise it could do what it liked and I wouldn't be able to stop it. I was no horseman – even Harry must've been able to see that.

But I'd have to make the best of it. We couldn't walk everywhere, it'd take too long. And, anyway, Harry was a gentleman, he couldn't go stomping about the place like an itinerant labourer.

So, out of Newcastle Emlyn we trotted, up Adpar Hill. I was sore, cold and so busy trying to copy what Harry did with his reins and his feet that I had no time to think about what we were going to say to Matt Tregorlais. Or whether he'd be watching for us. My hands were aching, the wind was singing in my ears where it was coming down the road from Rhydlewis and all I could think of was getting off that bloody animal.

So I nearly missed him. Matt. If he'd stayed bent over his spade, I would have. We'd've plodded on up to the farmyard and he'd have escaped. Just like yesterday. But he straightened up and I saw him. 'Over to your right,' I said to Harry. 'He's digging potatoes.'

I half expected Matt to run but he behaved as if he hadn't seen us. He had though. I could tell. He was working too hard at not looking up.

'Morning, Matt!' Harry hadn't asked how I knew the *plwyfwas* and I hadn't wanted to tell him it was from the Drovers'. I didn't want him to think I was always in there.

Matt didn't stop his digging. 'Dad said you'd been up here looking for me, John Davies. What d'you want?'

I glanced across at Harry but he said nothing. So on I went. 'Mr Probert-Lloyd's been asked to investigate the death of the dairymaid at Waungilfach. Margaret Jones.'

Matt carried on digging. 'Has he now? Case he didn't notice, there was an inquest.' He stooped and shook the earth off a root of potatoes. 'Jury gave a verdict. That's an end to it.'

I looked around again. For all the reaction Harry gave, you'd've thought he hadn't understood a word. I just had to follow my nose.

'You *chose* the jury, Matthew Evans. And somebody intimidated them into saying it was accidental death.'

Matt still didn't bother looking at me, just hefted his spade again. 'Don't talk nonsense, John Davies.'

'You know it's not nonsense as well as I do! There was a letter. Signed "Rebecca". They all saw it.'

Matt dumped a huge clod of earth and potatoes on the wet ground, then straightened up and glared at me. 'Who says?'

He had a spade in his hand. If he waved it about, my horse'd go galloping off and there'd be damn all I could do about it. Except fall off. I gathered the reins a bit tighter in my frozen fingers and flicked a look at Harry. Was he just going to sit there? 'Never mind who says. What we want to know is who told you to pick jurymen who'd be easily threatened.'

He bent over the potato ridge again. 'Nobody tells me what to do, John Davies. I pick who I like.'

'So who wrote that letter, then? Was that you as well?' I was getting fed up with this. Matt needed to show a bit more respect.

'There *wasn't* any letter, boy. Somebody's lied to you.'

'Nobody's lied to us.' I was trying to sound as if I knew what I was talking about. As if I was one jump ahead of him, waiting for him to put a foot wrong then pounce.

'No? Seen it then, have you?'

Matt must've spoken to Parry. He knew the letter was gone. 'Never mind what we have or haven't seen. What we want to know is whether you told the jury what verdict they were supposed to bring in?'

Matt stamped the wooden spade into the ground and upended a whole potato root. 'Why should I do that?' He bent over the ridge and pulled the plant towards him by the leaves. 'What's it to me whether she pulled the tree down on top of herself?'

She. Not 'the girl'; not 'Margaret Jones'. Harry caught it, too. 'Did you know her?' he asked, suddenly.

I was watching Matt. He faltered – just for a moment. Hadn't expected Harry to speak, I don't think. Especially not in Welsh.

'What?' he asked, as if Harry's question'd been too hard for him. Playing for time, he was. Probably only just realised that Harry'd understood every word he'd said.

'I'm asking,' Harry replied, still in Welsh, 'whether you knew Margaret Jones.'

Matt riddled earth and potatoes through his fingers. 'Why should I know her?'

I don't know what shocked me more, the insolence of him or Harry standing for it.

'You went to Treforgan chapel. So did she.' Harry's tone was mild but his message was clear: *Jumpy, aren't you, Matthew Evans? I wonder why.*

'No. Church, I am.'

'But you *weren't*. Not then. You used to go to Treforgan with Davy Thomas.'

Matt stared hard at him when he said that. 'A lot of people went there.'

'Yes,' Harry agreed with him, 'Nathaniel Howell was a very popular minister.'

The wind was gusting hard. Swept across the side of the hill like a flock of starlings. I shivered.

Matt moved away up the row. Harry nudged his horse after him and mine followed.

'Did Nathaniel Howell make an impression on you?' Harry asked. 'Most people seemed to find his preaching very powerful.'

Matt grunted. 'People soft in the head, maybe. Didn't fool me.'

'Didn't *fool* you? You don't think he was sincere?'

Matt glanced up. Fortunately, Harry's eyes were turned the right way. 'Nathaniel Howell was a fraud.'

'What d'you mean by that?' Harry's tone was sharp.

I heard the metal lip of the spade go into a potato. Matt cursed, using the ruined potato as a reason not to answer.

The question'd seemed important so I asked him again. 'Matt? What d'you mean he was a fraud?'

He dumped a clot of earth and potatoes on the ground and kicked at it to break it up. He wasn't a big man, Matt, but he was one you wouldn't want to cross. 'He's gone. Leave it at that.'

I flicked a glance at Harry but I couldn't tell what he was thinking. 'No,' I said. 'I want to know what you meant.'

'Well you'll have to want, then! Ask somebody else your questions.'

'We're asking *you*, Matthew Evans!' I flinched at Harry's tone. He might've been speaking to a dog. 'And I would appreciate it if you would do me the courtesy of answering.' He'd dropped the dialect. It was Bible Welsh now. Formal. Intimidating. 'I have been asked, by a party concerned with the case, to investigate further in the hope of finding new evidence and reopening the inquest. And, whether or not you tell us what you know, I *will get* that information and I *will* see the inquest reopened. And, when I do, I'll know who to call and to put on oath. Now – I'm going to ask you again, Matthew Evans – did you or did you not know Margaret Jones?'

Matt bent over the potato row. With a grunt, he turned over another spade's worth. It was a good imitation of contempt. If it was an imitation. Harry waited.

'If you're hoping we'll go away you're going to be disappointed,' he said. 'Did you know her?'

Matt threw a potato in the direction of the basket and missed.

'Matthew Evans! Did you know Margaret Jones?'

It's hard to break, the habit of obedience to your betters. But Matt wasn't going to give Harry any more than he had to. 'Not as well as you knew her,' he muttered.

'How *dare* you?' Harry was livid. White with rage.

Matt straightened up from his digging. He looked quite calm. As if he thought Harry couldn't touch him. 'Quite handy for you when she disappeared, wasn't it?'

I half expected Harry to get off his horse and take his whip to him. 'It was convenient for *somebody* but that somebody wasn't me, Matthew Tregorlais.' He was back to sounding local again. 'And you can be damn sure I'm going to find out who that somebody was.'

'You should listen to the jury. It was an *accident*. She died while she was trying to bury her bastard.'

Harry's horse was getting restive and he bent forward, stroked its neck. 'If that's true, why is Beca so afraid?'

Matt drove his spade into the ground. 'Take your questions

somewhere else. I've got nothing more to say. And if you have another inquest and try to make me give evidence, I'll have nothing to say then, either.' He bent over a clump of potatoes and earth. But Harry wasn't finished.

'You were one of Nathaniel Howell's Becas, weren't you? You were part of his crusade?'

Matt wiped the spade's lip on his boot and looked up at Harry. 'You should know, shouldn't you, Harry Gwyn?'

Harry

As our horses picked their way down the stony track away from Tregorlais and towards the road, I could feel all the questions John wasn't asking; they buffeted me along with the wind.

How much gossip had he heard about my involvement with Margaret? I knew how rumour bloomed from the smallest seed and I did not imagine for a second that my doings were excluded from people's speculation; John must have asked himself about my motives for investigating Margaret's death. And now, added to that, Matthew Evans had all but accused me of having dealings with Rebecca.

I turned my face to one side, offering the back of my head to the wind instead of my left ear which was beginning to ache. Though I could not see it properly, a broad swathe of the Teifi's wide and fertile lower valley spread out beneath us. A dozen shades of green and brown appeared around the whirlpool, the dunnish colours of leafless late November farmland, but, as to detail I was lost. Only my memory dotted the landscape with the white of limewashed cottages and byres, traced the high silhouettes of kites and buzzards, imagined the horizon as a watercolour wash where clouds hung heavy between earth and sky, blurring the boundary between them. Before my sight had failed, I could have stood in the stirrups and picked out landmarks beneath us; a fold in the landscape made Glanteifi mansion invisible from here but many of the farms which comprised the estate were laid out before us.

The mere thought of the estate and my place on it was enough to induce a feeling of wretched helplessness. Did my blindness really leave me no choice but to take up an unwanted duty as squire-in- waiting?

My father had made it very clear that my investigating the circumstances of Margaret's death would jeopardise any such future, my standing in local society being brought into disrepute by what others would see as an eccentric attachment to the lower orders.

As my neck muscles began to cramp, I resigned myself to earache and turned to face forwards again, acutely aware of John at my side.

We were several minutes away from the Tregorlais potato field, from Matthew Evans and his veiled accusation, and I had still said nothing. What could I say? *I rode out with Rebecca once but I don't remember Matthew Evans being there?* Explaining how I came to ride out with the Lady would, inevitably, involve explaining my association with Margaret and I was not yet confident enough of John to do so.

We rode on in silence, my mind busy with the memory of that night, seven years before, with Nathaniel Howell and his Rebeccas.

April 1843

As it has come to our attention that you are sympathetic to our cause, you are bid to help us in a pressing matter.

Be in the lane outside Treforgan chapel tomorrow night at half past ten o'clock. Come in a carriage, arrayed in every particular as a lady. In this you will show your sympathy to the unjustly treated amongst us. You shall see how you may be of service when you come.

It had not occurred to me to defy the summons. Not only was I excited, in a very young man's way, at being invited to ride out with Rebecca, I also wished to find out how my sympathy for her cause had been discovered. But I could not possibly assemble a carriage and pair on my own, nor drive them with any degree of competence, especially if I was to go dressed as a lady. So, I went to Davy Thomas.

'Good job I'm only a groom, isn't it?' His tone was somewhere between bitter and sardonic. 'If I was working with Ormiston I wouldn't know how to take you out in a carriage and pair.'

'You know I've tried,' I defended myself. 'My father won't make you under-steward until you prove an interest in the right things.'

Davy shook his head. 'Your father'll never see me steward here. He's never liked me, you know that.'

I sighed. 'He won't be squire forever, Davy. When he's gone and I'm in London, barristering, I'll need somebody I trust running the estate.'

'Somebody who looks the part, you mean?' He grinned and I knew he was referring to the often-recalled occasions when his mother had looked at the two of us, as little boys, dressed identically in clothes she had made herself, and pronounced that, on looks alone, there was not a soul alive who would not think Davy the master and me the servant. And she had been right. Always a head taller, Davy's dark features were striking in comparison to my own paleness and he had always been proud of the fact that girls would turn to him first, despite my being heir to the estate. We had gone about together from infancy never once acknowledging, between ourselves, what the world saw – the squire's son and his nursemaid's bastard.

But my insistence on treating him like a brother had been Davy's undoing. My father, still grieving for my long-dead brother George, had held us both to an exacting standard, and Davy had been found wanting, even more than I.

'If I had seen in him a determination to better himself, to avail himself of the advantages that have been bestowed on him and study diligently, develop an aptitude for the position,' my father had told me when I had complained of his failure to apprentice Davy to the estate's steward as I had suggested, 'then I would gladly ask Ormiston to take him on. Nothing would please me better than to have a local man as steward. But he will not exert himself. He wants everything with no effort.'

'Like me, you mean? I will have Glanteifi for no effort, won't I? I won't need to strive and learn and better myself, I will simply inherit.'

'It's different. You were born to it. You have been at school to be educated for it.'

'Then why didn't you send him to school with me? Why has he always been expected to do everything for himself?'

'Mr Davies's school was more than adequate for his purposes. And you know perfectly well that he would not have been tolerated at your school.'

But I believed, with all my callow heart, that if I were welcomed unquestioningly in barn and byre with him, then Davy should be as welcome in drawing and dining room with me. A year later, Oxford had done nothing to quench the flame of egalitarianism; I was a thoroughgoing rebel against the accepted order, ripe for Rebecca's picking.

'So… you're asking me to defy the magistrates,' Davy said when I asked him to obey Rebecca's summons with me, 'to break the law and risk transportation?'

'Are you telling me you haven't already ridden with the Rebeccas?'

He did not answer and, I confess, I was hurt. Did he think I would inform on him? 'It wouldn't be the first time we've broken the law together,' I reminded him.

'Poaching's one thing…'

I couldn't go without him and I was determined to go. 'Listen, if we're caught—'

'Caught?' He laughed with genuine merriment. 'Those soldiers couldn't catch a blind lamb in a small pen.'

'But if we *are*, I'll say I forced you to come. On pain of losing your position.'

He looked at me, his face guarded. '*Is* that what you're doing?'

The question dashed down spirits that had lifted with his laughter. 'Of course not. When have I ever forced you to do anything?'

He nodded, abashed at my vehemence, and rubbed his nose with the back of an index finger. 'You know what this summons is, do you? You know what the Rebeccas who meet at Treforgan chapel are about?'

In my ignorance, I had assumed that one band of Rebeccas was much like another. I shook my head.

'Hasn't your father complained to you about Nathaniel Howell's crusade against the new Poor Law? Denounced him for a subversive?'

'No.' My father had not so much as mentioned Howell's name.

'Hates the new law, Howell does. Especially girls in trouble going off to the workhouse. Calls the new law a seducer's charter.'

The minister was hardly the only one who held that opinion. I'd read as much in London periodicals.

'What does his crusade consist of?'

Davy looked at me, steadily, as he had used to when daring me. 'We'll find out, won't we?'

'You'll come then?'

'I'll come, but don't expect me to play the liveried flunky to your fine lady.'

Davy had promised to ensure that none of the stableboys came rushing out to confront us and, as we led out the carriage-pair, all was reassuringly still; no lantern bobbed its way towards us, no voice demanded to know what we thought we were doing.

Once the horses were between the shafts, traces fumblingly fastened in the inadequate light of our lanterns, I opened the carriage door, hung my light on its hook and threw in my valise.

'Who'd you borrow your lady's things from?' Davy asked.

'None of your business.' I was not going to tell him that I had gone up into the attic in search of my dead mother's clothes. Let him think my life replete with admirers.

'Not Margaret's, are they?'

I did not reply, my throat having closed up momentarily at the thought of her.

'Been to see her yet?' When I did not reply his tone became more serious. 'You should, Harry. She needs to see you.'

'Needs?'

'Go and see her.'

'You think my father's not angry enough with me for coming home – that I should step further over the line and go to Waungilfach?'

'So you won't go and see the woman you say you love, but you will ride out with a pack of felons?'

I stared, wordlessly, at his soot-blacked face. Finally, he jutted his chin at the carriage. 'You changing in there, then?'

'Warmer than out here.' Though he and I had been down to our linen together on countless occasions as boys, I had no desire to dress myself as a woman in front of him.

He climbed into the driver's seat. 'Get on with it, then, and we can be off.'

But I did not want to run the risk of being discovered in the stableyard. 'Let's get to the bottom of the drive. Then, if you can give me a couple of minutes, I'll sort myself out.'

Though the summons had instructed that I come to the rendezvous 'arrayed in every particular as a lady' I was determined that I would not arrive besprigged and beflowered in one of my mother's day gowns. I took out of the valise a dark green riding habit and short coat. It was then, stripped to the waist, that I encountered my first difficulty. How did women put their dresses on?

If Howell had summoned my brother, George Probert, to ride with Rebecca, he would have known. I had no doubt that George would have arrived dressed in a gown borrowed from his latest paramour, driving the carriage without assistance and flinging down the reins to take charge of the night's proceedings himself.

I stared at the buttons that ran down the front to the stiffened waist of my mother's habit. If I undid those, I should be able to step into the dress. Under no circumstances was I prepared to remove my trousers.

Buttons undone and the carriage at a standstill, I got both legs in through the waist only to find that I had to undo yet more buttons in order to pull the dress past my hips. Then another problem presented itself. In the attic, I had decided that the garment was only an inch or two short, a deficiency which I had remedied by taking my penknife to the stitching on the generous lower hem. But it seemed that my mother had been both diminutive and slight, for, once I had forced my narrow shoulders in, the edges of the habit's bodice would not meet across my chest.

Berating myself for not having made the necessary adjustments earlier, I wriggled out of the arms once more and fumbled for my knife. In the dark of the carriage neither seam nor stitches were easy to see and I was obliged to work by feel.

After a minute or so of cursing under my breath and nicks in the material, a thump landed on the roof of the carriage. 'What are you doing in there, making the damn clothes?'

Easy enough for him to be impatient, he had declined to wear the slightest element of female disguise. 'One minute,' I shouted, holding each edge of the half-opened seam and tearing the rest. With the back of the bodice gaping, I was able to put the habit on without difficulty. I fastened the buttons as quickly as I could and shrugged into the short coat which would cover my makeshift alterations. 'Done!'

The carriage creaked into motion again and I tossed aside the bonnet which matched the dress; I would not wear it for one moment longer than necessary.

Even from inside the carriage, the horses' hooves sounded loud in the silent darkness and I wished that I could be on the box with Davy, able to see and take steps against any threat that presented itself. But, dressed as I was, that was impossible so I attempted to compose myself for whatever lay ahead.

I did not have to endure long.

'Whoa, girls.' The carriage swayed to a stop as Davy pulled on the brake. Trying to convince myself that the quickening of my pulse was excitement rather than apprehension, I crammed the bonnet onto my head and opened the door onto the lane outside Treforgan chapel.

In the light of lamps and torches, I could see a group of two dozen or so men in the lane. Every one wore at least one item of female clothing and one or two wore a woman's Sunday hat.

Every face was blacked and every face was turned towards me. One man came forward.

'Good evening, Mr Probert-Lloyd,' he said, in Welsh, sweeping a ludicrous straw wig from his head, 'I am Nathaniel Howell.'

His blackened face made him as anonymous as he had been when he had led the *ceffyl pren* procession to Waungilfach to mend William Williams's ways. But I recognised his voice – a slightly husky light tenor, as if he'd been singing or preaching too hard.

I bowed, my mouth dry. 'My friends know me as Harry Gwyn.'

'Indeed,' Howell said, 'friends who include Margaret Jones of Waungilfach farm.'

I stared at him, my stomach tightening. 'I… We're…'

'I *know* what you are, Henry Probert-Lloyd.' He looked around at his men. 'We all know what you are. Please, do not attempt to justify your behaviour.'

It was as if he had slapped me across the face.

Howell gave a snort of laughter. 'Equality doesn't feel so noble when it's assumed by those on whom you wish to bestow it, does it? It doesn't feel as virtuous as telling your sweetheart that she's as good as a lady and you're no better than the working man, does it?'

There was a malicious gleam in his lantern-lit eyes and, despite myself, my knees began to tremble. How could I have been so stupid as to come? To assume that a gentleman would be welcome in Rebecca's ranks?

'But this is what equality before God *really* means, Harry Gwyn. That I – or any man here –' he flung out an arm to encompass the watching Rebeccas 'am as free to stand in judgement over you as you are over me.' He sucked in a sudden breath, as if bracing himself. 'Of course, the Bible tells us that we shouldn't judge each other – *Judge not that ye be not judged* – but when we see sin, constant and flagrant sin, we must act, mustn't we?'

'I haven't sinned—' my voice was a croak.

'Haven't you? Then you're a better man than any of us, here.' He waited for me to draw breath to defend myself and, when I did, interrupted me neatly. 'But don't worry, Harry Gwyn. Tonight isn't about punishing you, though your dalliance with Margaret has been noted. As has her condition.'

Her condition?

'Ah. I see you didn't know.' His voice had dropped; now it was for me alone. 'You must go and see her. Make amends.'

I shook my head, remembered to breathe. 'It's not mine. The child can't be mine.'

Head on one side, like a blackbird eyeing a worm half-pulled from the ground, he looked at me. 'And that's the only reason you'd have to make amends, is it?'

He waited while I took in what he'd said. 'Go and see her, Harry Gwyn. But not tonight.' He gave me his lantern to hold while he settled his grotesque wig back on his head. 'Tonight we have other fish to fry at Waungilfach.'

As we headed towards Williams's farm, I was reeling from the shock of Howell's words.

Margaret was carrying a child. Someone else's child. She had shrugged me off and taken up with another man.

She would be at Waungilfach. Would she come out when she heard us in the yard, as she and I had done when the *ceffyl pren* came for William Williams? I did not want her seeing me. Did not want her laughing at me in my mother's clothes; did not want her witnessing whatever humiliation might be meted out to me.

Margaret and another man. I writhed inwardly as I remembered her attempts to seduce me. How prim she must have thought me, how unmanly to turn away her offer of herself.

I heard a sudden shout and the carriage came to a halt. Deciding that it was better to be forewarned, I opened the door to see what we had stopped for, and a man, standing with his back to me, spun around at the click of the door. Bulging eyes and protrusive teeth are not easily hidden by soot-black, and I recognised Ezra Lloyd, one of my father's tenants. He said nothing but glanced back over his shoulder at Nathaniel Howell who stood a few yards away, in close-headed conference with a young woman.

The minister took his time saying whatever he had to say before bringing the young woman over to the carriage.

'This is Hannah Rees. She will be riding with you the rest of the way.'

Hannah Rees. Hannah the housemaid, much troubled the previous summer by the unwanted attentions of her master, William Williams.

Seeing my eyes on her, Hannah moved her hands protectively around the shawl-slung infant held fast to her breast.

I nodded and held out my hand for her, forgetting that I was supposed to be a lady. 'Come and take a seat. It's not the most comfortable carriage in the world, but it's better than walking.'

Once inside, Hannah backed into the shadowed corner furthest away from me and sat, cradling her swaddled child.

I let her be. We were not far from Waungilfach now and I was mute with apprehension.

Barely two minutes later, the carriage stopped. Before I could put a hand to the door, it was opened from the outside and I saw that we were in William Williams's farmyard, the whitewashed house and outbuildings pale and huge in the moonlight.

'Are you ready?' Howell asked.

He was looking past me at Hannah, his face sinister in the light of his lantern.

'No! I can't,' Hannah Rees sobbed. 'I can't give him up.'

'Hannah, I promise you he'll be well cared for. That he'll be brought up in every way as one of the family. As indeed he is, being Williams's son.'

'She'll be cruel to him! I know she will.'

'She will not.' Howell spoke with such authority that Hannah's sobs ceased.

'How do you know?'

'Because it is agreed. All the while Esme Williams cares for Samuel as her own, I will confirm whatever story she and her husband make up about how they come to have him. But, if I hear anything – anything at all – that tells me he's being unkindly treated, I will let the truth be known.' He gazed at her intently, as if willing her to trust him. 'Believe me when I say that neither she nor her husband is willing for that to happen. And – even if it's ten years from now – if I should hear of his being mistreated or unkindly dealt with, I will say what I know.'

Hannah took a deep breath. In the shadowy light thrown by the lantern, I saw her open the shawl and look down at her son.

'Come now,' the minister said, 'we must give him to his father and then I will take you to your new position.'

'At this time of night?' Hannah was momentarily distracted from her grief.

'It's all arranged,' Howell assured her. 'Now, be ready to come out with Lady Harriet here at my command. Do you understand?'

If Hannah gave any sign of comprehension or acquiescence, I failed to see it but Howell turned away, apparently satisfied.

I moved towards the open door and watched as he addressed the assembled men.

'First,' he said, 'as a sign that we're doing the Lord's work, and to ask his blessing on it, we'll sing a hymn.'

Unfamiliar with the tune they struck up, I turned my attention to the house. The windows were dark but I saw a brief sliver of light in one, as if a curtain had been twitched aside by somebody holding a lamp.

Singing is apt to make men forgetful of their surroundings and this was no exception. As the hymn's harmony filled the farmyard, it seemed to me that every eye, save those still hidden away inside the carriage, was on Nathaniel Howell. So, when the farmhouse door was flung open, the only people who saw Esme Williams's look of guarded unsurprise were Hannah Rees and me.

Williams's wife stood on the threshold fully dressed, a candle lantern in one hand. Either she was an exceptionally speedy dresser or she had been expecting us.

The hymn at an end, Nathaniel Howell turned to face her. 'Call your husband down, please.'

But, before she could turn around, Williams came out of the house, thrusting forward his lantern in an attempt to identify faces. 'What—'

Howell held up a hand. Unlike Williams he spoke in Welsh. 'Please, don't make yourself look foolish. You know how you have sinned and I don't doubt that you know, by now, how you will be required to make amends.'

'How dare you? I'm a gentleman—'

I could not see Howell's face but I could see anger in the rigidity of his stance. 'A gentleman.' It was not a question, it was a flat dismissal. 'Does a gentleman treat his servants with disrespect? Does he force himself upon a young woman again and again until she carries within her the consequences of his lust? Does he deny his own sin and deprive her of her livelihood?'

I looked over at Williams's wife, mortified on her behalf. But, eyes on Howell, her face registered no visible reaction.

Williams himself, however, showed all the indignation I would have expected.

'I won't stand here and be insulted by a man like you,' he blustered. 'I want all of you to leave my property. Now.'

Not an eye shifted from his face. Not a foot stirred. The Rebeccas' concerted lack of reaction was eerie; but, of course, this was not the first time they had been out on this errand.

Then, at the front of the crowd, Ezra Lloyd took a step forward.

Just one. And every other man followed suit. It was the most menacing thing I had ever seen.

Howell spoke into the silence. 'Mr Williams. Do not imagine that we will allow you to defy us. If you turn and go into your house we will come after you. If you bar your door to us, we will break it down. If you fetch the gun I know you possess, we will burn your house to the ground.'

I do not suppose a man present doubted that he would be true to his word; I certainly did not.

'Who are you to say such things to me?' Williams demanded. 'You stand in my yard and accuse me without evidence. You set yourself up to be judge and jury—'

'Not me alone. All of us. We are a jury of your peers—'

Williams waved a dismissive hand. 'These men are not my peers!'

'No!' Howell's fury sent his voice up half an octave. 'You're right – these men are *not* your peers. They are better than you! They are God-fearing men who know God's word and live by it!'

Not waiting for any kind of response from Williams, Howell turned towards the carriage. Suddenly, my mouth was like chalk and I could feel my pulse in my fingertips. I could not shake off the fear that I, too, was here to be judged.

'Bring her out, please.'

I stood and complied. One palm supporting her child, Hannah rose to my hand and I opened the door. Davy, true to his word, did not stir from his seat at the front of the carriage though I could feel his eyes on me, watching, as I lowered the steps and helped Hannah down.

Playing my part to the full, I tucked the young woman's free arm inside my own and walked her, side-by-side and sisterlike, to the waiting minister who bowed. Remembering myself just in time, I curtsied, clumsily, before standing to one side.

'It's time, now, Hannah,' I heard Howell whisper to the girl. 'Be brave. You know it's best for the child.'

Howell passed me his lantern and took the child from Hannah's arms.

'William Williams,' he strode towards the farmer, 'this is your son.'

Williams held up his lantern and looked down at the infant who, awoken and chilled by the removal from his mother's breast, began to grizzle. 'You can't just come here and father a child onto me!' he protested. 'How do I know it's mine? Any number of men could have had her.'

At this, one of the Rebeccas darted forward, stumbling slightly as his apron wrapped itself around his legs. He seized Williams by the lapels and forced him to his knees.

'You raping pig! You dare to lay the blame on my sister? She was a maid when she came here, an innocent!'

I nerved myself to look over at Mrs Williams. No matter how unsympathetic she was to her servants, she did not deserve to hear such lewdness on her own doorstep. But her face was without expression in the flickering darkness.

The child still clasped to his own chest, Howell stepped forward. 'Leave him be, Jac,' he said, quietly. Then, in a voice loud enough for all the gathered men to hear, he addressed Williams as the farmer pushed himself to his feet.

'You make your sin against this young woman even more reprehensible by refusing to acknowledge your responsibilities, and insulting her. You would do well to ask her pardon.'

'I will do no such thing! I am a gentleman – I will not apologise to that hussy!'

I did not see him move, the man who had claimed Hannah as his sister. There was just the sudden violence of a punch, and Williams staggering back, his hands to his face, moaning and swearing. His wife bent to the lamp he had dropped and, again, it seemed to me that she was unnaturally calm in the face of what was happening.

The crowd, meanwhile, broke into ragged encouragement and, if Howell had not held up a forestalling hand, I do not doubt that others would have surged forward to inflict a severe beating on Williams.

'Enough!' Howell's voice was raised to the point of shrillness; the situation was in danger of breaking out of his control and I saw him look towards Ezra Lloyd who came to stand at his side.

'Yes. Enough.' Mrs Williams pushed her husband to one side and came forward to address Howell. 'That's the first sense you've spoken since you've been here. What does Hannah Rees care for an apology? All she cares about is her child and whether he'll be looked after.'

I glanced at Hannah, who was still standing next to me. All eyes suddenly upon her, she gave a sob and rushed towards Howell, wresting the infant from the minister's grasp and clasping him to her.

Without her at my side, I felt exposed, at the mob's mercy.

Mrs Williams turned and spoke to Hannah, as if all the assembled men were of no account. 'Of course we'll look after him. You know we have only daughters in our house – we need a son.'

If Mrs Williams had held out her arms for the boy, I believe Hannah would have fled back to the carriage. But she did not. She simply stood and waited.

What choice did Hannah Rees have? If she kept the child, she would be in the workhouse till he was weaned, then she would be found work and he would stay there as an orphan.

As she had done before, Hannah kissed her son's forehead. For a long moment her lips seemed unable to part from his skin and I thought she would fail but, at last, she raised her head and looked into her erstwhile mistress's eyes. 'His name is Samuel.'

As Mrs Williams took the baby from his mother, her eyes darted to me and I felt a jolt of cold fear at the thought of being recognised. Then I realised; even if she knew me, she could not tell my father that Howell had paraded me. If she did, she would have to explain what I had been doing at Waungilfach.

A week or so later, my father asked me whether I had heard the news about Williams and his wife. They had, apparently, been so charitable as to take in the motherless child of one of her distant cousins.

I nodded, though my mind was filled not with the image of the child Samuel in his new mother's arms but with Howell's parting words to me.

'Do not give us cause to visit you, Harry Gwyn. For your father's position will not protect you.'

John

You should know, shouldn't you?

What had Matthew Tregorlais meant by that?

There was only one explanation I could see. Harry must've been on the receiving end of Howell's attentions. Was that why he was so keen to investigate? To get his own back on Beca?

The further we got from Tregorlais, the more I expected Harry to say something. Either to justify himself or distract me. But he said nothing. Not a word. In the end, it was me that broke the silence.

'Why would Matt leave the chapel and start going to church?' It was an oddity. Generally, if people were going to swap, they gave up church for chapel.

Harry answered without turning his head. 'The chapel at Treforgan – Nathaniel Howell's chapel – was very involved with Rebecca. Too involved perhaps. Howell left in a bit of a hurry and some people might've wanted to forget what they'd been mixed up in. Leaving the chapel would be one way to do that, I suppose.'

'But why church? Why didn't Matt just go to another chapel?'

'Perhaps he was worried about the family's tenancy, wanted the added respectability of going to church, getting the vicar on his side.'

That made sense. Added to that, Brongwyn was a small parish with few men to choose the *plwyfwas* from. If Matt had decided he needed more respectability, turning church was a good idea.

We reached a crossroads. Harry pulled up and looked round at me. 'I think we need to go and see Mrs Williams.'

I was taken by surprise. 'Esme Williams – Waungilfach?

Harry sighed as if he'd made a decision. 'Yes. It was she who asked me to investigate. She wants her husband's name cleared.'

'Ah, I see,' I said as if that explained everything. But it didn't, did it? Not everything. Not by a long shot.

The last time I'd been to Waungilfach farm, seven years before, I'd come by the footpath through the Alltddu, not along the road. The footpath led up to the farm's back yard, by the dairy. The front entrance was grander – a short, gated drive. We rode past an orchard on one side and a range of buildings on the other, down to Williams's tidy, two-storey farmhouse.

I was glad to be coming in the front way. I was already nervous enough about going to Waungilfach without having to go through the wood where Margaret Jones had died.

Esme Williams let her maid answer our knock, and the girl took us into the parlour. It was trying hard to be something else but it was still just the one decent room of a Cardiganshire farmhouse. Like my mother always said, you can put a pig in a dress but it's still a pig. It was also freezing cold and Esme had to call the girl back to light the fire.

'When you've done that, you can make us some tea.' Esme spoke to the girl in Welsh. The Williams's servants weren't in the same class as the Pridhams'.

Harry fidgeted while the maid brought embers from the kitchen fire and threw a shovelful of small-coal on top. His eyes were shifting about. Trying to get an impression of the room, most likely. What was it like, I wondered, being able to see that things were there but not being able to look at them properly?

Mind you, it was no loss in Esme Williams's parlour. The only thing to see apart from the fashionable furniture were those little china figures some women of a certain age love so much. On every flat surface, they were. Like pixies, watching you with their tiny, frozen faces. If I'd been William Williams, I'd've taken a stick to the lot of them.

Esme watched the maid get up off her knees and scuttle out in the direction of the kitchen before she spoke to us. The poor girl'd be cursing us for putting her behind on all her work. Esme Williams was the kind of woman who'd want everything done just so, visitors or not.

'Well then, Mr Probert-Lloyd,' she said, 'have you got some news for me?' Now that the maid was out of the way, we were back to English.

Harry shifted on the edge of the shiny sofa. I knew chintz was all the rage with houseproud women but it wasn't comfortable to sit on – felt as if it'd been lacquered. 'Actually, Mrs Williams, I have some questions.'

'Oh?' Esme shot a glance at me but I pretended not to notice. Didn't want her to know I was as much in the dark as she was.

'I need to ask you about the night little Samuel was brought here.'

'From my cousin's?'

Harry sighed. 'Mrs Williams, John Davies is my confidential assistant. He must know everything I know.' I was watching Esme carefully but she was keeping a tight hold of herself. 'It's necessary that he understands how Samuel came to be here,' Harry said. 'That he's your husband's natural son. His and Hannah Rees's.'

I waited for her to deny it but she kept quiet. Perhaps she realised I already knew. Me and the rest of Newcastle Emlyn. That cousin story had always been a fig leaf that drew attention to more than it covered up.

'And,' Harry was still using the same flat, don't-think-of-arguing-with-me tone, 'that Nathaniel Howell and his Rebecca band brought the boy to you.'

Now that *was* news to me. Then I remembered what Harry'd said about some of the Rebeccas rescuing young women who'd got into trouble. So… Nathaniel Howell the minister had been their leader, had he? Well, well…

Had Harry been caught up in that too? Had he had a visit telling him that when Margaret Jones's baby was born, he'd have to provide for it?

I watched him stand and warm his hands by the fire. I could see his reflection in the huge gilt-framed mirror above the mantel piece. It was far too big for the room, that mirror, but you could've said the same about all the furniture. Every stick of it was built for a drawing room rather than a parlour.

I turned and caught Esme's eyes on Harry's back.

'And is it *necessary,*' she burst out, suddenly, 'that he knows you were—'

'Mrs Williams!' The speed of Harry's turn was shocking, never mind the tone he used on her. 'If I am to conduct this investigation *on your behalf,* it is essential that *you* answer *my* questions, not that I answer yours.'

Esme Williams stared at him, red to the roots of her hair. Humiliation or rage? Either way, Harry'd made himself quite clear. He wasn't going to tolerate any tit for tat from her. Her secrets were fair game. His weren't.

He went back to the sofa and sat down. 'I need to know two things,' he said. 'Firstly, did you know they were coming that night – Nathaniel Howell and his Rebeccas?'

I watched her staring at him. I could see she was willing him to meet her eye. When he didn't, she turned her glare on me and I quickly looked away.

'Mrs Williams,' Harry wasn't giving up. 'Did you know that Nathaniel Howell was planning to bring Samuel to your husband that night?'

She looked away. 'Yes. I'd asked the Reverend Howell to bring him here.'

'You asked him to?'

Harry's tone was level – just making sure he understood – but the question itself was shocking. *You asked for your husband's bastard to be brought to you?*

Esme's chin came up. 'Yes. Waungilfach needed a son. I'd been with child three times and had three daughters. Childbirth is a dangerous business, Mr Probert-Lloyd, I might've gone through it another three times and had three more girls.'

Was she trying to embarrass Harry with the plainness of her speech? If she was, I couldn't speak for him but it was working on me. I didn't know where to look. A china clown was making a sad face on a little table at the end of the sofa and I knew exactly how he felt.

'How did you come to know Nathaniel Howell?' Harry asked.

'I didn't know him. I knew *of* him. Everybody in the parish was chattering about him.'

'And how did you go about contacting him?'

'He came here—' Esme broke off, clasped her hands and unclasped them again as if she couldn't find a comfortable place for them. Or as if she'd like to wring a neck. 'He came to tell me what had happened to Hannah Rees – after she left our employment.'

Left their employment? Got sent packing was what she meant.

'He told me the child would be brought up in the workhouse – or, more likely, would die there from lack of care – so I told him to bring the boy here.'

'Did he threaten you?' Harry asked.

Esme Williams's face coloured up again. Almost matched her purple dress. 'No he did not! He didn't have to – I know my responsibilities.'

'I just wondered… Howell was known for taking the *ceffyl pren* out and I know he'd made your husband ride it.' Had he indeed? And how did Harry know about it? 'Do you think Howell might have gone further if it hadn't been for your generosity in taking Samuel in?'

Generosity? Hah!

'What do you mean, might have gone further?' Esme's voice was sharp with suspicion. 'And done what, exactly?'

Harry's eyes seemed to be on the flowered tiles of the fireplace and the fact that he wasn't looking at Esme made it look as if he was just saying the first thing that came into his head. 'I don't know. Were threats made to your husband after that night? In a letter, perhaps? Threats related to his future conduct with his female servants?'

Just as well Harry couldn't see the look Esme Williams gave him, then. It would've stopped the blood in his veins. 'Are you suggesting that my husband killed Margaret Jones and put it about that she'd gone away because he was afraid of what Beca would do to him when it went round that she was pregnant?'

Old Schofield couldn't've summed it up more succinctly.

'I don't know what to think,' Harry admitted. Beneath his beard, he was chewing the inside of his lip. 'Nathaniel Howell left Treforgan very soon after Margaret disappeared. Do you know anything about that?'

'I heard he was offered the minister's job at a large chapel somewhere else,' Esme said. 'Why? Suspect him as well, do you?'

Harry gave an embarrassed half-smile. 'I had information that made me think he had plans to be here for some considerable time. He'd mentioned being here for ten years at least.'

Esme stared at him. 'Everybody has plans. And they often come to nothing.'

Our horses plodded back up the drive, past the huge doors of the threshing barn and the lower-roofed byres. I almost wished I was in one of the cowsheds sharing the steamy warmth of the beasts. I was shivering on my horse.

'Why did you want to know whether she knew Howell and his Rebeccas were coming that night?' I asked.

Harry's head turned towards me, away from the orchard's winter-bare apple trees. 'I think it's significant that Nathaniel Howell didn't just gather his men about him and ride out after dark. That he spoke to the people he was going to visit beforehand.'

'Why?'

'Because it's possible that he spoke once too often – to the wrong person.'

He stopped. From his expression, he was thinking hard. 'Perhaps Margaret Jones was made to disappear because somebody knew Beca was coming for him.' I waited while he thought some more. We passed through Waungilfach's open gates and onto the road. I didn't ask where we were going and the horses just turned towards home. 'Then there's Nathaniel Howell himself,' he said.

'What about him?' It felt awkward having to ask but there was no point just looking mystified and hoping he'd explain, was there?

'Matthew Evans said Howell was a fraud. That's the first criticism I've ever heard of the man. You'll be too young to remember but the Reverend Howell was something of a phenomenon – people came from all over to hear his preaching. And he carried a lot of people with him in what they called his Beca *crusade*.' Harry stopped. 'And then he left. Very suddenly. I must confess, I'm troubled by that.' He stopped, then said, 'I wonder whether, perhaps, he *didn't* leave.'

'What do you mean?'

He turned his face towards me. 'Everybody thought Margaret Jones had left. Run away. But she was here all the time.'

Harry

On our way back to Newcastle Emlyn, I pulled my horse up at the entrance to Glanteifi's drive. I must confess that the leaving of a *ceffyl pren* outside my room had unnerved me. I would be safer in my father's house; it was time to tell him the truth.

'I have some business up at the house,' I told John. 'Meanwhile I'd like you to do something for me.'

'Of course.'

'Firstly, I'd like you to find out the exact location of this chapel that Nathaniel Howell is supposed to have gone to. I think it was East Anglia somewhere. Then I'd like you to find out who the Treforgan chapel elders were while Howell was minister there. Try and establish who'd be the most likely to talk to us about Howell's involvement with Beca.'

I heard him take a breath, as if he was about to lift a heavy load. 'I'll do my best.'

'Oh, and see if you can find out who Stephen Parry's maid is, will you?' I needed to put a name to that grey-clad figure in the doorway. 'I don't know how long I'll be, so let's meet at the Salutation tomorrow. You can tell me what you've found out over breakfast.'

Reins slack, I let my horse find its own pace up the curving drive as I rehearsed what I needed to say to my father. I would have to take him into my confidence as to the exact nature and course of my association with Margaret; despite the fact that it might give him further cause to deplore my behaviour and my opinions, I saw no other option. I had let Margaret Jones down once, I would not do so again.

The Glanteifi drive was short and I had barely ordered my thoughts before I was in the stableyard, enduring the embarrassment of asking my father's grooms to tend to my by-the-hour hack, knowing that, as soon as I was out of earshot, speculation would rage about why I was back at Glanteifi.

I tried to leave my awkwardness behind with my horse as I slipped into the house through the servants' entrance, finger already to my lips lest any of the maids should come scurrying to greet me. I had deliberately chosen not to go in via the front door so as to avoid Moyle but, as luck would have it, he appeared in the hall at a smart clip just as I had made my whispering way through the servants' quarters and was standing before the door to my father's study.

'Mr Probert-Lloyd's not in there, sir. He's in the library. With a visitor.'

I turned. 'Oh. Who's that?'

Did I imagine a slight hesitation – a weighing-up of what it would be expedient to tell the temporarily estranged son?

'He's with Mr Williams of Waungilfach farm, sir.'

Moyle never failed to mangle Welsh names. Though he had been at Glanteifi almost a decade and could easily have submitted to learning basic pronunciation, he preferred to maintain some spurious kind of linguistic high ground.

'Then I'll wait for him in the morning room.'

I went into the faintly damp cool of the morning room and stood at one of the windows, gazing sidelong at the river view and wondering whether William's visit had anything to do with my investigation. My reverie was interrupted by one of the maids, a shovel full of embers in one hand and a coal scuttle in the other.

'Sorry, Mr Henry, I'll just…'

In my mind's eye I saw her nodding at the grate to finish her sentence. 'Of course,' I said, 'please.'

Why were servants trained to apologise when they came into a room to do something that was specifically designed for your comfort? It was foolish – as if my need for a fire should have been anticipated before anybody even knew I was going to be here.

'Will there be anything else, sir?'

I looked around and tried to smile directly at her, wanting to thank her for remembering that I preferred the servants to speak Welsh to me when my father was not present. 'No, thank you, Betty.' I was confident, now, in identifying all the servants by a combination of their voice and the impression they made on my peripheral vision.

She closed the door behind her and I moved over to the fire. The morning room had not changed since my childhood: the same delicate furniture, chosen by my father's first wife; the same long, striped curtains; the same pale rugs on dark floorboards.

So little had altered in this house during my lifetime. It was as if the whole period of my existence had been of little consequence, as if my father had lost interest in the house and everything in it with the death of his firstborn.

I contemplated this notion, looking at it dispassionately, wondering whether it accounted for my feeling that I had never belonged here, at least not in these rooms, furnished by a woman I had never known, many years before my birth. If I had ever felt at home at Glanteifi it had been in the servants' quarters, in the stables and out in the fields and farms of the estate.

My father must constantly have compared me with the son he had lost; the son whose portrait still hung in his dressing room. George Probert. He had my father's name as well as his heart.

My dead brother's face in that portrait was clear before me, my mind's eye unclouded by the whirlpool. It was a face full of ardour and strong will, an image so full of vitality that it seemed barely contained by its gilt frame, as if he was about to stride out and lay hold of life once more, to take it and drain it to the dregs before smacking his lips and laughing with glee at the sheer exhilaration of being alive.

As a small boy I had been fascinated by his portrait, sneaking into my father's dressing room when he was out on estate business to stand and stare at it. My brother. The son my father loved. Brave, fearless, manly George. But I had tried, in my childish way, to be those things, too. I had been brave when I was with Davy. Even though he was bigger and stronger than me, I had always accepted his challenges to wrestle, to race, to swim even though I was afraid, sometimes. Then I had been sent away to school and everything had changed.

School had been full of boys like George: laughing, swaggering, manly. Apparently admirable, I had soon learned that they were overbearing, headstrong and possessed of an unrestrained, animal sensuality. They had made my life miserable and I had learned to hate and fear them. After a single term, clandestine visits to my father's dressing room ceased, though George's image was never far from my mind. Now, however, his face seemed to sneer at me with the same cold contempt as my schoolfellows; his loud, commanding voice echoed their snide remarks about my accent; like them, he mocked my courtesy to the school servants. And when I was stripped and humiliated by older boys, when they laughed at my hairless nakedness and called me little Welsh maid, I saw his face amongst them.

207

But George's resemblance to my tormentors had done more than destroy my admiration for him. His memory, that portrait hanging in cherished privacy, had also hung between my father and me. It caused me to reject my father's ideas of what a gentleman should be and to take refuge in the radical philosophies espoused by a headmaster who had no notion of the barbarity being practiced by some of his students on their fellows.

Liberty. Equality. Fraternity. Those were the virtues I had cleaved to as I grew, the virtues I tried to live by. Finally done with school and looking to the future, I had wanted to be free to marry Margaret as an equal. I had wanted Davy to be my friend – my brother – not my servant.

Willfully choosing to believe that the principles that had brought about revolution in France and America were applicable to bucolic West Wales, I had ignored my father's remonstrations. But he had been implacable.

David Thomas cannot be your friend because he is not your equal. The lower orders look to us to provide for them, Harry, and that's what you are to him, somebody who can provide for him. You forget that at your peril.

But, to forget something, you must first acknowledge it and I had not. I had simply ignored what my father said. I had ignored it in my friendship with Davy and I had ignored it in my misguided but sincere attachment to Margaret.

And, now, I was nerving myself to explain that and to ask him to understand why I must find out the truth about her death.

The fire had barely begun to warm the morning room when the door suddenly swung audibly inwards, causing me to spin around. Some part of me still expected to be able to see whatever had startled me.

'Harry! Moyle said you were here.'

I wished he had not. 'I didn't intend to disturb you when you're busy, Father.'

'Not at all.' He moved further into the room. 'Are you well?' He sounded ill at ease.

'As well as can be expected when lodging in an hotel.'

There was a moment's fraught silence and I wondered whether I had gone too far but, when my father spoke again, there was no reproach in his voice. 'Your arrival is fortuitous, as it happens. William Williams is here.' He paused. 'I gather that his wife has informed him of your investigation.'

Williams had not been in the house when John and I were there. Had he seen us leaving Waungilfach and quizzed his wife as to the purpose of our visit? He could easily have ridden through the Alltddu and got to Glanteifi before John and I had reached the Newcastle Emlyn road, we had not hurried.

'I see. So he's come to ask you to bring me to heel?'

Was my father sufficiently far away not to notice that I was looking in his direction rather than directly at him? I heard him sigh. 'I would prefer that he explain his position to you himself.'

I shook my head. Williams would ask me, politely, to desist; I, with equal politeness, would decline. It was hard to see how my father could be a happy spectator at that conversation. I needed to say my piece about Margaret first.

'I'd prefer to ride over and speak to him later. There's something I'd like to discuss with you first, Father.'

'I would rather you spoke to him now, Harry, please. It would be churlish to send him away without seeing you when you are actually here.'

'Churlishness needn't come into it, surely? I could say, very politely, that I'll see him later today—'

'I would prefer it if you were to hear his grievance now. If you don't mind.'

I should have stood firm, refused to hear from Williams until I had said what I needed to say to my father. But, whoever made the observation that old habits die hard was right – as soon as my father spoke the words 'if you don't mind' I was a boy again, bending to his will.

Williams was standing in front of the window furthest from the library's door, as if he was afraid that I would take fright at the sight of him and flee before he could address me.

'Good day, Mr Williams.' I sketched a bow and went to stand in front of the fire, leaving him at his post in the far corner.

'And to you, sir.' His tone was chilly.

I was not going to help him. If he wanted me to give up my investigations he would have to broach the subject himself.

He began to make his way towards the chairs around the fire. 'You've been staying in the Salutation Hotel, I understand?'

'I have, yes.' Did he think that such a bald acknowledgement of my estrangement was going to embarrass me, put me at a disadvantage? I turned and bent to warm my hands. In my peripheral vision, I felt rather than saw Williams look to my father for help. But Justice Probert-Lloyd evidently felt he had done all that was required of him. Williams, still standing behind one of the chairs, cleared his throat.

'I gather that my wife has taken it upon herself to dislike the inquest's verdict and has asked you to become involved?'

I continued to cultivate chilblains so as not to have to look up at him. 'Mrs Williams gave me to understand that she was worried lest the verdict, not to mention the coroner's manner of questioning, had left an impression in the public mind that you might know more about Margaret's death than you were prepared to admit.' I heard myself slipping into barrister's rhetoric; a species of verbal armour, I daresay.

'She had no right to involve you,' Williams blustered. 'I mean to say, people – *some* people – will always gossip and find fault where there is none.'

I let him go on. People are surprisingly apt to tie themselves in knots if you give them a sufficient quantity of rope and no assistance.

'But I pay no heed to gossips,' he said, stiffly. 'Therefore, I require no investigation to be made on my behalf, thank you.'

I counted to five then, without turning around, straightened up. 'Very well.'

Again, I felt a look pass between Williams and my father.

'What do you mean, sir, by "very well"?' Williams was losing patience with me but I could have warned him that he would find no ally in the room if he went further and lost his temper. My father did not approve of shows of emotion as a means of winning an argument.

'I mean that I will not burden you or Mrs Williams any further with details of my investigation. Henceforth,' I rubbed my warm palms on the cold backs of my hands, 'I will conduct my investigations for my own sake and mine alone.'

I heard Williams's heavy tread as he moved around the chair towards me.

'I fear I have not made myself clear. I meant to ask you to cease your enquiries altogether. They are likely to cause me more embarrassment than any idle gossip could.'

I turned to face the spot he occupied. In my peripheral vision, he was difficult to make out against the shelves of books behind him. 'Mr Williams, let me assure you that if there is gossip about you as a result of my enquiries, it is none of my doing. At no point has your name been mentioned to anybody but Mrs Williams. In all other cases, I have merely stated that I have been asked to look in to events surrounding Margaret Jones's death. No suspicion can accrue to you from that.'

'Any further investigation simply prolongs people's interest. If you were to give up your enquiries, it would all blow over in a week and the gossips would find something else to chew over.'

'That may be true. But, though tongues might be stilled, suspicion would remain. My investigations will – ultimately – be to your benefit, Mr Williams.'

'I would appreciate your allowing *me* to be the judge of what will be to my benefit or detriment.'

'Do you not wish your name to be cleared, Mr Williams?' I asked, evenly.

'My name has no need of clearing. I do not stand accused of anything!'

'Not formally, perhaps.' I was quite aware that I was being provocative, now.

He took a step forward. 'Are *you* accusing me, sir?' The ragged edge to his voice told me that, had I been a man of a different station, Williams would have taken me by the lapels.

'Indeed I am not, Mr Williams.'

'Your failure to look me in the eye says otherwise!'

A sudden, reckless need to shock and embarrass him took hold of me. 'I'm afraid, Mr Williams, that I *cannot* look you in the eye. Neither you nor, regrettably, anyone else. I am going slowly blind, you see.'

The quality of silence that my words produced was not unlike that around a card table when a gentleman of previously impeccable solvency admits that he is obliged to offer a promissory note. It was, in other words, acutely uncomfortable.

'Blind?' Williams might never have heard the word before.

'Yes.' I felt entirely uncompelled to furnish him with specifics. 'Then how are you managing?' Again, I sensed a look flung in the direction of my father, seated on my other side.

'I hope you won't take offence, Mr Williams, if I say that that is my own affair.'

Williams now seemed at a loss. My father rescued him. 'Perhaps we should continue this discussion at another time.'

'Yes,' Williams moved towards him. 'Yes, perhaps you're right.'

As my father rang the bell and moved his guest in the direction of the door, I heard a low murmuring from Williams. He would, of course, be trying to secure my father's promise to persuade me away from my investigations.

A footman arrived to show him out and the door closed on our perfunctory farewells, leaving me alone with my father.

'I presume you didn't say that merely to deflect Williams?'

'No.'

'May I ask why you haven't seen fit to tell me before this?'

I sighed. 'It's only recently been confirmed. I thought perhaps it was over-work – eye strain – that it would go away eventually. But it just got worse.' I took a breath. 'Then I went to the eye hospital in London. An expert there tells me that it's a familial condition. It usually begins in late childhood though it can manifest in one's third decade, as in my case.' I hesitated. 'Did my mother suffer anything similar?'

'No.'

His abruptness stung me and I chose to match it. 'The upshot,' I continued, 'is that I have no useful vision for detail. I can't read or examine things closely or see faces. I can manage not to walk into things if I'm careful because I can see at the edges of my sight. But in the centre of my vision where, my eye doctor tells me, we do all our meaningful seeing, there's nothing but a blur. In short, I can *see* but I cannot look.'

'And what, therefore, are your plans?'

Unsure as to whether he was enquiring about the investigation or how I proposed to conduct the rest of my life, I did not know how to answer him. 'Plans have become… difficult,' I said, hearing the tightness in my own voice. 'In my immediate future, there is a journey to East Anglia in the company of the young man whom I have engaged as my assistant but I would like to ask…'

'Yes?'

'Whether I could move back to Glanteifi when I return.'

'Will you still be investigating this young woman's death?'

'That depends, somewhat, on what I discover during my visit to East Anglia.'

There was a long pause.

'My position has not changed, Harry. I cannot be seen to be at loggerheads with a legally constituted jury's decision. We shall have to reconsider the situation when you return.'

It was no good. His refusal to back down quashed any desire I had to lay my soul bare to him on the subject of Margaret. Or, indeed, any other.

I left the house, determination stoked by his continuing support of the magistrates' line. My feelings towards Margaret Jones had led to my exile from Glanteifi before, but this time I would not allow myself to be deterred from the course my heart dictated.

John

It wasn't hard to find out who Nathaniel Howell's elders at Treforgan chapel'd been. Apart from one who'd died, the eldership hadn't changed at all. But then, that's the way of the world, isn't it? Once a man's got a bit of power, whether it's being a magistrate or a *plwyfwas* or an elder in a chapel, he's not going to give it up without good reason. Like a cock crowing on a midden – only a stick, a worm or a willing hen'll bring him down.

Finding out where Howell'd gone was just as easy. *Ipswich* they told me. *Nathaniel Howell went to the Unitarian Chapel in Ipswich.*

I went back to my lodgings pretty pleased with myself.

As soon as I closed the front door behind me, my landlady was there in the narrow hallway with me. There wasn't much room for the two of us and I took a step back towards the door.

'Somebody's giving you airs,' she held a letter up with both hands, like a handkerchief she was pegging out. 'John Davies *Esquire*.' It was a point of pride with her, being able to read.

I put my hand out for it. In the end she had to give it to me and I put it in my pocket.

'Aren't you going to read it?'

Not in front of her I wasn't. Somebody'd sent Harry a warning with that *ceffyl pren* and this could be my warning. Then again, I was going to want some more lamp oil, later, so that I could get my notes written up for Harry. I needed to keep her sweet.

I pulled the letter out and tore the sealing patch. As soon as I'd unfolded it, I glanced at the foot of the text, heart going nineteen to the dozen. I was more than half expecting to see it signed 'Beca'.

216

Yours, I read *HP-L*

My guts unknotted themselves a fraction. Harry'd been using that apparatus of his. The results weren't perfect. The words were mostly readable and they sat on an even enough line but the letters were oddly spaced. Some drawn out, some squashed up together.

Dear John

I trust you have had a productive afternoon?

We have a great deal to do tomorrow and I would be pleased if, when you join me for breakfast, you would come with a bag packed and ready to travel. I consider it urgent that we speak to Nathaniel Howell as soon as may be.

'It's from Mr Henry Probert-Lloyd,' I told my landlady, folding the letter once more, 'I'm assisting him with some business at the moment.'

She didn't say anything but I could tell from the face she pulled that she was impressed.

I tramped up the stairs thinking about Harry's letter.

Come with a bag packed and ready to travel. So we were going to Ipswich, were we?

I'd never been further than Carmarthen in my life.

I'd been carrying Harry's notebook and pencil around in my pocket but, so far, I'd taken no notes at all. Harry'd decided it would be better for me not to write while we were talking to people. 'I need you to watch their reactions,' he'd said.

So now it was time to put what we'd done into the notebook. Old Schofield had trained me well. I didn't trust anything until it was written down where I could see it. Behaving itself.

I opened the book, turned it spine-topside and ruled three vertical columns. One for 'Name of Witness,' one for 'Summary of evidence' and one for 'New information'.

Then I sat and thought about the witnesses we'd questioned. Dic Jones the saddler. Parry the printer. *Stationer* as he called himself. Pridham the chemist. Matt Tregorlais – was he a witness? Of sorts, I supposed, but we'd definitely interviewed him. And Esme Williams.

Esme Williams who'd asked Harry to investigate. Harry. I had as many questions in my mind about him as I did about the murder. More, perhaps.

I decided to start keeping notes on him as well as our investigation.

Two columns – Information Gained, Questions still to Answer.

I flipped the notebook over and turned to the last page. It'd been written on.

How? I'd seen Harry flipping through it. Then I realised – he'd only flipped through the first few pages. He'd assumed that if they were empty, the rest of the book would be as well. But the book's cover was unmarked, there was nothing to say which was front and which was back. So when Harry'd checked it, by chance he'd riffled through it from the same end that I'd started writing in. But, sometime previously, he'd written on the pages at the other end of the book.

I stared at his writing. It straggled along unevenly, didn't sit neatly on a line.

I read the first few words – *I fear I am going blind* – then pulled the lamp closer. Fair play to Mr Schofield, he always made a point of us working in the bright light of sperm oil in the winter but my landlady made do with cheaper stuff. She didn't have clients to impress and she certainly didn't care if I ruined my eyes. Still, it gave light enough to see clearly when the book was close.

I fear I am going blind, I read again. *If it is a passing thing, I want to remember the fear and to value my sight as I have never done in the past. But if I am to be blind, I will set down here, for myself if nobody else, the things that trouble my conscience. They say setting things down on paper has the effect of relinquishing a burden. And I am burdened. Burdened by the knowledge that I betrayed Margaret. I betrayed my own love for her and whatever affection she had for me and trust she placed in me.*

Perhaps blindness is a just punishment for I did not see what I was doing. As they say, there's none so blind as those that will not see.

And that was it. That was all there was. Had he intended to write more? And if he had, what had stopped him? Failing sight, or an unwillingness to put the burdens on his conscience into words?

I betrayed Margaret.

What did that mean? How had he betrayed her?

I turned over the page and wrote: 'Harry – Questions' at the top of the left side of the page. Then I ruled a line down the middle and wrote 'Information' on the other side.

So far I had several questions and no information whatsoever.

I was going to have to do something about that.

John

'There are no places on the coach today,' Harry told me when I sat down to eat breakfast with him the next day.

I didn't know whether I was relieved or disappointed but Harry didn't give me time to think about it. While I was trying my first taste of devilled kidneys, he wanted to know what I'd found out.

'First rate!' he said when I'd told him. 'I knew you wouldn't let me down.'

Praise like that was enough to make me risk a question. 'Can I ask what we're hoping to find out from going to Ipswich?' I heard my own words. They sounded close to criticism but Harry didn't even blink.

'First and foremost, I want to know whether Nathaniel Howell actually went there or whether somebody just wanted his congregation to think he had, in order to explain his disappearance. Then, if he *is* there, I want to ask him why he left in such a hurry.'

I watched Harry loading his fork. Not being able to see what he was doing properly made him clumsy and half the food fell back onto the plate. 'Ministers chop and change chapels all the time,' I said, glancing up at the other people in the Salutation's dining room. None of them were looking in our direction, thank God.

'I know. But I have it on good authority that when he persuaded Hannah Rees to give up her son to Williams and his wife, Howell told her that he'd be on hand to keep an eye out for the boy. Why would he say that if he was intending to leave soon after?'

'Perhaps this offer from Ipswich was too good to turn down?'

'Perhaps. But I'd like to hear that from his own lips.'

I started on some thick bacon. There was more meat on the plate in front of me than I usually saw in a week. 'So are you more concerned *for* the Reverend Howell or suspicious *of* him?' I was bolder now that he'd answered that first question as if I had a right to know.

Harry sighed. 'It just seems odd that he should take Hannah off in the middle of the night.'

A ray of sunshine suddenly broke into the room, making the tired fake-marble wallpaper look even dingier than it had the moment before. Harry didn't seem to notice the sun. Looked as if his mind had wandered.

'Take her off where?' I asked.

He put his cutlery down and gathered his wits. 'After leaving Samuel at Waungilfach, Howell took Hannah Rees straight to her new position. Right then, at midnight or after. At least, that's what I was told.'

'Why wouldn't he wait until the next day?'

Harry nodded. 'That's the question, isn't it? I'd like to speak to Hannah Rees, make sure she actually got to her new position.'

I waited.

'She had a brother.' Harry sounded as if he'd just made a decision. 'Since we can't start out for Ipswich today, I think we should try and find him.'

As it turned out, Jac Rees wasn't hard to find. We just asked at the Treforgan chapel manse and the maid told us where he lived.

We rode back through town in weather that had cheered up a lot. The sun wasn't warm – it was the first day of December – but at least it gave a bit of life to the day. Everybody else seemed to think so too: 'Good days' came at us like flies in summer.

221

Somebody was making use of the good weather at Jac Rees's farm, too. We heard the thud of wooden mallets before we saw the two men standing in the yard, one on either side of a trough. Closer to, I could see they were beating gorse.

'My father always mixed his gorse with straw,' I called to them as we rode up. 'Do you do that or feed it by itself?' It was what Mr Schofield would've called a white flag – *I come in good faith.* The less they thought of Harry as gentry, the more they'd be likely to say.

The older of the two men – Rees himself, as it turned out – straightened up and I recognised him. Hannah's brother was the man who'd shouted out about Williams's bastards from the back of the ballroom during the inquest.

'Always mix it,' he said, so pleasant you'd never have believed he could look as angry as he had when Williams was giving his evidence. 'Makes the gorse last longer, doesn't it?'

I introduced us and Harry explained about his investigations, speaking Welsh as usual. 'We wanted to ask you about your sister,' he said.

'Which one?' Rees was tapping the head of his mallet up and down on the ground, wary now. The yard wasn't cobbled but it'd been made up in a rough way with broken stones so it wasn't just ankle-deep mud.

'Hannah,' Harry said. 'Where did she go after she left Waungilfach, Mr Rees?'

Rees turned to the younger man, his son from the look of him. 'You carry on while I talk to Mr Probert-Lloyd. Let's just go over here,' he nodded at the corner of the yard, 'out of the way of the noise.' He stopped next to a short row of pigsties. Far enough away from the beating-trough to make damn sure we couldn't be overheard.

'What do you want to know about Hannah for?' he asked.

To make sure she's alive and well. I didn't say it, just waited for Harry to answer him.

'After she left Waungilfach,' Harry said, 'the Reverend Howell found her a new place, didn't he?'

Jac Rees nodded. He was looking at Harry, now, but it was a calculating kind of look, as if he'd guessed about his sight.

'Where was that, Mr Rees?' I asked. Jac Rees glanced at me. I could see he'd been expecting me to keep my mouth shut now we were on to business.

'Out on a farm up the Lady Road,' he said. 'She was an outdoor servant there.'

She wouldn't want to risk going indoors at another house. Not after her experience with Williams.

'Is she still there?' Harry asked.

Jac Rees shook his head. 'No. One of the labourers on the farm married her and they've got their own little cottage. They do all right. Got two little lads.' He was nervous, answering questions Harry hadn't asked. Where were the nerves coming from – the scandal about Hannah and her bastard? Or did Rees know we were here about Beca and Margaret Jones?

'About the Reverend Howell,' Harry said. 'Did Hannah say anything to you about him? He went away very soon after she left Waungilfach.'

Rees shrugged. 'I know she was upset about him going because of—' He closed his mouth.

'It's all right, Mr Rees,' Harry said, 'we know about Hannah's child.' He gave Jac Rees a moment to take that in. 'Is that why she was upset?' For a moment, I thought shame would keep Rees silent. But he couldn't defy Harry.

'Yes. She didn't want to leave Samuel with Esme Williams. Afraid she'd be cruel to him. But the Reverend Howell said he wouldn't let that happen.'

Howell could have destroyed William Williams's reputation with a single word. *Bastard.* And he'd've been in a position to speak it into the only ears Williams cared about. The ones attached to the local gentry.

There was a sudden squeal from the sties. Sounded like an in-heat sow wanting the boar. Or perhaps she'd just heard us talking and thought we'd come with something for her. Jac Rees turned his head at the sound and, as he looked back at us, I caught his eye. He jerked his head at Harry and blinked, slowly and clearly, just once. Then he raised his eyebrows – *am I right?* I gave a tiny nod. Harry could see that sort of thing if his head was cocked, looking for it.

'Then he went off to England,' Jac went on. 'Quite quick after Samuel went to Waungilfach, like you say. Hannah was in a terrible state. At the finish, I had to say I'd go up there and make sure the boy was being looked after properly.'

'You went to Waungilfach to see your nephew?'

Rees looked at me. He'd've liked to slap the disbelief off my face, I could tell. 'Two can play at the game they were playing. When William Williams tried to order me off his yard, I told him Samuel might be a cousin to Esme on one side but he was nephew to me on the other and I was going to see him, else I'd make the situation known in the whole district.'

'And they let you?' Harry asked. He didn't make the mistake of sounding surprised.

'Didn't have a choice, Mr Probert-Lloyd. I go up there every few months. Just to keep an eye.'

Another squeal. I couldn't see the pigs because the sties faced the other way but the sties themselves were well-kept, with sound roofs and walls that weren't growing weeds. Jac Rees was a man who knew how to look after things. And he might've looked after Hannah, but that didn't mean he'd have been sympathetic to Margaret Jones. Even if your family turn out to be a pack of wantons and wastrels you can't just abandon them. But you can stick to your principles with everybody else.

'And how is Samuel treated?' Harry asked.

Jac Rees grunted. 'Only son, isn't he? If anything, he's spoiled. Going to be no use as a farmer, the way those girls pamper him. Your workers don't respect you if they don't think you could do what they do. Sorry, Mr Probert-Lloyd,' he added, 'I didn't mean to give offence. I'm not talking about a gentleman like your father, obviously.'

Harry smiled. 'I didn't take any offence, Mr Rees, don't worry. But there's something else I wanted to ask you about. You were one of Nathaniel Howell's Rebeccas, weren't you?'

Jac Rees looked at Harry as if he'd accused him of fucking his pig but Harry couldn't see that so he stared somewhere into the air, waiting.

'You must've wondered why he left so suddenly to go to Ipswich?' Harry said, when Jac Rees carried on saying nothing. 'One minute he was riding out at night with half his congregation, promising the likes of Hannah that he'd be there to look after them, and the next minute he was leaving.'

Rees started his mallet-tapping again. 'He had his reasons.'

'Do you know what those reasons were?' Harry asked.

A shake of the head. All of a sudden, Jac Rees wanted us gone as much as Stephen Parry had.

'What about somebody in Beca who was close to him?' Harry asked. 'Who was his Charlotte?'

Lady Charlotte was what they called the second-in-command of a Rebecca band. God knows why.

Rees shook his head again. Finding his mallet really interesting, he was. 'I don't know. I don't know anything about all that. It was a long time ago.' He looked up, but only to glance over his shoulder. 'I have to get back to work, now.'

Harry nodded. 'Thank you for your help.'

We mounted up – I was beginning to get the hang of it – and turned our horses down the track. 'So,' I said when we were out of earshot, 'Howell didn't run away because of Hannah Rees.'

'Apparently not.'

We were almost at the end of the farm track when Harry pulled up suddenly. 'You stay here. I'm going back to speak to Rees, again. He might tell me something if you're not there.' And off he went.

I watched him trot back down the lane, baffled. Why should he think Rees would speak to him and not to me?

He disappeared round the corner into the yard. I didn't like letting him out of my sight. Mr Schofield would hang, draw and quarter me if anything happened to Harry. I slipped off my horse's back and led him back down the lane, keeping him on the grass at the edge so his shoes wouldn't make any sound.

At the turn in the lane, I stopped. If I craned my head round, I could see the yard but I was pretty sure Harry wouldn't be able to make me out, even if he looked back.

He'd pulled his little mare up. But not so he could speak to Rees. The yard was empty but for Harry.

I waited. He just sat in the saddle, doing nothing. Nothing that I could see, at any rate. Sat there for two, maybe three minutes. Then, slowly, he pulled the mare's head round. I turned and ran my horse back up the grass and was waiting for him where he'd left me when he came around the corner again.

He was grinning. 'I got the name of Howell's Charlotte out of him,' he called.

What? The lie felt like a punch in the guts. 'Who was it?' My voice sounded normal but I was glad Harry couldn't see my face. He'd've been able to see I didn't believe him.

'Ezra Lloyd,' Harry said. 'I know him.'

So if he knew, why didn't he just tell me? Because of *how* he knew – must be – he'd been involved.

But did he ride out with Howell, or had the minister and his crusade come to Glanteifi?

If I was going to steer Harry the way I wanted to, I was going to have to find out.

Harry

Though I disliked hiding behind subterfuge, I still felt the need to conceal my first-hand knowledge of Nathaniel Howell's Rebecca band from John. I knew I had little hope of keeping my participation in Samuel Williams's repatriation from his ears permanently but I wished to do so for the time being, lest he feel that my investigation was compromised by my own involvement with Rebecca.

More and more, I was coming to believe that the actions of Nathaniel Howell and his Rebeccas were significant. Howell's name had been mentioned by both Dic Jones and Stephen Parry and I was convinced that his sudden disappearance was bound up with Margaret's death, in some way.

Had she gone to him for help? And, if so, was her murder connected with his sudden move to Ipswich?

Unless, of course, he was not in Ipswich at all, but in his own version of Margaret's makeshift grave.

'Good day to you, sir,' Ezra Lloyd returned my greeting when we finally tracked him down, hedge-laying in a field distant from his house. I had declined his daughter's offer to go and fetch him, suspecting that he would be better disposed to answer questions if he had not been dragged away from his work. 'It's good to see you home from London,' he added. 'If you don't mind me saying?'

'Thank you,' I said, seeing him stoop and hearing the almost fleshy sound his billhook made as he sliced it into the turf at his feet. The earth would clean the blade while we talked.

'I expect you've heard that we're looking into Margaret Jones's death?'

'I did hear something,' Lloyd acknowledged.

'I'd like to ask you about the Reverend Howell,' I said, deliberately leaving the sentence hanging to see what he might do with it.

Did he lick his lips uneasily? Did he look from me to John, trying to find a clue as to the question I was really asking? I had no way of knowing but I heard the tension in his voice when he answered. 'Mr Probert-Lloyd, I know you mean well, but the Reverend Howell had nothing to do with the girl. And anyway, it was an accident, wasn't it? That's what they said at the inquest.'

The smell of freshly cut wood was coming from the saplings he'd laid into the hedge. Though I couldn't see his work, I knew that the sycamore, ash and hazel which he would be laying grew long, straight poles that wove well into the bulk of a hawthorn hedge. I had cut one of those poles often enough, in years gone by, to furnish one of the thousand and one uses a boy has for a stout stick.

'Mr Lloyd, I'm not suggesting that the Reverend Howell was involved in Margaret Jones's death. I'm concerned about why he felt the need to leave so quickly. Has anybody had any word from him since he went to Ipswich?'

I tried to keep my eyes fixed on the spot where I estimated Ezra Lloyd's face was likely to be, so as to encourage him to answer; but I was acutely aware that the oddness of my gaze might well have the opposite effect. His answer was stiff, guarded.

'No, nothing. But we didn't expect it.'

'Why?'

Lloyd hesitated. He was clearly reluctant to speak about the Reverend Howell which I found strange, given the esteem in which the man had been held.

'Before he left, he asked us not to write to him.' His words were flat, devoid of emotion; he would tell me what I wanted to know but he would not allow me to see his own feelings on the matter. 'He said that it wasn't his choice to leave but he was going where he felt he was being called.' He hesitated, then forged on, as if he had decided that I might as well hear everything. 'Said that hearing about folk here would only make him feel the loss of us even more. He'd thought he'd end his life here, where he'd been so happy. But it wasn't to be.'

'End his life? Nathaniel Howell was a young man.' My confusion was made worse by my inability to see Ezra Lloyd's expression, see how he delivered the words. Was he telling the truth? I thought so but, until sight is denied you, it is easy to underestimate the constant scrutiny one makes of a face as its owner is speaking.

'You're right, Mr Probert-Lloyd. Reverend Howell was barely twenty-three when he came to us. But he always had the feeling that he would be called home young. Even had a plan to go and live with his sister when the time came.'

'The time?'

'I took him to mean when his last illness came.'

I waited and, as I had anticipated, Lloyd felt the need to explain. 'I believe he must have been given knowledge of his own death.'

At that moment, I would have sacrificed a week of my life to be able to share a look of scepticism with John. I felt trapped behind my own blind eyes, denied common communion with my fellow men. 'Do you know where this sister lives?' I asked, my mouth bitter with something a little less than grief but more than frustration.

'No. And she never came to visit him – it was always just, "I'll go to my sister's when the time comes".'

The high clouds shifted, uncovering the sun and flooding the oddly shaped little field with a warm, low-angled light. Despite myself, my spirits rose a notch. 'I know Nathaniel Howell had a faithful congregation who were prepared to defend the weak with him,' I said, not wanting to invoke Rebecca's name unless I had to. 'Did something happen, on one of those nighttime outings, something to make him feel afraid? Was that why he decided to leave Treforgan?'

I caught a glimpse of Ezra Lloyd running a hand over his face. 'No.'

I waited, but he said nothing more.

'Did the Reverend Howell's band ever take part in other Beca activities?' John asked.

'What other activities?' Lloyd's voice was taut with suspicion.

'Well, gatebreaking, I suppose…'

I heard the farmer take in a long breath. 'I couldn't say,' he said, finally. 'I know *I* didn't.'

Was he protecting himself or was that the truth? 'Did he make enemies,' I asked, 'defending young women? I'm sure not everybody agreed with him?'

'Mr Probert-Lloyd.' It was almost a plea. 'What has any of this got to do with the girl who was killed by that tree falling?'

'Wasn't she just the kind of young woman the Reverend Howell's crusade was for?' John asked.

I pictured Ezra Lloyd looking this way and that between me and John, like a boy left out of the game watching his friends play catch. I felt John's eyes on me. He was throwing the ball back.

'The reason I asked about enemies,' I said, 'is that if somebody was threatening the Reverend Howell – if, perhaps, that encouraged him to take up the offer from Ipswich—'

'I've told you! It was God's call – he wouldn't have run away!'

231

'Not run away, no. But, perhaps, if there was opposition to his views…?'

'There's always opposition to those who dare to challenge sin.'

'If somebody was threatening him,' I suggested, 'whoever it was might have been a threat to the girls he was trying to help, too. Girls like Margaret Jones.'

'We didn't have anything to do with Margaret Jones! Nothing!' He was desperate to be believed. Because he was telling the truth, or because he was lying? Ezra Lloyd took off his cap and wiped his forehead. He was sweating and I doubted very much that it was a result of the exertions we had disturbed.

'If I were you, Mr Probert-Lloyd,' Ezra Lloyd's voice shook slightly, 'I'd let the dead rest in peace.'

Which was just what Rebecca wanted. What her threats to Stephen Parry and the rest of the jury had been calculated to achieve. 'There is no peace,' I said, 'not when an innocent life is taken and nobody is brought to justice.'

'Margaret Jones was no innocent. David Thomas must've told you that she—'

I had moved before I was aware of it. 'How dare you—'

'Harry!'

It was John's use of my Christian name that stopped me as much as his restraining grip on my arm.

'Take my advice, Mr Probert-Lloyd.' Even as Ezra Lloyd's voice shook there was a kind of latent menace to it. 'Don't rile Beca. Let her be. Because, believe me, you don't want her to come after you.'

Harry

Though we had not seen each other for seven years, it still dislocated something in me when I heard Davy's name.

David Thomas must've told you... I shivered. Davy *had* told me.

And I had not wanted to know.

I recalled the conversation we had had on the night of Samuel's delivery to his father. On the way back from Waungilfach, I had asked him to stop the carriage so that I could put my own clothes back on; then I had climbed up to sit outside with him as he drove home.

'Why didn't you tell me Margaret was pregnant?'

Davy kept his eyes trained on the darkness ahead of us. 'I said you should go and see her, didn't I? It was her business to tell you, not mine.'

'Davy, I'm not the child's father!'

That made him look round; his blackened face showed no expression in the dark but his white eyes stared into mine. 'I know that's what you told Howell but you don't have to lie to *me*, Harry.'

'I'm not lying! The child isn't mine.' I hesitated, strangely unwilling to admit it. 'It can't be.'

Davy said nothing. I was relieved; I had braced myself for mockery at the admission that I had failed to deflower Margaret.

'Why didn't you write to me?' I blurted. 'If you thought it was mine, didn't you think I'd want to know?'

The carriage swayed under us. 'I knew you'd come home when I told you about Beca threatening your father. I thought there'd be time enough, then, for you to see you needed to clean up after yourself.'

233

I winced at his choice of words. As if fathering a child was equivalent to trailing mud thoughtlessly into the house.

'How did you hear?' I asked. 'About the baby?' He would have no reason to go to Waungilfach and Margaret barely ever left the farm but to go to chapel.

'I've started going to Treforgan.'

'But all the se—' I stopped myself. 'Everybody at Glanteifi goes to church.'

'Not *all* the servants do.' His voice was bitter. 'And not *me*, anymore. There's no law that says I have to go to church just because that's what your father thinks is proper. Times are changing.'

We had been silent the rest of the way home, leaving me time to think unwelcome thoughts. Margaret was carrying another man's child; yet still I wanted her. In fact, now I knew she was not virtuous, I wanted her in a way I had not before.

I sat there, on top of my father's carriage, imagining another man doing with Margaret the things I had not allowed myself to do. Who was he, the man she had given herself to once I had been banished to Oxford? Some labourer who had reckoned on her receiving favours from me? Might she even have encouraged such a belief?

Harry's in love with me, he won't see us destitute.

I felt the humiliation of being played for a fool. And yet… William Williams had been very keen to denounce me to my father. Had he taken advantage of Margaret as soon as I was out of the way? Knowing she was without family or protection, had he forced himself on her as he had on Hannah Rees?

My mind flitted back to the scene we had just played out on Williams's yard. Had he recognised me? Had his wife? Her eyes had been everywhere, missing nothing.

Was I to anticipate another visit to my father from Williams?

I feel it my duty to tell you, Probert-Lloyd, that your son has been keeping dubious company once more.

No. Williams would not wish to incriminate himself. But any one of the men under Howell's command might betray me as they had nothing to fear. No crime had been committed; no *ceffyl pren* had been carried, no property destroyed. A child had simply been taken to his father and a message delivered. *Take your son and sin no more.*

But what message had I been intended to take from my involvement? My presence, along with my father's carriage and pair, had, without doubt, served Rebecca's purpose and made Howell's message to Williams plain – *those whose acceptance you crave see you for what you are and hold you to account just as much as those whom you consider beneath you.*

And yet, had I not been given a warning, too? Though every man gathered outside Treforgan had been in women's garb, did my being required to appear 'arrayed in every particular as a lady' not set me apart, set me up for ridicule, just as much as my confinement in my father's carriage had done? *You are not one of us and you never can be.*

I had been used by Howell. Cleverly used.

You must go and see her and make amends.

There and then, I had decided that I would go nowhere near Margaret Jones.

I was not Nathaniel Howell's to command.

John

Harry leaned forward and banged his forehead on the scruffy table. Just once. 'Are we ever going to get anybody to speak plainly to us?'

We were back in The Lamb and – thank God – he'd accepted Nelly James's offer of something to eat with our beer. It was well into the afternoon and I could hardly think for the growling in my belly. There wasn't any hot food – The Lamb wasn't an inn, only a public house – but Nelly knew better than to let one of the gentry go hungry on her premises.

I looked at him, sitting there with his head on the boards. It was all very well him going on about nobody speaking plainly to us but I'd've welcomed a bit of plain speaking from him. First he'd gone out of his way to lie to me about how he knew Ezra Lloyd'd been Howell's Charlotte, and then he'd reacted like a bar-room brawler when he thought Lloyd'd spoken out of turn.

If I hadn't grabbed his arm, he'd've hit Ezra Lloyd. I'd felt the blow coming as if he'd aimed it at me.

He sat up and sighed. I wondered if the question going round in my head was still nagging at him, too.

What did Ezra Lloyd know about Margaret Jones and her innocence or otherwise?

But I had another question as well. One Harry wouldn't be asking. *Who was David Thomas?*

Harry put his elbows on the table and looked down at it so he could see me – sort of – over the top of his blind blur. I had to lean forward to hear him when he spoke. There was a conversation going on not three yards from us and you'd've thought that the men having it'd taken a vow to be heard in the street outside.

'Why did you ask Ezra Lloyd whether Howell ever took his men out on ordinary Beca outings?' he asked me.

I glanced towards the back of the room. Nelly was standing there but I didn't think she'd hear us over the loudmouths. 'Because if the Reverend Howell was a proper Rebecca, he'd've been less likely to make enemies. But if he was using the name for his own ends...'

'Some people might not have taken kindly to that.'

'Exactly.' I watched his face. 'Was the Reverend Howell a man who had enemies?'

'He was a great boy for all men being equal in the sight of God.'

I wasn't sure I'd heard him right. 'I beg your pardon, Mr Probert-Lloyd?'

'Harry,' he said. 'You called me Harry when you were trying to stop me laying hands on Ezra Lloyd.'

I felt myself going hot. 'I'm sorry. I just thought—'

'Don't *apologise!* It did the trick and stopped me. And anyway, I should have asked you to call me Harry before this.' He sounded serious, as if he'd given it some thought.

'Thank you. Harry.'

His smile was sad. One of those you give a child who's parroted something serious that he doesn't understand. 'It shouldn't be a matter for thanks.'

'You're a gentleman.'

'I'm a *man*. And you're a man – or very nearly so, anyway. How old are you, actually?'

'Nineteen.'

'Not far off, then. Right. When we're just the two of us, we shall be Harry and John. When we're out and about, I shall leave it to you how you address me.'

I couldn't fathom him. One minute his lips were locked and he was leaving me guessing, the next he was treating me like a trusted friend. But if he didn't want to stand on his dignity, why was he trying to keep Margaret Jones a secret from me? What else wasn't he telling me?

'What you just asked,' he suddenly said, 'about whether Howell had enemies?'

'Yes?'

'Ezra Lloyd said something about there always being opposition to those who challenge sin.'

'Just one of those pious things people say, isn't it?'

'But what if it wasn't? What if there was *actual* opposition to Howell's crusade? Not just grumbling – men prepared to deal with young women in a very different way? Teach one of them a lesson so the rest didn't come to Howell for help, for instance.'

I looked at him. 'You think it might've been Margaret Jones they tried to teach the lesson to – and it went too far and they killed her?'

I had to say *they*, didn't I? So as not to give away what I knew. But it wasn't a gang that had killed Margaret Jones. Just one man. Was he the one who'd got the short straw?

'But why would that have made Nathaniel Howell leave?' Harry asked. 'D'you think he felt responsible – felt that he should've seen how things would turn out?' He thought again. 'That is, of course, if he *did* go to Ipswich. If he's still alive.'

Just then Nelly brought us a plate of cheese, bread and cold meat. After she'd left us to it, I asked, 'Do you think William Williams really asked you to stop investigating just because he's finding it socially awkward?'

Harry shook his head. 'I can't see Williams as a killer.'

I cut some cheese. 'No, but d'you think he might've had *something* to do with it?' Just then a huge laugh came from the men behind us and I was reminded to keep my voice down. God alone knew who was listening and who they were telling.

Harry'd stopped eating and was just staring at nothing. Thinking about what I'd said. 'He might have wanted to get back at Howell, I suppose, after he was forced to take Samuel in. Especially if he knew Esme'd been plotting with Howell to have the child brought to Waungilfach.'

'Didn't dare take it out on her so he went for Howell instead?'

Harry nodded, chewing. 'Yes. I don't think Mrs Williams would stand for much from her husband.'

Common gossip agreed with him but there was more to it, as well. 'It's not just that. There's talk that it's only her money – which is to say, her father's money – that's keeping Waungilfach from bankruptcy.' That was news to Harry, I could see it in his face.

'Having Samuel brought to his door was the second time Williams had been humiliated by Howell,' he said, slowly, as if he was changing his mind about something.

I cut a lump of cold beef into small pieces and waited.

'Before Beca started –' he said, 'the summer before – Howell brought the *ceffyl pren* to Waungilfach. He told Williams that if he didn't mend his ways, he'd make him ride it up Newcastle Emlyn high street. William Williams had more reason than most to hate Nathaniel Howell.'

I took a swig of my beer. 'Brought' the *ceffyl pren* he'd said, not 'took'. So. He'd been at Waungilfach when the *ceffyl pren* came. He'd been with Margaret Jones at night. A *scandal*, like Mr Schofield had said.

'There's somebody we haven't thought of in connection with the murder,' I said, my heart jumping against my ribs as if it was trying to attract my attention and shut me up.

'Who?'

My heart was loud, now. *Be quiet!* But Harry was keeping things from me. If I was going to steer him to the truth, I needed to know what he was hiding so it didn't trip me up. 'The father of Margaret's child,' I said.

His brows came down and I felt a sudden fear. But the words he'd written in the notebook were still fresh in my mind. *I betrayed Margaret Jones.* There had to be a good chance that he was the father of her child. And that would explain why he hadn't given evidence at the inquest. Old George Probert-Lloyd would've had a fit at the thought of that coming out.

Harry owed me now, for not letting him hit Ezra Lloyd. So I pushed it. 'Somebody must've known who the father was,' I said. 'At the inquest, Rachel Ellis said she didn't but I'm pretty sure she was lying about that. Out of fear.' Rachel Ellis had definitely been afraid of something up there in front of Coroner Bowen.

Harry chewed his lip. 'It comes back to William Williams then. Williams was known to take advantage of his female servants so if he was the father Rachel might've been afraid to say so.' He bit off a chunk of bread and chewed for a bit. 'I think it'd be worth paying her a visit. Do you know where she and her husband live?'

'I can find out. Dai Penlan – the one who gave testimony at the inquest – drinks at the Drovers'. He's worked for Williams for years – he'd know. I could go and see if he's there tonight, if you like.'

'Yes. Do that. Thank you.'

Perfect. I'd planned to be in the Drovers' that night, anyway. I wanted to see if I could get some of my other questions answered.

Harry

John had not managed to find out who Stephen Parry's maid was so, as we were barely a hundred yards from the stationer's on leaving The Lamb, I decided that we should try and speak to her directly.

Parry's premises, however, proved to be locked up and his neighbour, emerging in response to our persistent knocking, told us that one of the Parry children was sick.

'Taken her to his mother-in-law's, he has, to be looked after.'

'What about his maid?' John asked. 'Is she still here?'

'No,' the woman said scornfully. 'He wouldn't trust her here by herself. Sent her home, hasn't he?'

'Where do her parents live?' I asked.

'The Morgans? Up on Moelfryn.'

John was already wincing from saddle soreness so I decided against the ride. Time enough to speak to the girl later, if it proved necessary. As there was little we could do until we had found out where Rachel Ellis lived, I felt it would be politic to send John back to Charles Schofield for a few hours so that both he and I stayed in his employer's good graces.

Once we had parted, I walked into the Salutation, intent on arranging for my laundry to be done, only to hear a polite greeting as I stepped into the hallway. 'Good afternoon, Mr Probert-Lloyd, sir.'

I looked around and was able to see the figure of a man near the door. I had the impression that he had recently stood up, as if he had been sitting, waiting for me.

'Good afternoon,' I said, keeping my tone neutral, hoping that he would give me some clue as to who he was.

'It's Twm, sir, from the stables. At Glanteifi.'

Was he just assuming that a gentleman recently come from London would not make the effort to learn one servant from another, or had my father warned him that my sight was failing and I might not recognise him?

I was suddenly sick of having to guess what people thought.

'I'm sorry, Twm.' I spoke in Welsh, though he had used English. 'I'm going blind, you see, and I didn't recognise you.' His answering silence was understandable; what was the proper form when the man who would one day be your master announced such a thing? 'You were waiting for me, were you?'

'Yes, sir. Your father sends his compliments and asks if you could spare him an hour of your time.'

Dusk was turning swiftly to dark as I trotted up the drive at Glanteifi on the horse Twm had brought for me, and I wondered how I would get back to the Salutation later. But, perhaps, what my father wished to tell me was that he had relented and I was free to come home?

Leaving the horse with one of the grooms, I made for the back door and poked my head in to the early lamplight of the north-facing kitchen and scullery.

'Is Mrs Griffiths in?'

Now that Twm knew of my blindness it would be common knowledge amongst the servants five minutes after his return and I wanted to tell our housekeeper myself. I knew I could count on her to deliver both the news, and my request that none of the servants should treat me any differently, with infinitely more discretion than Moyle would.

Isabel Griffiths had been housekeeper at Glanteifi since before I could remember and she stood like a symbol of constancy behind every childhood memory I had of the servants' quarters. At the back of the house, she was queen and her determination to run her realm as she saw fit had never wavered before any behaviour of mine; she had administered reprimands with as liberal a hand as she had slices of bread and butter. I had absolute faith in both her judgement and her affection for me.

So, having explained my loss of sight, I was not in the least surprised when, instead of offering futile sympathy, she asked a sensible question.

'Is that why you've employed that young man from the solicitor's office?'

'Yes.'

'Hah! I told them it wasn't because you didn't know people here anymore. I told them, just because he's been making his fortune in London doesn't mean Harry Probert-Lloyd isn't one of us. He is.' I smiled at her unashamed partisanship. 'Mr Moyle won't like it – me knowing before him.'

'You'd better make sure you tell him, before he has to hear it from Twm or one of the others. But he wouldn't expect to hear it from me, in all honesty. There's never been any love lost between us.'

'Yes. Now why *is* that?'

I suppressed a grin. The question – and her refusal to beat about the bush – was typical; Isabel Griffiths had always wanted to know the whys and wherefores of things. I could see the exact look she would have on her round face: eyes narrowed in a wrinkled frown that said she had yet to understand something she felt she should already know, top teeth drawing in her bottom lip as if she could squeeze the answer out of it.

'He disapproves of me,' I said, baldly.

'It's not for him to disapprove of you – or to approve for that matter – you're the heir to the estate.'

I noticed that, honest to a fault, she did not say there was nothing to disapprove *of*. 'Moyle is loyal to my father,' I said, 'which does him credit.'

I knew Isabel Griffiths would be pursing her lips at that. It was time I made my way to my father's study but, as I began to make my apologies, she spoke again.

'Has anybody told you that Mari Thomas is dying?'

I felt a shock go through me, as much at the name as at the news. 'Dying? How long has she been ill?'

'Some time.' I almost heard Mrs Griffiths's mouth clap shut on that piece of news.

'Why didn't anybody tell me?'

Mrs Griffiths did not answer me, and, in the silence, I was aware of an ember shifting in the grate. Things were changing at Glanteifi. Time was passing here just as it had in London, and it was taking the people who had filled my childhood with it. The bed in the corner of Isabel Griffiths's room was new. Either we had more maids than previously or she had decided that she no longer wished to leave the warmth of her little sitting room of an evening and climb two flights of stairs to an unwelcoming bed. The thought that Mrs Griffiths might be getting old struck a chill into me.

'You and Mari didn't part on the friendliest terms,' she said, finally. 'Blamed you, didn't she? For Davy. For being left with no son to care for her in her old age.'

I sighed. Yes, that would be like Mari Thomas, however unjust. 'I should go and see her. Whatever has come between us, I'll always owe her my life.'

My father had asked for an early dinner for the two of us, but it soon became clear that this was not on account of the volume of things he had to say to me; candles lit across the width of the long dining room table, we ate in virtual silence. 'I would rather not impair either of our digestions if you don't mind,' he had said when I attempted to find out why I had been summoned. 'Let's do justice to this first, shall we?'

I do not know whether my father was able to savour his food but, for myself, I tasted very little. Apart from being unable to examine what I was eating and, therefore, ending up several times with a mouth considerably fuller of mutton fat than I would have liked, it was unnerving to imagine my father watching me and asking himself why he had not noticed the strange way in which I held my head while I ate, the way I seemed to look away from my wine glass before I picked it up. *How*, I imagined him asking himself, *could I not have realised that the boy was having trouble seeing?*

'The worst thing,' I found myself saying into the silence, 'when eating anyway – is that it's almost impossible to clean one's plate properly. I always feel like some churl who doesn't know any better, leaving my plate in an unseemly mess.'

Listen to yourself burbling, I thought. *Is this what you and he are reduced to – table etiquette?* It was not as if what I had said was even strictly true; though mildly discomfiting, a failure to arrange one's plate neatly was nothing compared to being unable to bone a fish. What on earth would stop me telling him that?

'I imagine the courtesies, generally, become difficult,' he said. 'They are built on such finely judged nuances, are they not?'

I was surprised. Not simply at his joining me in my meaningless prattle but at his perceptiveness. 'Yes,' I said. 'Yes, they are.'

Over the last few months I had actually begun to wonder whether my diminishing sight would render me mute. Until I became unable to see properly, I had not appreciated just how much of what we say is dictated by what we observe: a look of embarrassment causing a change of topic, a flush of enthusiasm and a bright eye egging one on, a new dress or hat demanding a compliment, confusion prompting a clearer explanation. Would things become easier now that I was beginning to admit to my difficulties? I feared not; so much emotion, so much thought, is simply not articulated. We are a visually acute species and our social intercourse is predicated on that sense.

Suet pudding consumed and dishes removed, my father reached for the decanter of port and poured for us both. Barely able to distinguish his movements, I felt myself at a huge disadvantage; my peripheral sight diminished in proportion to the available light and my father had never favoured a brightly lit dining room.

'Vaughan of Aberdwylan came to see me today.'

I felt myself tense. Vaughan sat on the magistrates' bench with my father. It seemed that we had arrived at the reason for my being here. 'I suppose he dislikes my investigations?'

'He does. He came to ask me, in the strongest terms, to force you to desist.'

As I drew breath to reply, I heard my father sigh. 'Please, do not simply refuse without hearing me out.'

I was taken aback, his tone was almost pleading.

'Vaughan came to see me because he, in his turn, had received a visit. From Roberts of the Salutation Hotel.'

At the mention of Roberts's name I was filled with the same sense of enraged mortification that I had felt when he tried to browbeat me. *Some criminal has invaded my hotel after dark. I cannot have that happening. Nor can I have the other guests in the hotel put to fright by such grotesque appearances.*

'Roberts informed him that an offensive object had been left outside your door in the hotel.'

'Yes, a *ceffyl pren,*' I said, exasperated that he could not bring himself to articulate the words.

'An object of rebuke,' he insisted. 'And of intimidation.'

'That was its intention, certainly, but I confess to being less than intimidated.'

I jumped as a thud made the glasses and the decanter rattle. My father had slapped the table in his irritation. '*Must* you be so solipsistic? I warned you that your intentions risked a resurgence of Rebecca activity and that is exactly what you have brought about.'

'What *I* have brought about?'

'Was it not you who insisted on an inquest?'

'How could there *not* be one?'

'Very easily! As Bowen pointed out, it was scarcely in the public interest. How does it benefit anybody to have all this raked up – all the old enmities and fears?'

'So because the men who killed Margaret are now trying to warn me off,' I tried to glare at him, 'you find *me* to be in the wrong?'

'The magistrates made a decision. The jury's verdict should be allowed to stand. The *jury's* verdict, Harry, not the magistrates.' I tried to interrupt, to point out that he had not answered my question, but he spoke over me. 'The jury wanted to draw a line under the whole affair. Could you not simply have acceded to their wishes?'

'But it *wasn't* their wish! It wasn't *their* verdict.'

Another sigh. 'You surely don't believe the rumours of jury tampering—'

I could have screamed with frustration at my inability to see his face and it made me more combative than I might have been. 'I believe what I was *told!*' I did not quite shout but I knew I was being more forceful than my father would find acceptable. 'By Dic Jones, the saddler, one of the dissenters on the jury.' My eyes to one side, I tried as hard as I could to get some idea of what my father was thinking but I could see no movement, no expression. 'He told me that a letter was circulated amongst the jury threatening that their houses or businesses would be burned down unless they brought in a verdict of accidental death.' I paused for his response but my father said nothing. 'Did you know that?' I pressed him.

When, eventually, he replied, his voice was low, almost confiding. 'Harry, you haven't been here – haven't *lived* here – since the riots. You don't know the remorse, the *fear* with which people look back on those events. What started as a response to a genuine grievance turned into something monstrous – farmers hid amongst their corn so as to escape the messengers that would summon them, they paid proxies to go on Rebecca's illegal errands rather than risk transportation.' He took a restorative breath. 'It was madness, Harry. Authority was defied on every hand. And people *don't want to remember it.*' He punctuated this last phrase with light thuds of his fist on the table. 'They want Rebecca – even the *memory* of it – to die. Why do you think nobody but you wanted that inquest? Nobody wanted to give evidence – indeed, the witnesses scarcely *gave* evidence! Were we one jot the wiser at the end than we were at the beginning? No. But it had all been stirred up again. Rebecca had been resurrected.'

He stopped, abruptly, and the silence in the wake of his speech was stifling. I could scarcely breathe for it.

'There hasn't been a sniff of the *ceffyl pren* for years,' he went on, 'and, now, you have one deposited at your door. Is this really what you want, Harry? To unleash the madness of insurrection and intimidation all over again?'

I did not know how to respond. He was right, of course. Nothing had been heard of Rebecca since 'forty-three. After that extraordinary summer, whatever impulse had brought Rebecca forth had subsided again and, improbable though it had seemed, life had resumed its former pattern.

'You say I've resurrected Rebecca,' I said, 'but that would imply that she'd died. And, however devoutly people might wish that she had, Rebecca cannot die while those who killed Margaret Jones remain unpunished. While the secret of her death is being kept, Rebecca is merely in hiding.'

'Dead or in hiding, it makes no difference. The phenomenon had disappeared entirely from view. And now you are flushing it into the open, making people afraid.' I could feel his earnest gaze fixed on me, beseeching me to agree with him. 'Fear is dangerous, Harry. People who are afraid do desperate things.'

The nape of my neck prickled at his words. Had somebody been afraid of Margaret Jones? Of something she knew? Was that why she had been murdered?

'I can't give up now,' I told him. 'If I do, fear and intimidation have won. Rebecca won't go away if I give up – whoever threatened the jurors and put that *ceffyl pren* outside my door will simply conclude that they can do what they like. There may be no more trouble now – possibly not for months. But the next time somebody's afraid of a verdict, what's to stop them using Rebecca's name? This *has* to be seen through to the end.'

In the light of the candelabra in the middle of the table, I saw his hand reaching for the decanter and heard the sound of more port being poured into our glasses. My father pushed my glass towards me but said nothing. And as he continued not to speak, I found my attention focusing itself on the unhurried tick-tick-tick of the long-case clock that stood in the corner of the room. It suddenly seemed intrusive, louder and more insistent than before, as if the silence between my father and me had somehow amplified it.

Tick-tick-tick-tick.

Since becoming more reliant on sound, I had begun to hate the way in which a room could be filled with the beat of time being meanly parcelled out, ticked off into sightless seconds. *You can count on me to tell you the truth; everything else is blind guesswork.*

Tick-tick-tick-tick.

I was sick of it; sick of not being able to see, sick of the caution which I had allowed my condition to inflict on me, sick of the violence which I could feel building inside me like steam heat. Violence which had almost boiled over at Ezra Lloyd's accusation. Damn it, if blindness was my lot, it was time to start using it to my advantage.

'I can't see your face, Father,' I said, 'so I have no idea what you're thinking. You'll have to tell me.'

His voice, when he replied, sounded old, weary. 'You do understand that you're making a future as squire of Glanteifi impossible for yourself?'

I sighed. I had no more idea how to respond to this charge, now, than I had when he had first made it on seeing me depart for the Salutation.

When I did not answer him, his voice sharpened. 'While you were

250

a barrister you could avoid coming home and shouldering your responsibilities. But you quite clearly haven't that recourse any longer.'

That impotent heat rose in me again. I *would not* allow him to bring me to heel by pointing out my dependence. It was not possible to think of being master of Glanteifi on that basis. 'I may not have the faculties to practice at the bar.' I was trying, sadly less than successfully, to keep the emotion out of my voice. 'But I think I could make a tolerable living as a solicitor.'

'A *blind* solicitor?'

How *dare* he taunt me with it? 'I believe so. If I was to avail myself of the right clerk.'

'Somebody like young Davies, you mean?'

'Yes, somebody exactly like John.'

'Are you paying Mr Davies for his assistance?'

I felt the heat of my rage doused by a mortified kind of shame. In point of fact, I could not afford to pay John and I knew that, in persuading Mr Schofield to help me, I was exploiting my position as heir to the estate. But naming myself a hypocrite did nothing to deflect my resentment away from my father who inferred the answer to his question from my silence.

'So Charles Schofield is, effectively, funding this enterprise?'

Would he stoop to putting pressure on Mr Schofield to withdraw his support for me? I thought it possible; I had failed to reveal my true motives for this investigation and he was obviously suffering under increasing pressure himself.

'How long can you remain solvent in your own right, Harry? How long before you cannot afford to live at the Salutation anymore?'

'I hope to conclude my investigation before my savings dwindle quite to nothing.'

He sighed, perhaps hearing the truth behind my stiff reply. 'Father, I would like you to understand,' I held up a hand as he tried to interrupt. 'No, let me finish, please. I'd like you to understand why I feel compelled to do this. I know you believed that you were acting in my best interests when you sent me up to Oxford early. But, in doing so, you set in train a set of circumstances which, I believe, ultimately led to Margaret Jones's death.'

I had expected him to object but he said nothing.

'I know it was a young man's unwise affection,' I chose my words with the utmost circumspection, 'but I did care very much for Margaret Jones. I am aware that you will see it as further evidence of my immaturity – as did she, incidentally,' a sad smile pulled at my mouth, 'but I wished to marry her.' Again, I was forced to hold up a forestalling hand, desperate to make him understand. 'Then you sent me away and, when I came back, it was to discover that she was ruined.' Somehow, I could not say *pregnant*. 'Despite my affection, I chose to believe ill of her, chose to believe far worse of her than she deserved. I did not help her when I could have and, in doing nothing when I should have acted, I believe I was complicit in her murder.' I paused but, now, he seemed to have nothing to say. 'I will not,' I concluded, 'be complicit in her murderer's escape from justice.'

John

I was glad to escape to the Drovers' that evening. I'd run out of polite ways to tell Mr Schofield that I couldn't discuss Harry's investigation, and I needed a pint of beer.

But, when I walked in, I didn't get the friendly welcome I was used to. What I got instead was a lot of suspicious looks and eyes turned away. Working with Harry wasn't winning me any friends. I was *persona non grata* as Old Schofield would've enjoyed telling me.

I swallowed a hard lump in my throat. Sod them! I was here to do a job for Harry and I was going to do it. Dai Penlan was sitting in a corner with Ianto Harris. They saw me coming over and the two of them looked about as guilty as a cat with its face in the cream. After the inquest, everybody knew they'd been going to steal the root wood from the fallen tree. Mind, you'd've sworn they'd murdered Margaret Jones the way they looked at me.

Made my job easier, of course. When I told them what I wanted, the words fell out of Dai Penlan's mouth before I'd even offered to buy him a drink. Didn't ask why I wanted to know, not him nor Ianto. But then, everybody knew what me and Harry were up to, didn't they? I made a note in my book, just to let them know they'd given me official information, then nodded my thanks and got out of their way. You could've heard their sighs of relief on the street outside.

Good, now I knew where Rachel and Aaron Ellis lived and I still had the money Harry'd given me to *make Dai well-disposed enough to tell me*, as he'd put it, so I fetched a drink for the man I'd really come here to speak to. Daniel James.

Daniel and I had been at Mr Davies's school together. Now, he worked for Glanteifi's estate lawyer and he was in the Drovers' almost every evening. Said it was *professionally useful* to keep his ear to the ground.

'How's business, Daniel?' I shuffled myself onto the bench and put a second mug of beer in front of him.

'What do you want, John Davies?'

'Daniel! So suspicious!'

'If a man buys me a drink, he wants something.'

I grinned. 'You're right, I do need a favour. But it's not for me, it's for my boss. My *temporary* boss.'

He picked up the beer and spat in it. 'Now you can't take it away when I say no.'

I made a face at the childishness of the gesture but we both knew I'd've done the same.

'So by "temporary boss", I suppose you're talking about Harry Glanteifi?' he gave me a sly grin. 'Heard he'd managed to persuade old man Schofield to let you work for him for nothing.'

That was Newcastle Emlyn for you. You could share a confidence in the morning and it'd be town gossip by the evening.

'Yes, well, the person who's asked him to make enquiries isn't paying,' I said, looking sideways at the men nearest to where we were sitting. Didn't want anybody paying too much attention to us.

If Daniel noticed, he didn't follow my lead. I think he'd already had a couple and his voice was louder than I'd've liked. 'So, what favour does your temporary and not very well-off boss need? Why isn't he well-off, anyway? I heard he was some big lawyer in London.'

I shrugged and raised an eyebrow at the same time. *I know but I can't tell you.* We lawyers' clerks knew how to value discretion as much as information. 'I can't talk about Harry's finances—' I stopped. Daniel was asking a question.

'Is that what you call him? Harry?'

I shrugged. 'What else would I call him?'

'To his face?'

'No, to his arse! Yes, of course, to his face.'

Daniel gave me a look. Half of him didn't believe me, the other half was unwillingly impressed. 'Well then? What's the favour?'

'We need – that's to say *Harry* needs – some information from the Glanteifi estate records.'

He watched me over his beer, waiting.

'An address,' I said, 'that's all. There was an old boy – a groom, Harry can't remember his name,' he'd believe that, a gentleman not remembering the name of a servant, 'who retired a few years ago. He wants to talk to him, see if he remembers some things from back then.'

Daniel looked at me over his pint. 'What's that got to do with me?'

'The old chap'll have a pension from the estate, won't he? There'll be an address attached to his name on the records.'

Daniel put his empty mug down. Then he looked into it and up at me. I picked it up and waved it at Mrs James, who wandered over with her jug and refilled it. Refilled mine while she was at it.

She flirted with us for a bit, like women of a certain age always do with young, unmarried men, then she went to fill somebody else's mug. I waited till she started speaking to them, then turned to Daniel. 'Well?'

'You want the name and address of a groom who's been pensioned off in the last few years?'

'Yes.' I'd picked a groom because, once or twice, a stable lad had been mentioned in connection with Harry's youth. A man employed to work in the stables would know who this lad was. Ezra Lloyd had talked about a David Thomas. Was he the one Harry'd gone about with as a boy?

If Harry was right and there had been a Beca band that wanted to teach young women a lesson, what Lloyd had said made me think this David Thomas might've been one of them. So why weren't we asking him questions?

'How will I know whether I've got the right one?' Daniel wanted to know.

I thought quickly. 'There can't be that many grooms who've been pensioned off in the last ten years,' I said, throwing my net fairly wide. 'Just bring me the names of any grooms who've been given a pension since the end of the riots.' I knew that mentioning the riots would get his interest. 'Yes, since eighteen forty-three. From what Harry said that should do it.'

'And why should I do this for you? Or for him?'

'Because when Harry's the squire of Glanteifi and I'm his lawyer, I shall employ you, Daniel James.'

He raised a dubious eyebrow but I could tell he half-believed me.

And I hoped that meant he'd get me the information I wanted.

I needed to know what Harry wasn't telling me about David Thomas.

And why.

Harry

Despite a certain *rapprochement* occasioned by my father's invitation to spend the night at Glanteifi rather than return to the Salutation in the dark, our earlier argument had left me feeling restless and frustrated. Lying in my own bed, I could not help but feel that part of me had marooned itself stubbornly in the past, forcing me to go over and over my association with Margaret, wondering how things might have turned out had I acted differently.

It was not a pleasant experience; the sifting and weighing of my own youthful actions prompted a shame so profound that continuing to investigate the circumstances of Margaret's death in spite of my father's wishes seemed almost insufficient as a response. The journey to Ipswich would not, I knew, be long or arduous enough to represent any form of penance – Australia would scarcely have been far enough – but I hoped that it would furnish me with a modicum of clarity on whether it was possible that Margaret had become caught up in the rivalries of Nathaniel Howell's Rebecca crusade.

Nathaniel Howell. He had all but commanded me to go and see Margaret – to *make amends* – but I had resisted him, adamant that he should not order my affairs as my father did.

And yet I *had* gone to see Margaret. Not at Howell's instigation, but at Davy Thomas's.

Two or three days after Hannah Rees and her son had ridden to Waungilfach with me in my father's carriage, Davy had been waiting for me as I led my little mare, Sara, to the stables on our return from church.

'You're in trouble, Harry.'

I looked at him, apprehension blooming like a blush. 'Why?'

He waited until we were inside the stable, looking about lest we should be overheard. 'The sermon Nathaniel Howell preached this morning was about you.'

'*What?*'

He shook his head, dismissing my horror. 'He didn't mention you by name, obviously – the man's not a fool. But anybody who knows you were courting Margaret knows it was you he was talking about.'

He watched my trembling fingers sliding stirrups up leathers and undoing Sara's girth. 'Want to know what he said?'

I pulled the saddle towards me off the mare's back. 'No. Not at all. But you'd better tell me.'

'Yes, I'd better. What's that English phrase you used to like so much? *Forewarned is forearmed.*'

The words sounded odd, coming from him. I could not recall him speaking English to me – even so short a phrase – since the days when I was teaching him to read. I dumped the saddle on its stand. 'Go on then,' I said, unbuckling the mud-spattered girth so as not to have to look at him.

All the apprehension I would have felt had Howell himself been standing in front of me was coursing through my veins. I truly did not want to hear whatever humiliating things the minister had said about me. But Davy was right, I needed to be forewarned.

He took a breath to tell the story and I steadied myself for whatever I was about to hear. I knew he would not summarise to spare my feelings; Davy was a raconteur and he revelled in the role.

'*Imagine,*' he said, adopting something of the minister's lighter tone as he quoted his words, '*that there's a rich man* – Howell didn't say "gentleman", that's not the language of the Bible, but everybody knew gentleman was what he meant – *imagine there's a rich man who falls in love with a poor girl* – he didn't say servant but he didn't have to – *and she falls in love with him, though she knows it's a foolish thing to do. And he tells her he loves her and he wants to marry her. She knows it would be a disaster for him and she tells him so. She saves him from his own folly. But still he declares his love. His undying love. And then the rich man is sent away on a long journey. He's away for a long time, with no word to the poor girl. Not a single word. She expects to see him back after a month or two but he stays away and stays away. And still no word.'*

Expressly prohibited from coming home at Christmas, I had spent a barely tolerable fortnight with a college-mate in Radnorshire, wallowing in my own self-pity. It was only now that I understood how Margaret must have looked for my arrival, day after day.

I slipped off my coat, picked up a brush and began rubbing Sara down.

Davy went on. *'And so, the poor girl knows that he's forgotten her. His was not an undying love at all, merely the lust of a young man. He is gone and she must forget him as he has forgotten her. And then it happens that the young woman finds herself with child. The man who's got her so is unwilling to marry her—'*

'Is he?' I asked, resolutely brushing at the sweaty, saddle-flattened hair on Sara's back. 'Is the father of Margaret's child refusing to marry her?'

Davy shrugged. 'You'd have to ask her. But the Reverend Howell seemed to think that was the story. D'you want me to go on?'

I nodded, unwilling to say yes or even to look at him.

'*So*, Howell says, *it comes to pass that the rich young man finally returns home. The poor girl, desperate by now, decides to go to him and ask for his help. Now, brothers and sisters – the rich man, seeing that she has been possessed by another, feels no love for her any more. His heart is hard. In his own mind, he has no responsibility here.'* Davy paused to let these words sink in. *'But the gospels tell us differently, do they not? The words of our Lord are not "if somebody offends you, you may have nothing more to do with them," the words of our Lord are, "even if somebody is your enemy you must love him". The rich man may say he does not love the poor girl any more, but that is not the love our Lord meant. The rich young man is responsible for the poor girl. Not because he once fell in love with her. Not because he is the father of her child – for he is not. But because he led her to believe that she could trust him. The rich man has been given great wealth. And with great wealth comes great responsibility.'*

I stopped, the brush still on Sara's back, and leaned against her. Her warm solidity was comforting. I had no doubt that Davy had rendered the story almost verbatim; though he had been no quick study when learning to read and write, he had an excellent memory for what he heard and a merciless ability as a mimic.

'I thought you were going to see her?' he challenged.

I stepped back and moved around to Sara's far side, putting her between Davy and me. 'No. You told me I *should* go and see her. So did Howell. I never said I *would*.' I heard my own petulance and felt a swell of self-loathing.

'Harry, you don't want to make an enemy of Howell. He could make things difficult for you.'

I lifted Sara's mane and began working on her neck. 'What about the father of Margaret's child? Is Howell pursuing him, as well?'

'He doesn't know who it is. Margaret hasn't told him. That's why Howell's going for you. Everybody assumes it's yours.'

'Why hasn't she told Howell who it is?'

I glanced at him and saw an expression that I wasn't sure how to read. Discomfort? Embarrassment? Unease?

'Perhaps she doesn't know herself.'

My hand stopped moving as if it had registered Davy's words along with my ears. I stared at him, refusing to believe what he was implying, trying to force him to say something which would offer me an alternative explanation.

'Harry.' His voice was unusually soft, almost hesitant. 'Everybody knew about you and her, you must know that. And everybody assumed you'd—' He stopped, didn't say *had her*. 'I mean, *I* assumed you had. So you can imagine how men flocked about her after you'd gone. And, with you going like that, without a word – I don't think she cared what people thought or what she did.' He stopped, eyes on me. 'I'm sorry. I thought she was trying to father your bastard onto whoever she could but, if it isn't yours—' He stopped. 'Perhaps she wanted them to think there was a baby, so they'd think they could get favours from you if they married her.'

Bile rose up in my throat and I had to swallow hard to stop myself from throwing up all the hurt and rage I felt. 'Were you one of them?' I asked. He had always had an eye for the girls, and they for him.

His eyes went dark, as if a light had been blown out behind them. 'You think I'd do that?'

Heartsick, I had no answer for him. I began to move the brush again, mechanically, over Sara's shoulder, eyes fixed on what I was doing. But Davy had a point to push home. 'Never mind you being my friend, I'd've been mad to get involved with her, wouldn't I? I can't run the risk of having to marry somebody like Margaret. I need a woman with more about her. You might've thought *you* could go against convention but I've always known I couldn't. I have to behave myself if I want to get on, do the right thing. Margaret Jones is a pretty girl but she'd've been a disaster for my prospects.'

I could not bring myself to speak but I knew that what he said was true.

'And I've got bigger fish to fry, now, anyway.' I looked up, surprised, and he shrugged. 'You'd hear soon enough, I daresay. I'm courting Elias Jenkins's daughter, Elizabeth. Halfway down the aisle, already.'

'I see.' I swallowed. I could not find it in me to congratulate him. He nodded, then returned to the business at hand. 'Go and see her, Harry. Set her up in a cottage with a cow and a pig – it's what she'd've been expecting when she set her cap at you, you know it is.'

I let the hand holding the brush fall to my side. I felt weak, suddenly; inadequate. 'It wasn't her that set her cap at me.' I forced myself to meet his eye, make him see the truth of what I was saying. 'It was me that set mine at her.'

He shook his head. 'That's what women want you to think. They convince you that it's your lust when, all the time, they're leading you on.'

He put a hand on Sara's back and looked over at me. 'I'm sorry, Harry. I know you were fond of her but you need to see what she's really like. If you'll take my advice, you'll do something for her, and quickly. Before she has the child and Howell brings it to you.'

Harry

Over breakfast with John, the following morning, I told him about Vaughan's visit to my father and the magistrate's request that I give up my investigations.

'What do you think?' I asked. Though he was too young to have taken part in the disturbances, he had grown up in the shadow of Rebecca and could be expected to know her covert power. On the other hand, he was a lawyer's clerk who, according to Charles Schofield, *cleaved to the law as if to his very salvation, my dear Mr Probert-Lloyd*. I felt he had a right to know what the magistrates' opinion was.

He put his knife and fork down. 'I'm sorry, Harry…' I heard the slight hesitation before the use of my Christian name and experienced a mingled sense of irritation and, regrettably, gratification; clearly, some unsuspected, patrician part of me agreed that my inviting him to call me Harry was deserving of gratitude. '…are you asking me whether I agree with the magistrates – that we should give up our investigations?'

I nodded and sipped at my breakfast tea. 'Yes, I am. According to my father, if we go on, we risk turning everybody against us. Apparently, nobody wants Margaret's murderer brought to justice. Sleeping dogs, it seems, are preferred.'

There was a brief silence in which I could discern no movement from John. Then he spoke, paying his words out painstakingly, one after another.

'But, if a dog runs mad and savages the sheep it's supposed to guard, it's not allowed to sleep, is it? It's put down without a second's thought.'

I nodded. Encouraged, John leaned forwards. 'If we give up, now, we're no better than the jurors who brought in the accidental death verdict. Cowards.'

Though I was gratified to hear him say it, I could not let him make a decision without a proper awareness of the possible consequences. 'You do know that this could affect you, too – defying the magistrates?' No immediate reply came, and I fought down a sudden fear. If John chose not to continue to work with me, then my investigation was at an end. Alone and blind I would be next to useless. As my assistant, he did more than simply compensate for my lack of sight; he gave my investigations a gravitas which I could never achieve by myself.

But I need not have worried. I heard a smile in his voice when he spoke. 'If the magistrates don't like what I'm doing, I shall just have to blame you, shan't I? After all, when the heir to the Glanteifi estate crooks his finger, what choice does a lowly clerk have but to do as he's told?'

John

Harry couldn't stop talking. Prattled on and on as we got the horses and rode out of Newcastle Emlyn. We were halfway to Aaron Ellis's cottage before I realised he was babbling from relief. He'd been afraid I was going to tell him I didn't want to carry on working with him. That I was too afraid of Beca. Too afraid of the magistrates. But I couldn't have said that, even if I thought Mr Schofield would've let me get away with it.

The dreams were waking me, night after night.

Take this message to Mr Williams at Waungilfach.

Rain, pattering down, running down the roots of the tree on to me.

His relentless voice. *This is your fault, Margaret – you've brought this on yourself… You said you'd do it. You said you* had *done it. But you were lying…* Her hands, pulling at his; her body slumping.

His voice as he chased me. *I'll find you boy! I'll kill you!* Would the dreams stop if Harry could uncover the truth? I had to believe they would.

A good angel might've pointed out that Harry'd get to the truth a lot quicker if I told him what I knew. But, if I'd ever had a good angel, he'd been silent since that night. Silenced by fear.

Fear obviously took Harry the other way. His tongue was running away with him.

'The magistrates think they can bring me to heel by threatening to bar me from the bench. It doesn't occur to them that I might not want to be part of their self-satisfied clique!'

Be a squire and not a magistrate? He might as well try and be a dog and not bark.

'They seem to think that the way they do things is indisputably the right way – the only possible way! I think they've forgotten that there's been a revolution in France, that in America they're forging an entirely new way of thinking of land ownership – that every man should own the land he works.'

On and on. And then, suddenly, he stopped. We were coming down to the bridge over the little river Ceri, just before it joined the Teifi below his father's house. Was he imagining his father's eyes on him?

'Thinking of home?' I asked, feeling daring.

'Just thinking that Glanteifi is about the right size of house for a man living on the home farm acreage,' he said. 'Not too big.'

'Is that what you'd like to do?' I asked. His nonsense about not being a magistrate was making me bold. 'You'd like to live off the home farm?'

'Yes, why not? That or make my living as a solicitor.'

Was he speaking *hypothetically*, as Mr Schofield would say, or did he really think he could manage the job without being able to see? I soon found out.

'I know it seems an oddity, a blind solicitor, but I believe that with the right kind of clerk it could be done.'

The right kind of clerk.

My thoughts began to race, then. I might leave Schofield's and work with Harry. He might article me. I could be a solicitor in my own right one day. I could *be* someone.

Did my silence make him realise what he'd said – what I might be thinking? I don't know. But something brought him back from what my old schoolmaster, Mr Davies, used to call Utopia.

'That gift we've brought for Rachel—' he said.

A visiting-gift for Rachel Ellis had been my idea. Either the gentry thought their neighbours were well-enough off without visiting-gifts or he just hadn't thought of it because Mrs Ellis was a servant.

'What about it?'

'Should we give it to her straight away or at the end as a thank-you?'

'Straight away. It's not supposed to be a reward.' Going ratting with stableboys and courting dairymaids hadn't taught him much. 'You just give it to her. *Hello Mrs Ellis, nice to see you again, I brought a small thing for you.* Like that.'

Harry twisted his mouth, chewing the inside of his lip.

'Everybody knows what we're doing' I told him. 'The minute she opens the door and it's you, she'll know what you want. Bringing something can only help.'

He nodded. 'True. At least if I don't come empty-handed that's one thing she can't hold against me.'

What is she holding against you, then? I wanted to ask. *What is there between you and the servant who was Rachel Evans?*

We found Rachel Ellis digging potatoes with her children. The cottage was right next to the road so they were easy to see on their little plot. Just as well to get the potatoes up. The weather hadn't been bad but much more rain and they'd start to rot in the ground.

I watched her notice us. She straightened up, one hand on her back, and sent her little boy running off. I didn't know whether Harry'd been able to make out what was going on, so I told him.

'She'll have sent him off to get her husband,' he said.

We dismounted and walked the horses the last few yards. Rachel was trying to look busy with her little girl and the basket of potatoes they were carrying between them but she couldn't keep the fear off her face. I'd seen that fear before. When she was answering Bowen's questions.

'Good morning to you, Mrs Ellis,' Harry called, stopping at the edge of the potato rows.

Rachel Ellis put the basket down and pinched her nose, just like she'd done at the inquest. 'Good morning. Fine weather, isn't it?' Her speech still sounded odd.

Her daughter looked up at her. 'Who are they, Mami?'

'Shh. Go in the house,' her mother said, giving her a little push to send her on her way. 'Wait there till your brother comes then the pair of you can go and fetch some water.'

The little girl did as she was told but she looked back at us when her mother wasn't looking. Wondering who we were and what we wanted. I watched her go into the neat, whitewashed house. It had a glassed window and good thatch. How many cattle in the byre end, I wondered. From the size of it, not more than two. But if Rachel Ellis made butter to sell – and there was definitely more money coming in than just a labourer's wages, judging by that glass window – they'd need more than one to keep the milk coming all year.

Harry'd dismounted and was getting the visiting-gifts out. 'I didn't want to come and take up your time and not bring something for you,' he said. 'Tea, sugar and flour,' he put the packages in her hands, 'I hope they'll be useful?'

With both her hands occupied, she couldn't pinch her nose but 'thank you' doesn't take much understanding.

'You've got a tidy place, here,' Harry told her. I wondered how much of it he could see. Could he tell that, beneath the limecoat, the house was built of *clom*, not turf? I doubted it. He'd just see white.

Rachel didn't reply, just stood, watching him look about. It wasn't cold but she was shivering. Or shaking.

'And two children – you must be very proud.'

When he got no answer to that, Harry came to the point. 'You know we're trying to find out what happened to Margaret?' She nodded and I wondered if he'd seen. 'I don't believe the jury's verdict,' he said. 'I think they were told what to say. Threatened.' Then he stopped, tried to look her in the eye. 'You don't believe Margaret would have killed her own child, do you, Rachel?'

Rachel Ellis didn't reply. She just shifted the packages he'd given her so that she was holding them in the crook of her arm, like a newborn. To give her a hand free to pinch her nose.

Over her shoulder, I saw that the little boy'd found his father. Aaron Ellis was striding towards us along the road, a billhook in his hand. From a movement of Harry's head I knew he'd seen him too.

Did Rachel see us both looking past her at her husband? I don't know but she started speaking quickly, her voice low. 'You should give this up, Harry Gwyn. There's no good can come of what you're doing. Not for you.'

Harry Gwyn?

We could hear Aaron's boots clumping now, and Rachel half-turned towards him.

'Why, Rachel?' Harry took a step towards her and she backed off, shaking her head. 'Who thinks I should give it up?' he asked. 'Not you, surely?'

'I can't tell you anything about Margaret's baby, Mr Probert-Lloyd,' Rachel said, loud enough for her husband to hear.

'Mr Probert-Lloyd!' Aaron Ellis had reached us. 'Good day to you, sir.' He put a hand on his wife's arm. It looked like reassurance but perhaps it was a warning, too.

As Harry gave him his 'Good day' back, Aaron's eyes were on me. 'And Mr John Davies from Schofield the solicitor's, is it?'

I inclined my head, never taking my eyes off him. I wasn't going to let him stare me down. He wasn't a handsome man, Aaron Ellis – his face was narrow and thin and his top teeth stuck out. To be truthful, there wasn't much to recommend husband or wife as far as looks went.

'Mr Probert-Lloyd, if you're here to ask my wife questions about Margaret Jones, I'm sorry but you've had a wasted journey. She doesn't know anything.' Aaron was speaking Welsh. He'd probably come to the end of his English with 'Good day'. 'She told Mr Bowen everything she knew at the inquest and that's all there is. She doesn't know anything else.'

'If I could just speak to her for a minute—'

'I'm sorry. She doesn't know anything more.' He turned to Rachel and spoke with a gentleness that surprised me. 'Give me those.' He held his hands out for Harry's calling-gifts, 'and go in the house now. I'll speak to Mr Probert-Lloyd.'

His wife turned to go, but Harry stepped forward, put out a hand. 'But Rachel and I are old friends, aren't we, Rachel? I'm sure she won't mind—'

'I beg your pardon, Mr Probert-Lloyd,' Aaron Ellis kept his tone the right side of courtesy. 'I know you were acquainted with my wife, years ago, but there can't have been a friendship. Not between the squire's son and an outdoor servant. Go on, Rachel, go in, now.'

Harry was good at hiding his feelings, I understood that by now.

Came from being a barrister, I suppose. But I was looking for a reaction to Aaron Ellis's flat contradiction so I saw it. The little muscles around Harry's eyes tightened, his jaw muscles bunched up under his short beard. He didn't lose control like he had when he nearly hit Ezra Lloyd, but he was still angry at being defied.

'Why?' I asked for him. 'Why don't you want us speaking to your wife, Aaron Ellis?'

Aaron pulled his lips over his teeth and swallowed, his Adam's apple stretching his scrawny throat. 'You see my house, John Davies?' His finger pointed at the cottage his wife was making her way towards, his eyes never leaving mine. 'I built that house with my own two hands. I rent this land fair and square. I put food on the table because I work hard…'

'But you don't own any of it,' I finished for him. 'It's William Williams's land and he could have you off it in a blink if he wanted.'

Aaron said nothing, but the look on his face told me I'd got it right.

Harry was there too. 'He's told you not to speak to me, hasn't he? What's Williams afraid of? The truth coming out, or Beca's threats?'

Aaron stuck out his chin. 'I'm sorry Mr Probert-Lloyd but there's nothing I can tell you.'

Harry nodded. 'Very well.'

Aaron held out the parcels he'd taken from his wife. 'You must take these, too. We haven't earned them.'

Harry shook his head. 'Nobody was meant to earn them. They were a visiting-gift.'

'You know every sip of that tea will stick in Aaron Ellis's gullet?'

Harry turned to me in surprise. 'Why should it?'

I turned my eyes back where they belonged – on the road between my horse's ears. I couldn't ride without thinking about it, not like Harry. 'Because he knows he's made his wife keep things from you. He'll already feel less of a man for standing there and lying to you, without you leaving him decent grocer's food.'

'You think she did know something?'

'I'd put money on it. If I had any. But I'd bet even more that Williams has told them to say nothing.'

Harry looked away from me. I knew it was just so he could see me better but it looked as if he was staring at the mill, down on the meadow by the little stream. 'You told me everybody knows Williams's father-in-law is giving him money to keep the farm going?'

'Yes. Common knowledge in town.'

He chewed his lip a bit. 'Well then, what if Esme's father has told Williams that if he hears one more piece of scandal about him and a young woman that he'll cut off his financial support?'

A picture of Esme Williams's father appeared in my mind's eye. Thomas Owens. Didn't look like a successful man. Thin as a vagrant, he was. And he had a beard that was almost white when most of the hair on his head was still dark. It was like looking at a skinny badger. But still, looks can be deceptive. He'd made a lot of money through shrewd investments. He might still be known as Owens the grocer but most of his money came from elsewhere, now.

'Do you think he'd do that to his daughter?' I asked. 'Make her husband bankrupt?'

Harry chewed the inside of his lip. 'I don't know. Maybe Esme's sick of trying to be a lady when Williams isn't up to the job of being a gentleman. Maybe she'd rather face a few weeks of being the talk of the town if she could go back to queening it in her father's house. You're too young to remember, but her mother died when Esme was a girl and she grew up as the lady of the house. I'm sure she thought marrying into land would raise her father's social standing as well as her own but she miscalculated with Williams.' He stopped, half-turned towards me. 'Is Esme Williams using me?'

'*Using* you?'

His teeth pulled at his lip. 'Yes. She says she wants to clear her husband's name but what if what she *really* wants is to find out how far he's implicated in all of this so she can use his involvement as a reason for going back to her father's house?'

I looked up at the cold, pointing fingers of the winter trees in the hedge. A little wind found its way in around my collar and made me shiver.

At first glance, the idea was ridiculous. Women in Esme's position didn't just abandon their husbands. Too much to lose. But then, I wondered. Harry was right – Esme would know she'd be the subject of gossip either way, so she might well choose to be the wife who wouldn't put up with her husband's waywardness any more. Better than being the put-upon woman who'd been married for her money and been made a fool of by a lout dressed as a gentleman.

'Do you think she knows he *was* involved,' I asked, 'and just wants to find out how far?'

Harry shook his head. 'I don't know. But Williams wants me to stop, so, at the very least, there's something *he* doesn't want us to find out, isn't there?'

Harry

That evening, after dining and making arrangements for the following morning, I fell into bed and quickly succumbed to a deep sleep. But it was not to last. I woke, suddenly and completely, to the vast silence that presses in upon the world in the small hours and knew that I had been dreaming about the last time I saw Margaret.

After enduring Davy's rendition of Nathaniel Howell's sermon, I had realised that I had no choice but to go and see her. I knew from Davy that, fearful of being judged, she no longer attended chapel so I had decided to visit Waungilfach on Sunday morning, when Williams and his wife would be at church.

I found Margaret Jones much changed.

She saw the shock on my face as she turned from the butter churn at my greeting; I tried to hide it but I saw from her reaction that I had failed. Some women blossom when they are carrying a child and I suppose I had expected buxom Margaret to be one of them. But I could not have been more wrong. The young woman before me had shrunk and withered. Her eyes had lost their sparkle, her cheeks were pallid and thin. Even her arms, previously plump and strong from carrying buckets of milk, were thinner. It seemed to me that the child in her womb was sucking the life out of her.

She crouched over her work, hiding her face from me. She said nothing and, standing there in the chill of the sunless dairy, I found myself at a complete loss as to how to proceed.

Had I really expected that she would throw herself on my neck, weep with contrition and beg my forgiveness? I was appalled at my own self-delusion.

I watched her shoulders heaving the churning-handle and tried to summon up some appropriate words for her. Contrary to the impression Davy had given me, Margaret clearly had no desire to see me; her back said that she wished only for me to be gone. And the cowardly part of me felt the same, it wanted nothing more than to flee, to ride back to Glanteifi and never see her again. But something, some glimmer of a nobler impulse kept me there, my eyes on what had become of her.

As if my gaze were controlling her movements, the churning slowed; finally, it stopped.

I moved so that I could see her in profile. The size of her swollen belly was a surprise even though I had been expecting it.

'When will it be born?' I despised myself for sounding so querulous. She must think I was afraid she might deliver her child there and then, on the damp flagstones.

'Midsummer,' she said not moving her gaze from the churn. She made to start turning the handle again but I put a hand on her arm.

'No!' She shrugged me off. 'Don't look at me.'

'I only want to—'

'Go away! I don't want you to see me like this.'

At her words, all the kind and conciliatory things I had wanted to say, the forgiving and gentlemanly tone I had practised, vanished, and the hurt and bewilderment that had collected inside me found voice. 'Carrying another man's child, you mean?'

She did not turn around, but she spoke softly. 'I wish it was yours. I wanted it to be yours. You know I did – you know I wanted you.'

'Yes, so that you could have a cottage and a cow and a pig off me.'

She turned then, eyes wide, mouth open but I gave her no time to deny it. 'That's what you were after, wasn't it? Right from the beginning? You thought that if you could have my bastard, I'd set you up in a little cottage and take care of you. You virtually said so – all I can ever be is your mistress, you said, so let's make the best of it. Well, you were certainly hoping to make the best of it, weren't you?'

Her eyes on me, her face seemed to collapse in on itself and she dropped her head and wept.

'Don't think you'll get round me like that, madam,' I said. 'Your tears are as false as your affection was.'

She looked up at that, and, for the first time, her eyes held something of their old passion. 'I never said a false word to you, Harry. Never.'

'I don't believe you.'

'It was *you* that came after *me*!'

I remembered Davy's words. *That's what they want you to think.* 'Was it?' I asked. 'Whether it was or not, you saw straight away that you could get something out of me.'

'Do you blame me? I have no family. No prospects of a comfortable marriage—'

'So you admit it? You played me for a fool?'

'It was me that was the fool! I let myself believe you. I let myself fall in love with you. Even though I knew it would bring me nothing but pain—'

'You fell out of love with me damn quickly! The very day I left for Oxford by the look of you!'

As if I had threatened the child, her hands went to her belly.

'You left without a word,' she was sobbing now, and it would have been clear to a harder heart than mine that her tears were genuine.

Snot flowed from her nose and spittle from her mouth as she flung words at me. 'You left without telling me you were going or when you'd be back. You *abandoned* me!'

I felt sick. What she said was true. I had been so wrapped up in my own wretchedness that it had not occurred to me to ask myself how she might be feeling. Had I really believed that she would simply go back to being Margaret the dairymaid when she had, briefly, been Margaret the beloved?

Feebly, I tried to defend myself. 'I couldn't write to you, could I?'

'You could have written to David Thomas! Could have asked him to bring me news. But no. Not a word.'

She was right. I could have done as she said. I should have. But I had been so ashamed of being sent away in that summary fashion that I had said nothing to Davy. I had not even written to him from Oxford; not until Christmas when I had felt the need to tell him that I would not be coming home.

'I waited and waited. I thought you'd be home at Christmas, that you'd come and see me, but there was nothing. Not a word...' Her sobbing seemed to consume her and I became concerned that she would collapse.

Taking a bucket I upturned it and put it next to her. 'Sit for a moment. Calm yourself.'

She put her apron to her face and did as I bid her.

'Didn't Davy tell you that my father had forbidden me to come home at Christmas?' I asked. 'That he'd forbidden me to come home at all during my first year?' She said nothing, her face still hidden in the striped wool of her apron. I remember thinking, with horrible triviality, how little the wool would absorb her tears and snot compared to the handkerchief in my pocket. I still regret, to this day, that I did not give it to her. It would have been such a small thing and the kindness might have induced her to confide in me.

I squatted down on my haunches next to her. 'Margaret, I want to help you. If you tell me who the father of your child is—'

She shook her head and wept harder. 'I can't. I can't tell you.' So. Davy had been telling the truth.

Everybody knew about you and her, you must know that. And everybody assumed you'd— When Margaret's pregnancy started to show, everybody assumed it was my child. Howell clearly had. As had Davy. And Williams?

I stood and addressed her covered face. 'I shall make sure Mr Williams knows this child is not mine,' I said. 'What he decides to do then is his business.'

In telling Williams that the child was not mine, had I removed from Margaret the one last protection that might have saved her?

PART 4: IPSWICH

John

Harry and I got off the coach in Carmarthen and made our way straight to the docks. If there was a chance of catching a steamer that day we didn't want to miss it – Harry wanted to be in London and then Ipswich as quickly as he could. The quickest way – the mail – had had no spaces so here we were. It was steamer to Bristol for us, then train to London.

Steamer! Train! I'd hardly even been in a coach before.

I'd never been near Carmarthen docks, either, but their reputation was shocking. Well, it was in Newcastle Emlyn anyway. As far as people like my landlady were concerned, the docks were a hive of murderous gangs and shameless prostitutes. But perhaps that was just after dark, because all I could see was a businesslike quayside, with things coming off and going on to ships under the eye of men with bills of lading in their hands. It all looked about as scandalous as Owens the grocer's warehouse.

Mind you, busyness was almost as much of a problem for Harry as dodging criminals would've been. It wasn't easy for him to watch his step while he was making his way between piles of merchandise, wooden landing piers and lines of barrows and carts. More than once he had to grab at my coat to stop himself being pushed over.

'Along here?' I skirted past barrels coming down a gangway onto the quayside.

'Yes. But I'm not sure which building. You'll have to ask.'

Ten minutes later, the ticket clerk was telling us that we were just in time – a steamer would be leaving in half an hour.

How did people travel to America and live to tell the tale? The Bristol Channel almost did for me. According to Harry, the sea was calm for the time of year but my stomach didn't think so. Not at all. And it wasn't just the sea. When we came down the gangway on to Bristol docks, my legs turned to string. I'd been yearning for firm ground underfoot but, when I got it, I found myself stumbling to my knees on the solidity of it. How did sailors manage after weeks at sea? Why weren't Bristol docks full of staggering men?

Harry almost fell over me. 'Are you hurt?'

'No,' I muttered. 'Just slipped on the wet stones, that's all.'

'Just stand still for a minute,' he said. 'Your body still thinks it's on the steamer. Let it settle to being on land again.'

It was all right for him, he wasn't reeling around like a drunkard. 'You need something to eat,' he said, after I'd managed to stand up straight for four seconds in a row. 'Let's find out what there is before we see about a train for the morning.'

It was amusing to see Harry standing in the street eating a pie of eels and oysters out of his hand as if he'd done it every day of his life.

'D'you like it?' I asked.

'Bit salty. But when you're hungry anything will do, won't it?'

I doubted whether Harry'd ever known real hunger in his life. Not that belly-shrinking hunger you get when you've had no food for two or three days. But I didn't say that.

And I kept my mouth shut when we had to stay the night in the same cheap room, too. If Harry could lie down in his shirt and breeches, so could I.

But both of us were scratching in the morning.

The Bristol railway station was huge. Bigger than I'd ever imagined a building could be. It was hundreds of yards long and the span of the roof was immense – that's the only word for it – with gigantic, curving iron ribs supporting the glass of it.

Harry obviously saw me looking up. 'Magnificent, isn't it? It's so big even I can see it. Detail's irrelevant.'

What he wouldn't be able to see was that the roof's acreage of glass was grey with smoke from the locomotives' long chimneys. And it wasn't just smoke the roof kept in, either. The noise of trains and people was held down, too, close to the iron rails and the platform, battering at your ears. The whole place echoed and rang so much my head throbbed.

It was a relief to hear the guard shouting the off. I spotted him, sitting high up on the coach at the back of the train. Just like being outside on a normal coach. 'Close all the doors, gentlemen! All those not travelling, kindly step aside. We are embarking. We are embarking!'

I can't say the train's seats were as comfortable as the ones on the Carmarthen coach but they were no more uncomfortable than the stools in Mr Schofield's office so I had nothing to complain of on the journey to London. Nothing except hunger anyway. And we could move about. There was some empty bench space on the other side of the carriage so, if the view from one side got boring, I could move to the other. Harry asked what I was looking at but I didn't know how to answer him. I'd never been further than Carmarthen in my life so I was looking at everything. Because everything was different. The houses, the fields, the villages, the towns, the rivers. Everything. It all looked prosperous and fat and well-tended. Every house seemed to be built of brick or stone and, everywhere, houses were two-storeyed, like in Carmarthen, only this was the countryside. Where were the labourers' cottages, I wondered. But I didn't ask. I didn't want Harry to think I was ignorant.

Mind you, I wasn't the only one staring. Every time Harry and I opened our mouths and spoke Welsh the other passengers gawped at us. I felt like a freak in a show. *Roll up, roll up, see the men who talk nonsense and yet understand each other perfectly!*

'We've got a good chance of getting to London in daylight and finding something near Shoreditch,' Harry said. 'That's where the trains for the east coast go from.'

Shoreditch. I mouthed the word. 'What shore is it on?'

Harry made a face. 'I've never thought about it. It's not on a shore, actually. Not even on the bank of the Thames. Maybe it was once – on a shore, I mean – London's got some very marshy areas. And had more before it was drained, I dare say.'

'Odd,' I said, 'the name not being anything to do with the land around.'

'Yes. I've never thought of it but it's not like at home, is it?'

I thought of the places associated with Margaret Jones's death. Glanteifi: the banks of the Teifi, where Harry's home was. Alltddu: the dark wood, where her bones had been found. And Williams's Waungilfach: the meadow with the little hiding place. It had been hiding Margaret Jones. Was it still hiding secrets?

The place where the train stopped in London was called Paddington. The station there was nothing like the huge glass-house at Bristol. It was all soot-blacked red brick and brown-painted wood. Outside, a thick fog lay low to the ground.

I coughed. 'Why does this fog taste of coal dust?'

'The smoke from all the fires gets caught up in it. They call it a London Particular.'

I was glad we didn't have to spend more than a night in London. Breathing that air, day in, day out, would have killed me in a month. Harry stood, chewing the inside of his lip. I knew he was fretting about the light. It was almost dark and we weren't going to be able to find our way to this Shoreditch very easily.

Finally, he made up his mind. 'John, can you see a Hansom cab anywhere?'

I wasn't going to admit I didn't know what a Hansom cab was. 'What do they look like?'

'Small. Two wheels, one horse.'

'Sounds like a gig.'

'Hansoms are closed.'

I looked about, squinting into the Particular. There were gaslights at the side of the road but they seemed to make it more difficult to see, not easier. The fog around them glowed so you couldn't see beyond it.

Then I heard a faint sound. A metallic scrape and jingle. I moved forward until I could see.

I turned to Harry. 'There's one of your Hansom cabs just up the street.'

'Lead on then.'

The driver – *cabbie* Harry called him – turned his face to us as we approached.

'Evening, gents.'

Harry gave him his greeting back and I thought how different he sounded in English. Just like what he was – the squire's son, a gentleman.

After I'd passed our bags up to the cabbie, I heard a thump and the doors at the front of the cab opened for us to get in.

'He's got a lever up there,' Harry told me in Welsh, 'and he won't open the doors to let us out until we've paid him.'

'Not very trusting.'

'That's London for you.'

When we were in and the doors had closed in front of us, a little hatch opened in the roof of the cab. 'Where to, gents?'

Harry gave an address, the cabbie called to his horse and we were off.

'Is that a guest house?' I asked as the horse began to trot.

Harry grinned. 'Not exactly. It's the home of my friend, Augustus Gelyot.'

The smartest house in Cardiganshire would've looked shabby next to the Gelyots' tall, modern house. Everything in it looked as if it'd been invented last week. It was all fresh and new and shiny, from the door knocker to the patterned tiles of the entrance hall and the wallpaper on the way up the stairs.

'I see Mrs Gelyot has embraced the new fashion for turquoise?' Harry said as Gus Gelyot led us up the grand curve of the staircase. He'd come bounding down when we were announced, like a boy let out of school.

'My mother *embrace* a fashion? My dear Harry, she *started* it.'

I studied the wallpaper which was bright in the hissing gaslights. Turquoise. An odd word for an odd colour. Not green or blue but a mixture of both. It made the curling white vine pattern that ran up it seem to stand out, as if it was sculpted instead of painted on.

'Have you dined?' Gus wanted to know.

'No. Nothing since a pie in Bristol,' Harry said, with feeling.

'Then I'll have something brought up and you can tell me what on earth you're doing here.'

We sat in the Gelyots' blue and gold dining room eating curried beef – the first time I'd heard of curry, never mind eaten it – while Harry told Mr Gelyot about our investigations.

In a day of new experiences, sitting in the Gelyots' house felt like the strangest. All the rest were what the newspapers would call *marvels of engineering* – steamers, stations, locomotives. This was somebody's *house*. But it was a different way of living entirely from what I was used to. Bright-as-day gaslights, food from the other side of the world that made your mouth burn, colours I'd never seen before.

Harry, who was used to it all, I suppose, ignored our surroundings after his comment about the wallpaper. He was too busy telling Gus how things stood at home. 'My father,' he said eventually, 'is keen to point out my insolvency but less keen to ameliorate it.'

Gus Gelyot's eyes moved from Harry to me. They'd been doing that since we arrived. He wanted to know what I was doing there.

'Harry, might this be an appropriate moment to have Mr Davies shown to his quarters?'

'What, so he can lay out my clothes for the morning?' Harry's voice was suddenly sharp, as if Gus Gelyot had insulted me. 'He isn't my valet, Gus, he's my assistant in this investigation. And, I may say, my friend.'

Gus's eyes were on me again. 'Be that as it may,' he said, 'I'm sure he would be more comfortable if certain things were left unsaid in his presence.' He wanted me to do the right thing and save Harry from himself.

But Harry wasn't having it. 'If you think John is going to be shocked at the idea that I have no money and am going to ask you to lend me some, then you're wrong.'

Gus Gelyot was still looking at me. Nervous now, I shrugged slightly. *You know what Harry's like, he won't be told.* He turned away. I'd disappointed him.

'P-L, do you not see what an invidious position you put Mr Davies in by having these discussions in his presence?'

'Invidious? Hardly. It's *I* that am at a disadvantage, here, not John.'

'Oh, for the love of God!' Gus Gelyot rolled his eyes. 'What disadvantage? This boy has no power over you at all.'

'Except the power to tell the world that I had to beg for money.'

'Oh, and that would result in the good burghers of Cardiganshire being better informed than they find themselves, now, would it? Don't be ludicrous, P-L, they already know that you've fallen out with your father and are living in a rented room – it would hardly startle anybody that he's not funding your eccentricity!'

Harry turned his face to me and drew a steady breath. 'Do you feel that I'm acting unfairly towards you, John?' I could tell he was trying to meet my eye but he missed by about a foot.

'Don't ask *him*!' Gus Gelyot was almost shouting, now. 'He's the last person who can give you an honest answer!'

'On the contrary – he's the *only* person!'

'Harry, you're a fool. The world won't alter to suit you, however much you want it to.'

The silence that followed Mr Gelyot's words was filled with nothing but the gas lamps' hiss. You forgot they made a noise until there was a silence, then they seemed overly loud and you wondered how people stood it. Not to mention the smell of them.

'Am I not allowed to order my own life in the way I wish, Gus?'

'No. Because the ordering of your life impinges on the way others are obliged to order theirs.'

I could see they weren't going to agree. If Harry needed to borrow money to finish our investigation, it would be best if they didn't argue any more. I stood up.

'The ordering of disparate lives notwithstanding,' I said, using the best English I knew, 'it's been a very tiring day or two. We've been conveyed hundreds of miles by diverse means and, though I know none of that is new to Harry' – I might be falling in with Gus Gelyot's wishes to keep the peace but, by God, I was going to call him Harry! – 'it's all new and strange to me and I'm falling asleep where I sit. If you could ask somebody to show me where I'm to sleep, Mr Gelyot, I'd be grateful.'

If Harry thought I was taking the coward's way out then he could tell me to my face tomorrow. We could have an argument about it, then, if he liked. As equals, seeing as that seemed to be what he thought we were.

Mr Gelyot turned to the footman standing in the corner of the dining room. But before he could speak, Harry was on his feet.

'Don't even think about putting him in the servants' quarters, Gus. Please.'

Gus didn't look around at his friend. He glanced at me without changing his expression then said, 'Fred, please see Mr Davies to the room you put Mr Probert-Lloyd's bags in. And ask a maid to make up the room next to it for Mr Probert-Lloyd. You can fetch Mr Davies's bags down while you're at it.'

Harry

I was glad to put the city behind us. Everything about it – the sounds of Paddington Station, the familiar tang of the Particular in my throat, the Cockney tones of the cabbie, even my argument with Gus – had been a painful reminder of my former life. Gus's house, so familiar despite his mother's constant changing of furnishings and decoration, had almost undone me. Once, I had imagined that the life of a barrister would allow me to own such a house, to live in it with a family of my own. No more.

Did Gus understand the jumble of emotions that had led to my outburst? I doubted it; he had been too taken up with what he saw as my eccentric attitude towards John. But what choice did I have, now, but to embrace what he saw as eccentricity? I had to fashion a new life for myself and, though it might be lived out beneath my father's roof, I was damned if it was going to be lived after my father's example.

From Bishopsgate station we travelled on the Eastern Counties railway to Colchester and, from there, on an Eastern Union train to our final destination. The fares were steep – had I not persuaded Gus to lend me some money John and I would have found ourselves without the means to get home and I tried not to think about how I would live if our investigation went on much longer.

Once we were out of the railway station – which was, like all railway stations, grimy, sooty and laden with coal dust – Ipswich had a different smell from London or even Bristol or Carmarthen. Perhaps it had to do with the stiff easterly breeze that was blowing from the North Sea, but there was an unfamiliar flavour to the air.

John asked the way to the Unitarian chapel and was given directions over a bridge into the middle of the town.

'How far is it?' he asked.

''Bout ten minutes.'

Ten minutes if you knew the way, perhaps. Half an hour later, after stopping twice more to ask which street we should follow, we found ourselves in front of a large building which stood, from what I could make out, on the far side of its own graveyard.

'This is his chapel,' John said. 'What now?'

'Let's see if he's here.'

A brief reconnaissance revealed neither minister nor any other person.

'His house can't be far away, I'll ask.'

I stood aside while John knocked at a door close to the chapel and asked whoever had appeared if they might be able to tell him where the Reverend Nathaniel Howell lived.

'Who?' a female voice asked.

'The Reverend Howell. The minister at the Unitarian chapel.'

'That's Reverend Mudge.'

'Oh. I see. Well, could you tell me where he lives, please?'

Brief directions were given and I saw the door close as John came down the steps towards me. 'This way,' he said and picked up the bags which he had left at my side.

'Did you hear?' he asked. 'She said the minister's called Mudge, not Howell.'

'Yes, I heard.'

'Do you think this Reverend Mudge will know where he's gone?'

'I sincerely hope so.' I also sincerely hoped that Nathaniel Howell's absence did not presage a dead end; in either sense.

We walked no more than two minutes before John said, 'Here we are. This is what she said – black painted railings, blue door with an oval window over.'

We both approached the door and John gave the knocker a couple of good raps. A short while later the door opened and I heard a woman's voice say, 'Yes? Can I help you?'

The local accent was very different from London. Oddly, it resembled the speech of Bristolians more than anything that was to be heard around the capital.

'We'd like to speak to the Reverend Mudge, please,' John told her.

'Master's away. Won' be back till 'omorrow.'

I felt my spirits plummet.

'Your mistress, then?' John extemporised.

'Gone with 'im.'

I stepped forward and looked up the steps to where the servant stood. 'We were actually hoping to speak to the Reverend Mudge about his predecessor, the Reverend Howell.'

'The minister who was here before the Reverend Mudge,' John explained, presumably having inferred from her expression that she did not know what a predecessor was.

'I've not bin 'ere long. I'll fetch th'housekeeper, Mrs Spicer.' I discerned that she had turned to go when I heard her speak again. 'Wai' there, if y'please.'

'Not been here long and not been trained very well as yet,' I said, acutely aware that, had it not been for my blindness, John and I would simply have exchanged a knowing look. Words felt clumsy in comparison.

A minute or so later a figure appeared in the doorway. 'Good afternoon, gentlemen. I am Mrs Spicer, Reverend and Mrs Mudge's housekeeper. How may I help you?'

'Mrs Spicer,' John said, 'my employer and I have come all the way from Cardiganshire in South Wales because we were told that the Reverend Nathaniel Howell was minister here.'

'I see,' the woman replied. 'You've waited a while to pay him a visit – it was years ago that poor Reverend Howell was due to come to us.'

Poor Reverend Howell. I did not like the sound of that. 'It's become necessary to speak to him, urgently,' I said.

'Well, I'm afraid you've had a wasted journey. The Reverend Howell died before he could get to us.'

'Died?' John and I spoke almost simultaneously.

'Yes. Took ill on the journey. Never was strong, according to Miss Howell – that's his sister.'

The sister with whom he had envisaged ending his days; sooner rather than later according to Ezra Lloyd. 'Where can we find Miss Howell?' I interrupted.

'If you had let me finish, sir,' she said, in mild reproach, 'I would have told you. Miss Howell lives here. She's governess to the Reverend Mudge's children.' Mrs Spicer allowed a small but pointed silence to form. Teaching me manners. 'If you'd like to speak to her, perhaps you'd be so good as to step inside?'

Chastened, I allowed her to show us into the drawing room. It was chilly, presumably because the master and mistress of the house were away and the fire had not been lit.

'I'll tell Miss Howell you're here,' the housekeeper said. 'Who shall I say is calling?'

'Mr John Davies and Mr Henry Lloyd,' I said.

The housekeeper closed the door behind her. Neither of us sat down.

'Henry Lloyd?' John asked.

'We don't know what Howell told her. I don't want Miss Howell taking a fit of the vapours and refusing to see us.'

'D'you think she'll know anything?' John asked.

I took in the stillness of him at the edge of my vision. Of course, this could not possibly matter to him in the same way that it mattered to me. 'We'll soon see.'

'Why didn't she write to the elders at Treforgan to tell them her brother was dead?' he wondered. 'They'd've wanted to know, wouldn't they?'

'No doubt she'll tell us.'

I tried to form an impression of the room but, aside from the fact that the wallpaper was green, the windows were small and the chairs and sofa were upholstered in yellow, I could make out very little with any accuracy. A piano stood in the corner but its lid was down as if it was played infrequently.

The door opened behind me and, before I could turn, a voice spoke.

'*Prynhawn da, boneddigion.* Or is it good afternoon, gentlemen?'

That voice! The shock hit me like a wide-armed slap and I spun around. 'Nathaniel Howell!'

'Harry!' John's voice sliced through the air between me and the person who had just entered the room. 'This is *Miss* Howell.'

The begowned person who had greeted us, however, said nothing and my thoughts raced. Middling height, stocky. Padding could easily flesh out a womanly form. And Nathaniel Howell's Rebecca had worn women's clothes with a nonchalance none of the rest of us could muster. I had only ever seen him at night, his face blacked, so I could not speak of the condition of his beard but I imagined that a great deal might be done with a keen razor and women's powder.

Though bodies are easily disguised, voices are generally harder to change; but Howell's voice, a light tenor in a man, needed no alteration to become the low contralto of a well-built woman. 'Nathaniel Howell,' I repeated.

I heard a sigh. 'Henry Probert-Lloyd. The last time we met, we were *both* in women's clothing.'

I said nothing and the sigh came again. 'Please, sit down. I'll ring for some tea.'

While we waited for our refreshments, I decided to make my blindness clear.

'Perhaps you'll allow me to explain why I can't look you in the eye.' I spoke in Welsh though Howell had not. I did not want him to be able to hide behind the careful diction of English; I wanted him speaking the language of Rebecca.

A brief explanation of my condition concluded, I saw Howell nod. 'That's how you recognised me. You weren't confused by my appearance.'

I schooled myself not to smile at his replying in Welsh. 'At last,' I said, 'an advantage to blindness.'

My quip was greeted with silence. Good. I could turn his embarrassment to my own advantage; embarrassment can be led by the nose to garrulousness if it is managed correctly.

'Why disguise yourself as a woman?' I asked. 'For the same reason that you didn't want the congregation at Treforgan writing to you – because you were afraid?'

Before Howell could reply, John spoke, his tone careful as if he was speaking to me but looking at the other man. 'Harry, I'm afraid you've made a mistake.'

'How so?'

John did not reply straight away and I wondered what kind of look was passing between him and Howell.

'What Mr Davies means, Mr Probert-Lloyd, is that though your hearing has correctly identified me as the person you knew as Nathaniel Howell, you are mistaken in assuming that I have disguised myself as a woman.'

I turned my head so that he appeared at the edge of my vision. He was clearly dressed in women's clothing.

'*Nathaniel* was the disguise. My real name is Lydia.'

So, then, it all came out. The whole history of how Lydia Howell had become Nathaniel. Children of the manse, she and her brother had been orphaned when Lydia was twenty and he twenty-two.

'When our father died,' she said, 'Nathaniel had already completed his ministerial training and been asked to come and preach at Treforgan with a view to becoming minister there. We were travelling down together – with Father gone, we'd intended that I would go to Treforgan with my brother as his housekeeper. I wanted to see the house and what it would need. Then, on the way, Nathaniel fell ill with a fever and died at Milford Haven.'

She stopped but I had the impression that it was out of respect for her brother's memory rather than from any remaining grief.

'He'd always been delicate. Not like me.' I heard the smile in her tone and tried to see Nathaniel Howell as a woman. I remembered a square face with a definite nose. Not a feminine face but one with character. And shrewdness.

'My brother's death left me alone in the world with no obvious means of supporting myself. I was as educated as he had been and I'd always been more interested in the finer points of theology. He'd followed our father into the ministry as a dutiful son but he didn't feel half the passion for the calling that I did. He knew that, and we both knew that I'd be writing his sermons for him. I'd already written the one for his preaching visit to Treforgan before he died. '

I was finding it difficult to reconcile the voice I could hear with what it was telling me. It was Nathaniel Howell's voice and yet it belonged to a woman. I tried my utmost to get a proper impression of Miss Howell but I could see nothing beyond a face framed with brown hair. What had Nathaniel Howell looked like under his soot black? I remembered a wolfish smile but any smile will appear outsized in a face blackened to the hairline. I had never seen the minister in ordinary clothes, only as a carrier of the *ceffyl pren* and a Rebecca. And disguise always lends a menacing cast to any figure.

'But how did nobody guess?' John blurted.

There was a shrug in Lydia's voice. 'People see what they want to see. They saw a preacher – and preachers are men, aren't they? Even if they don't grow much of a beard.' She paused. 'I was careful to make it clear, from the beginning, that I was called to the celibate life and wouldn't be looking for a wife, so there wasn't too much pushing of daughters at me.'

'But, servants and so on…' John clearly had the more intimate aspects of life in mind.

I heard the suggestion of a wry smile in Miss Howell's reply. 'I didn't employ a housekeeper – there would have been things no woman living in could fail to have noticed – but I had Naomi and Peter Williams's deaf-mute daughter in every day as maid-of-all-work.

She was grateful to be out of their house and she wasn't able to blurt out any secrets.'

'Were you not afraid of being found out?' I asked.

Lydia Howell drew in a breath. 'Never *afraid*, Mr Probert-Lloyd. Not until...' she stopped, redirected herself. 'Before Rebecca, there were times when I relished the thought of being discovered, of watching all those pompous elders realise that the sermons they'd praised to the skies, the wisdom they congratulated themselves on discerning in me, despite my youth, had all come from a woman. A weaker vessel, incapable of abstract thought.'

'So why did you revert to your real identity when you came here?'

She hesitated; she had not been required to articulate this before. 'In the end, I discovered that it's only possible to be somebody else for just so long. I was weary with vigilance. I wanted to be myself again.'

Her words produced a moment of strange fellow feeling as I realised that I longed to be myself again, too. This blind person was not me and I did not know how to be comfortable as him. Like Lydia Howell, I was tired of the eternal vigilance required by my changed state. 'But it wasn't *just* a wish to be a woman again, was it?' I asked. 'Your preaching had got you into trouble – or, at least, the *result* of your preaching. You were running away. And, if Nathaniel Howell had died, then he was nowhere to be found. Not by anybody. Even Rebecca.'

Without warning, she was on her feet and moving across the room to the window. At one and the same time I found myself taken aback at the suddenness of her movement and aware that, had she been a man, it would have been less worthy of comment. Men act; ladies remain composed.

I had read Mary Wollstonecraft's views on the education of women and I wondered whether Lydia's father had, too. What must it have been like for Lydia in dead Nathaniel's clothes, able to put to use the learning she possessed, to act as she saw fit and not as her gender dictated?

'Is that why you're here,' she asked, keeping her face to the window. 'Because of Rebecca?'

'We're here because Margaret Jones was murdered.'

She turned then. 'Margaret Jones – William Williams's dairymaid?'

'Yes.' Briefly, I outlined the finding of Margaret's remains, the farcical inquest verdict, and our subsequent investigation.

'And what do you want to know from me?' She had returned to looking out of the window but her voice seemed distant, as if part of her – the part that had been most Nathaniel, perhaps – was, once more, back in Treforgan.

I spoke carefully. 'Well, we know, obviously, about the Rebecca band that you led.'

She made no response.

'It caused opposition, didn't it – your crusade?'

Still she said nothing and, as the silence lengthened, it became clear that she did not intend to.

'Is that why you left in such a hurry?' I persisted. 'Because those who opposed you were threatening you with harm?'

'I was a fool,' she said, her voice still somewhat distant. 'I embraced Rebecca with the zeal of an innocent. Not that I blame myself for that, many people saw Rebecca as a force for good at the beginning – finally, it seemed, we had discovered a way of standing against injustice for ourselves.'

I heard my father's voice in my head. *The lower orders are not fit to*

*wield power – they are not bred to it and do not understand the limits
that must be put on it.*

'So you embraced Rebecca?' I prompted. 'Then what?'

'I had ridden out with the *ceffyl pren*,' she said, slowly, 'and I
thought that riding under Rebecca's banner would be the same, only
with greater moral purpose. And so it was, to start with.'

She faltered again and I wondered what she was seeing in her
mind's eye.

'Almost every man from Treforgan rode with me – and with no
coercion on my part. I didn't want anybody to be able to say that I'd
used my position to force him into breaking the law. But then...' She
sighed. 'Rebecca excited men. Particularly young men. Being able to
do what they wanted while the special constables and militias ran
around looking for them went to their heads. I began to notice other
men joining our band. Men who weren't from Treforgan.' She stopped.
Was she looking for a response from me? I opened my mouth to ask
who these men were but, before I could speak, she went on.

'At first, I was pleased – I made the mistake of thinking they were
all there as staunch opponents of the Poor Law.' She made a sound
of self-derision.

'I soon realised my mistake. I should have known that some men
– not all, but some – would use Beca for their own private reasons.'

'So why didn't you stop them?' John's tone was belligerent; had I
not known that he was far too young I would have suspected him of
being on the receiving end of what Lydia Howell was describing.

'I thought I had. I told the men of Treforgan that I didn't want
anybody but them – my own flock – riding out with us. And I
prevailed. Our band shrank back to members of our own
congregation.'

'But another band formed, didn't it?' I asked. 'A band that wanted revenge on women.'

Lydia moved away from the window but did not resume her seat. Instead, she went to stand in front of the fireplace, as if the unlit grate could warm her.

'They said that some girls were threatening men with a visit from Rebecca. That they'd forgotten their place. That they needed teaching a lesson.'

'And was one of those girls Margaret Jones?' I asked.

Did Lydia Howell nod? Shake her head? Shrug? John's voice broke into her silence.

'Miss Howell, can I remind you that Mr Probert-Lloyd can't see? You need to give him an answer.'

I saw her turn but, if a look passed between them, it stayed between them. 'Margaret Jones came to see me,' she said. 'In great fear.'

'Fear for her life?'

'Fear of harm, certainly. From the men I'm talking about.'

'Because she had been free with her favours?' I asked. It was all I could do to articulate the phrase.

'Because the rumour had been *spread* that she had been free with her favours,' Lydia Howell corrected. 'William Williams's other outdoor maidservant had overheard a conversation between two young men that she relayed to Margaret. One had been telling the other that he should be careful or Margaret would try and father her child on to him. He protested that she couldn't – he'd had no carnal knowledge of her. But, according to the servant, the other man said something to the effect that it would make no difference – she'd been intimate with so many men that no one would believe he was innocent.'

'Did she say who these young men were?' I asked.

Her failure to answer immediately brought a sound of impatience from John. 'Who are you protecting, Miss Howell?'

'Myself, Mr Davies. I left Treforgan to escape these men. I don't want them coming after me now.'

'Why should they?'

'For the same reason that they threatened me then. I'd made fools of them.' When neither John nor I replied she was forced to explain what she meant. 'They discovered that I was a woman,' she said. 'From that moment on, I was in grave danger.'

As she told us the story of how her secret had come to be discovered, it became clear that Lydia Howell had had no choice but to leave Treforgan.

'I soon realised that cutting men out of our band – sending them away – had been a mistake. While they rode with us, I'd been able to exert some control over them. Once they were free of me, there was no brake on their activities.'

I wanted to press her for details but instinct told me to hold back, to wait.

'At first,' she continued, 'they went after girls who were known to tempt men in the hope of getting favours or gifts, you know—'

I did. My father had suspected Margaret of being exactly that sort of girl and Davy Thomas had implied it.

'But, soon, they started on other women who'd offended one of them in some way. Landladies who refused to have habitual drunks in their houses, sour wives, women who'd rejected suitors.' I heard her take a breath, as if she was panting through her story. 'I tried to stop them. I preached against them and explicitly said that if anybody knew of their actions, they should report them to the magistrates.'

Another mistake. The men who rode with Rebecca hated informers above any other class of person.

'That was foolish, of course,' she admitted. 'Words – preaching – had been my weapon once, but I'd shown them the power of taking action and men were not disposed to listen to words any more. After that sermon, one of my congregation came to me and told me as much.' She paused for a moment. 'He also told me that I should not worry too much, that no real harm would come to any individual. He would see to that, he said.'

'How?' John asked.

'He rode with them.' Lydia said, simply. 'Though I'd excluded men outside my congregation from our band, I hadn't tried to forbid Treforgan men from riding with any other. I couldn't have done – I knew that some rode to gatebreakings – but I didn't expect any of my own to continue harassing young women.' She paused momentarily, then said, 'He led me to believe that he rode with the other band so as to rein in the hotheads amongst them.'

At the edge of my vision, I saw her turn back to the cold fireplace as if she could not bear to look at me.

'He wasn't very successful, was he?' I asked.

'On the contrary,' she said, her voice quiet, 'until you came here, today, I had reason to believe that he wielded a good deal of influence over the band.'

'Because there were no reports of violence?' I asked.

She did not reply straight away, nor did she turn around. 'No,' she said eventually, 'because he stopped them violating me when they discovered my true gender.'

Surprisingly, as if that shocking statement had freed her from some constraint, she turned and came to sit down once more. She did not speak again immediately but, discerning a degree of purposefulness in the way she had returned to the sofa, I did not press her.

'It was after I preached the sermon against revenge and intimidation,' she began again after a minute or so. 'He warned me to expect a visit from Rebecca. Telling my congregation to go to the magistrates if they knew that girls were being harried had incurred the Lady's displeasure.'

'What did you do?'

'What could I do? Nothing. I simply waited.'

'They came,' she said, 'two days after he'd given me the warning. At some time just before midnight – late, anyway.'

It had been late of necessity; the time she was speaking of had been barely a month before high summer when full dark is a long time coming.

'I don't know what they'd expected – the doors barred, some of my congregation there with me, perhaps. Or simply that I'd take steps to arm myself. They clearly had not expected me to open the door to them and stand there, unprotected.'

I caught a movement which might have been her clasping her hands in her lap. I tried to remember what her hands looked like – what, I should say, Nathaniel Howell's hands had looked like. I did not recall thinking them especially effeminate and I wondered how they looked in the lap of a woman.

'What they could not know – what, I believe, no one can understand unless they have experienced the same thing – is how protected I felt by my masculine dress. Over the few years I had lived at Treforgan, it had become my armour, my defence against the world. No one looked beyond it to see Lydia. The clothes *were* Nathaniel –

they gave legitimacy to my preaching, to my authority at chapel, to my very conversation. You can have no idea, you men, how much more attention is paid to the words of a man than to those of a woman. If I had spoken as Lydia, no one would have given my words the slightest credence. But because I was Nathaniel, my words were heeded. More than heeded – they were hung upon, Mr Probert-Lloyd. People hung upon my words!'

Did her vehemence indicate how much she felt she had lost in becoming Lydia once more? Did she regret her reversion to womanly form?

'So you stood before them,' I said, 'unprotected and unarmed. Weren't you afraid at all? You must have been aware that other Rebecca bands had manhandled clergy – beaten them even?'

'Yes, but those were Anglican clergymen. What with tithes and the restrictions placed on dissenters, Rebecca had no love for the church of England. But there'd been no violence offered to any chapel ministers.'

'Because, by and large, they stood shoulder to shoulder with Rebecca,' I pointed out. 'But you had stood against her. Or, at least, against some of her actions.'

'Yes.' The word was flat, uninflected. 'And I was foolish enough to continue to do so, even as they stood on my doorstep.'

I shivered, suddenly chilly in the unheated room. The very notion of those men standing there, silent and soot-blacked, their faces ghastly in the torchlight, was like icy feet walking over my grave.

'I told them that they brought dishonour on the name of Rebecca, that they encouraged the magistrates in their belief that we Welshmen were not fit to manage our own affairs, that they'd allowed their own personal grievances to overturn what should have been a proper concern for the good of the whole community.

'And that's when the hissing started.' Her voice dropped away as she spoke the sentence, as if she could barely bring herself to articulate it. 'As I spoke, one man began to hiss. Faces turned away from me, to him. And, when they looked back at me, they were hissing, too.'

From the tone of her voice, I could tell that she was seeing the scene she described in her mind's eye.

'That hissing—' she faltered, 'it's hard to explain its effect on me. Here was a group of men – some of whom I knew – who had turned into something I didn't recognise.

'Disguise has a profound effect,' she went on. 'I saw it every time we went out – the blacking of faces, the putting-on of clothes not your own – it masks who you are. It allows you to do things you'd never do undisguised. And, of course, it was dark…'

I heard her composure waver, waited for her to collect herself. When she resumed, her voice was firm once more.

'They may have looked like women in their aprons and tall hats but they sounded like a pack of wild animals. Worse than wild animals – wild *men*, men detached from all civilising influence. It was utterly chilling. Then one of them stepped forward. '*You must be taught a lesson,*' he said, '*you must ride the ceffyl pren.*'

In the silence of the room, I heard her swallow.

'They brought it up then – the *ceffyl pren*. There was no head, no sheet. It was just a pole.

'I watched them as they came up with it—' She broke off but my mind's eye was able to flesh out the scene from what I had observed when she and her own congregation had brought the *ceffyl pren* to William Williams. Half a dozen men would have approached the person they knew as Nathaniel Howell – two holding the wooden horse between them, two quickly moving behind him to stop him

306

from retreating into his house, two to manhandle him onto the torturously thin pole.

'If I had allowed them to lay hands on me and put me on the pole, all might have been well.' Lydia's voice was firm, once more, as if she had made up her mind to what she must say. 'But I didn't. Something in me – some propriety that I thought I'd overcome, some fear or outrage – would not allow it. So I fought them.'

I could see the scene, all too easily. The men, tense with that peculiar kind of anxious exhilaration that Rebecca's illegal sorties brought, would have welcomed Howell's resistance as an opportunity for violence.

'It was a stupid thing to do. There were too many of them. Of course they'd prevail. But my resistance wasn't rational. A punch stunned me and I was barely aware of what happened next. Two of them lifted me up but another stopped them, made some disparaging remarks about my manhood – told them to take my trousers off me so they could see what a celibate –' she hesitated momentarily '– organ looked like.'

I could almost smell the animal scent on the air which the brief outbreak of violence would have caused. The urgent need to humiliate, to gaze and to mock. And voices echoed in my head.

Get his drawers off, let's see what the little Welsh maid has between his legs. Let's see if he's as much of a girl below as he is in his pretty little face!

'I could do nothing,' Lydia said. 'I had no strength in my limbs to resist them.' She broke off and, for once, I was glad I could not see her. I had no wish to be a witness to such mortification as she must be feeling and I hoped John was showing sufficient decency to keep his eyes elsewhere.

'At first,' she said, her voice curiously flat, 'I believe they thought

I'd been mutilated. That I was a man despite the evidence of their own eyes. Then one of them—' she broke off again and I knew she would not continue. Even a woman who had lived as a man for several years could not be expected to speak of an action which ascertained that she was, in fact, female.

'Once they understood that I was a woman, pandemonium ensued.'

Pandemonium indeed – not least the demon of lust, I imagined.

'I'd always known that, if I were to be discovered, there would be anger and disgust – revulsion, even. But I hadn't anticipated their hatred. Their need for revenge, for punishment.'

Punishment for impersonating a man. I saw her covering her face with her hands. There could only be one punishment when she was lying there, stripped of the trousers that had conferred masculinity, her true sex revealed. Rape must have leapt into the loins of more than one man. A woman! And a woman who had preached at them – a woman whose preaching they had listened to, obeyed! A woman who had claimed power over them.

She drew in a deep breath and was mistress of her own emotions once more.

'But they were prevented from—' John stopped, the question clear enough.

'Yes. By the man I spoke of earlier.'

An uncomfortable silence developed as we waited to see whether she would name him. When it became obvious that she would not, I asked, 'And who was he, this man?'

'Isaac Morgan.' Her voice was steady again and I wondered at her fortitude.

'Was he one of your congregation?' John asked.

'Yes, an elder, though he comes from some distance away. From the hills up towards Hermon. He'd argued with his own minister about the Holy Spirit and, when he heard that I was a Unitarian, he came to Treforgan.'

The ease with which Lydia Howell slipped from the most horrifying recollections to an acknowledgement of lay disagreements on points of theology was extraordinary; a demonstration of the strength of character she had needed in her life as Nathaniel.

'He called them to heel. Told them that I'd be no further trouble. Told them to go. He was the last to leave.' She hesitated. 'Just before he went, he came to me. "Do not think you can preach another Sunday," he said. "If you're still here on the Sabbath, I will not stop them."'

John

I'd thought Gus Gelyot's money meant I wouldn't have to share a bed with Harry again but I was proved wrong. Maybe he hadn't asked Gus for enough. Or maybe he was just taking care of what he'd borrowed. Either way, one bed was all he paid for in Ipswich that night. Granted, it was a better bed than last time, and we didn't get bitten. But that wasn't much comfort in the middle of a sleepless night.

Carrying our luggage about the place had left me stiff and sore. And, on top of that, I was lying on a lump in the mattress. I could've sat up and punched it out but then Harry'd have known I was awake and he'd have started talking. And I didn't want to talk. Especially not about what Lydia Howell had told him as we were drinking our second pot of tea. The look on his face had been pure shock and I didn't want to have to pretend I hadn't seen it.

Lydia Howell. *Nathaniel* Howell. I'd never clapped eyes on so-called Reverend Howell so I didn't know what kind of a man Lydia'd made. But it was hard to imagine. Not that she was a beauty – too thick through the body and square in the face for that. But there was no question that she was a woman. If Harry'd been able to see, he'd never have made the mistake he did. But then, who'd guessed the truth, sitting in the chapel at Treforgan?

Lydia was right: people accept what you tell them. When I'd turned up on Mr Davies's schoolhouse doorstep he hadn't questioned the information I'd offered. I told him I was from Cynwyl Elfed, that my parents were dead, that I could read and write, and I wanted to learn.

310

I'd chosen to ignore the previous six months. To pretend they'd never happened. And Mr Davies never found reason to doubt me.

I would've been very glad if I could've pretended to *myself* that they'd never happened. That I hadn't seen what I saw in the Alltddu. That I hadn't run away, back to Cynwyl Elfed, in terror. That I hadn't got back to our farm to find my parents and sister dead. All of them. Dead.

'Lucky you weren't here, boy,' one of our neighbours told me when I turned up, 'else you'd be dead of the typhoid, too, for sure'. Maybe he was right. But luck hadn't saved me from the Alltddu had it? Luck would've given my fate to somebody else. Another messenger would've taken the note to Waungilfach that day, not me. A different pair of eyes would've seen what I'd seen. Somebody else would've been tormented with nightmares.

Those nightmares. At least that was one good thing about being sleepless – no chance I'd wake up shaking and panting in terror. How would I have explained that to Harry?

I listened for his breathing. It was quiet. Too quiet for somebody who was asleep. He must be thinking about what Lydia'd told us. The truth about Margaret Jones and her child.

After she'd told us how her disguise came to be discovered, Lydia Howell had gone to fetch more tea and Harry leaned back on the sofa, shaking his head.

'I'm sitting here, listening to Nathaniel Howell's voice but the person speaking is wearing a woman's clothes – even I can see that. I can't put the two together, John. Tell me what she looks like.'

I stared at him. His eyes were on an angle to see me but I knew he couldn't tell that I was looking at him. 'She's… well, she's not slim, but not fat either.' She had none of that soft roundness that fat women have. 'She's... solid, I suppose you'd say.'

'And her face?'

'Not one that would stop you in the street – not either way. Pleasant enough.' I sighed, frustrated with myself. 'Quite a mannish chin, I suppose. And a big mouth.' Generous, I should have said, but big was the truth.

'Eye colour? Hair?'

'Eyes? Not sure. Greyish, I think. And her hair's a kind of light brown. Not properly fair, no red in it, it's like...' I tried to think of a good comparison. 'The colour of a mouse, I suppose.' But that gave him a false impression – small, scurrying, anxious. I tried again. 'Or like oat straw.'

The door opened and Lydia Howell came back in with a fresh pot of tea. If she wondered what was like oat straw, she didn't ask.

After the story she'd just told us, I thought Harry'd treat her a bit more gently. But no, he was straight back to the questioning. Perhaps he felt she'd made a fool of him as much as the other Rebeccas.

'You said Margaret Jones came to see you in fear of her life, Miss Howell. When was that?'

Lydia kept her eyes on the tea she was pouring. 'Unfortunately, it was the day after I'd been discovered and I was—' she made a sound halfway between a cough and a laugh. 'I was going to say I wasn't myself but I didn't know who or what I was after Beca's visit. I'd been Nathaniel for so long... I *wanted* to be Lydia again but I'd almost forgotten how.'

She met my eye. I knew she was only looking at me because Harry couldn't see her but it still made me feel important.

'You might imagine that, on my own in the evening, I became

Lydia again. But I didn't. I was Nathaniel morning, noon and night. I wore his clothes. I read his books. I even used his razor on my face though all I got for that was sore skin.'

She stopped and looked from Harry to me.

'In as many respects as I was able, I *was* Nathaniel. Being discovered left me no choice but to flee but I didn't know whether I should leave as Nathaniel or as Lydia.' She stopped, took a steadying breath. 'It was only Margaret Jones's own agitation that prevented her from seeing that something was badly wrong.' She glanced at me. 'She'd received a visit the night before, too. In fact, I believe they must have gone on to Waungilfach from the manse. Given the state they were in, it's a wonder they didn't do the poor girl some injury. As it was, they'd frightened the wits out of her.'

I glanced at Harry; he was sitting very still. 'What did she say?' I asked. 'What did they do to her to make her so afraid?'

'They told her that she must stop accusing different men of being the father of her child. Or else they'd come and see to it that she wasn't capable of making trouble anymore.'

'They threatened to kill her?' Harry interrupted. 'In so many words?'

'No. In just the words I've told you.'

'And what did she want you to do?' he asked.

'To begin with, she wanted to tell me it wasn't true. She said she'd never accused *any* man of being the father of her child apart from the man whose child she knew it to be. She hadn't attended chapel for weeks,' Lydia explained. 'She didn't know that rumours had been growing like mushrooms at Treforgan.'

'She denied having been intimate with more than one man?' Harry asked. Lydia didn't answer. 'Miss Howell?'

Her eyes moved over to me. 'Mr Davies, perhaps it would be better if I spoke to Mr Probert-Lloyd alone?'

I was halfway to my feet when Harry spoke. 'No.'

Just one word. Like a stone dropped onto a pile of sacks to keep them in place. I sat down. This was Gus Gelyot all over again.

Lydia wasn't going to give up. 'I really think it would be more suitable—'

'No. John will stay and hear whatever it is you've got to tell us. I insist.'

I was curious about what she had to tell him – of course I was – but, at the same time, I wished he'd let me go. There was something between him and Lydia Howell. Secrets. Resentment. I wondered again whether he'd had a visit from her Rebeccas.

'Very well,' Lydia said. 'I'll tell you what Margaret Jones told me.'

I tried to imagine the state Margaret had found Lydia in. Still in breeches and coat. Still Nathaniel. But nervous, agitated. Had she already started packing up to leave? Had there been piles of books tied with string, bundles of papers?

'As I said,' Lydia began, 'the first thing she wanted was to convince me that she had not been free with her favours—'

Harry held up a finger. *Stop.* 'You mentioned that the servant Rachel Ellis – Rachel Evans as she was then – told Margaret that she'd overheard two young men talking about her, about how she'd try and get Rebecca to father her child onto one of them?'

'Yes.'

'Who were they – the two men?'

'One was Matthew Evans – I believe his father was a tenant of yours – and the other was your groom, the one who came with you on the night we visited William Williams. David Thomas.'

When Harry was prepared, he could keep his face from showing any emotion. But sometimes – like now – his face was an open book.

A very simple book. And mine must've looked the same. *The one who came with you on the night we visited William Williams.* Harry'd been one of them. A Rebecca. I stared at him. At the shock on his face.

'Matthew Evans from Tregorlais farm?' he asked.

'Yes.'

'And Rachel said she'd heard him warning David Thomas that Margaret would try and father her child onto him?'

Lydia shook her head. 'No. The other way around. David Thomas was warning Matthew Evans.'

'No. That can't be right.'

'I assure you, that's what she said.'

Harry looked as if he wanted to argue but he got a grip on himself. 'Very well then. What was Matthew's response? According to Rachel.'

'I don't know. I was getting this from Margaret herself, don't forget. I wanted her to tell me only what she felt she had to.' Lydia stopped for a moment and I wondered what she was remembering. 'I could see that Margaret was hurt that David Thomas was saying such things. Refusing to marry her was bad enough but blackening her name in that way seemed unnecessarily cruel.'

'Refusing to marry her?' Harry made it sound like an outlandish suggestion. 'Why should David Thomas marry Margaret?'

'Because he was the father of her child.'

His whole face changed then, as if somebody'd pulled a string and tightened every sinew. 'No, he wasn't! Did Margaret tell you that? It's a lie.'

Lydia glanced at me. If she was asking for help, she was out of luck.

I didn't know what was going on in Harry's head. Or who David Thomas was. Not yet, at any rate.

'I can only tell you what Margaret told me,' she said, 'and I have every reason to believe that she was telling me the absolute truth.'

'And I have every reason to believe that David Thomas told *me* the truth!' Harry almost shouted. 'I asked him outright. He swore to me that he had no carnal knowledge of Margaret.'

Again, Lydia's eyes met mine. I shook my head at her this time.

Honestly, I know nothing more than you do. Less, if anything.

'Mr Probert-Lloyd, I'm afraid I don't find it difficult to believe that David Thomas lied to you. He lied to everybody. If he thought there was something to gain by it, he lied.' Lydia bent her head, as if she was at prayer, or collecting scattered thoughts. 'Soon after he started attending Treforgan,' she said, 'he began courting a young woman. Elias Jenkins's only daughter. His only child.'

She gave those last two words more than their due weight. Making sure Harry understood. The man who married Jenkins's daughter would become his heir. Inherit his tenancy.

'Yes. I know. He told me.'

'But do you know that he told Elizabeth he would be *steward of Glanteifi* when you were squire?'

Harry nodded. 'Of course he'd tell her. That was the understanding between us.'

A sudden shaft of sunlight came through the window and shone straight into his face. He put up a hand to shade his eyes, dazzled.

'You and a groom had an understanding that he would become steward?' Lydia asked, careful now, as if she thought Harry might be unbalanced.

'Miss Howell. David Thomas was an educated man. He was only a groom because my father believed he should prove himself.'

I expected Lydia Howell to object. To say that Glanteifi's tenants would never take a man who'd been a groom seriously. That they'd make a mockery of David Thomas and a bankrupt of Harry. But she didn't.

'I see.'

Her tone made Harry defensive. 'David Thomas wasn't *lying* to Elizabeth Jenkins, Miss Howell. He was telling her what had been agreed between us.' I waited for him to demand evidence of other lies, but he didn't. Just asked a question I didn't understand.

'Did you send a letter – an anonymous letter – to Elias Jenkins warning him not to let his daughter form an attachment to David Thomas?'

Lydia stared at him.

'Well?' Harry demanded, 'Did you?'

Her chin came up. 'Yes. When Margaret came to see me I told her there was nothing I could do, that I had no influence any more, that I was leaving because of it. But, on the journey here, I realised that the facts could speak for themselves, as long as they were not seen to come from me. So I wrote to Elias Jenkins.'

I watched Harry trying to see her, trying to bring her into view in the corner of his eye. What was that anonymous letter to him?

'You said you had every reason to believe that Margaret was telling the *absolute truth*,' his voice was cold, distant. 'What were those reasons?'

Lydia was wary of him now. You could see her listening to every word before it left her mouth. 'She told me things about herself that she would not have divulged unless she had to. Facts which rang true, in the circumstances, in a way which her supposed promiscuity didn't.' She picked up her teacup.

'What facts?' Harry was scornful. 'What did she tell you?'

Lydia put her cup back in the saucer, glanced at me, and took a breath. 'That she was your dead brother's daughter.'

Harry blinked, as if what she'd said had clouded his sight. 'George? Margaret told you she was George's *daughter?*' He couldn't've looked more shocked if she'd pulled out a knife and stabbed him in the guts.

'Yes. She said that was why your father sent you away when Williams told him what was going on between the two of you—'

'What Williams *believed* was going on! The man's a lecherous—'

Harry stopped, caught hold of himself. 'I'm sorry. Please. Carry on.' Lydia looked at me again but I had nothing to say. 'William Williams knew that Margaret was your father's illegitimate grand-daughter,' she said.

'No. My father would never have taken William Williams into his confidence over a matter like that!' Harry sprang to his feet. 'Never!'

'I don't think he necessarily did take him into his confidence. My understanding of the situation was that your father asked Mr Williams to find a place for her in his household and, seeing an obvious resemblance to your brother, William Williams guessed at her identity.'

That seemed to calm Harry down. He still didn't like Williams knowing, but at least he'd only guessed.

'Margaret told me that she'd had no idea who her father was until Williams spoke to her. With you home again, he felt she had to know. So that she could prevent anything – *untoward* from occurring. He was anxious that your father's prohibition might not be sufficient to stop you seeking her out.'

Harry moved towards the window, his back to us, head down.

I turned to Lydia Howell. Silently, she held up an index finger.

318

Say nothing for now. She'd become Nathaniel again, dishing out instructions.

A minute is a short time if you're laughing and joking with friends, but a very long time if a man is standing in front of you, silent with shock. My mouth was dry. I picked up my tea cup and drained it to the leaves.

'So,' Harry's voice was tight, 'David Thomas was the father of *Margaret's* child and my late brother George was *her* father. David Thomas was putting out vile rumours about Margaret which people seem to have found it all too easy to believe and you took it upon yourself to write to Elias Jenkins accusing David of abandoning Margaret. She subsequently disappeared because, as we now know, she had been murdered. Is there anything else?'

I could see that Lydia Howell disliked his tone. I would've, too. 'From what Margaret told me, you found her promiscuity all too easy to believe yourself!'

Harry turned away from the window. 'The evidence was there in front of me!'

'No, Mr Probert-Lloyd. The evidence was there that she had succumbed to *one man*. And that one man was David Thomas!'

'She *claimed* it was David. Why should I believe her word over his?'

Before Lydia could answer him, I forced myself to speak. We needed to get away from all this hearsay and back to actual facts. 'Miss Howell – what did Margaret Jones say when you explained that you couldn't help her? What was she going to do?'

Lydia Howell stared at me. I could see she wanted to slap me for interrupting. She *wanted* an argument with Harry. Wanted to shout at him, lose her temper, tell him exactly what she thought of his hypocrisy in investigating Margaret Jones's death when he'd done

319

nothing to help her while she was still alive. He probably deserved it, but none of that would help me.

'Miss Howell?' I wasn't taking silence for an answer. 'What did Margaret say?'

Lydia Howell gathered herself together. When she spoke, her voice was flat. 'That she was ruined. That she'd be in the workhouse once the child was born. That her life was over. Everybody would believe the rumours and she could not defend herself for fear of what the men from Rebecca would do to her.'

'And what advice did the *Reverend Howell* give her?' I asked.

Lydia Howell stared at her lap as if the word of God was written there. 'I said that the best thing she could do' – her voice shook slightly – 'was to go to Mr Probert-Lloyd, here, and confess everything.' Harry didn't move, didn't speak.

I tried to find some moisture in my dry mouth. 'And what did Margaret Jones say?'

Lydia Howell looked up directly into my eyes. 'She said she would rather die.'

Harry

The countryside between Colchester and London was sufficiently novel and fascinating to keep John's head turned perpetually towards the window of our carriage; either that or – and I acknowledged that this was infinitely more likely – he did not know what to say to me after the previous day's revelations. We had scarcely spoken after leaving Lydia Howell, so wrapped up had I been in the past and its self-recriminations and I had spent a sleepless night alternately reliving my last conversation with Margaret, miserably wishing that she could have told me the truth, and dreading an onslaught of questions from John, wakeful at my side.

Trying for the umpteenth time to quell my tormented conscience, I directed my peripheral vision towards the landscape but could make out little beyond the colours of winter, an impression of trees and fields, scattered buildings of indeterminate purpose. Unlike the majority of my travels which were undertaken over long-familiar routes, here in these eastern flatlands I could not rely on memory to fill in the blurred and barely distinguishable world outside the train. Denied distraction, I was at the mercy of remorse and self-reproach.

Finally, I could keep silent no longer.

'Perhaps I was right all along. Perhaps Margaret did kill herself.'

John gave a perceptible start at my side. 'What makes you say that?' he asked. There was caution in his voice; he was unsure of me, now.

'She had nobody to turn to! Everybody thought she was a slut and, in a few weeks, she'd have been in the workhouse. She had nobody and nothing.' A coldness seized me at my own words. 'What did she have to live for?'

I could hear John drawing in a long breath, giving himself time to think before he answered. 'If she killed herself,' he said, carefully, 'how did she come to be buried like that?'

I had been giving consideration to this. 'I think Williams must have gone looking for her and found her, hanging from a tree. If what Lydia Howell told us about her being George's daughter was true, he'd've been desperate when she went missing. What would he have told my father? So I think he just cut her down and buried her there. Pulled the tree down on top of her. Avoided any awkward questions.'

'That doesn't sound very likely to me,' John said. 'I mean, if you were William Williams and you'd buried her there – would you ask your labourers to chop the tree up?'

'He did tell them not to dig up the roots.'

'But still…'

I was glad of his doubts. I did not want it to be true, did not want Margaret to have despaired.

'What about this David Thomas?' he said, abruptly.

My stomach contracted. 'What about him?'

'If he was the father of Margaret's child but had his eyes on a bigger prize…' he let the implication hang.

I shook my head 'No. David Thomas wasn't the father of her child.'

'How can you be so sure?'

'If we believe Lydia Howell when she says that Margaret wasn't promiscuous, that she only knew one man, then it wasn't David Thomas. He couldn't have been the child's father.'

'Couldn't?'

I knew I had to explain myself to him if we were going to waste no more time on a consideration of Davy as Margaret's killer.

'As you must be aware by now, I had a romantic attachment to Margaret Jones.' I swallowed. 'But I didn't father her child. However, David Thomas believed that I had. And, when I told him that I couldn't be the child's father, he was obviously surprised.' I paused, hoping that John would see what I was implying and spare me the need to be more explicit. But he said nothing.

'What I mean to say is,' I could feel the heat rising beneath my beard, 'if David Thomas had seduced Margaret, he would have known that she was a virgin. He could not possibly have believed that I was the child's father.'

'Perhaps he was faking surprise.' John's voice was subdued, presumably by embarrassment.

My mind flitted back to the moment; to Davy's black face, to the itch of my own skin from my mother's green worsted riding habit. He had been surprised; I had no doubt of that. Even in the dark, the silence with which he had greeted my pronouncement had been one of re-assessment. It is hard to dissemble with silence.

'No. Until I told him otherwise, he'd genuinely believed that I was the child's father.'

'Well somebody's lying! Either it's David Thomas or it's Margaret Jones. Or Lydia Howell, I suppose. Who's your money on?'

When I did not answer, he gave a frustrated sigh. 'You know, I think we've allowed ourselves to fix our eyes too much on Margaret Jones and not enough on Rebecca.'

'Go on.'

'We know now, for certain, that there were two opposing Beca groups dealing with girls in trouble. Howell's and the one made up of men he'd kicked out. And we know that Beca must be involved in Margaret's death somehow. Beca didn't want the inquest. She doesn't want us investigating.'

I nodded. 'True.'

'What if Margaret Jones was killed for some other reason? Nothing to do with the baby?'

'What sort of reason?'

'I don't know,' he admitted. 'But I think we should speak to one of the men who discovered Lydia was a woman and ask.'

'Why should they tell us anything? Nobody's been prepared to give us the time of day so far, why should they suddenly start giving us information that could see them prosecuted?'

'Because, in return for their information, we guarantee that they *won't* be prosecuted.'

'We can't do that. How will we know we're not offering immunity to the murderer himself?'

John was silent. Obviously, he had failed to think of that.

PART 5: UNRAVELLING

John

All the long way back home from Ipswich, I kept hearing the words I'd heard in the Alltddu. Kept hearing the killer's voice. Kept seeing him bending over her, knee in her back.

'This is your fault, Margaret – you've brought this on yourself... All you had to do was one thing. One simple thing. You said you'd do it. You said you had *done it. But you were lying, weren't you? Lying!'*

I was sure those words held the reason for Margaret Jones's death. But I couldn't tell Harry. Not without admitting that I'd been there.

It was clear to me that Margaret Jones had been involved in some kind of Beca plan. That she'd been given something to do and had failed to do it. Worse, that she'd lied and said she *had* done it. Beca was no lover of liars.

Beca had ordered her death, and that's why the inquest jury had been told not to find for murder. The Lady wanted no more questions to be asked.

But what had the plan been? And how had Margaret Jones been involved?

I thought I knew how I could find out. But, first, I had someone to talk to.

'Daniel!'

Daniel James looked around at me as he came out of his employer's office door. 'Oh, it's you.'

Harry and I had come in with the mail early that morning. He'd ridden straight out to Glanteifi and a confrontation with his father and I'd gone to my lodgings for a couple of hours' kip before coming to lie in wait for Daniel.

Jervis and Evans were more modern than Mr Schofield – they shut up shop at midday on a Saturday.

Daniel set off down the street as if he hoped I'd go away. No chance. I fell into step with him. 'I'll buy you a drink.'

'Too right you will. And something to eat. You owe me. It wasn't easy getting that name you wanted. Not easy at all.'

By two o'clock I had the name of a retired groom and an address to go with it. Trouble was, the address was in Rhydyfuwch, just outside Cardigan, a good three hours' walk away. I could do it and be back in time for my landlady's curfew at nine but it would be a stretch. Or I could do what Harry'd do and hire a horse. Not a cheap option, especially when I was already out of pocket after feeding Daniel James.

In the end, it came down to this: I'd spent the last four days travelling in style and I didn't fancy going back to tramping the countryside. I decided that, while I worked for Harry Probert-Lloyd, I was going to play the part. Even if I was still riding about in my clerk's clothes.

By that time, I'd got the hang of controlling a horse and I quite enjoyed the ride to Rhydyfuwch. Not that my arse wasn't sore when I got there, mind, but it was less sore than my feet would've been.

I dismounted outside a little row of cottages and knocked on the first one. A youngish woman opened the door.

'Good afternoon. I'm looking for Edward Philips. Does he live here?'

The look on her face told me she didn't generally get callers with a horse. She didn't know whether to be flustered or afraid. 'Yes, he's inside.'

'I need a few words with him, if he can spare the time.'

'You can have your words and welcome, but I'll warn you – his mind's not what it was. Can't be relied on to remember so much as to take the kettle off the fire and make tea when it's boiling.'

I went cold. I'd just spent all the money I had until Mr Schofield paid me again and this woman was telling me that the man I'd come to see wasn't all there. 'What about his life at Glanteifi,' I asked, 'does he remember that?'

'Oh yes. Can't get him to shut up about that.'

I reached into the small pocket of my waistcoat and pulled out the penny I'd put there earlier. 'Is there somebody who can make sure my horse doesn't wander?'

The old man and I took a short walk to Cardigan common. 'You can't have a private conversation in this house,' Edward Philips had said. 'Too many children.'

I could've wished for somewhere more comfortable. On the common there was no cover against the sly little wind that got between your buttons and I was already cold from the ride over. If I was going to make a habit of riding, I needed a topcoat and riding breeches, not to mention long boots.

Edward Philips settled himself on an old tree stump as if it was a regular sitting place for him. I stood with my hands in my pockets. I wasn't going to sit on the ground and get a wet arse.

'Did my niece tell you I was going soft in the head?'

I didn't want to start off on a sour note. 'Well… not really. She just said your memory wasn't what it used to be.'

His grin was full of gaps. 'That'll do.'

I stared at him.

'It's like this, boy. She's a nice enough woman and she's more than happy to have my pension coming into the house but she's always after me to do things around the place – make the tea, mind the children, kill the pig. Well, I've had enough of work, haven't I? I want a rest before they put me in the ground. So I let her believe my memory's going – that I can't be trusted – and then I'm free to do what I like.'

Cunning old bastard. I told him about Harry's investigation.

'*Duw*, yes. I remember when the girl went. Talk of the parish.'

I decided to take a risk. 'I'll be honest with you, Mr Philips. Harry Probert-Lloyd doesn't know I'm here.'

His eye was almost as beady as Mr Schofield's. 'What is it you want to know, boy?'

Two could be blunt. 'I want to know who David Thomas is.'

His eyebrows shot up. 'David Thomas! There's a name I haven't heard in a month of Sundays!'

The small wind swirling around the common pushed cold air down the back of my neck. I looked down towards the town but couldn't see it clearly. It was a dull day and I wondered if the wetness in the air was hanging on to the smoke from everybody's fires. A tiny version of the London Particular. I hunched further down into my jacket. 'So who is he?' I asked. 'Does he work at Glanteifi?'

Edward Philips narrowed his eyes at me. 'If you're working with young Mr Harry, why don't you ask *him* who David Thomas is?'

'Because every time the name's mentioned, he changes the subject. He doesn't want to talk about him.'

'So you're asking *me* to tell you what Mr Harry wants to keep to himself?'

I looked him in the eye. 'Yes.'

The old man gave a bark of laughter. 'Damn me, you're a cheeky one, aren't you?'

I risked a worried-feeling grin. 'The truth is, Mr Philips, I think we should be talking to this David Thomas. If Harry's protecting him, I want to know why.'

'He's not protecting him.'

'How do you know?'

'Because David Thomas isn't here to speak to, boy. He left for America seven years ago.'

'You're young,' Edward Philips began when he'd relented and agreed to tell me what I wanted to know, 'so perhaps you don't know but Harry Probert-Lloyd never knew his mother – she died in childbirth.' I nodded. Mr Schofield had told me that much. Philips pulled his scarf up around the back of his neck. There was an edge to the wind, now, that felt like rain coming.

'Well, by rights, Henry should have died with her. Came before his time, see. There was no wet nurse waiting, so there was a panic, then, to find a girl who could feed him.' He sniffed and ran his palm up his nose to wipe a drip. 'Well, it happened that a maid had just been turned out of the house for having a child. Had it there, in the servants' attic, she did, and nobody'd've been any the wiser if the child hadn't cried the second he was born. I daresay she was going to do away with the baby and get on with her work as usual. Well, she couldn't, then, could she, not once he'd been seen? So, out she went. But then, when Harry came, they fetched her back, took her on as the wet nurse.'

I stared at him. A disgraced maid brought back to wet nurse the squire's heir? 'There must have been a *proper* wet nurse available, surely?'

The old man looked at me. 'Maybe, maybe not. But there was more to it, you see, with this girl.'

'What sort of more?'

Edward Philips coughed and spat, as if he was clearing his wind for a long story. 'You know Probert-Lloyd the magistrate was married before?' He took a pipe out of his pocket and knocked it on the heel of his boot. I should have brought him some tobacco. 'Well,' he said, eyes on the pipe, 'Mr Probert-Lloyd had a son with his first wife. George, he was called.'

George the father of Margaret...

Philips hesitated. 'Like I said, you're young, you won't have heard all the scandal about young George but he was—' the old man stopped, like a dog that'd reached the end of its chain. 'Put it like this, he had an eye for the ladies.'

'An eye?' I asked, shifting my cold toes in my boots, 'Or some other part of him?'

He gave me his gap-toothed grin again. 'Quite right, boy! Well, one of the girls he'd taken a fancy to was this girl who'd just had the baby. Mari her name was.'

I frowned as I sifted through the implications of what he'd just said. Edward Philips knew what I was thinking.

'No, George wasn't the father of Mari's child. He'd been dead two or three years by the time she was thrown out. Plenty of time for other men to take an interest since he'd been gone. But... Probert-Lloyd the magistrate knew that George had taken her virginity. He might've had her sent home when she had the child but she made sure we all knew she wasn't being sent away without money. Ruin money, it was. Guilt money.'

'So,' I felt my way, 'Mr Probert-Lloyd fetched this Mari back to wet nurse Harry because he felt the family owed her something – because George had seduced her?'

The old man pushed his bottom lip out. 'That's what she told people, at any rate. Then again, p'raps she was the only wet nurse they could find at a minute's notice. But she always said that making her Harry's nurse was the least Mr Probert-Lloyd could do.' Philips looked me in the eye. 'She was fond of telling anybody who'd listen that young George had promised her marriage before he'd gone and broken his neck.'

He spat very accurately at the damp brown stalk of a dock. 'Easy to say when the boy was dead and gone, wasn't it? Lies it was, though. Young George wouldn't've promised marriage to a housemaid any more than he'd have promised it to one of his dogs.' He looked into his cold pipe again. 'Not that he mightn't've said things to lead her on – always had a flattering tongue on him, George Probert did.' He sniffed again and put the pipe away. 'But she couldn't say he'd forced her – everybody in the place knew she'd set her cap at him.'

'Why?' I asked. 'What was in it for her?'

'Being the favourite. Being the only maid in his bed. He was a good-looking boy, George Probert was. All the maids had an eye for him but the rest were cowed by the housekeeper. If they so much as looked at the men in the family they'd feel the lash of her tongue – and probably more than that, too. Known to be free with a nasty little cane she kept in her sitting room, the old housekeeper was.' His eyes looked past me and I knew he was looking into that time before Harry was born. He could probably see that better than he could see me, if the milkiness of his eyes was anything to go by.

'Of course, she went when Mari was brought in as nursemaid –

333

the old housekeeper I'm talking about. Made the mistake of going to Mr Probert-Lloyd and saying she couldn't be in charge of the household when Mari was defying her and mocking her at every turn. Thought he'd send Mari packing. But it was her that went, in the end.

'Don't look at me with your mouth open like a dead fish, boy! It's the truth – not six months after Harry was born, the old housekeeper was gone and Isabel Griffiths had arrived. Still there, she is.'

I shook my head. Perhaps the old man was going soft, after all. 'Mind you,' he said, 'Mari would have it that he'd given her his word – Mr Justice Probert-Lloyd. And, fair play, I don't know that it wasn't the truth. She said he'd promised her that if she could rear young Harry to his first birthday, she'd have a place for life at Glanteifi. For her and her son.'

'Her son?' Momentarily, I had forgotten her illegitimate child.

Then light dawned 'So that would be—'

'David. Yes. David Thomas was Mari's boy.'

The way Edward Philips told the story, Mari and David became Harry's family. She'd insisted on having her son with her in the nursery while Mr Probert-Lloyd rattled around the rest of the house by himself, in the cold.

'The squire was still mourning his poor wife, see,' the old man said. 'Hadn't been married a year when she died, they hadn't, and he was so sick with grief that he didn't see what Mari was doing. By the time he gathered his wits and took notice of his son, the boy was walking and talking. And he was talking in Welsh, not in English. As far as Harry was concerned Mari was his mother and Davy – they always called him Davy – was his brother.

'And Mari encouraged that. She never made any distinction

between the two of them. She made all their clothes so she could dress them just the same. She used to bring them out into the stableyard for Harry's riding lessons and she'd say, *'look at them – if you didn't know better, you'd think Davy was the gentleman, wouldn't you?'*

'And would you?' I interrupted.

Edward Thomas gave me a sharp look. 'You might've, as it happens. Mari's boy was tall for his age, and strong. She never said who his father was but there'd been a sailor about the place at one time, wanting harvest work. Well, you know how it is when the weather's right and the barley's got to come in – everybody's out there, even the housemaids if they know how to tie a stook. I always thought Davy had a look of that sailor – tall and dark. Had a tongue on him, too, the sailor did – knew how to talk his way round things – and Davy was just the same.'

'What about Harry?' I asked. I had to bring him back from his reminiscences before I lost him.

'Oh, quiet little scrap, he was. If Davy was the stableyard cat, Harry was the mouse. Mind, he was the sweetest-natured child you'll ever meet, Harry. Mari called him Harry Gwyn – we *all* did – and he loved that, never took it as disrespect. *I am Harry Gwyn,* he'd say to any visitors we had in the yard. And he'd give a little bow, as if the people were gentry, like him.'

'So he was always in the stableyard with you?'

'Often as not. He loved it – helping us with the tack and rubbing the horses down and even shovelling shit and straw. Never once said "I'm not doing that." The other one did, mind.'

'David Thomas?'

'Yes. To be fair, that was when they were older. When they were little, they were tight as peas in a pod.' His eyes glazed. He was back there again. I wished he'd get to the point, if there was one. I was stiff with cold and my teeth were clenched together to stop them chattering. It was all right for the old man, he had a scarf and a coat he'd got from somewhere. An old soldier, from the look of it.

'Mis-matched peas, mind,' he went on. 'Harry was a sunny child, always smiling. But the other one—' He broke off, coughed up a sigh. 'Davy Thomas was a watcher. He'd watch young Harry, as if he was trying to catch the trick of being a gentleman.'

I raised my eyebrows at him. 'Did he manage it?'

'No. Couldn't, could he? Has to be in the blood.'

I wasn't sure Harry'd agree but I nodded anyway. 'What did Davy do when Harry went away to school? Was that when he started working in the stables?'

Edward Philips rolled his eyes. 'No. Young Davy got an education. Harry wanted him to go away to school with him, said he wasn't going unless Davy went as well. We got all this from Mari,' he added, 'always preened herself like a she-cat on heat, she did, when Harry stuck up for Davy. Never stopped telling us all that Harry looked on him like a brother.'

Over the old man's head I watched a listless boy driving a draggle of sheep towards the edge of the common. They were going home. It was getting late, dusk was dimming the air and making the cold bite. Perhaps a lifetime in the stableyard had given Edward Thomas cold-weather skin but I was used to a fire in Mr Schofield's office. I rolled my shoulders. They were stiff from the way I had to hunch to keep my hands in my pockets but I needed my fingers to work on the way home. Couldn't afford to give the horse its head.

'Anyway,' Philips finished, 'for once, the squire put his foot down, said it was about time Harry started learning how to be a gentleman and Davy started learning how to make a living.' He grinned. 'You can bet we didn't get that from Mari! That came from one of the maids who'd overheard the row between Harry and his father.' He winked. 'Surprising what you can hear when you're polishing the floor outside the study door.

'So, Harry went away to school and Davy went to Mr Davies's in Newcastle Emlyn.'

I felt spider-feet walk over me at the mention of Mr Davies. Odd to think of this David Thomas at the school that'd been my home for four years. I shifted my numb feet.

'I've heard Harry talking about some agreement that David Thomas would be steward when he became squire. That's not true, is it?' Harry had assured Lydia Howell that it was. I wanted to see whether anybody else at Glanteifi had known about it.

Edward Philips rubbed his nose with the back of his hand. I watched his hairy nostrils being alternately squashed and pulled open. 'Mari was always going on about that – how her boy was going to be steward. She was behind the idea, for sure.'

'Harry said David was an educated man. I see what he meant now. Mr Davies's school.'

'Wasn't just that, boy. Harry wanted his friend to know everything he did – he was always trying to teach Davy what he'd learned away at school. Mind, he'd been the same since they were tiny. As soon as his tutor'd taught him to read and write, Harry had to pass it on to Davy. Sums, the same. Not that young Davy was much of a scholar – used to rage at Harry that he was a bad teacher, that he wasn't explaining things properly. Didn't like not being as sharp, see? Brought out the nasty side in him.'

He looked away and I knew he was looking into the past again. As long as he was looking at David Thomas that was all right with me. Except that I might freeze solid before he'd finished at the rate we were going. The boy with the sheep had disappeared. Probably inside by now. I envied him.

'There was one time,' Edward Philips said, 'they'd've been eight or nine, I suppose – and Davy'd decided to get his own back for the lessons. Said he was going to teach Harry to wrestle. Only it was wrestling according to his rules and Harry got beating after beating from him until I told him that if he didn't stop, I'd take a stick to him.'

A shiver went through me. 'Not a man to cross then.'

'No,' Edward Philips said. 'No, you wouldn't want to cross David Thomas. Him and his mother were a pair well matched in that respect. Best to keep on the right side of them.'

If we didn't move soon, I wasn't going to be back in Newcastle Emlyn before it was completely dark. 'Why did he emigrate to America?' I asked.

'That was a surprise, that was. There'd been no talk of it at all. The boy'd been courting seriously – a girl with a good farm coming to her. And then, all of a sudden, that was all off and he was going to America.'

'How did he get the money?'

Philips sighed and unfolded his old bones from the tree stump. 'Harry I suppose. I mean, I know they'd argued but Harry was always a loyal friend.'

'They argued – Harry and David? What about?'

He turned his lips down. 'Don't know. But they came to blows over it, whatever it was. Right there in the yard, in front of everybody.' I felt a spot of rain. I hoped it wasn't going to come to much. Without hat or coat I'd be drenched in no time.

The old man turned for home and I moved to his side.

'Mari was very bitter when Davy went,' he said. 'Blamed Harry for losing her son. Mind you – she'd always been a difficult woman. Never knew where you were with her. Sweet as you like one day, caustic as lye the next.'

'Does she still work in the big house?' I heard myself slip back into the language of my childhood instead of referring to Glanteifi by name.

'No. Squire was glad to pension her off when the boy went to America.'

'So where can I find her?'

'If you take my advice, boy, you'll leave well alone.'

John

All the way home I wondered about two things.

Lydia Howell's anonymous letter, and the argument Harry'd had with David Thomas.

I couldn't shake the feeling that those two things were connected, that Lydia's letter to Elizabeth Jenkins's father had caused the argument. Otherwise, why had Harry been so keen to ask her about it?

Did David Thomas believe that Harry'd had something to do with that letter? If he did, they'd've had reason to come to blows. The accusation that he was the father of Margaret Jones's child had ruined any chance David had of marrying Elizabeth Jenkins. No wonder he'd decided to emigrate.

But what, if anything, did that have to do with our investigation? Try as I might, I couldn't see that either the letter or the argument had any bearing on Margaret's Jones's murder. That was down to Beca – I knew that from the evidence of my own ears.

I could still hear the rain pattering on the leaves, the killer speaking as he forced Margaret Jones to her knees. An ordinary voice, as if they were just having a conversation. Except she didn't answer. Couldn't answer. It was just him, talking, on and on, to the back of her head, his knee between her shoulder blades.

'This is your fault, Margaret – you've brought this on yourself… All you had to do was one thing. One simple thing. You said you'd do it. You said you had done it. But you were lying, weren't you? Lying!'

I'd seen him shake her then, like a man shaking a disobedient puppy by the scruff of the neck.

'*After you saw Howell, you were going to go to Probert-Lloyd, weren't you? You were going to tell him – save your own miserable skin...*'

There had been a plan, that much was clear. And the killer had thought Margaret was going to tell the magistrates. But had it been a Rebecca plan? I'd always believed it had. But now I was starting to ask myself whether that was just because of the way I'd come to witness Margaret Jones's murder.

Cardiganshire, May 1843

Uncle Price called me over.

You want to help Beca don't you?

Of course I did! There wasn't an eleven-year old boy in the county that didn't want to be a part of Rebecca's cause. And my head was still full of the gatebreaking I'd seen weeks before in Cwmduad when I'd looked for my father in the crowd.

Yes, Uncle!

Good. Then take this to Mr Williams at Waungilfach.

Only a message? In broad daylight? No face-blacking, no torches? I stifled my disappointment and took the message from my employer.

Put the message into Mr Williams's own hand. Give it to him and nobody else. Don't give it to a servant.

Yes, Uncle.

I shouldn't've hankered after a nighttime assignment because I near as damnit got my wish. As a *gwas bach* I was at the bottom of the farm's pecking order. I was at the beck and call of every other servant and no amount of telling them that I had a message to take for Uncle would stop them wanting me to run errands for them. So it was getting towards dusk by the time I set foot on the path through the Alltddu to Williams's farm.

When I climbed over Waungilfach's back gate, a man was standing there, dressed as if he was going to chapel.

I've got a message for Mr Williams.

Give it to me, then.

Are you Mr Williams?

He came towards me, then, a hand raised. *Don't cheek me, boy! Give it to me now.*

What else could I do? I was a *gwas bach* and he wasn't dressed like a servant. So I gave it to him.

When he read it without moving his lips, I relaxed. He hadn't learned to read at Sunday school with a pointing finger and words read aloud. He must be a gentleman, then. He must be Mr Williams.

Then he glanced up at me.

Tell your uncle all right.

All right. I'll do what this letter says. I'll do what Beca wants.

I'd watched Margaret Jones die, not half an hour later, as I sheltered from the rain.

Of course, it was years since I'd realised that the man I'd given the note to hadn't been Williams Waungilfach. William Williams had come to our office one day and Mr Schofield had told me his name, so that I'd know the gentleman again.

If my shock showed in my face, nobody'd thought it was worth mentioning.

I'd put that shock away. I'd tied it up with all the other secrets and put it to the back of my mind. But his face – the killer who was not William Williams – had been in my nightmares.

Tell your uncle all right.

My 'uncle'. I was going to have to persuade Harry to go and talk to him.

Harry

'Harry, what a pleasant surprise!'

My father came from behind his desk towards me. He sounded sincere and I was somewhat taken aback; after our last encounter, I had expected a certain *froideur*. But I had not come to Glanteifi to exchange pleasantries.

'Why didn't you tell me that Margaret Jones was my brother's daughter?'

The hand on my shoulder fell away. 'Williams,' he muttered, bitterly. 'I suppose he told you in an attempt to steer suspicion away from himself?'

'No. Williams is blameless, for once.'

John and I had agreed that we would not reveal Nathaniel Howell's secret. If it proved necessary to explain how we had come by our information, we would simply say that the minister had died on his way to Ipswich and that we had spoken with his sister. However, I did not propose to offer my father any further explanation unless I was forced to do so.

'It doesn't matter who told me,' I said. 'What matters is that you didn't.'

He lowered himself on to the button-backed leather settee which had stood in the same position for as long as I could remember. 'Please sit down, Harry.'

'I'd rather stand, if it's all the same to you.'

My father's voice was low and tired. 'I know you can't see me but I can see you and I would rather not have you glowering down at me. Please, sit down.'

I perched on the edge of a chair. 'Well,' I repeated, 'why didn't you tell me?'

I heard my father's sigh. 'As soon as I realised that you had formed an attachment to the girl, I took steps to separate you—'

'Yes, you sent me away to Oxford. But why didn't you tell me who she was?'

'I had no way of knowing how far things had gone between you,' his voice was quiet. 'And I did not want you to feel disgust at yourself.'

Disgust. Was that what I had been feeling since Lydia Howell's revelation? No. What I had been feeling was anger, pure and simple. 'Is that the truth, Father?' I heard my witness-harassing tone and tried for a more conciliatory one. 'Are you sure it wasn't because you didn't want me to think less of George?'

'Think less of *George?*' My father sounded baffled by the idea. 'You never knew him – what opinion could you possibly have had of him, one way or the other?'

'People had been lauding him to the skies as long as I'd been alive! He was so tall and strong and fearless and handsome. He rode to hounds in the most dashing manner possible. He was the beating heart and soul of any gathering. He would have been bound to marry well, make our branch of the Young family as wealthy as your elder brother's – and so on and so on *ad infinitum!*'

The silence that greeted my words only emphasised how wildly I had been speaking.

'Is that what people said of him?' my father asked.

'You know it is!'

My father made no response. Was he thinking his own thoughts, his mind full of memories of my dead brother? Or was he looking at me, trying to fathom my thoughts, my presence here?

'I tried to be like him,' I had never mentioned George in my father's presence before but, now I had begun, I seemed unable to stop. 'I couldn't be big but I tried with all my might to be strong and hardy. To be dashing and fearless, like him.'

'But why, in God's name?' my father cried. 'When had I *ever* given you to understand that I wished you to be like him?'

'You didn't have to! I was quite clearly a disappointment to you. You barely spoke to me, barely had anything to do with me. I was obviously an inferior creature in your eyes.' My mouth seemed to have grown a mind of its own, articulating things that I had never acknowledged to myself, even in the darkest of moments. 'You left me in the company of servants! What was I to think but that I deserved no better? That I was unworthy of the company of gentlemen, unworthy of *your* company?'

'Harry!' The voice was not my father's; it was the voice of a man in pain. 'How could you possibly think such things?'

'Isn't it true? Did you *not* leave me in the company of servants?'

'Only because I thought that was what you wanted, that you were content there! Your mother was dead and I was at a loss as to what I should do for the best. You seemed happy with Mari Thomas!'

'It was *all I knew*! I grew up thinking I was a little Welsh boy. That Mari was the mother I had been given and Davy the brother. Then, later, you complained of it when I wouldn't relinquish them! You gave me no other teachers, no other friends and then you found fault with me when I loved them, when I learned the lessons they taught me!'

'Harry...' my father's face was turned away from me, towards the fire, as if he had forgotten that I could not see in his features the pain that was all too audible in his voice. 'I couldn't bear to be disappointed a second time,' he said, so softly that I barely heard.

I waited for him to explain. His hesitation indicated that he was unsure how – indeed whether – he should continue. 'What do you mean?' I prompted.

He drew in a long breath before turning to me. 'George was brought up in every way as a gentleman should be. English nursery maids and governesses. My own riding master brought from the family home. Tutors who were required to instill habits of mind as well as learning. He had no contact with the household servants. He might as well have been brought up in Worcestershire.'

He stopped but he had not finished. Turning away once more, as if he could not bear to look at me and speak at the same time, he went on in the same flat, deliberate tone.

'He became a little princeling who saw deference – no, not simply deference, adulation – who saw adulation as his due.' He faltered, then stumbled on. 'You say he was considered *dashing* – but where others saw courage I saw foolhardiness. Others might see charm and ease but I knew those qualities as duplicitousness and deceit.'

Feeling slightly dizzy with the effort of trying to see him, I shuffled further back in my chair.

'He lied without compunction, ran up debts, borrowed incessantly from his friends and was a shameless womaniser. Twice, I was forced to remove him from school and he was sent down from his Oxford college – no, not the one to which I sent you – for maintaining a woman in his rooms.' He stopped, abruptly. His breath was coming hard, as if he had been exerting himself. 'When you were born, it was my dearest wish that you would not grow up to be like George. Not in any way. I was ashamed to have fathered such a person.'

'Then why did you keep his portrait in your bed chamber?'

There was a beat of pure silence, as if every sound in the already

346

quiet little room had been driven out by the force of my words. Then I heard my father swallow. 'His mother had it painted for his coming of age. I removed it from the main hall after her death and put it in my bedchamber until I could decide what to do with it. When you were born – when you survived against all the odds – I made up my mind that I would not let you grow up to be like him and I hung his picture on the wall so that I should be reminded, daily, that your upbringing must be different.'

I do not know how to describe the mental upheaval that my father's words caused. All my life, I had believed myself a disappointment to him; believed that I had failed, in some essential way, to be the son he wanted. I had seen him as grief-stricken both for my mother and for my brother, the son who was so close to his heart that he had placed his portrait where nobody but he could see it.

My every opinion, my every understanding, my every action had been formed and moulded by that belief and, now, to understand that it was wholly erroneous, that my father had chosen to allow my upbringing to proceed in a certain fashion with the express intention of producing *a better man* than George was utterly bewildering.

'Of course,' my father's voice was heavy with self-reproach, 'time revealed that I had failed you just as I had failed your brother. I had failed to instill in you the duties and responsibilities of a gentleman. You had no true esteem for your own position. Though I had allowed George to nurture too great a degree of self-regard, I erred just as badly in allowing you to nurture too little.'

I could not respond. I had not the slightest idea what to say to him.

John

When I got back to my lodgings, my landlady was waiting for me. 'Another letter,' she said, holding it out. 'I suppose you think you're somebody now.'

I didn't answer, just took it from her and climbed the stairs.

Dear John

As you will see, this hand is not mine. My father is kind enough to write for me as I do not have my apparatus to hand.

His father's hand was cramped, barely easier to read than Harry's uneven efforts.

I will be staying at Glanteifi tonight and will not be at the Salutation till later in the day tomorrow. Perhaps you would be so kind as to come and meet me in my rooms on Monday morning at eight o'clock?

H P-L

I smiled to myself. Probert-Lloyd the magistrate writing a letter to a solicitor's clerk. But I had another reason to smile as well. With Harry at Glanteifi, I'd be able to catch Matt Tregorlais after church the following morning. I could try and find out what Beca plan Margaret Jones had been mixed up in without Harry wanting to know how I knew about it.

The following day, I stood outside Brongwyn church, waiting for the service to finish and watching dark clouds gathering over the tiny Gwenffrwd valley. It was only half an hour's walk from Brongwyn back to town but you can get very wet in half an hour and I didn't want to spend the rest of the day drying my clothes in front of the tiny fire in my room.

Matt was one of the first to come out at the end of the service and he and a couple of other men went and stood out of the wind against the east-facing wall of the little whitewashed church. I walked straight up to them and didn't wait for a gap in the conversation.

'Hello, Matthew.'

He made a point of finishing what he was saying before turning to me. 'John Davies.'

'A word, if you please.'

He shook his head. 'You can tell the magistrate's son I don't do parish business on the Sabbath.'

I stuffed my hands in my pockets. 'I'm not here on Harry's say-so. I'm here to bring greetings from a friend, as it happens. An old friend.' I saw a quick flicker of concern when I said that. Good. He'd be wondering who I'd been talking to. I helped him out. 'That friend of yours who went to live in Ipswich a few years ago. We had a *very* interesting chat.'

He plastered a look of surprise onto his face. 'Oh, him!' He looked about at his audience. 'Old chapel friend, from before I was reformed, boys.' He took me by the elbow. 'Come on then, you can tell me how he's getting on.'

The painful pressure of his fingers was a warning and I heeded it, said nothing more. He steered me to the edge of the sloping churchyard, far enough away from his cronies' curious looks, then he let my arm go. 'What do you want, John Davies?'

I moved off the wet grass and on to the path before my boots got soaked. 'Harry and I know about Nathaniel Howell's little secret. *Her* little secret.' I glanced back towards his friends, making a point.

He couldn't help looking in the same direction. Making sure they weren't taking too much interest. 'So?' His voice was tight.

Two women walked towards the little gate near where we were standing. Both of us nodded politely and waited till they were gone. '*So,*' I said, 'it would be very embarrassing for the *plwyfwas* if people were to hear how he used to take orders from a woman. That he'd followed her out at night, broken the law for her, and all to help other women.'

Matthew's eyes narrowed. 'Don't threaten me, John Davies.'

'Why?' I took a step towards him. 'What will you do?'

He didn't back off. 'You'd do well to remember,' he said, voice low but every word as clear as print, 'that the last person who knew about the *Reverend Howell,* ended up buried under a tree.'

The hair stood up on the back of my neck. If I'd been a dog I'd've bared my teeth, the way they do when their hackles go up and they're trying to pretend they're not frightened to death.

'You're saying Margaret Jones was murdered because she knew about Nathaniel Howell?'

'I'm *saying* that when Margaret Jones disappeared, I was told it was a good thing. Because if she wasn't here, she couldn't be going around telling everybody what she knew.'

I shook my head. Lydia'd said nothing about Margaret guessing the truth about her. 'Were you the father of Margaret Jones's child?' I asked, hoping to catch him off guard.

'*What*? No!' He'd forgotten to keep his voice down and people looked over at us. I didn't make the same mistake.

'You were overheard being warned that she'd father the child on to you.'

He turned so that his back was facing the church and only I could see his face. 'She was trying to father it on anybody with a cock! She'd already been to see Howell to try and get him to make David Thomas marry her and she was going to try the same trick with me.'

'Is that why your little anti-Howell Beca sect paid her a visit?'

'What are you talking about?'

'I told you. We've talked to Howell. We know about your group. Isaac Morgan was reporting back to Howell. He joined you to try and keep control of what you got up to.'

Nobody was watching us now. There was rain ready to fall and everybody was keen to get home. I moved to shelter under the old yew tree that stood on the southern wall of the churchyard. Matt followed, shaking his head. 'Morgan wasn't doing anything for Howell.'

I wasn't taking any of Matt Tregorlais's nonsense. 'He was. We had it from Howell not three days ago.'

'Well Howell was lying, then. Or Morgan was lying to him. Her,' he corrected himself. 'Isaac Morgan didn't join us. He *led* us.'

If that was true, Morgan would've known about any plan involving Margaret Jones. Might've come up with it himself.

All you had to do was one thing. *One* simple *thing*.

'I heard Beca had a plan that Margaret Jones was part of. What was that about?'

He shook his head. 'Don't know where you got that. It's rubbish.'

He thought it was the truth. I could tell. I took my spectacles off and wiped them. 'Maybe they kept you out of it,' I said.

'Don't talk nonsense, John Davies. You don't know anything about it.'

But I did. I knew things he didn't because I'd been there and he hadn't.

After you saw Howell, you were going to go to Probert-Lloyd, weren't you?

Specs back on and the world was sharp again. 'What if she said she'd go to the magistrates?' I asked.

He looked at me but didn't answer. He didn't have to. Threatening to go to the magistrates would've been the most dangerous thing Margaret Jones could possibly have done.

'Why are you doing this, John Davies?'

The question took me by surprise. 'Harry Probert-Lloyd came to Mr Schofield's asking for a clerk. What choice did I have?'

'But why are you *here*? Now? Without him?'

'He's busy—'

'I don't believe you. Why are you here? What's all this to you?' He took a step towards me. 'How are you *involved*, John Davies?'

My legs were suddenly shaking. 'Need to stay in Harry's good books, don't I? Never know when I might need a job.'

I could tell he didn't believe me. And I was afraid of who he'd take his suspicions to.

It wasn't long before I found out. When I went back to my lodgings a few hours later, another letter was waiting for me. And, this time, it wasn't from Harry.

Harry

When Moyle announced John and showed him into the library on Sunday afternoon, my first thought was that my letter had failed to reach him, but he assured me otherwise.

'It arrived in good time, yesterday evening,' he said, speaking English in deference to my father. 'I wouldn't have disturbed you but, since then, I've received another letter. One which concerns us both.' A pause, then my father spoke. 'Don't distress yourself, Mr Davies. I have matters to attend to elsewhere.'

What had passed between him and John – an anxious look from the latter or something more substantial? Whatever it was, none of us broke the silence as my father made his way to the door. The library was not an over-large room but it might have been a hundred yards long, as far as I was concerned, and my father travelling at the pace of a centenarian.

Finally, the door closed behind him and John moved to my side. 'It was waiting for me at my lodgings.' He held it out to me. 'I think it's a Beca letter.'

'Well, I can't read it, can I?' I despised my own tetchiness; for John to have forgotten himself so far as to offer me the letter, he must be profoundly disturbed.

He withdrew his hand without apology. 'It's written on the back of an auction notice,' he said.

He was still speaking English as if being in my father's house demanded it but I reverted to Welsh. 'It's Sunday,' I reminded him. 'Whoever wrote it obviously had no choice but to use what was to hand. Go on, read it to me.'

I heard him take a breath. *'If you want to know what plans Beca had for Margaret Jones, come to the beginning of the path leading to Waungilfach through the Alltddu tomorrow evening at seven. Bring Henry Probert-Lloyd with you.'*

'Is that all?' I asked. 'No threats about what will happen if we don't go?'

'No. It's not signed, either.'

So perhaps he was wrong in assuming the hand of Rebecca. As I recalled, the Lady had not been chary of putting her name to a summons. 'Read it to me again, will you?'

John did so and a phrase struck me. 'What does it mean "what plans Beca had for Margaret Jones"?' I heard him take a breath, as if he was about to answer, but he said nothing. 'John?'

'I went to see Matt Tregorlais this morning. He talked about a Beca plan.'

I did not know whether to be more surprised by John's acting on his own initiative or by the implication that Matthew Evans had volunteered information. 'Do you mean he told you about it of his own accord?'

Again there was a hesitation before his answer came. 'Not exactly. It came out by accident. More or less.' He seemed unsure how to go on. 'I just asked something like, *So what was the plan with Margaret Jones?* Meaning, how were they going to warn her off? But Matt misunderstood – started bleating about not knowing anything about the plan. That it was nothing to do with him. All that.'

I frowned. It sounded as if we had finally been granted a stroke of luck; which made John's discomfort all the more baffling. Perhaps he felt he had failed to capitalise on it.

'I take it you asked him what the plan was and he refused to give you any more information?' I guessed.

'Exactly. I tried to be crafty about it but he realised I didn't know what he was talking about and shut up completely.'

But Matthew's blurting out of Rebecca's secret had obviously resulted in the letter now in John's hand. Was John worried that, in stumbling upon this plan, he had put us in danger?

'Do you think it's too risky?' I asked. I was not utterly naïve: this could be a Rebecca trap. The isolated location would allow us to be molested unobserved. However, anybody who had ridden with Rebecca and was now willing to disclose information would be putting himself at considerable risk; such a person would obviously not wish to be seen or overheard speaking to us.

'For myself, I see no option but to go,' I said when he did not reply. Whatever the risk, I knew I would find no peace if I stayed away.

I watched, sidelong, as John folded the letter in half, then half again and put it in his pocket.

'I know I have no right to ask—' I left the question unfinished, hoping that he would rush to tell me that of course he would come with me. But he did not. 'I know it's a risk,' I began again, 'but could I persuade you to come with me?'

After a silence too long to be called a hesitation he took an audible breath. I waited. 'Can we go armed?' he blurted, finally.

'Only if you own a weapon. For obvious reasons, I've no use for firearms or blades.'

The enormity of what I was asking of him was not lost on me. My family name and connections might protect me from harm but the same was not true of John; he had far more to fear from Rebecca than I did.

'However' I said, a solution suggesting itself, 'weapons aside, I believe I can find a way to keep us safe.'

Harry

When we met the following morning in the Salutation's dining room, I detected a constraint in John that made me uneasy. Loath to spend the day waiting for him to tell me that he had changed his mind, I challenged him while we helped ourselves to breakfast from the sideboard.

'Have you had second thoughts about meeting with Beca tonight?'

'No. No.' He manoeuvred something that I could not see onto his plate and shook his head but the denial was not altogether convincing. 'I was just awake half the night thinking about it.'

I picked up my plate and sat down. I was already sufficiently interesting to the servants at the Salutation, if not to the guests, and I did not want our conversation overheard. 'We need to find out what we can about this plan before tonight' I murmured, once John was seated opposite me. 'The more we know the less we can be hoodwinked.'

John picked up his cutlery and addressed himself to his breakfast. 'What kind of plan do you think they'd've wanted Margaret Jones to help with?' he asked.

It seemed likely that any Rebecca plan unknown to Lydia Howell had probably been conceived after the discovery of her true gender. 'What if, after Margaret'd been to see Lydia and been told she could expect no help there, some of the Beca boys paid her a visit?' I suggested. 'Offered her a way to get back into Beca's good books?'

My eyes on my plate, I saw John lift his head to look at me. 'What kind of way?'

'Something to do with Lydia? I don't know. We should go and see Isaac Morgan – see if we can clear up this business of whether he was reporting back to her or not.'

John sawed vigorously at what was probably a chop. 'If Matt Tregorlais was telling the truth and Morgan *led* the other group, he's not going to tell us anything, is he? And another thing – if he *is* the leader, don't you think Morgan might be the one who wrote the letter calling us to this meeting?'

'Quite possibly, so it's worth seeing him today while we've got the element of surprise. But, first, I think we need to talk to Rachel Ellis again. If anybody'd been to see Margaret, Rachel would've known.'

A figure passed by our table. 'Morning to you, Mr Probert-Lloyd.'

I smiled. 'Good morning.' Who the devil had that been? No day allowed me to go long without another reminder of the extreme social disadvantage my blindness inflicted on me. Would it get easier as people became accustomed to it? Would they announce themselves to me or would they simply walk past, spared the obligation to be civil?

John broke into my unproductive thoughts. 'I think, if you want to talk to Rachel, we should take William Williams with us. We need him to give her and Aaron permission to talk to us, otherwise it'll be the same story as last time.'

I had not spoken to William Williams since our meeting at Glanteifi when he had tried to persuade me to give up my investigation, so it was with some unease that I approached Waungilfach to ask for his assistance.

'Mr Williams,' I began, once the maid had shown us into the *soi-disant* drawing room and the master of the house had been found, 'I do apologise for disturbing the beginning of your week—' I stopped, conscious that there was little point expressing regret for the disturbance if I did not intend to offer the slightest excuse for it.

Williams made no reply to my truncated apology but his wife, who had come bustling in on his coat-tails, was less reticent. She seemed unaware that her husband had asked me to desist from my enquiries.

'Do you have news, Mr Probert-Lloyd?'

I turned towards her. She was attempting to present a united front, sitting with Williams on the sofa, while John and I were in straight-backed chairs on either side of the empty fireplace. 'We're making progress, Mrs Williams.' I leaned forward, confidingly. 'It seems that Margaret Jones may have become involved in some Rebeccaite plan...' I left the thought hanging, to see if either of them reached for it.

Mrs Williams obliged. 'But why would she get involved in anything Rebecca was up to? She had no friend *there*, did she?'

'My dear,' Williams interrupted, 'are you quite certain that the children can be trusted to get on with their lessons without you? Would it not be better for me to speak to Mr Probert-Lloyd while you attend to them?'

'Excuse me, Mr Williams' – though I was fairly sure his wife would disregard his suggestion, I wanted him to understand that I would not allow him to thwart me –'may I just detain Mrs Williams for a moment longer?' I turned without waiting for him to answer. 'Mrs Williams, when you say Margaret had no friend in Rebecca, are you referring to a visit the Rebeccaites made to her, here, to warn her about her behaviour?'

'Yes, I am.' I imagined Mrs Williams looking defiantly at her husband and heard him drawing breath to silence her. Before he could speak, I slid a question into the gap. 'Did you *see* the men who were here that night, Mrs Williams?'

'I did. I could see them quite clearly. When they came clattering in, they had enough torches with them to light up the dark from now till Christmas.'

'And did you recognise any of them?' I tried not to sound too urgent.

There was a small silence. I imagined her shaking her head regretfully, her eyes on me, pitying my state; I had no doubt that her husband would have told her about my sight.

'No, every one of them was blacked up. It makes it so difficult to recognise a person. I don't believe I'd know my own children if their faces were blacked.'

'And you, Mr Williams?' I asked. 'Were you able to recognise any of them?'

Williams was clipped. 'I was not.'

'My husband went out to try and send them on their way,' Mrs Williams proclaimed, 'and the ruffians laid hands on him and held him with his face to our own back door so that he shouldn't see anything. Disgraceful!'

I had to admire Mrs Williams's subtle undermining of her husband. Under the pretence of abhorring the Rebeccas' treatment of him, she had provided us with a humiliating picture of his impotence.

'Did they lay hands on Margaret?' I asked her.

'They didn't touch her. She only came out to the top of the steps – and they wouldn't dare go into the loft – it's one thing coming on to the yard but it's another thing to go invading somebody's buildings.'

'That didn't stop them firing my barn a few days later!' Williams challenged.

I had quite forgotten that Rebecca had burned one of the

Waungilfach barns to the ground. It had happened in the days immediately after Margaret's disappearance and had been of little consequence to me in comparison.

'Mrs Williams,' John broke the sudden tension, 'did you see anybody lingering after the rest of the Becas had left the yard? Anybody that might have spoken to Margaret after the rest had gone?'

'No. They all went off, all of them. And she went back inside the loft.'

'If our information about Margaret's involvement with Beca is correct,' John continued, 'somebody must've spoken to her very soon after that night. She couldn't read so they must've come here to see her.' He paused, allowed them to take this in. 'Did you, possibly, see anybody around the farm on the days before she disappeared? Anybody at all?'

Did they look to me? I had no idea so I let John's words stand. 'There are always people coming and going,' Mrs Williams said. 'But I don't remember anybody out of the ordinary.'

The words had barely left her mouth when her husband spoke, as if he was affording her the smallest feasible degree of courtesy. 'I don't know if it's relevant, but somebody was *supposed* to have come who didn't.'

'Who?' I asked.

'A messenger was supposed to have been sent but failed to turn up.'

'A messenger? Who from?' This was Mrs Williams.

'Price over at Pant Yr Hebog said he'd sent a messenger.' I could tell that Williams's face was turned towards me, answering his wife's question whilst appearing to do nothing of the kind.

Mrs Williams was undeterred. 'Price? What did he want?' I was keen to know that myself.

Williams's tone, when he answered, spoke of an old grievance.

'According to him, he sent a message summoning me to appear at a Rebecca gathering.'

I was taken aback. 'For what purpose?'

'For the purpose of forcing me to take part in their illegal activities!' Williams failed to control his irritation. 'To make me their accomplice! To ensure that I was implicated in activity that would haul me up before the bench if ever I was tempted to see justice visited upon them!'

It was easy to see why Williams might be bitter. Though he could not plausibly have informed on the men who had brought Samuel to his door, Morgan's band might well have been afraid that Williams would take what he knew of their intimidation of Margaret to a magistrate. Involving him in illegal activity would not absolutely have ensured that he would make no accusations, but it would have put him in an acutely compromising situation; compulsion is a weak defence at best and he would have done his dubious social standing no good whatsoever by protesting it.

'You said *according to him*?' John echoed Williams's earlier words. 'Did you have some reason to disbelieve what Mr Price said, Mr Williams?'

I heard Williams's fierce intake of breath, as if he was about to leap up and grapple with John. 'Yes. I did! Price maintained that the Rebeccas fired my barn as punishment for not coming when I was summoned. But Price would have done it anyway, just because he could.'

'What makes you think that?'

'I'll tell you what makes me think that, *Mr* Davies. When I went out to the fire that his men had set raging in my barn, Price was still there. His henchmen were long gone but he'd stayed. He had the gall to stand there as my barn burned and tell me I'd brought the whole thing on myself.'

I wondered whether his anger had been as poorly disguised that night. If so, Price can only have considered his job well done.

'Said if I'd only come when I was bidden then neither of us would have been standing there.'

'But, as far as you were concerned,' I suggested, 'you hadn't *been* summoned. Is that right?'

'Exactly! According to Price he sent a *gwas bach* over with a message for me. Said he told him to put it in my hand and mine alone. Liar!'

'Did you ask to see the *gwas bach*?' There was an edge to John's voice. Clearly he thought he already knew the answer.

'I wouldn't lower myself,' Williams spat.

'Mr Williams,' I began, 'what night were you supposed to have ridden with Rebecca?'

The farmer hesitated. 'The night before the barn was fired, I suppose. Yes, it must've been. Price accused me in those terms – you weren't with us last night.'

'So was the *gwas bach* sent with the summons for that same evening, or for the following day?'

'He was *supposed* to have been sent the day before. At first, when Price said he'd sent a boy over, I told him it was no wonder I'd missed him because we'd all been turning the place upside down looking for my missing dairymaid. But he said I couldn't use that as an excuse, he'd sent the boy the previous day.'

'Then the messenger came on the same day that Margaret disappeared?'

'I've told you, there *was* no messenger!'

I held up a quieting hand. 'Let's just suppose, for a moment, that Price was telling the truth. That there was a *gwas bach*. Perhaps the boy brought a message for Margaret at the same time? A message that told her to meet somebody in the Alltddu?'

'But why would Price want Margaret killed?'

'We don't know,' I said. 'That's why we need to speak to Rachel Ellis.'

John

Williams came with us to the Ellis' cottage. I was glad of it. Having him riding between us kept Harry from speculating about Price's *gwas bach*.

But that didn't stop me wanting to grab Williams by the lapels and shake him till his teeth rattled. To tell him that Price *had* sent somebody with a message. *Me.* It was a real temptation, just to see the astonishment on his face.

But then I'd've had to explain everything, wouldn't I? Explain to Harry that I'd seen her die, I knew what had happened.

Except that I didn't, I reminded myself. I didn't know. Not really. Not everything.

I knew Margaret Jones had been murdered but I couldn't tell Harry *why*. I couldn't put a name to the face I saw in my nightmares. The face of a well-dressed, fluently literate man.

Or *could* I?

Things Edward Philips had said kept coming back to me.

She made all their clothes so she could dress them just the same. As soon as his tutor taught him to read and write, Harry was teaching Davy.

David Thomas. Educated. Well-dressed.

Had he been the man who insisted on taking Uncle Price's letter from me?

And, if it had been him, *what had he read?*

I could've read that letter myself. Even then, I knew how to read – I could have opened the letter and read it.

But no. It had come from Beca. I would no more've opened it than spat in Uncle Price's eye.

364

This time, it was Aaron we found digging in the potato field. Patches of blue sky overhead or not, the wind made it colder than when we'd found Rachel out here and the three of us dismounted and stood next to our warm horses as soon as we could. Aaron was in his shirtsleeves, jacket folded over one end of the potato basket. Digging's hard work.

His 'Good-day' was civil enough, and he got it in before Harry or Williams spoke. But his eyes told a different story. Cold as the earth he'd been turning over. Wary as hell.

Harry'd asked Williams to speak first and he spoke to Aaron in Welsh. Even though he wasn't a real gentleman, it sounded wrong.

'Aaron, previously I asked you not to speak to Mr Probert-Lloyd about anything Margaret Jones might have told your wife.' Williams looked pretty uncomfortable at having to explain himself but Harry'd insisted. 'Circumstances have changed, now. There's no need for you or your wife to keep silent. I'd like you to give him any help you can.'

Aaron kept his expression blank but what man likes being told what to do? Especially on his own land.

Harry piped up. 'It's really your wife we'd like to speak to, Mr Ellis.'

Aaron turned to him. I could almost see his thoughts. *My wife, the woman you think you were friends with. If you ever so much as laid a hand on her...*

'I'm sorry,' he said, without sounding it, 'she's not here.' Then he added, 'She's gone to the weavers with the wool.' Didn't want us to think he was being unhelpful.

Harry was trying not to look confused but I knew what Aaron meant. My mother used to spin, too. Most women did, for the extra income. Some of the weavers would collect the yarn but you got paid extra if you took it to them.

'You can ask me your questions, if you like.' Aaron offered. Harry's smile looked as if it'd been pulled into place by a string.

'Unless you were there the night Rebecca came to threaten Margaret Jones, I doubt you'd be much help, Mr Ellis.' Then his expression changed. 'Or perhaps you *were* there?'

It was possible. Aaron and Rachel could easily have been courting seven years ago. Their little boy looked to be at least five.

Aaron wanted to say he'd been there. I could see it flit across his face. The temptation to lie, to keep Harry Gwyn and his questions away from Rachel. But he was a good chapel man and he couldn't have a lie like that on his conscience.

'No. I wasn't.'

'Will Mrs Ellis be back before dark?' Harry asked.

'I can't say, Mr Probert-Lloyd. The days are short now, aren't they? Once she'd been paid, Rachel said she'd go into town for some bits.'

Town. Newcastle Emlyn. Rachel would be glad to stop there for a while, rest her feet, have a gossip while she bought her tea and soap and mending thread. A brief memory of my mother doing the same while my sister and I looked at sweets we couldn't have made me feel heavy and sad.

'In that case,' Harry said, 'we'll come back tomorrow, if you don't mind.'

What could Aaron Ellis say? He wasn't allowed to mind.

Harry

When William had taken his leave and cantered away, John and I walked our horses back along the little road out of the Ceri valley in silence. In between the sudden tugs of a gusting wind, the stillness of winter was everywhere; no birds sang in the newly bare trees, crickets and grasshoppers were dead or burrowed deep into the matted grass, people were indoors if they could manage it. The only thing to be heard was the quiet, inexhaustible seeping of water through soil, along ditches and down banks.

As we approached the junction with the road to Newcastle Emlyn, John spoke up.

'Harry, I know we need to see Isaac Morgan, but it's been a week since I've been into Mr Schofield's office. I should go and pay my compliments to him. Feed him some tidbits to keep him happy.'

I smiled. John had changed since London; he was much more confident, more open. 'Yes, do,' I said. 'Shall we meet at the Salutation at two o'clock? That will leave us enough time to get out to Morgan's place and back in daylight.'

I was loath to accompany him into town and simply wait at the Salutation, so I decided to return to Glanteifi and beg lunch from Isabel Griffiths. My father would be in Cardigan on county business so I knew I would not risk his displeasure by appearing there, again, despite my continuing investigation. Besides, I felt we had achieved something of a *rapprochement* in finally talking about George. Certainly, there had been a sufficient thawing of relations to allow my father to suggest that, instead of constantly using livery nags, I should take Sara and her stablemate Seren with me when I returned to the Salutation the previous evening.

Now, with the scent of home in her nostrils, the little mare began to trot once we'd set foot on the drive but, before we came within sight of the house, I pulled her up and sat, looking – as best I could – through the trees and down the slope to the bend in the river.

The Teifi seemed swollen with recent rain and I knew there would be little white eddies here and there where the brown water caught on something beneath the surface and was whirled around before rushing on its way. I imagined twigs and leaves and other detritus snagged in the reeds at the water's edge, pushed there by the swing of the river around its wide meander.

I jumped, startled by a sudden cry. A pheasant panicking its way into the air in the woods behind me, shrieking its foolish, tinplate cry. Davy had loved to go thrashing through the woods putting up pheasants and mocking their strangled alarm. He had called them the stupidest birds alive. *Even more stupid than pigeons* he'd say. *At least pigeons've got the sense to come and steal grain off the yard.*

The times we had spent in these woods, setting snares, looking for eggs, taking frogspawn out of a puddle, lying in a sunny patch watching little lizards bask and then flick away when they saw a hand move towards them. Davy had always lost interest in the eggs once we'd taken them home, leaving me to do the blowing and labelling and storing. *Thrush. Woodpecker. Blackbird. Rook.*

Likewise, once hunted down and brought home in triumph, the frogspawn failed to hold his attention until the bucket in the stableyard began to roil with tadpoles. Then he would spend whole afternoons taking out two at a time and poking them into races down one of the cobbled drain channels. The fact that they ended up wriggling to death in the mud and shit beyond the wall of the yard did not disturb him at all. As far as he was concerned most tadpoles died so it did not matter if he hastened the demise of a few. It was a pragmatism that was hard to argue with without seeming girlishly sentimental.

David Thomas.

Everything seemed to come back to him.

That spring, the spring when Margaret had died, the spring when Rebecca had woken into black-faced life, his letter had drawn me home, even though he must have known that I could do little to influence my father.

I knew you'd come home when I wrote to you about Beca threatening your father. I thought there'd be time enough for you to see you needed to clean up after yourself, then.

There was a question I had been asking myself since Ipswich; a question I kept, defiantly, answering in the negative. Now, it nagged at me again and I was no longer so sure of my answer.

Was it possible that Davy had written the threatening Rebecca letters to my father, himself, in order to force my return?

I had certainly found no justification for the urgency in his letter when I returned home. Rebecca had taken no actions against Glanteifi and, as far as I was aware, no further threats had been made.

But, supposing Davy *had* written the letters – what had been his motive for bringing me home? Was it possible that he was part of whatever plan Margaret had become embroiled in?

I had never stopped wondering why Davy had chosen to emigrate so suddenly.

Now, as I trotted Sara up the drive, I had to ask myself whether I was being wilfully blind; whether his emigration to New York was not very simply explained – as the flight of a murderer from the scene of his crime.

John

I'd lied to Harry. I wasn't going to see Mr Schofield. I wanted to see David Thomas's mother, Mari. Wanted to know why her son had gone to America.

My watch – Harry's watch, I should say – read five minutes after eleven as we parted company. Almost three hours till we'd arranged to meet at the Salutation.

Plenty of time, even if I was going to have to put Seren in the hotel's stables, like I would've done if I'd really been going to the office.

Edward Philips had told me where Mari lived – her cottage on the turnpike road to Cenarth would be an easy stroll from town. But the old man'd warned me that if I was set on talking to her, it'd be better to keep any good opinions of Harry to myself. 'She's very bitter against him. Blames him for her son going off to New York.'

'Blames Harry? Why should she?'

'Because that's what she's like – always looking for somebody to blame when things go against her.'

I also knew from Mr Philips that Mari was ill and not going out much. Still, it was a relief when she answered the door.

'Who are you?' she peered at me, one hand gripped on to the doorjamb. 'Do I know you?'

I had to stop myself staring. I'd never seen a living person so thin, right to the flesh of her face which had shrunk back onto the bones. I swallowed. 'My name's John Davies. I'm a solicitor's clerk.' I stopped. If she went to the shops or the market, she'd have heard about Harry's investigation. But perhaps her illness kept her to herself because she just stood there, waiting for me to explain what I was doing on her doorstep.

'I'm working for Mr Henry Probert-Lloyd,' I said.

'Well, you can go from here now, then,' she stepped back to close the door on me. 'I've got nothing to say to Harry Gwyn or any friend of his.'

I put a hand on the door. 'I'm no friend of his, Mrs Thomas. That's why I'm here.' The lie – and calling him Henry not Harry, as if he was nothing to me – made me feel ashamed, disloyal. But it was the only way to get into her house. I put my hand into my pocket and took out the quarter of tea I'd been back to my lodgings for. 'I brought some tea for you. Can we drink a cup together?'

She narrowed her eyes at me as if she was trying to bring my motives into focus. 'What do you want, John Davies?' I got a whiff of her breath as she spoke. It was so foul I had to stop myself taking a step backwards.

'Just a little chat. That's all.'

Inside, the house was small but well-furnished. You could tell money'd been spent on it. There was a proper *siment* floor, not beaten earth like I'd expected, and the room was divided in two unequal halves by a good-sized dresser – table and chairs on the larger side, bed and press on the smaller. The table was decent – polished not scrubbed – and it had proper chairs tucked under it. No stools or benches for Mari Thomas. The rocking chair by the fire had cushions and there was a bit of a carpet in front of it. Not bad for a woman who'd never married and who'd been living on a pension for six or seven years.

'Sit down.' Mari Thomas nodded at one of the chairs by the table. 'I'll make the tea.'

She shuffled over to a narrow door at the back of the room. A little pantry, north-facing and cool. Any minute now, she'd open another door and I'd see a water closet.

Mari brought a jug and put it on the table. Living where she did, she wouldn't have to go into town for her milk – one of the Newcastle Emlyn milk sellers'd be bound to pass by her door every morning.

I looked around for her teapot. It was on the hearth, waiting for the tea. I'd been half expecting something fancy, but the pot was a serviceable blue-and-white just like we'd had at home. Perhaps she had a fancy one for best in the small cupboard under the window.

I wouldn't get best, that was for certain. Not somebody who worked with Harry Gwyn.

She made the tea, stirred it and poured. Then, after she'd given me my cup, she lowered her bones painfully into the rocking chair and glared at me.

'Well?'

Edward Philips hadn't exaggerated Mari Thomas's sourness. Caustic as lye he'd called her and I didn't want that lye taking my skin off. I was going to have to go carefully.

'I expect you heard about the inquest that happened in town, a couple of weeks ago?'

'You can see I'm not deaf, can't you? Of course I heard about it.'

'So you'll know the verdict caused a bit of a stir.'

Mari pulled a face which poured scorn on the whole inquest – jury and coroner and all. Or, then again, perhaps it was me she was pouring scorn onto.

'Henry Probert-Lloyd didn't like the verdict,' I said, watching her.

She sipped some cooled tea from her saucer. That wasn't a habit she'd learned at Glanteifi.

'So he's looking into the whole thing,' I pressed on. 'He persuaded my employer – Mr Schofield – to loan him my services.'

She was watching me over the saucer, wary as a yard cat.

'Well,' I let myself sound just a bit aggrieved, 'I don't like being loaned out like some *gwas bach*. I wanted to know why Henry Probert-Lloyd was so interested in some servant girl's death. But he won't tell me – I'm just a servant, he's not going to tell me anything, is he? But I keep my ear to the ground.' I gave her a look – *we servants can be sly when we have to, can't we?* 'I heard there was something between him and the dead girl – Margaret Jones.'

She carried on staring at me. My mouth had gone dry, and it wasn't from talking.

'Well…' I took a sip of my own tea. 'I thought you'd know the truth. You brought him up, didn't you? And, from what I've heard, his closest friend was your son, Davy.'

She put her cup on the empty saucer, eyes on it the whole time as if she didn't trust her hand to get it there safely. 'Yes. I do know the truth. And you won't get it from Harry Gwyn.'

I leaned forward. The very picture of eagerness, I was. 'So was he involved with her? With Margaret Jones?'

Mari grunted as she put her cup on the floor. She was in pain and trying to hide it. 'That girl was always going to come to a bad end.'

I raised my eyebrows. *Tell me more.*

'No good, she was. Very free with her favours.'

Rich, I thought, coming from a woman who'd warmed the bed of her employer's son and given birth to another man's bastard.

'Set her sights on *Henry Probert-Lloyd*,' she sneered, 'and he was too silly to know what she was about. Got her with child, he did, and then panicked and—'

Her mouth shut with a snap. *And* what?

'That's what I wanted to ask you, really,' I said, treading carefully. 'Henry says we need to find out who the father of Margaret Jones's child was – says that's who must've killed her. That makes me think he wasn't the child's father—'

'He can say what he likes. He *was* the father. My son told me. Came home one day full of it. *Harry Gwyn's done it now,* he said. *He's got a girl with child and his father's packing him off to Oxford early.* And he was right. The boy was gone the following morning. Davy said not to tell anybody that was the reason. Harry'd told him, of course, but his father didn't want the servants to know.'

She couldn't help herself. She didn't really want to talk to me but she wanted me to know that she knew these things. Wanted me to understand that the reason she had *privileged information,* as Mr Schofield would've called it, was because her son had been like a brother to Glanteifi's heir.

'So there's no question? Henry was definitely the father?'

'Oh yes.'

I nodded as if that was an end to it. 'Is there another cup in the pot?' I asked.

She shuffled to the hearth and bent to pour me a cup.

This time it actually tasted like tea. She'd put so little in the pot that the first cup had tasted like watered milk. I couldn't see the point in her scrimping. From the look of her she'd be lucky to last longer than the quarter of tea I'd brought.

As I sipped away, I made sure she saw me looking around the cottage. 'George Probert-Lloyd must have been very grateful to you,' I said.

'So he should be. Without me he wouldn't have a living son. I reared that boy from hours old. They all thought he'd die without his mother, but I reared him.'

From the way she said it, you'd've thought she'd stood at the side of Harry's cradle and fought off death's scythe with her bare hands.

'I see. No wonder the squire sees you so well provided for.'

'This?' her eyes went round the room. 'This isn't George Probert-Lloyd's doing. My son, this is, sending me money from America.'

I raised my eyebrows. 'So he's doing well there, then?'

'Yes, no thanks to anybody here.'

'Why's that? I thought Henry gave him the money for his ticket.' It was what Edward Philips believed and I had no reason to question it.

Her death's-head snapped up. 'What? Is that what he told you – that he paid for Davy's ticket?' I couldn't get my mouth open to answer her before she was blackening Harry's name. 'Henry Probert-Lloyd's a liar! I didn't bring him up to lie but his father sent him off to that fancy school and when he came back he was a different boy. He wasn't ours any more. But that's what his father wanted, of course, to make him one of them, one of the *crachach*.'

'To be fair to Henry,' I said, hoping for more about Harry's supposed dishonesty, 'it wasn't him who said he'd paid for David's ticket. It was an old servant from Glanteifi.'

She sneered. 'That's as maybe but he lied about plenty of other things. And the worst kind of lies – ones that got other people into trouble so that he wouldn't be blamed.'

The trick had worked once, so I defended Harry some more. 'Like I said, I'm no friend of Henry Probert-Lloyd's but I haven't heard him—'

She didn't want to hear it. Her rage against Harry was boiling over like a too-full kettle. 'You've been talking about his biggest lie already – that girl's child!'

'Margaret Jones?'

'Yes! He tried to persuade my boy to marry her, to make himself feel better. Well, Davy was looking for a better marriage than that – he'd been brought up as a gentleman, he wasn't going to marry a dairymaid who was no better than she should be!'

'No. Of course. Henry'd promised him he'd be steward to Glanteifi, hadn't he?'

'And that's the other thing!' Mari was beside herself now. Her sunken face was alive with malice. 'When Davy wouldn't let Henry father his bastard on him, he told Davy could forget being steward. Said their friendship was at an end.'

I arranged my face into an expression which was supposed to tell her I was shocked but not entirely surprised. 'That must've been a terrible blow – to lose the prospect of being steward.'

She held up a bony, listen-to-me finger. 'No. And I'll tell you why. Because my David didn't need the Probert-Lloyds to give him a place in the world. He was courting a girl whose father was looking to take another farm on so they'd have enough land for them all. They'd have been married, for sure, if it wasn't for Henry and his lies. Do you know what he did? No, of course you don't, who'd tell you? He wrote a letter to the girl's father, telling him that David had fathered Margaret Jones's bastard and that he was refusing to do the right thing and marry her. Well, of course, a tenant would believe Henry Probert-Lloyd wouldn't he? Whatever Davy said only made things worse. So the engagement was off.'

'Is that why your son decided to go and try his luck in America?'

Her eyes were fixed on mine. I could almost feel her hatred for Harry being transferred to me. '*Luck*? It wasn't luck that made him his fortune. Davy's got a good business head on his shoulders. That's why he's made his fortune in New York. Nothing to do with luck.'

'I'm sorry,' I stammered, 'I didn't mean – it's just a turn of phrase, isn't it? I didn't mean that he didn't know what he was doing.' She stared at me. I could feel her contempt for my nervous babbling but I wasn't sure whether she really believed in it. 'He's obviously doing very well,' I let my words tumble eagerly over each other, every inch the boy trying to make amends. 'What line is he in?'

She unbent a notch. 'He owns a livery stable. But that's not all. He's started buying and selling *commodities*.' She used the English word which made me wonder whether she knew what it meant. Did she think 'commodities' was a specific type of goods? I wondered what David Thomas was trading in. And how legal it was.

'He must be quite the successful man of business these days then.'

'He is. You can see if you like.' Without waiting for an answer, she forced herself out of her rocking chair and pulled a drawer from the dresser.

'It's one of those new image-maker pictures,' she said, as she unfolded the letter. 'It's not painted – this is what the box did. This is my Davy.'

With great pride, she handed over the first photographic portrait I'd ever seen. It was a seated picture of a dark-haired man in a high-buttoned coat, a dark necktie around his white collar. He had a neat beard and moustache and deep-set eyes.

The beard and moustache were new but the eyes I had last seen looking at me in Waungilfach's yard.

Tell your uncle all right.

Harry

As I rode slowly into Newcastle Emlyn after enduring a solitary lunch (Isabel Griffiths having refused to countenance my eating in the servants' hall) my thoughts were drawn back, inexorably, to my suspicions. I could not reconcile myself to the thought that Davy might be a murderer. Everything in me protested that he could not have done such a thing; and yet... Unwelcome recollections of our last encounter were a bitter reminder that I had not known him nearly so well as I had always believed. In my mind's eye, I saw him standing over me, shouting.

'What gives you the right to ruin my life, Henry Probert-Lloyd?'

'What are you talking about?' I lurched up from the ground where his fist had put me.

'You stopping me from marrying Elizabeth and taking over Jenkins's tenancy! You're still holding on to that childish idea of yours about me being steward – you think if you can stop me marrying Elizabeth I'll have no choice!'

'*What?*'

'You've always wanted to be in charge of me. Read this, write that, learn the other. Be my steward. Marry Margaret Jones.'

His words pulled me up short. '*What?* When have I ever told you to marry Margaret?'

'In that bloody letter you wrote to Elias Jenkins! Telling him to go to the Treforgan elders and get them to force me to marry her because I'd made her pregnant!'

Perhaps it was the effect of his fist but I could make no sense of what he was saying. 'I didn't write any letter to Elias Jenkins!'

'*Don't lie to me*! Who else would write it? Who else would believe that I was the father of her bastard?'

'Why should *I* believe that? She never said you were.'

'Of course she did! And you believed her, didn't you? You believe anything that lying little hussy says.'

I stared at him, striving for a calm I did not remotely feel. 'She isn't a lying hussy, Davy. And she didn't tell me that you were the father of her child.'

He chose to hear only part of what I had said. 'Not a lying hussy? You don't know her like I do. But then you couldn't, could you? She's just a servant, isn't she?'

He was on the floor before the pain registered in my knuckles. He put a hand to the ground to push himself up, but I forced him back down with a boot on his shoulder.

'You take that back, David Thomas! You *know* she was never just a servant to me! I was in love with her.'

He took hold of my boot and wrenched it aside, throwing me off balance.

'You weren't in love with her! If you had been, you'd've fucked her like a man. But you were too prim to put your cock in her, weren't you? Didn't want to dirty yourself. Wanted to save yourself for a lady.'

I leaped at him, pushed him backwards with both hands. 'I was saving myself for my *wife*. I wanted to *marry* Margaret.'

He threw back his head and laughed without mirth. 'Marry her?'

I thrust my face at him, breath seething through my teeth. 'Why not? I was in love with her, she was in love with me—'

'Margaret Jones was never in love with you.'

He spoke the words with such assurance that they stripped me to the bone. Davy must have seen the confusion in my face for he carried on, his expression set as if he was doing something distasteful but necessary.

'Margaret Jones was in the same case as me – neither one of us was in a position to say no to you. You think I wanted to trail round after you all the time when I was a boy? You think I wouldn't've preferred to be with the other lads out here?' he motioned at the outbuildings and stables behind us.

'My mother was always pushing me to be with you. *Stick to him like glue*, she used to say, *or we'll be put out of our place. Be his friend, or we'll have no home to go to.*'

'That's not true! My father would never have put you out of Glanteifi!'

'He tried to get my mother and me out of the nursery when you were weaned – brought in some English nursery maid!'

I could not deny that, it was part of Glanteifi lore – how I had cried and cried for Mari and would not be consoled until she was reinstated in the nursery. 'But you weren't sent away – Mari was just given other duties.'

'And had to farm me out!'

We stared at each other, he choking with resentment at a childhood full of obnoxious obligation, I struggling to reconcile his words with my memories.

'After we were brought back, she said to me *We're never leaving here again – you are going to be his friend from now on. His only friend. You're going to be like a brother to him.* And that's what she did, *Harry Gwyn*, she made you into a little brother for me. You should have heard her going on about it – *Look at the little gentleman going around speaking Welsh. His father won't like that, will he?* And she made you mind your manners with all the servants in the house and the yard – made you be polite to them, say please and thank you and excuse me to them as if they were *crachach* like you. She used to laugh at the way you spoke to the maids and the grooms. She'd made you into one of us!'

Until that moment I had believed that it was my mother's Welsh blood, calling out along my veins and in my tongue, that had fed my affinity with the people who were Glanteifi's tenants. But it seemed that the truth was a good deal less romantic, that I had been led by the nose to my own most cherished opinions.

I looked about me, now, as well as I was able, at the fields and woods and meadows that I had loved so dearly as a boy. Despite my early attachment to the place, an attachment I had considered unbreakable, I had returned to my father's house infrequently in the years after Davy had left for America. I am sure my father attributed this estrangement to his handling of my association with Margaret Jones and I did not know how to disabuse him of that belief without telling him the truth – that I had no idea how I might find the peace of mind to live at Glanteifi after her disappearance.

John

Harry was waiting for me outside the main entrance to the Salutation. I saw him, sitting there on his little mare, as I came down Bridge Street.

Shit! Now he'd know I hadn't been to Schofield's. The solicitor's office was in the other direction entirely.

'Been for something to eat?' he asked.

I nodded. 'I'll just nip in and fetch Seren, then we can be off.' I just hoped he hadn't been up to the office to look for me.

Harry was quiet as we trotted out of town. I was glad, I couldn't stop thinking about that picture of David Thomas. The man in Williams's yard. The man in Sunday best who'd read Beca's note. The man who'd strangled Margaret Jones with his bare hands.

Tell your uncle all right he'd said. But what had he meant?

In the light of what I'd witnessed, I'd assumed he must've meant *all right I'll do it, I'll kill her if that's what Beca wants*. But *was* that what he'd meant? What if it meant *all right, I'll pass the message on?* What if killing Margaret had nothing to do with Beca?

Mari Thomas and Harry could believe what they liked but it still seemed to me that if Margaret Jones had told Nathaniel Howell – or Lydia Howell, rather – that David was the father of her child, then he probably was. Had Margaret threatened to go to Elias Jenkins and tell him what kind of man David Thomas was? That would've been the end of his plans to marry well and have a farm to rival William Williams's. That could be a motive.

But no. That couldn't be right, could it? Elias Jenkins knew about

David Thomas being the child's father, anyway, because of the anonymous letter.

But then it came to me. *When* did he know?

When had the anonymous letter reached Elias Jenkins – before or after Margaret had disappeared?

There was only one way to find out. I took a deep breath and clutched the reins hard to stop my hands shaking.

'That anonymous letter you asked Lydia Howell about,' I said.

Harry moved his head in my direction. 'What about it?'

'Did it arrive before or after Margaret Jones went missing?' I could feel myself placing one word after another, like a man on a circus tightrope does with his feet.

He was silent for a few moments. 'A few days after. Why?'

I hesitated. 'Because the threat of Elias Jenkins finding out about David Thomas being the father of Margaret's child might've been a motive for murder.'

Harry pulled Sara up. The sound of rushing water suddenly made me want to piss very badly. We'd passed the workhouse and were riding up the hill towards the common land on the top. On our right-hand side the road dropped away into a steep-sided little valley, covered in stunted oak trees. I could hear the little stream at the bottom. The sound of it seemed to fill my bladder and I squirmed in the saddle, waiting for Harry to speak.

'Who have you been talking to?'

I could've lied. I was a good liar, a practised one. But that wasn't going to help. We had to have this out. 'I went to see Mari Thomas. Just now.'

'You went to see *Mari*?' He didn't say *Without me*? but it was there in his voice.

'I didn't think she'd speak to you,' I blurted.

'Why not?' his voice was flat, cold. 'Why on earth would you think that Mari wouldn't speak to me?'

'I heard she blamed you for her son going to America,' I said.

'You *heard*?' I felt myself tighten with fear. I'd given myself away. It was Edward Philips who'd told me Mari blamed Harry for David emigrating. I wouldn't have known anything if I hadn't been to see him. 'And who exactly did you hear it from?'

I made myself look at him. The knowledge that he couldn't see me made me braver. 'People kept mentioning David Thomas's name, but all you'd say about him was that he couldn't be the father of Margaret's child,' I said. 'I thought I should make up my own mind.'

'Who did you *hear it from*?'

The way he asked it seemed to pull the truth out of me. 'A groom who used to work for your father. Edward Philips.'

'Old Mr Philips?' He sounded disbelieving. 'He's been retired for years – he lives in Cardigan with his niece – where did you bump into him?'

I took a deep breath. I was so far in now, there was no point stopping. 'I didn't bump into him. I went looking for him.'

'How *dare* you? I've trusted you—' He broke off, brought himself under control. 'I've put my life in your hands,' his voice was rough, as if he had something in his throat, 'and this is how you repay me? How *dare* you go around behind my back asking about me—'

'I wasn't asking about you! I was trying to find out who and what David Thomas was.'

'And what did you find out, may I ask?'

I hesitated, thinking how to put it. 'That he had a grudge against you – or his mother did, at any rate. She blames you for everything that's happened to her son. She's convinced that you wanted to force him to marry Margaret because you wouldn't marry her yourself.'

That stopped him in his tracks. 'Mari thought I should be marrying Margaret? She thought I was the father of her child?'

'Yes. According to her, as soon as your father sent you away to Oxford, David told her that you'd made Margaret pregnant.'

'But she wasn't even pregnant then!' He stopped abruptly. It didn't take a mindreader to see that he was asking himself whether that was true.

I remembered what the midwife'd said at the inquest. About when the baby was supposed to come. Margaret had disappeared at the beginning of May and her baby'd been due a week or two later. I worked backwards nine months from the middle of May, surreptitiously counting on my fingers so Harry wouldn't notice. August.

'When did you go off to Oxford?' I asked. 'The middle of September.'

So. She *had* been pregnant, then. When Harry'd been sent away to Oxford to stop his dalliance with Margaret, she'd already been carrying another man's child. I was still trying to work out what that meant when Harry pulled Sara's head round and kicked her into a canter back down the hill.

Seren turned to follow without any instructions from me. 'Where are you going?' I shouted.

He didn't even turn in the saddle. 'Go back to Mr Schofield's. He'll be expecting you, now.'

So he had been to Schofield's to find me. My guts were like jelly. I felt like I'd just made the biggest mistake of my life. 'What about tonight?' I called, kicking Seren after him.

He spurred Sara on, trying to outride me. 'It's me they want.'

True or not, I couldn't use that as an excuse, keep out of harm's way like a weanling hiding behind his mam's skirts. I pulled up to let him go. 'I'll come anyway,' I shouted after him.

If he heard me, he didn't turn.

Harry

Even as I urged Sara into something that was recklessly near a gallop, I knew I was behaving like a petulant child. But I could not help myself. I felt compelled to put as much distance as I could between me and what John had said.

Later, I would appreciate the courage it had taken to admit that he had sought out Edward Philips and Mari Thomas but, at that moment, all I could feel was the need to be nowhere near him.

As I came into Newcastle Emlyn and pulled Sara into a walk, I strained my ears into the air behind me but could hear no hoofbeats. John had not followed on my heels.

Unable to bear the thought of riding down the main street, I skirted the top of town and rode on towards Cenarth. I had no clear aim in mind, I just did not wish to be seen or forced to speak to anybody. I was scarcely able to tolerate my own company and could not abide the thought of anybody else's.

By the time the sun began to set, hunger had driven me back to the Salutation. The gnawing in my stomach had become more and more insistent, amplifying the bite of the cold air, magnifying my self-loathing. Though I had little hope that a hot meal would restore me, I gave Sara to one of the ostlers and went inside to ask whether there might be a private room where I could eat an early dinner. When my account with the hotel came to be settled, I would pay dearly for avoiding my fellow lodgers but that could not be helped. I did not have it in me, at that moment, to be civil.

Boiled mutton is not, I believe, generally recommended as a restorative but when combined with a bottle of claret, it made me feel a little more like myself. Sated, I sat back and stretched my legs towards the small grate.

Was I going to keep my rendezvous with Rebecca, as I had implied to John?

I had begun this investigation partly in order to establish to what extent, if at all, I was responsible for Margaret Jones's death. If David Thomas had killed her – whatever his motive – I had my answer. David was a creature of my family's making. He and I had been raised as brothers; I could not disavow an obligation to bring his crimes to light, if crimes there were.

I shivered, despite the heat of the little fire. What else might a meeting with Rebecca uncover that might better be left undisturbed?

At half past six, as I had arranged, one of the Salutation's stableboys came to tell me that Sara was saddled and waiting and I went out into the chill of the yard.

A boy handed me the reins. 'Has John Davies been for the other Glanteifi mare?' I asked.

'No, sir.'

So. He was not coming. At least now I knew.

I walked Sara quietly out onto the street, hoping that my own apprehensiveness would not communicate itself to her and make her skittish. As a lantern would not materially help me, I was relying on the little mare's sight and my knowledge of the road to guide us. I was almost truly blind once night fell.

While Sara picked her way along the silent road, I kept nerves at bay by considering the ease with which we could have remained ignorant of Beca's recruitment of Margaret. I might dislike John's tendency to go behind my back but, had he not taken it upon himself to go and question Matthew Evans, Rebecca's plan – and David Thomas's role in it, whatever that might prove to have been – was unlikely ever to have come to light.

Given the speed with which John had received the summons to tonight's meeting, Evans must have gone straight from their encounter at the church to his Rebecca confederates. Or had he simply ridden to confer with Isaac Morgan, alone? Lydia Howell had trusted Morgan as a moderating influence but he seemed, at best, to have had divided loyalties. Had he been the instigator of the plan Evans had unwittingly revealed?

Sara and I made our quiet way over the Ceri bridge, up the hill and past Glanteifi's drive. I thought of my father sitting in his study and wondered whether things might be different between us in the future. Past the forge, down the steep hill to the looming white of Nathaniel Howell's little chapel. Next to it, sluicegates to the mill-race closed, the cascade of the little stream was tumbling freely at the side of the silent wheel, the sound of falling water loud in the darkness.

I had not come this way since the day Margaret's remains had been found, and I felt a chill of apprehension. Who was waiting for me at the bottom of the path that had taken us to her makeshift grave?

A great, white shape suddenly swooped through my side-sight and a blood-freezing cry turned my bowels to ice. I let out a quiet oath and took a firmer hold on reins I had almost dropped in an instant of sheer terror. A screech owl. Though I had used to love standing at the rickyard gate watching their pale forms hunting for voles in the twilit field behind the stableyard, once night fell, the owls seemed to take on a different, more sinister form. No wonder old folk regarded them as birds of death; darkness gives a morbid significance to everything.

I was just beginning to recover from the sudden shock when I had another.

'Harry. I'm here.'

A low voice in front of me and to the right, beneath the hedge. John had come after all.

'Have you walked?' It was a stupid question but it seemed to break the ice between us as I heard a low laugh from John.

'Yes. Nice to know I've still got the use of my legs after all this riding around like a gent.'

There would be time for more fence-mending later but, for now, it was enough.

'Have you seen anybody?' I asked.

'No. Only been here a few minutes. If they've got any sense, they'll be waiting for us further up.'

We were keeping our voices down but, now, I lowered mine even more. 'Let's hope Twm and the boys were here before them, then, or we're done for.'

My plan to keep us safe involved the grooms and stableboys of Glanteifi, hidden – all being well – in the meadows to our left.

'Come on then,' John said. 'Let's go and see if they're waiting for us.'

As we made our way along the path, I turned my head this way and that, willing perception into the imperfect edges of my vision. Who was there? Were there eyes in the darkness, watching?

'Harry.'

I jumped at the sound of John's voice. 'What?'

'There's somebody on the path ahead.'

Try as I might, I could see nothing. 'One man or more?'

'Only one that I can see.'

'Good.'

'We're not there yet.' In a louder voice, he called, 'Good evening!'

'Good evening to you, John Davies,' came a voice. 'And to you, Henry Probert-Lloyd.'

Bring Henry Probert-Lloyd with you. Why had the letter gone to John and not to me? The question came with a nauseating surge of suspicion. No! I snuffed out the spark of nascent mistrust before it could start a holocaust in my mind. The letter had gone to John's lodgings as it was easy to put a letter under a door, or hand it to a scullion who would not think to ask who was bringing it.

'Good evening to you,' I called back, answering the voice I had not recognised. 'Who am I speaking to?'

There was no response but, with an abruptness that almost stopped the blood in my veins, figures suddenly crowded in from all directions and I felt hands on me.

I kicked out and reached into my greatcoat pocket for my father's hunting horn. A single blast would bring the men of Glanteifi to our rescue.

But, as my hand drew the horn out, a voice called, 'He's got a pistol!' and I was pulled from Sara's back. My right hand still entangled in my coat and my left flailing in the air, I was powerless to prevent myself from being dragged to the ground.

As I fell, I heard a muffled shout from John, as if somebody had a hand partially over his mouth. Then there was a horrible crack and a cry of pain.

From the other side of Sara, I heard movement. Had John been knocked to the ground?

Some other hand now pulled the hunting horn from my pocket.

'A horn. There's help waiting somewhere.' Another voice I did not recognise.

I was manhandled to my feet and held up by my lapels. 'Shout to whoever's out there that everything's fine.' His voice was harsh from fear or anger. And it came from above my head. He was taller than me by several inches. 'Tell them you don't need help.'

When I made no immediate response my captor shook me. 'Do it, or young Davies'll get a kicking.'

'All right, all right.' I took a breath and turned my head in the direction of our would-be reinforcements. 'Stay back,' I shouted. 'We're fine.'

'In the meadow, are they?' I was turned, roughly, through ninety degrees. Only the hands restraining me kept me upright against the sudden violence of the action. 'Again, then. Louder.'

I did as I was bid, cursing myself for not having foreseen this and agreed a code. The horn had seemed like such a simple solution; one blast and help would come.

'Get him on his feet.'

There was a scrabbling which I took to be John being dragged upright.

Things took shape, then, with disconcerting swiftness. Sara was led off, and we were pushed into a circle of black-faced men. As far as I could make out, each man was wearing an apron and shawl. Clearly, they had not come here to talk about what happened to Margaret.

Abruptly, we were pushed to our knees. Water struck through my trousers and ran into my boots.

Eyes fixed on the ground, I detected movement that might be feet coming to stand directly in front of us.

'John Davies and Henry Probert-Lloyd.'

Did I know that voice? It spoke again. 'Brothers, why have we brought these men here?'

Accustomed to singing together in chapel, the voices around us fell into an easy unison as soon as they began speaking.

'To tell them their sins and make them repent.'

There was something profoundly disturbing about this chorus. Individual wills had been subsumed into something collective, something less than reasoningly human.

'And what are their sins?'

Feet moved a step forward to our right and a thud on the ground indicated that a hefty staff had been brought smartly down. I felt a gut-loosening wrench of panic at the thought that every man might be carrying a similar stave.

'Henry Probert-Lloyd. Guilty of the sin of fornication,' a voice intoned.

I knew there was nothing to be gained by protesting. Nothing but blows and scorn.

The staff came down again. 'Guilty of refusing to acknowledge fatherhood of his own child.'

Was it Matthew Evans's voice? I was almost certain of it.

A third time the staff embedded itself wetly in the ground. 'Guilty of refusing help to the mother of his child.'

That cut me close. Though help had not been sought, I should have been man enough to offer it.

'Guilty of trying to blame Rebecca for the *accidental death* of Margaret Jones while she was trying to bury his own child.'

A picture appeared in my head at these last words: Margaret kneeling in the rain, scrabbling frantically at the earth, a swaddled bundle lying next to her. Margaret, her long auburn hair slicked to her head in the downpour, reaching in to slide the bundle down beneath the roots, looking up as she heard a groaning, crashing sound. The tree's roots, tearing themselves free of their hold on the bank; the tree coming down, bringing soil and stones with it, collapsing and cascading down the slope; stones bouncing down onto the path, soil and rock and roots burying Margaret with her child. I saw it all in a terrifying heartbeat; as clearly as if I had stood there and watched.

The man I took to be their leader spoke. 'Got anything to say, have you, Henry Probert-Lloyd?' His speaking Welsh to me was not a sign of acceptance and camaraderie but of contempt. I was being addressed in familiar form, like a child or a servant.

I was acutely aware of John next to me. I had promised him he would be safe, yet he was already wounded and in danger of further violence. However, though I was well aware that any denial on my part would provoke our captors, I could not bring myself to confess to things I had not done.

'I should have done more for Margaret Jones,' I said, keeping my eyes submissively on the ground. 'Though the child was not mine and I am not guilty of fornication,' I was forced to raise my voice as the outrage around me began, 'I should have recognised my responsibilities and provided for her.'

'You dare to deny a father's name to this child, still?' the leader asked, his voice full of scorn.

Unwise or not, I had to stand up. I would rather bear their blows than kneel there in the mud while they looked down on me. But, though I managed to stumble to my feet, I had not straightened up before I was gripped by both elbows and had my feet kicked from under me. I was borne to the ground once more, this time face down.

I turned my head so that my cheek met the mud rather than my nose and mouth.

'Hold him there,' I heard the leader's voice behind me. The smell of mud and water and wet stones filled my nostrils. I could hear a trickling through the earth as my ear was forced down into it. In seconds I was soaked through to my skin.

'John Davies,' a voice said, and feet moved forward. 'Guilty of being a magistrates' informant.'

I flinched as a heavy stick slammed into the ground inches from my face. *What?* Did they think we were investigating at the magistrates' behest? In other circumstances it might almost have been amusing.

'John Davies.' Thud. 'Guilty of conspiring with Henry Probert-Lloyd to say that Margaret Jones was murdered by persons connected with Rebecca.'

I remembered John's response when I had warned him that the magistrates might not like his working with me. *I shall just have to blame you, shan't I?* He had been blithe, certain that he would not be blamed for my annexing his services.

I tried to force myself to my feet. 'You can't blame him—'

A foot was placed, very deliberately, on the side of my head and pressed down so that my ear squelched into the mud and my nose filled with water. 'Keep. Your. Mouth. Shut.'

John

'Anything to say, John Davies?'

I was afraid to speak. Afraid I'd choke on my own vomit.

'Guilty, then.' The same voice.

'No.' A croak. But he'd heard.

'No? Not an informant? Or are you saying you and Henry Probert-Lloyd *didn't* invent a plan Beca was supposed to have made up with Margaret Jones?

'Misunderstanding,' I managed.

'Oh! *Misunderstanding* is it?' It was Matt Evans, Tregorlais. He was enjoying this. Like a cat with a mouse. Bastard.

'So you *weren't* accusing Rebecca of making a plan with Margaret Jones then killing her because of it?'

There *must* have been a plan. I could see the killer in my head. Hear him. *All you had to do was one thing. One simple thing. You said you'd do it. You said you* had *done it. But you were lying, weren't you? Lying!*

I couldn't think straight. My heart was beating too hard and fast. *Shit*. Run. Can't.

Are they going to kill us?

Shit!

'Were you?'

Was I what? What was the question?

'Yes! No – I don't know!'

I could feel tears. Did *not* want to cry.

I didn't want to die, either. Were they going to kill us?

'Confused is it?' Him. Not Matt Tregorlais. The leader. 'Telling lies

397

does that to you. Makes you confused. You don't know what's true anymore.'

A sudden blow between my shoulder blades. I fell forward. Put my hands out just in time to save my face. A boot came down on my back. Pinning me. Pushing me down till I was lying in the mud, like Harry.

'Well, listen, and I'll tell you the truth,' the leader's voice said.

'Rebecca did *not* ask women to do her work for her. Margaret Jones had *nothing* to do with Rebecca and her *death* had nothing to do with Rebecca. It was a judgement on her. She'd done away with her child in secret, as she thought. But God Almighty sees all. And, because of His righteousness, He buried her as she had thought to bury her sin.'

I knew he was lying. But I wanted it to be the truth. With my whole being, I *wanted* it to be the truth.

But I knew it wasn't. I could see him. Knee in her back. Hands round her throat.

After you saw Howell, you were going to go to Probert-Lloyd, weren't you? You were going to tell him – save your own miserable skin…

If there wasn't a plan, what had Davy Thomas thought Margaret'd been going to tell the magistrates?

'Do you understand, John Davies? Do you understand what the truth is now?'

My face was in the mud. I couldn't speak. But I made a noise. 'Good. Right.' His tone changed. He wasn't talking to me anymore. 'Bring them up.'

The boot left my back. I didn't move. What now? A kick in my side. 'On your feet.'

I did as I was told. Water trickled down under my clothes.

Shrivelled my balls.

I thought my legs wouldn't hold me up. They felt like they had on Bristol docks. Not mine to control.

'Move.' A shove in the back showed me which way. I staggered forward and my legs carried me. Just.

A gust of wind. Chill. I shivered, clamped my jaw shut.

'Up there.' Another push in the back. Off the track, up into the trees.

I couldn't see where I was going. Just followed the boots of the man in front of me. Harry was somewhere ahead. His sight was much worse in the dark. Did they know he was blind?

I fell, slipped, got dragged back to my feet.

'I told him we should've brought a light,' somebody muttered.

Him. The leader. I didn't know who he was. They all looked the same. Black faces, shawls and aprons. They'd've looked like fools in daylight. In the dark they were terrifying. The man in front of me stopped. I put a hand out to stop myself crashing into him and he turned, knocked my hand away as if I'd infect him with something.

'Bring them here.'

I was shoved over to my right. Again, I put my hand out to steady myself.

'Get off me, magistrate's boy!'

I stumbled, got pushed upright again.

Something was shoved at me. 'Take it.'

A spade.

'Dig. Both of you.'

Neither of us moved fast enough for them. I got a shove in the back.

'Go on! Dig.'

I heard the sound of a spade being dropped. Then Harry said, 'I'm not digging my own grave.'

'Who said grave? You came here looking for the truth. We're going to show you the truth.'

A shove in the back almost sent me onto my face. 'Dig!'

I saw no help for it. I shoved the spade into the ground and pushed. The earth was soft and easy to shift. Just as well, I was shaking so much I could barely keep a grip on the handle.

'And you.'

Harry's spade went into the ground too.

A thought came to me. Could I swing the spade at somebody's head? No, they'd hit back. I could almost feel the blows from those sticks they were carrying. On my back, swung against my legs. At my head. I'd had one of those already and my head was throbbing.

We dug further and further into the bank. We were in each other's way. We tripped over the earth we'd taken out. And with every spadeful I heard Harry's words. *I'm not digging my own grave.*

Blisters were filling up on my palms. The hole was deep into the bank, now. Any second, the top would start to give way.

Eventually, one of them said, 'Enough.'

I dropped my spade, felt about on my left palm. Two of the blisters were broken and there was a sticky wetness. Like blood.

'*This* is the truth,' the leader's voice said. 'This is where Margaret Jones tried to bury her child. And this is where God saw fit to bury *her* and take *her* life. The jury brought in an honest verdict. Accidental death. This was her grave.'

My heart was galloping in my chest. But I couldn't run. I wouldn't get more than two steps.

The open blisters on my palm were stinging with sweat-salt. With all that digging I wasn't cold any more.

'Come forward.'

My heart kicked in my chest and I looked around as the leader spoke but he wasn't talking to me and Harry. One of his men stepped forward and hands pulled away from the hole we'd dug. Me to one side, Harry to the other.

'Spit in the grave,' the leader said. 'Then swear, "The inquest verdict was true".'

The man spat and said the words.

'Now you.' Another man came forward and did the same.

Then another. And another. One by one, they all spat and swore.

'Now you, Henry Probert-Lloyd.' A hand in the back pushed Harry forward. He took a step towards the hole to stop himself falling over but then he just stood there.

'Spit in the grave and say the words.'

'No.'

'If you swear, you can go. If you don't, we'll tie you up and leave you in the hole. Margaret Jones found out that digging in these banks makes them come down pretty easy. You might be lucky, or the roof might come down and bury you. Spit in the grave and swear that the inquest verdict was true. Then you can go.'

'No.'

He turned. 'John Davies.'

Hands pushed me forward. I couldn't swear. Not because it wasn't true. I didn't care about that. It was Harry. I couldn't have him thinking I was a coward.

I didn't dare to open my mouth. Wasn't sure what would come out.

So I shook my head.

'Spit. Swear!'

I shook my head again. I could almost feel their sticks on my back, feel them beating me to the ground, tying me up, throwing me in the hole. And that overhang – it wasn't safe. It'd never last till morning. It'd collapse and we'd die, drowned in earth. And nobody'd know we were there. Just like Margaret Jones. My breath caught in my chest.

'Tie them up. To each other.'

Hands grabbed us, spun me round. Next thing I knew, I was back to back with Harry. A rope went around our chests, pulled us together, arms pinned tight.

'On the ground.'

Before I could move, my feet were kicked from under me for the second time. I hit the ground, Harry with me. We fell over sideways and somebody held us down with a boot. Then I felt a rope go round the wet trouser legs of my ankles.

'Put them in.'

They shoved us into the hole. Shoulders against the back wall.

'You'd better pray the roof doesn't fall in before somebody finds you. You've been warned. It was accidental death. If you spread any more rumours, next time we'll make sure the roof collapses.'

I thought he'd turn and go then but he still had something to say.

'And if I hear any scandal about the Reverend Nathaniel Howell I'll know who to come after for it.'

Then there was just the sound of them sliding and clumping down the bank to the path.

When we couldn't hear them anymore, I felt Harry's head turn.

'I'm sorry, John.'

I didn't reply. Too afraid how my voice'd sound. My throat was tight with fear.

'You should've done what they wanted,' he said. 'Then they'd've let you go.'

Suddenly, a voice called out from down the slope. 'Mr Probert-Lloyd?'

'Twm!' Harry shouted, startling me almost out of my wits. 'Up here!'

Without lamps they couldn't see us so we kept calling out till they found where we were.

'I'm sorry, sir,' Twm panted while one of the other men cut the ropes around us, 'we crept up but when we saw how many of them there were we knew we just had to wait.'

Something fell on my head. A stone. Then another, and a trickle of earth.

'Get out!' I scrambled onto my knees, pushed myself towards Twm. 'Quickly! Get out!'

We were only just in time. I'll never forget the sound of the bank giving way, crashing down into the hole where we'd been lying. I'd heard the same sound before. When David Thomas pulled the bank down on Margaret Jones.

Harry

The following morning, John and I followed our newly established routine and met for breakfast in the Salutation's dining room.

The clothes he had worn to the rendezvous in the Alltddu would, like my own, be unfit for decent company, and I had told him to bring them with him to the hotel so that I could have them laundered at Glanteifi. Consequently, he informed me, with some mortification, he was dressed in clothes that he had assumed would never see a weekday again.

'You couldn't even call them second best. You're lucky you can't see people's pitying looks. They're thinking you've come down a long way in the world to be associating with somebody whose trousers are so baggy around the knees, there could be a pair of rabbits living in each leg and nobody'd ever know.'

I was grateful that he was capable of making light of the situation after the previous night's terrors.

'I don't know about you,' I said as we ate, 'but two things strike me about the events of last evening.' We had had no opportunity to discuss the threats and mistreatment we had endured, as Twm and the others had insisted on accompanying us all the way into town and seeing us to our respective doors. 'Firstly, they were very anxious to tell us there wasn't a plan. And, secondly, they're still desperate to pass off Margaret's death as accidental. So much so that I began to wonder whether they actually believed it.'

John's knife and fork came to rest on either side of his plate as he gave me his whole attention. '*You* don't believe that, though?'

I did not. Not rationally. And yet, I had believed for so long that Margaret must have come by her own death that a remnant of such a belief could not help but linger. John saw my hesitation.

'Harry, think about it. We had a pretty easy time of it digging last night, with those spades. But how easy d'you think it would've been to dig into the bank with your bare hands?'

Before I could reply, he supplied his own answer. 'It would've been a damn sight harder. Hard to impossible, I'd say. So where was Margaret Jones's spade? If she dug a hole big enough to bring the tree down on top of her, what was she using to do it?'

He was right. No spade, nor anything resembling any part of a spade had been found with her remains.

'So you still think Margaret fell foul of some botched plan, then? A plan that somehow ended in her death?'

'Yes! Why else would they try and shut us up? If she'd really died accidentally, why would they care?' He gave a derisive snort. 'All that "spit and swear" nonsense. Like a lie'll be true if enough people tell it.'

He seemed completely sure. It was something to hold on to when we confronted Isaac Morgan.

John

The rain kept us quiet on the ride up to Morgan's farm. There's something about the way rain falls on your head – all those little taps – that keeps you shut in on yourself. Harry'd made me go back to my lodgings for my old cap. And he'd brought an overcoat for me, from Glanteifi. I was glad of it, I can tell you.

'You see those sheep?' he asked, suddenly.

I peered into the rain. There was a flock of ragged ewes on the other side of Morgan's farm lane. 'What about them?'

'Black faces or white?'

'Black.'

'Thought so but I couldn't be sure. The sheep's head on the *ceffyl pren* that was left for me was black.'

'Doesn't prove anything.'

'I know. But still.'

I rubbed my hands together to try and dry them. The black-faced sheep might mean that Isaac Morgan was behind the *ceffyl pren*. But, then again, they might just be sheep.

We clopped over the brow of the hill and Morgan's farmyard came into view. 'Not a bad-looking place,' I told Harry. 'House is a decent size, the windows have all got glass in them and there's a couple of windows in the eaves, too.'

Harry nodded. Windows like that meant that Morgan had gone to the trouble and expense of putting boards over the kitchen to make a second storey. Might even have gone as far as raising the roofline. Not a hand-to-mouth tenant.

'And the roof's tiles, not thatch,' I told him. 'Barns and byres look well-kept too.'

'Any sign of anybody around?' Harry asked.

My mouth was open to say no when I saw a boy coming out of one of the outbuildings.

'Hey!' I called out to him. 'We're here to see Isaac Morgan – is he here?'

The boy stopped where he stood. He took in our horses and clothes, turned on his heel and went back into the shed. A few moments later a middle-aged man appeared.

'Mr Probert-Lloyd. Good day to you.' Polite. In English. I stared at his face. No sign of any lingering black streaks. Was that the voice from last night? With him speaking in English, I couldn't be sure.

'Good morning, Mr Morgan.' Harry. Just as polite but in Welsh. 'May we have a few minutes of your time?'

Isaac Morgan didn't answer straight away so Harry pushed him along. 'I'm sorry if anything about me seems odd to you. You may have heard a rumour that my sight is failing. It's quite true. I'm going blind.'

I saw Morgan's embarrassment and I realised Harry'd done it on purpose. Announcing his blindness put Morgan on the wrong foot, made him uncomfortable. Especially if he'd been leader last night. Hopefully, now, he'd be thinking about all the humiliations he'd dished out to a blind man.

'Come inside,' Morgan said. Invitation or instruction? The way he said it, it was hard to tell. He turned to the boy who was standing on the threshold of the barn, watching us. 'Don't stand there like a simpleton! Come and hold the horses.'

We followed him into the house. His wife scurried in through the door ahead of us and swung the kettle over the fire. 'You'll take some tea with us, Mr Probert-Lloyd, Mr…?'

'John Davies,' I said.

'Mr Davies – you'll have some tea?'

'Thank you, Mrs Morgan,' Harry said, 'you're very kind.' We took seats on the settle at the side of the fire.

'Go and finish your work,' Morgan snapped at his wife. 'The water'll be a few minutes yet and the gentlemen don't want you hovering.'

She went.

'I won't waste your time or ours, Mr Morgan,' Harry said. 'I expect you know why we're here?'

I hoped Morgan was pissing himself with fear that Harry'd say he was going to be up before the bench for what he'd done last night. But if he was, it didn't show. He just shook his head, eyes wary. 'No.'

'I'm looking into the murder of Margaret Jones.'

Morgan blinked. Then, as if he couldn't help it, he looked at me. He was holding something in but I couldn't've sworn as to exactly what. Shock, fear, anger?

'There wasn't a murder,' he said, eyes back on Harry. 'They said. At the inquest. Accidental death.'

And then I knew. Without a doubt. It *had* been Isaac Morgan the previous night. I could hear the words he'd used.

This is where God saw fit to bury her and take her life. The jury brought in an honest verdict. Accidental death.

Harry's tone didn't change. 'I don't believe that. I believe the jury was intimidated into bringing in that verdict.'

Morgan grunted, but his eyes never left Harry's face.

'We know there was a group of men that broke with Nathaniel Howell's Rebeccas,' Harry said.

Morgan wasn't surprised. I was watching.

'We also know that they paid a visit to Margaret Jones – to warn her off. And we know *you* were there – that you rode with that band so that you could restrain them and so that you could report back to Nathaniel Howell.'

Harry was ignoring what Matt Evans had told me about Morgan being the leader of the group. Why? Keeping the truth in reserve in case he needed to threaten Morgan with it? Or just playing a careful game?

'And we *know* that there was some kind of plan that involved Margaret Jones.'

He made a point of that 'know'. He knew Morgan had been our accuser last night, too. 'We believe that, whatever that plan was, Margaret Jones died because of it.'

Morgan moved towards the fire and nudged the kettle with his foot. As if he could bring it to the boil quicker, give us our tea and get us away. 'I don't know what you're talking about, Mr Probert-Lloyd.'

'You're saying you didn't know about the plan?'

'I didn't know about *any of it*. I don't know where you got the idea that I went out with Rebecca.'

'Nathaniel Howell told us,' Harry said. 'Or rather, *Lydia* Howell did.'

Harry was goading him. And there were no henchmen, no surrounding dark to escape into, here. Morgan's eyes flicked towards me. Ha! I thought. Not so cocky now, are you, you bastard?

'We don't want to make trouble for you,' Harry said, 'or for anybody who followed the Reverend Howell. We're only interested in whoever killed Margaret Jones.' He was dangling a carrot. *Nobody ever needs to know. Not about Lydia. Not about last night.*

Morgan stared at him, then at me. '*Nobody* killed Margaret Jones.

It was an accident. And, whatever the person calling themself Nathaniel Howell says, I don't know anything about Rebecca, either. If a person is wicked enough to deceive us all in that way, I'm surprised you believe a single word that comes out of their mouth.'

Behind Morgan, I saw a flutter of something in the open doorway. Something grey, near the floor. Mrs Morgan's apron. She was standing there, just out of sight, listening.

'Mr Morgan—'

'I've got nothing more to say,' Morgan stood up. 'You'll find nobody who'll stand in front of a magistrate and say that I rode with Rebecca. And if you bring that person back from England and she stands at an inquest and tells her lies, do you think anybody's going to believe her after what she did?'

He laid hold of the hat that he'd taken off as he came indoors and stuck it back on his head. 'I'll send my wife in to make the tea. She'll like to have news from you for a few minutes, I'm sure.'

'Mr Morgan—'

I put my hand on Harry's arm, making him look round at me, as Morgan went out of the door. 'His wife was listening,' I hissed. 'She might know something.'

Almost before I'd finished speaking, Mrs Morgan was in and scurrying towards the fireplace.

'Oh, look at the kettle boiling away there and none of you men taking any notice of it!' She swung it off the fire and, with it still on the hook, tipped its spout into the teapot. Her eyes flicked to me, then to the door. I went and peered out. Morgan was going back to the barn he'd come out of.

I turned back, I cocked my chin at her. *What have you got to tell us?*

410

'We'll have to be quick,' she said. 'He won't like it if you're here too long.' She reached for milk and cups, talking as she went. 'He's been worried ever since you went to see Stephen Parry. Our eldest girl's maid-of-all work there. I didn't want her to go, Parry's known to be very free with his fists but my husband said he'd deal with that.' She glanced at me. 'Anyway, she heard you talking to Parry. Said he was beside himself. A fire at his shop and he'd've been in the workhouse. Him and his children. He was terrified that whoever burned that *ceffyl pren* in his yard would hear that you'd been talking to him and they'd come back and finish the job.'

'Did Parry know who sent him that threatening letter?' Harry kept his voice low to match hers.

'No. But it wasn't my husband. He can read but he can't write.'

'A gang of men threatened me and Mr Davies, last night. Did your husband go out, Mrs Morgan?'

She shook her head. 'I can't say about last night. But I know he's been worrying himself into the grave about a visit from you.'

Her eyes flicked back to the still-open door. 'He can keep telling you he doesn't know anything till he hasn't got a breath in his body,' she said, urgently. 'But it's not true! He knows what happened to Margaret Jones!'

'How?' I asked. 'Did he—'

'She came here,' Mrs Morgan said, cutting off my accusation, 'to tell my husband that it was all lies – what people were saying about her. She asked him to help her.'

'And what did he do?' Harry asked.

'Sent her away with a flea in her ear. Said she might be able to charm young men who kept their sense in their trousers but she couldn't charm him.' Eyes on the door, she cut him off before he

411

could ask another question. '*Then* somebody else came here. A man.' She shook her head at a question we hadn't asked. 'I don't know his name. I'd seen him at Treforgan chapel a few times but he was just one of the young men and I didn't bother with them. Anyway, he came here one day shouting for Isaac.'

She poured the tea. Her hand was shaking. 'I was pulling weeds in the garden behind the wall out there,' she nodded at one end of the house and I remembered seeing a chest-high wall that would keep the wind and the animals out of the family's vegetables, 'and he didn't see me. Isaac was in the yard and he came as soon as he heard his name being shouted. They didn't go in the house because the children were in there – they had the chicken pox that summer – so they just stood there on the other side of the wall. I could hear every word.'

Before saying anything more, Mrs Morgan went to the door again and looked out.

'He was very angry.' She turned back to us. 'Giving my husband the blame for something.'

Her teacup rattled as she picked it up.

'He was shouting at Isaac. Said he'd gone too far. *I don't know what you said to the poor girl* he said – and those were his exact words, Mr Probert-Lloyd I remember them, clear as day – *I don't know what you said to the poor girl, but you went too far.*'

I looked over at Harry. His face was giving nothing away.

'He said that, the night before, he'd been to see Margaret Jones but she wasn't there. He'd been walking home through the Alltddu and stopped under the trees for a few minutes to shelter from the rain. *And do you know what I saw, Isaac Morgan?* he said.' Mrs Morgan's voice dropped as she realised that she'd almost been shouting. '*Do you know what I saw?*'

I could feel my heart going in my chest: run-run, run-run, run-run.

'I saw her hanging there, from a tree. Margaret Jones. Dead. You frightened her into that, Isaac Morgan he said. *You drove her to take her own life.'*

I stared at her.

'That's what happened to Margaret Jones, Mr Probert-Lloyd. My husband and his Rebeccas drove her to despair. So she killed herself. You don't know how that's been weighing on my conscience all these years. Every time the minister preached about not keeping secrets it felt like he was pointing a finger right at me!'

She was quivering. She believed that what she'd just told us was the truth and she was glad to get it off her chest. But I knew that whoever came here that day had been telling a pack of lies.

Mrs Morgan was waiting for something from Harry. 'My husband isn't a bad man, Mr Probert-Lloyd. He didn't mean for her to do away with herself. He would never do anything like that—'

'What did he say next, Mrs Morgan?' Harry asked. 'The man who came to see your husband? What did he do when he found Margaret Jones hanging there?'

Again, Mrs Morgan's eyes were on the door. I could tell she wanted to get up and look again, to check that her husband couldn't hear what she was telling us. But she stayed where she was. 'He said he cut her down and buried her, there, in the woods. In a hole under a tree.'

Harry didn't answer straight away. He looked as if he was seeing it all in his mind's eye. 'And then?' he asked, eventually. 'Did it all stop? The riding out to threaten young women?' His voice was pulled in tight.

'Oh yes. There was no more after that. But that wasn't why he'd come. Whoever he was. He wasn't here to warn my husband – he wanted something.'

'What?'

'He said he was in danger. Somebody'd seen him burying her. A boy.'

My heart had been running before. Now it started to sprint. So hard it hurt.

I've seen you boy and I'll know you again! Say nothing, boy, or I'll kill you. I'll find you and kill you!

'What boy?' Harry asked.

'He didn't know him – it was too dark to see. But the boy had seen what he was doing.'

Harry wasn't interested in the boy. 'What did this man want your husband to do, Mrs Morgan?'

'He wanted help to get away. So that, if the boy went to the magistrates, he'd be safe.'

'And did your husband help him?'

'Yes. He said he'd pay for his ticket to America.'

Harry

Mrs Morgan's account of what had happened filled me with self-loathing because, whatever Isaac Morgan and his renegade Rebeccas had done to make Margaret despair, I knew that I had done ten times worse.

As we rode away, the wind buffeting us like the shoves of a hostile crowd, I felt like a lunatic doused in cold water to bring him to his senses. The past clung to me with all the discomfort of wet clothing and I did not know which way to turn.

Was my despair obvious? I know that, when he spoke, John's voice seemed forced. 'Isaac Morgan might want to convince us there was no plan but I'll be surprised if Rachel Ellis agrees.'

Surely he could not believe we still had more to discover?

'What's to be gained in speaking to Rachel? There was no plan. Margaret killed herself.'

'No!'

I turned towards him, my gaze drawn by his vehemence, and he disappeared into the whirlpool.

'There *was* a plan! I *know* there was.'

He sounded like a boy desperate to avoid a beating. 'You put that much faith in Matthew Tregorlais's version of events?'

'More than I do in David Thomas's—'

'You never *knew* David Thomas!' My words – a roar of anguish – silenced him. What was he doing? Looking away in embarrassment? Watching me with pity? God, how I loathed not being able to see what people were thinking!

'Don't do that!' I shouted, causing Sara to throw her head up in alarm, jerking the reins in my hands. 'Don't just *stop speaking!* Dear God, I never knew what a weapon silence could be until I met you!' I shut my mouth, grinding my teeth to stop any further petulance escaping.

When he answered, John's voice was unsteady. 'I may not have known David Thomas, but I do believe there was a plan. And I believe that Margaret Jones was killed because of it.'

'She wasn't killed! She committed suicide!'

'So *David Thomas* said! You agree that it *was* him – the man who went to see Morgan?'

'He certainly went to America.'

'Yes, and all of a sudden, according to Edward Philips. From what he said, David Thomas'd never so much as *mentioned* emigrating. Then, suddenly, he was off!'

Was he waiting for me to tell him that was not true, that Davy had had a long-cherished plan to emigrate?

'I don't think the notion of Margaret Jones hanging herself fits with what we know,' he insisted.

Without meaning to, I had pulled Sara up, and Seren had stopped at her side. Though I could see little of the landscape, three counties were laid out below us and the wind that had swept over the Irish Sea and up the Vale of Teifi rushed at the slopes of Moelfryn as if to repel us.

And yet, despite the cold and the despair that had threatened to overwhelm me a minute before, John's words had sparked a tiny lick of hope.

'What do you mean it doesn't fit with what we know?'

'Well, to begin with, if she meant to take her own life, why did she

416

take all her belongings with her? Why not leave them for Rachel? She'd've known how useful they'd be to her.'

I did not want to think about Margaret packing her meagre possessions in her shawl, leaving the loft for the last time. I wanted to knock him down for his cool, analytical tone. Instead, I nudged Sara into motion once more.

'She wouldn't have wanted anybody going to look for her, stopping her,' I told him, not looking round. 'She needed to make them think she'd taken her things and wasn't coming back.'

To my left, I saw Seren throw her head up restively in the wind, causing Sara to sidestep suddenly.

'No!' I thought John must be admonishing his mare, but it soon became clear that his emphatic tone had been meant for me. 'Nobody would have gone looking for her after dark! If they were going to look, they'd've left it till daylight.'

Was that true? John certainly thought so; he was not making suggestions now, he was speaking as if from knowledge. I had not asked about his life before he had been taken in by Mr Davies at the grammar school; had he spent his early childhood sleeping in lofts, like Margaret?

'Then, think about where she was buried,' he went on. 'David Thomas said he buried her in a hole under a tree. But what if he already knew about that hole. What if he took her into the woods and killed her there because he knew he wouldn't have to dig a grave?'

I drew in a steadying breath. Though I had begun to fear that Davy might be guilty of Margaret's murder, I had not allowed myself to imagine the details of what might have taken place; John's bluntness had conjured up scenes in my mind that, try as I might, I could not un-see. 'So you think he killed her, then went to Morgan with that story about the boy because he knew that, if he said he'd been seen, Morgan would help him?'

John leaned towards me. 'What if there *was* a boy?' he said. 'Price's boy from Pant Yr Hebog. The *gwas bach* that Williams didn't believe in.'

'If there *was* a boy, if he saw what happened, he'd have told somebody, surely?'

'Not if his life was threatened! He'd've been too scared. And rightly so if he'd just seen somebody murdered!'

I took a breath, tried to separate the tangle of hope and misgiving in my mind. 'Yes. You're right. We should go over to Pant Yr Hebog, talk to Price.'

'If you don't mind me making a suggestion?' John was suddenly tentative again. Was he afraid he had gone too far? 'I think it would be a good idea to see Rachel Ellis before talking to Mr Price. I know Morgan said there wasn't a plan but I think he was lying. He lied to us about other things – said he never rode with Howell when we know for a fact that he did.'

'All right.' I urged Sara into a trot, then a canter. 'Let's go and see Rachel.'

John

It'd stopped raining before we got back to Newcastle Emlyn, thank God. It was cold enough without being wet as well. Mind you, the wind was almost as bad as the rain. The crows that always follow sheep about in the winter were getting blown ragged and the buzzards were having to flap their wings for once – no warm air for them to stretch out in and go up and up in their lazy circles.

I shrugged myself down into the coat Harry'd brought and concentrated on keeping my wits about me. I'd pushed him into going to see Rachel Ellis and I needed to make sure I didn't say anything that'd give me away.

Mind, I didn't need to worry overmuch. Harry was too taken up with his own fears to give any thought to me.

'Even if there was a plan,' he said, 'Margaret might still have killed herself. If the plan went wrong she'd have been afraid of what Rebecca would do to her. Add that to the shame of having a child with no father and it's not difficult to see why she might have fallen into despair.'

We trotted past the workhouse and I couldn't help shivering a bit. 'Let's just wait and see what Rachel's got to tell us, eh?'

I'd half expected Aaron to be there, waiting for us, but Rachel Ellis was on her own with her children.

'Aaron said you were coming. He had to go. He got the offer of some work.'

And a man like him couldn't turn down work when it was offered. Not even to protect his wife.

Rachel looked nervous but not terrified like she had at the inquest. She'd sent her children into the house, out of the way, and we were standing in the washed-out sun that was peeping out from behind the clouds.

Harry took his time. 'Before I ask you anything,' he said, 'first I must tell you something, so you don't wonder why I'm not looking you in the eye while you speak to me. I can't see you properly. I'm going blind. I can see you're there, but I can't see the expression on your face, or where exactly your eyes are.'

Rachel looked from Harry to me. She seemed less nervous now she knew he couldn't see. Which was what he'd wanted, of course.

'I don't want to waste your time,' he said. 'We know that Rebecca came to Waungilfach to see Margaret. To threaten her. What we don't know is who stayed behind that night. Who talked Margaret into getting involved with whatever Beca was planning.'

Rachel Ellis didn't reply but her eyes moved back to me again. 'We know some of the men who were there that night,' I said, 'Matt Tregorlais, Davy Thomas. Did one of them get her involved in Beca's plan? Men who rode with Beca back then have tried to stop us finding out what happened to Margaret,' I told her. 'Whatever this plan was, they don't want it coming out. They're protecting somebody.'

Rachel's eyes moved away from me to Harry and his face turned towards her, like a flower turning to the sun. 'You know something, don't you?' he asked.

Rachel shook her head. 'There was no Beca plan.'

Harry heard the edge to her voice as well as I did. 'Rachel, we know there was a plan. It's all right if you know nothing about it but we need to know who stayed on that night—'

'Nobody stayed on. Margaret had nothing to do with Beca and her plans.'

She was lying! I heard David Thomas's words again. The words he'd spoken as he killed Margaret Jones. *All you had to do was one thing. One simple thing. You said you'd do it. You said you* had *done it. But you were lying, weren't you?*

Rachel put one arm across her body, as if she wanted to fold her arms. But she needed one hand to help her speak so she just clutched her elbow instead. 'I don't know anything about that night,' she said. 'Only that they came and said things about Margaret. Things that weren't true. She didn't know what was happening to her.'

'But Matthew Tregorlais said—'

Suddenly she was shouting at me. Waving her hands. Raving almost.

I stepped backwards without thinking, almost knocked Harry over. 'I can't understand what you're saying!' I shouted, angry that she'd startled me like that.

Rachel got hold of herself, pinched her nose. 'Matthew Tregorlais can say what he likes. And he can think what he likes but he knows *nothing* about Margaret Jones,' she said. '*Nothing.*'

'And Davy Thomas?'

She shook her head at me. 'I've told you everything I know.'

'No,' Harry's voice was harsh, 'you haven't! What about Margaret and David Thomas?' Rachel stared at him like a foot-snared rabbit that sees the club coming down. 'David Thomas was the father of her child, wasn't he?'

I saw Rachel swallow, saw her hand shake as she lifted it to her face. 'I can't talk about this with you here, Mr Davies.' She turned away from me to Harry. 'This is for you, Harry Gwyn. Only you.'

421

'Then tell me! We can go into the house. John can stay out here.'
I'd never heard Harry so close to begging.

I watched Rachel's face. She was suddenly calmer, she'd made a
decision. 'Yes. All right. We can speak English so the children won't
understand.'

With the children there, she and Harry'd be chaperoned. She
wouldn't want them telling Aaron that Mami had shut them out of
the house while she was inside with a strange man.

Harry

Rachel opened the door to her cottage and stood aside for me to enter. 'Welcome to our house.'

I was thrown, we had never spoken English to each other before, but I knew why she would not speak Welsh to me: there were things that small ears should not hear.

'Thank you.' I was wretchedly conscious of the barrier that English would put between us but I was also forced to acknowledge that, from Rachel's point of view, a barrier had always been there, irrespective of language. Imagining otherwise had been part of my own self-delusion.

The children, presumably having watched their mother's encounter with the gentlemen through the window and seen her turning towards the house, were sitting quietly beneath the window, working away at something. I had the impression that they were stripping rushes but I could not be certain.

'I can make some tea.'

I did not want tea, but I knew that she would feel more at ease if she was doing something. 'Thank you.'

She began speaking as soon as she went towards the fire. 'There was a plan but it was not a plan of Beca.'

It was said quickly, as if she was afraid she would lose courage otherwise.

'Then what kind of plan was it?'

I saw her swirling the teapot, heard the old leaves being dumped in the swill-pail. 'A plan of David Thomas.'

Davy. I tried to calm the thrumming of my nerves with a deep breath. 'Please, Rachel, tell me what it was.' In Welsh, it would have felt more like a request between equals; English gave it the force of a command.

I heard her draw breath, saw her hand move upwards. 'You remember the bidding of Hepzi Jones and Tom Roberts?'

I nodded. 'Yes.' I was quite certain I would remember it to my dying day.

'David Thomas saw you with Margaret. He saw you—' she fumbled for the phrase, 'that you liked her – you know. He knew—' she stumbled again, 'he knew how it goes with men and women, always. So he came with a plan to Margaret.'

A plan. A plan of David Thomas. Somewhere inside me a gash of fear split open.

'He said to her that you will speak a lot of nonsense. He said you will believe you was in love with her. That you will say it to her. But he said to her not to listen to your nonsense because love cannot be with somebody like you and somebody like her. That she was a servant, always, and you was the squire's son.'

How many times had I tried to persuade Margaret that I did not have to be the son my father wanted? That she did not have to be a servant?

David had been right, I had spoken a lot of nonsense. He knew me so well. And he had used that knowledge against me.

I heard the sound of boiling water being poured into the teapot and swilled around to warm it. 'He told her he was—' I could feel her translating what she wanted to say in her mind, 'that he was a long time tired of being a groom, that you said he can be the steward of Glanteifi, but it is not true.' She paused again. 'He said to Margaret that he cannot be steward. Instead,' she hesitated and something in her voice told me that she was looking for confirmation that she had used the right word. She had forgotten that I could not see that she needed a nod. 'Instead,' she repeated, 'there was a plan with him.'

I waited, apprehension stealing over me like hoar frost.

'*If you give Harry a child,* he said to her, *he will look after you – he will give you a cottage and a cow and a pig.*'

I swallowed a gulletful of bile at the memory of his using exactly those words to me.

'*But I am his best friend,* he said, *and if I marry you and say I will bring up his child like my own, he will give us a farm. A good farm. And not rent. Give. Our own farm.*' She paused for a second. 'That was his plan. Margaret only had to make sure that you gave her a baby.'

I unstuck my tongue from the roof of my dry mouth. 'How do you know?'

'I heard. Remember, I was in the loft with Margaret.'

And out of sight is out of mind, as I knew only too well. I tried to order my darting thoughts. 'I know David didn't want to be steward,' I said, 'he told me that himself. But he still had ambition – he still wanted money,' I amended, lest she did not know what ambition meant. 'I don't think he would have married somebody like Margaret.'

'Not Margaret by herself. But Margaret with a good farm from you is different.'

I tried to conjure up a picture of her face from the take-it-or-leave-it tone of her voice. Was she looking at me with pity, knowing I couldn't see her?

'David Thomas wanted a farm from you. So there must be a baby. He said to Margaret that you must think it belonged to you but he will not rear any man's bastard. He said if anybody is putting a child in her it is him. But you must think it is yours.'

I swallowed. That was why he had not been surprised to find her a virgin. He had quite deliberately taken her virginity before I could. No wonder she had tried so hard to seduce me; I had to believe that her child was mine.

'She started to grow after you went away,' Rachel said, 'and David Thomas put his hand on her stomach and laughed every time he came to Waungilfach. He said to her when you come home, he is coming to you with the plan. To tell you he's willing to wash your pots for you.'

Wash your pots. Clean up your mess. I knew, then, that Rachel was telling me the truth.

'Don't think bad of Margaret,' she said, a practical sort of kindness in her voice. 'She thinks she can stop him telling you the child is his. That she can change him. Make him a good man. Stupid, she was. David Thomas wanted to take something from you. To pain you.'

To pain me. To *hurt* me.

He had certainly hurt me often, physically, when we were children but I had always put that down to his being bigger and stronger; of course I would get beaten in a fight, of course I would fall over as we bumped together in a race.

I had been an innocent in so many ways.

'But what about Elizabeth Jenkins?' I asked. 'Was David really courting her?'

'Yes. He was waiting for you to come home at Christmas but you didn't come. Without you there was no plan.'

The course of events was clear, now. In the face of my persistent absence, Davy had written, telling me that I had to come home to defend Glanteifi from my father's misguided defiance of Rebecca, hoping that his plan to become a landowner could still be rescued, believing, still, that I would accept the child as my own. And, meanwhile, he had hedged his bets with Miss Jenkins. A rented farm might not be as good as one owned outright, but it would have fitted Davy's self-conceit far better than grooming Glanteifi's horses did.

'Did Margaret know about him courting Elizabeth?' I asked.

'Yes. She asked him why he was sniffing after Elizabeth when he was promised to her.' Rachel paused. 'David Thomas said to her if she could get a farm off you, he would have to see. *It depends if it's a good farm*, he said.'

And then, on the carriage ride home from Samuel's presentation at Waungilfach, I had told him that, whoever the father of Margaret Jones's child was, it could not be me.

I had sealed her fate.

All Davy had to do in order to have Elizabeth Jenkins and her father's farm was to traduce Margaret and ruin her reputation. And it had been so easily done. Even I had believed him.

Margaret had seen no choice but to take her own life. She had hanged herself in the Alltddu and Davy had found her.

Had he gone to Waungilfach with the intention of punishing her for lying to him, for allowing him to assume that I would accept the child as mine? Perhaps that fear, in the end, was what had pushed her into self-destruction. If so, there was a bitter kind of justice in him finding her body.

'Stupid to believe him, she was.' There was resignation in Rachel's voice; this is how people are, her tone seemed to say, they believe what they want to believe. 'But she thought it was a chance for her. A good chance.'

I could feel her looking at me and I submitted to her gaze without knowing whether it was one of judgement or compassion; it was the smallest kind of penance I could do.

'A gentleman, you are,' she said. 'You don't know what it means for a girl like Margaret to think of having a farm and a husband – not to have a fear of the workhouse.'

Although she meant it kindly, she was wrong; I had known Margaret more than well enough to know what such a prospect would mean to her. I had simply been too selfish to offer it.

'She knew you could not marry her. She had to make her own way.'

I nodded, unable to speak. Margaret had used those same words to me. *I have to make my own way in the world.*

'After you came to see her the last time, she cried. That night. And she said to me that she loved you. She said she tried to stop herself, because of her plan with David Thomas but she couldn't stop love. *He was such a kind boy* she said to me *and I made him cruel.*'

Cold fingers wrapped themselves around my heart. Yes, I had been cruel.

There was one last thing I needed to know. 'Rachel, why didn't you say any of this at the inquest? The coroner asked you whether Margaret was courting and you said no. You could have said all this then.'

I heard a sigh. 'Mr Williams, it was. Before the inquest, he said to me not to say anything that will...' she searched for a word, 'upset you.'

'Upset?' I asked. 'Do you mean embarrass?'

'Yes. Embarrass.'

'And are you sure he meant me, not my father?' Again, I felt her eyes on me.

'It's the same thing, isn't it?'

But it wasn't. William Williams, having no way of knowing whether Margaret had confided the details of her parentage to Rachel, would have been desperate to keep that embarrassing revelation from emerging at the inquest and bringing my father's wrath down on his head.

Whereas he would have given no consideration at all to sparing my feelings with regard to Margaret and David Thomas.

Feelings which were now threatening to unman me entirely.

John

When he walked out of Rachel Ellis's house, Harry looked as if he didn't know where he was putting his feet. Or didn't care.

'Harry?'

He held out his hand for Sara's reins. I passed them to him and moved Seren aside so he could mount up.

He turned the mare's head and walked away from Rachel's cottage. I scrambled into the saddle and followed. What the hell had Rachel Ellis said to him?

At the road, instead of turning right and heading for Price's place, he turned left, towards Newcastle Emlyn. Or Glanteifi.

'Pant Yr Hebog is the other way.' My voice sounded too loud, too sudden.

'There's no point going to Pant Yr Hebog. She killed herself.'

'No—' I had been going to tell him what I knew. *No she didn't, David Thomas killed her*. But he interrupted me.

'Yes! She did, John! There was no Rebecca plan – just one cooked up by David Thomas. But he reneged on it and turned on her. Spread lies to ruin her reputation. And nobody would help her! Howell was fleeing to Ipswich. Morgan and his gang believed David Thomas's lies. I thought—' he stopped. 'Everybody was against her. She had no choice but the workhouse or death.'

I didn't like the way he numbered himself among the sinners. He was giving up. 'You don't *know* that!' I told him.

'I do. I knew *her*. There was no way for her to make her way in the world anymore.'

'Harry—' I put my hand on his arm, to stop him.

He pulled Sara up and looked at me with eyes that couldn't see I was there.

'I thought it would help if I could find her murderer,' he said. 'If I could find the one person who'd betrayed her more than me. But there *is* no help.' He turned away. 'I'm going home. I suggest you go back to Mr Schofield. I can do you no good.'

'No.' I said it as forcefully as I dared. 'I'm not going back to Mr Schofield's until I'm satisfied – *completely* satisfied – that we've done everything we can to find out the truth.'

'We have.' His voice had a weariness that Mari Thomas, near death as she was, hadn't had. It frightened me.

'No, we haven't! We haven't been to Price's and asked him about this boy. For all we know he could still be working there and we can ask him ourselves!' I heard myself pleading.

'There's no point.'

'There *is*, Harry – there *is* a point! You don't see it, now, but in a week, a month, a year, you'll start to have doubts. Is that really how it happened? Did I make a mistake? Should I have gone to see Price?'

I knew what I was talking about. I'd had those doubts for seven years. 'Pant Yr Hebog is only a few minutes away. What will it cost us to satisfy ourselves that we did everything – *everything we could* – to get at the truth?'

If Harry'd had all his wits about him he'd have been suspicious. I'd never pushed him like that. As it was, he just nodded. 'If that's what you want.'

It wasn't far to Price's from the Ceri valley but Harry's silence made it feel like a day's journey. The rain kept off but the air was damp and thick, the low clouds stopping you seeing far. A day to drive you into yourself.

In Price's yard, we found my former uncle in the big barn, talking to two labourers holding threshing flails. He sent them off before either Harry or I could speak. He knew why we were there.

'Mr Price,' I said, my chest tight, 'good day to you.'

He looked me in the eye without a flicker. 'Good day to you. Good day, Mr Probert-Lloyd.'

Harry nodded but said nothing. He was going to leave this to me. I took a breath. 'Mr Price, I'm John Davies from Mr Schofield's office in town – I'm working with Mr Probert-Lloyd as his assistant. You've probably heard that we've been looking into the circumstances of Margaret Jones's death, after the inquest?'

Price gave a tiny nod. 'Yes.'

'There's something we wanted to check with you.' I stopped, fixed my eyes on Price, willing him not to look at Harry. Never mind why he's not speaking, *look at me*. 'It's difficult,' I said, 'because it concerns Rebecca.'

Price's expression slipped.

'We're not interested—' I stopped. 'That's to say *Mr Probert-Lloyd* isn't interested in the activities of Rebecca for their own sake – only in so far as they have to do with Margaret Jones. He's not going to be giving names to the magistrates or pointing the finger. That's not why we're here.'

Price's gaze shifted to Harry. He wasn't comfortable with the squire's son letting a clerk speak for him. Not at all. But he couldn't very well say *Hey, Probert-Lloyd, why's your boy doing your talking for you?*

'We've spoken to Mr William Williams,' I told him. 'Several times, in fact. He's been very helpful. Held nothing back, even when it's been embarrassing to him.' I looked meaningfully at Price. *We know all about Rebecca's visits to Waungilfach.*

Price just waited. He was back in control of his face.

'One of the questions we asked Mr Williams was whether anybody'd come to the farm on the day that Margaret went missing, and he said that there was somebody who was supposed to have come to Waungilfach that day – somebody who hadn't turned up.' I took a breath. 'You sent a boy with a message. A message telling Mr Williams to come to a Rebecca gathering the following night.' I was almost bursting with the effort of willing him to speak but Price was keeping hold of himself.

'When Mr Williams didn't come to the meeting, his barn was burned down.' I stared him in the eye. 'Like I said, we're not interested in Rebecca. We're here because Mr Williams says he never got the message. That he doesn't believe a message was ever sent.'

That was as good as calling Price a liar. I thought that'd get a reaction from him but he just carried on staring at me. Did he know about Harry's sight? Was he giving me dumb insolence because he knew Harry couldn't see?

A shaft of sunlight came slanting down on us from a high shutter, setting the air in it alive with tiny specks of chaff dust. I swallowed a sudden need to cough. 'Mr Williams says that you stood there watching his barn burn and told him it was his own fault because he'd ignored the summons from Beca.' I was beginning to hate the sound of my own voice. 'He told Mr Probert-Lloyd that you swore you'd sent a messenger. And Mr Probert-Lloyd sees no reason not to believe that,' I added. 'Nobody would accuse you of being the kind of man to see a farmer's barn burned to the ground unjustly.'

'Nobody except William Williams anyway.'

The relief at hearing his voice was immense. Thank God – I'd finally got a reaction out of him! 'You did send a messenger, didn't you, Mr Price?'

Price sucked his teeth, as if he was thinking. Or perhaps he was trying to keep his mouth shut so no more words escaped.

'Mr Price,' Harry said, 'I'd be glad if you'd answer Mr Davies's question.' Hearing him speak Welsh jolted Price's mouth open.

'Yes. I sent a boy. Jac Wap.'

Jac Wap. Quick Jack. That'd been me – always quick. Quick to scurry about, quick to understand things. Well, if I'd been quicker to get away from the other servants that day, or quicker to get home in the rain, I wouldn't be standing here now. I'd believe what Harry believed – that Margaret Jones had taken her own life. That David Thomas had saved Isaac Morgan and his Beca band from any blame by burying her. But I hadn't been quick enough and I knew, for a fact, that those things weren't true.

'And what happened?' I asked. 'Didn't he go?'

Price turned to Harry. ''Course he did. Keen to help Beca, wasn't he?'

My heart started its racing again. It knew what I was about to ask and it wanted me to run away again instead. But I'd done enough running. 'What happened to the boy, Mr Price?'

'He doesn't work for me anymore if that's what you mean.'

I could hardly draw the breath into my lungs to say it, I was so nervous. 'No. He ran away, didn't he?'

Price frowned. I thought he was going to ask me how I knew but he just nodded. 'Yes.'

'Were you worried? Did you go looking for him?' In my fear that the killer would come looking for me, I'd run hard and far. I'd imagined dogs on my trail. *I'll find you boy!*

Price shook his head. 'I asked around the other farms for a few days – had anybody seen him, you know.'

'But nobody had?' He shook his head.

'What did you think'd happened to him?'

He shrugged and I wondered whether me disappearing had given him a minute's real concern.

'Ran home, I expect. Boys like him do.' Boys like him – what did that mean?

'And you've never seen him again?' I asked.

'No.'

My hands were shaking so much I was surprised Seren's bit didn't jangle. My knees were weak, too. I knew I had to say it before I fell over. 'You're looking at him now. I'm Jac Wap.'

'*You?*'

'*What?*'

Harry and Price asked their questions in the same moment. I didn't dare look at Harry so I kept my eyes on Mr Price. I dropped Seren's reins. With one hand I took my spectacles off. With the other I brushed my hair over my forehead to bring to mind my ragged, eleven-year-old's fringe. Price peered at me, his face full of doubt. Seven years is a long time and I'd only been on the farm a few months when I ran away.

'You got me from the hiring fair in Newcastle Emlyn,' I said, desperate to convince him. 'My father was with me. We'd come down from Cynwyl Elfed. My father told you not to leave me in charge of any dogs,' I said, pushing him into certainty, 'because I'd been badly bitten once, and I was afraid of them.'

Price stared at me. 'Good God, it is you! How in Heaven's name did you come to be a solicitor's clerk?'

I wasn't going to stand there and tell him the story of my life. It was enough that he'd confirmed that I was the *gwas bach* with the message. The missing boy.

'Thank you, Mr Price.' Harry said.

Price looked at him and suddenly remembered his manners. Stammered out an invitation to come into the house but Harry declined, politely. 'Mr Davies and I have a great deal to discuss,' he said, 'and I'd rather not delay.'

In other words he wanted to tell me exactly what he thought of me and he didn't want to put off the shouting until after he'd drunk a cup of tea in Price's kitchen.

We mounted up and left Price on his yard, watching us go.

Harry didn't head for home. At the crossroads, instead of turning down the hill towards Treforgan, he rode straight over, into the little Gwenffrwd valley. And he said nothing for a good half a mile. Not a word. Could he tell that I kept glancing over at him? Probably. But his expression didn't change.

In the end, he pulled up outside Brongwyn church. And he spoke just two words.

'Tell me.'

John

For weeks after the gatebreaking I'd seen in Cwmduad I couldn't think of anything but Beca. Of going out after dark, face blacked. Of marching with an axe on my shoulder.

With all my heart, I wanted to be a part of it. Not to be just a *gwas bach*, doing what I was told. I wanted to be like my father. Because I'd convinced myself that he'd been there, he'd been part of that band who'd dared say 'enough'. And I wanted the chance to do that as well.

So when Uncle Price had come to me and said, 'You want to help Beca, don't you?' I'd felt a stab of that same terrified excitement that'd woken me in the loft in Cwmduad all those weeks before.

'Yes, Uncle!' I'm willing to bet he'd never seen me so eager to do anything for him.

'There's a letter I want you to take.'

Did he see the disappointment on my face? He must've because he turned stern, then. 'It's important, this letter. You have to give it to Mr Williams at Waungilfach. And make sure you put it in his hand. Only his. Don't give it to a servant.'

All the rest of the day that letter was like a hot stone in my pocket. I couldn't think of anything else. What if I lost it? What if the wind blew it out of my hands? What if somebody stole it from me?

I was desperate to get off, get to Waungilfach and give the letter to this Mr Williams and be rid of it. But I couldn't. Every time I saw a chance to go, one of the other servants wanted me.

Fetch this. Find that. Move the other.

I've got a job to do for Uncle, I kept telling them. But they didn't care. It was always, *Well you can do this first.*

All day, I was looking out in case Uncle Price saw me and asked me if I'd delivered the letter. I couldn't tell him no or I'd get a hiding. But I couldn't tell him that the other servants had stopped me going or I'd get a hiding off them for getting them into trouble. Every five minutes my hand went into my pocket to make sure the letter was still there, that I hadn't lost it without noticing. By the time I handed it over, it must've been filthy from my worried fingers.

The sun was thinking about setting and I still hadn't had a chance to go. I didn't know what to do. It was supper time soon and I was starving hungry. Would it be better to have supper and then go, or miss supper and go while there was still good light? The worry of it was churning my belly almost as badly as the hunger.

In the end, I decided to look in and see if Uncle Price was going to be at servant supper. Sometimes he was, if he wanted to check something. Most days, it was just Aunty. If he was there, I'd have to miss supper and get over to Waungilfach.

Well, in the end, he was busy. So I got my supper then I was off. *Got an errand to do for Uncle*, I said. Knew nobody'd try and keep me back then, not with Aunty standing there.

It's not far from Pant Yr Hebog to Waungilfach. Twenty minutes if you look sharp. But the sun was almost down and it was beginning to get dark.

I trotted along, letter in my hand in case it worked its way out of my pocket somehow. Looking at the heavy sky, I knew there was a storm coming. The wind was coming up and there was rain promised on the edge of it.

What light was left was stormy – a kind of yellow in the air that stained the clouds – and the hawthorn blossom glowed strangely in the hedges. The trees, all fat and towering with new leaves, were huge and dark against the dimming sky. It felt as if things were closing in on me. Ordinary things that'd bring a smile to your face in full daylight grow shadows in the dusk. And things hide in the shadows, waiting to come out. Just like fear hides in the sunlight, waiting for the dark to stalk through your mind.

The clouds that'd been piling up all day had brought night on quicker. On a sunny day it'd still have been almost full light after supper but, now, I knew I was going to be coming home without much light to guide me. And in the rain.

I shivered and trotted a bit faster.

Everything was quiet. The birds knew there was rain coming and they were roosting, hiding from it. The only thing I could hear was the sound of my boots on the ground and my own panting.

A few minutes later, I stopped, caught my breath. I had to decide whether to go down to Waungilfach by the road or take a shorter way through the Alltddu. Longer or darker?

Just then, a gust of wind blew a stray raindrop into my face. A big, fat drop. The rain that was coming was the kind that'll soak you in a minute. I didn't want to have to sleep in wet clothes so I'd just have to whistle my way through the wood. Whistle the shadows away. And find a stick.

There was nobody on the square at Treforgan as I ran down the hill. The forge fire was out and every door was shut against the rain. I felt like the only person in the world. I could see a light in the mill-house but that made me feel worse. There'd be no lights when I got back to Pant Yr Hebog. Just my dark corner in the stable loft.

I felt homesick. I wasn't thinking of Dada going out with Beca anymore. I was thinking of Mam. Of the warmth of her. Of the way that, when she brushed my hair out of my eyes, her fingers smelled of onions and earth. Of home.

I tried to remember the men marching to the gatebreaking. To think of Beca and remember that I was working for her. I had a job to do. An important job, Uncle Price'd said.

But I wanted my mam.

Up the hill I went and into the woods. Into the almost-dark of clouds and trees over my head. Had to keep my eyes on the ground else I'd've tripped over a root or put my foot in a hole. But I hadn't found a stick to carry and every sound made me look up. That's how I saw the tree with the cave underneath. Well, not really a cave, a hole under the roots where the earth had fallen away down the slope.

I slowed down and looked at it. A black mouth under the tree. Full of shadows. What else might it be full of? I didn't want to think of that. Just wanted it to be a shelter for me if the rain really came on.

Uncle Price had said that the way through the Alltddu was a shortcut but it seemed long to me. Far too long. And it was getting darker and darker. Every time a tree creaked in the wind, fear went through me like a stab. Fear of ghosts. Fear of vagrants. Fear of what I couldn't see.

By the time I left the woods behind me and crossed Williams's rickyard, I was as jumpy as a stray cat.

It was late. I was afraid Mr Williams would've locked up for the night and I'd get a thick ear for disturbing the family. I didn't know, then, that people like the Williamses could afford lamps and candles enough to be up half the night if they wanted to.

What a relief when I went to climb over the back gate and saw a man standing there in the gloom. Leaning on the gable wall of one of the outbuildings, he was. The dairy by the scrubbed-clean look of the step.

It wasn't till years later that I understood why David Thomas had been standing there. He'd've been invisible from the house and the farmyard. I'd only seen him because I'd come the back way.

Over the gate I went, and into the rickyard.

'Good evening,' I said.

He didn't reply straight away and I thought it was because I was only a *gwas bach*. But then I wondered. I didn't know Mr Williams but I knew he was a gentleman. Perhaps he couldn't speak Welsh.

My English wasn't very good in those days but I did the best I could manage. Told him that I had a message for Mr Williams.

He held his hand out. 'Give it to me, then.' He spoke English as well.

I didn't know what to do. Uncle Price'd been very clear about this letter. *Give it to Mr Williams at Waungilfach,* he'd said. *And make sure you put it in his hand. Only his. Don't give it to a servant.*

This man wasn't dressed like a servant. But I had to be sure. I didn't want to let Beca down. And I didn't want a beating for not doing what Uncle Price said.

'Are you Mr Williams?'

He came at me, then, hand raised. 'Don't cheek me, boy! Give it to me. Now!'

What choice did I have?

I watched him read. And then I knew it was all right. This man must be Mr Williams because he was a gentleman – you could tell because he didn't move his lips when he read. Everybody I knew moved their lips, except our minister. Even I did and I was the best reader in our chapel.

He finished reading and looked up at me. 'Tell your uncle all right.'

Good. He was going to do whatever Beca wanted. I was relieved. Sure to've got the blame, I was, if he'd said no. Uncle Price would've been furious.

I nodded and climbed back over the gate. Glad to be leaving him behind. He frightened me.

I went faster on the way back but the rain came down properly before I even got to the wood. Hard, heavy rain that was going to soak me to my skin. I began to run. Down the path, looking up the slope. Looking for the cave tree.

The rain pelted the leaves, splatted onto the ground. The air was full of the noise of it. I could feel rain soaking through on my shoulders and my knees.

Then, there it was. Right above me. The cave.

Bramble thorns ripped my hands and the rain was running down my neck but, inside a minute, I was scrambling into the dark of that mouth under the tree.

A flash of lightning came as I was crawling in under the roots. Then the thunder. Almost straight away. The storm wasn't moving down the valley. It was right over me.

Lying there on my side, I was completely sheltered from the rain. I was still wet and cold, but I wasn't getting any wetter. The rain came down on the leaves in front of my face, steady and hard. Like the sound of barley pouring out of the sack into the rolling mill.

Lightning came, again and again. And every time, it was as bright as noon. Brighter. But only for a moment. Then your eyes went dark. Darker than before while they adjusted again.

I don't know how long I'd been there when a flash showed me a movement. Somebody was down below. On the path.

I stared until my eyes remembered how to see in the dark again and I could see two people. Standing under a tree. A man and a woman.

What were they doing out in this weather?

I watched them. They just huddled there doing nothing for a while. Then the rain got softer. Maybe the storm was moving after all.

After a little while, I saw the woman put a hand out from under the branches. Looking to see how hard it was still raining. She must've got the answer she wanted because they came out then. Her and the man. Started walking down the path away from Waungilfach.

Down the hill they came and I saw the woman put one hand on the man's arm. She had a little bundle in the other.

They were closer, now, and I could see it was the man I'd given the letter to. The man who must be Mr Williams. I'd thought he was saying all right to a meeting. A gatebreaking. But Beca must want to see this woman for some reason. He must be taking her to a meeting. I couldn't think what the reason might be for a woman going to a Beca meeting but that didn't matter. Beca did what Beca did.

They got nearer and I heard the woman ask, *Why won't you tell me where it is?*

Because it's a surprise, the man said.

He'd sounded English before, like any gentleman would. But, now he was speaking Welsh, he sounded like one of us. I'd never heard of a gentleman being able to speak Welsh so well.

Then I heard the woman speak again, clearer this time, because they were closer, almost directly beneath me.

Are we going to walk all the way? That was what she said. But the man didn't reply. Instead, he seemed to stumble, sort of. She let go of his arm and he was a pace or so behind her. Then, before she could turn, his hands were round her neck.

What was he doing?

I didn't know but I think I understood, even from that first moment, that something terrible was going to happen.

He pushed her forward, hands still around her neck. Then he put his knee in her back and she fell forwards. Her bundle dropped to the ground and I could see her hands pulling at his, trying to get his fingers away from her neck.

Then he spoke. He said, *No, we're not walking there.* His voice was different than before. Tighter. Harder. *There is no there. Did you think you deserved a farm of your own? Did you?*

I shivered. Cold or fear I couldn't tell you.

Why couldn't I take my eyes off them? I didn't want to see what was happening but I couldn't take my eyes off the two of them.

He shook her then, as if he was annoyed that she hadn't answered him.

No, he told her. *This is what you deserve.*

She was still trying to pull his fingers away. And she tried to kick out at him but her legs were folded back because he had her on her knees.

He pushed her further down, still talking.

This is your fault, Margaret. You've brought this on yourself. Words were just coming and coming out of him. As if he'd been waiting for her to be quiet so he could speak. *All you had to do was one thing. One simple thing. You said you'd do it. You said you* had *done it. But you were lying, weren't you?*

I wanted to look away but I couldn't. I could barely blink.

And he was still talking. Talking, talking, talking. As if he expected her to answer. As if he was angry that she was so quiet. I remember thinking that it was unfair – how could she answer? Stupid, the things you think when you're watching somebody die.

After you saw Howell, you were going to go to Probert-Lloyd, weren't you? You were going to tell him. Save your own miserable skin!

How long do you think it takes to strangle the life out of somebody?

Whatever you say, you'll be wrong. It's longer. Far, far longer.

Finally, he let her body fall to the ground and stood there, one hand in the small of his back as if he'd done nothing more out of the ordinary than clip the fleece off a ewe.

Then he squatted down. Rolled her over on her back and put a hand on her breast.

I closed my eyes then. Why? What made me watch him kill her and then shut my eyes as he made free with her body? It made no sense!

Except he wasn't making free with her, was he? He was feeling for a heartbeat. Or breath. Making sure she was dead.

Her little bundle was still on the ground where she'd dropped it. He reached over and grabbed it, shoved it under his waistcoat. Then he took her arms and pulled her up. Bent his legs, got under her and she was on his back. A grunt like lifting a heavy sack and he was upright.

I hadn't seen her belly till then. Her huge, huge belly. Now it stuck in his face, made him walk with his head to one side.

Because that's what he was doing, now. Walking. Walking with her on his back. Not back up the track. No. Up the slope. Coming up through the wet, sodden leaves, ducking under low braches. Coming towards me.

Then I understood why he'd killed her there. Because of the cave where I was lying. He was going to put her there. He was going to bring the tree down and bury her in the cave.

445

Get away!

I knew that's what I had to do. But I couldn't. My legs and arms were numb with terror.

Still, he was coming up. Getting closer. I heard him slip. Saw him almost fall on his face. But he put out a hand and saved himself. Her body slewed round to one side, almost had him over, but he shrugged her back again and kept on coming.

I could feel water dripping onto my neck from the roots over my head. Smell the wetness of the earth. Move! I told my body. *Move!*

He was so close, now, I could hear his breathing. Finally, panic and action clasped hands and I was moving. Rolling out from under the tree. Grazing my shins on the stones at the lip of the cave. I knew the pain was there but I couldn't feel it.

He swore in shock as he saw me and the sound of his voice terrified me. I tried to stand upright, lost my footing, almost fell backwards on him. With the strength of terror, I just kept my balance. Threw my trembling bones sideways, scrambled on hands and toes.

He came after me and only the weight of her body on his shoulders stopped him catching me. He slipped, she pinned him beneath her dead weight and I was gone before he could get a hand out towards me.

I've seen you boy! And I'll know you again! I heard the rage in his voice and almost pissed myself. *So say nothing or I'll kill you. I'll find you and I'll kill you!*

It must've been that same rage that gave him the power to pull a whole tree down on top of her. Even as I tumbled down the slope and spilled out onto the path, I heard the creak and groan and fall of it. It was almost more terrifying than his words.

Say nothing or I'll kill you.

Harry

All the while John was speaking, I found my mind snagging on the most mundane details: the scrubbed cleanliness of the dairy step; the hunger of a small, overworked boy; the fact that Davy had not moved his lips as he read the note meant for William Williams. But the most poignant detail, the one that seemed to have taken painful root, was the image of Margaret standing under that tree and holding out a hand to see how wet she would get if they started walking again. That little, unthinking action seemed to represent all the things that violent death had stolen from her, the ordinary acts of daily life as much as the larger events that mark a person's passage through the years.

I shifted my gaze until John's face was in my peripheral vision. 'How can you be sure it was Davy?'

'His mother showed me a portrait he'd sent her from America. One of those photographic things.'

'I see.' The hope that he might be wrong had been faint at best.

'I'm sorry, Harry.'

'Don't be. Without you, I would never have known the truth.'

The arbitrariness of John's being there, in that tree cave, had struck me very forcibly while he was speaking. Everything we had done together rested on his decision to go to Waungilfach by one way and not another: the whole concatenation of circumstances that had led from that rainy evening to his being present at Schofield's office when I called in to solicit the lawyer's help.

'If you hadn't sheltered beneath that tree,' I said, 'there would be nobody, now, who knew the truth. I would have left Isaac Morgan's house convinced that Margaret had taken her own life. That the only thing David Thomas was guilty of was trying to keep the scandal from Rebecca's door and extorting the price of a ticket to America.'

John's eyes were fixed on me, I could feel his gaze. Did he believe me?

The mew of a buzzard overhead turned my attention to the clouds. But I would never see a buzzard again. No more than I would see Margaret Jones. Though the bird might still wheel and cry in the valley while Margaret was reduced to bones, the sight of both existed now only in memory, for me; it was not only the dead that were gone from my sight.

'Why tell me now?' I asked. 'You could just have let me believe that Margaret had killed herself. I'd have let you go back to Mr Schofield with a good report and nobody need ever have been any the wiser.'

John did not reply immediately but his silence had the weight of a decision being made. His mare, impatient at this standing about, tossed her head, her bit jingling.

'Right from the beginning,' he began, 'I was determined *not* to tell you. I was terrified of you finding out. I was scared that I'd lose my job. That Mr Schofield wouldn't trust me anymore – that he'd think I was a liar and a fraud for not coming forward before. So I kept telling myself that you didn't *need* to know what I'd seen. That I didn't have to tell you.'

'And yet you have.'

He drew in a long breath. 'I thought we'd find out the truth. That you'd find out what had happened without me having to tell you. But we didn't.' He seemed to wrestle with himself, with how to express himself, perhaps. 'At the beginning, I didn't know you. But I do now.

448

And I couldn't have you believing David Thomas's lie,' he managed, finally. 'Because Margaret Jones didn't kill herself.'

'No thanks to me. I still let her down.'

'But you'd've made sure she was all right, in the end, wouldn't you? You wouldn't've just left her to go to the workhouse.' He was pleading now, wanting me to prove that I was worthy of the truth he'd given me. 'And David Thomas took that away from you. He took the chance to make amends away from you.'

That, at least, was true. Whether or not I would have done as John believed, her murder had deprived me of the opportunity.

By unspoken consent, we moved off again and, as we began to descend the steep hill towards the tiny Gwenffrwd stream, John suddenly spoke, as if he felt the need to have all his questions answered, now, before it was too late.

'Do you know why David Thomas killed her?'

'Yes.' I said no more. What Rachel Ellis had told me was nobody's business but my own.

He obviously heard the finality in my voice. 'What I don't understand,' he said, moving tactfully to more recent events, 'is why Morgan and the others were so afraid of our investigation. Afraid enough to threaten the jurors.'

I took a breath, tasting the scent of wet road stone and damp leather. 'I think Morgan must have been panicking that things were getting beyond his control, even before Margaret's death. Once Nathaniel Howell had been chased away, there was nobody to keep Morgan's group in check. It had been formed in rebellion against Howell and, with Howell gone, it became rudderless and dangerous. I think Isaac Morgan was afraid that Margaret's death would be laid firmly at his door. His group had persecuted her and he, personally, had refused to help her, leading to what he believed was her suicide. Not only that but, if her death were to be investigated, all the activities of that group would be brought to light and he'd be at risk of being gaoled or even transported if the magistrates associated him with Williams's barn being burned down. Not to mention the ridicule he'd endure if the truth about Lydia was made public. I think the fact that he paid for David Thomas's ticket shows you how desperate he was to have the whole business of Margaret tidied up out of harm's way.'

Because, if Isaac Morgan knew David Thomas at all, he must have known that if he was denied what he wanted, he would become a very dangerous enemy.

We rode on, the silence between us broken only by the liquid sound of the little, winter-full Gwenffrwd rushing to meet the Teifi. I watched it in my edge-sight, remembering it in summer, sunlit pebbles as bright as semi-precious stones beneath the shallow flow. Margaret and I had walked along this tiny road one sun-filled Sunday afternoon in July and I remembered picking a stem of red campion for her. I could still see her tucking it into her shawl with that dimpled smile of hers.

'If Lydia Howell hadn't fled to Ipswich,' John said, pulling my attention back to the present, 'none of this would've happened. If she'd still been here – as Nathaniel – Margaret would have come to you, told you everything.'

'Possibly. But you can't blame Lydia. She was afraid. Not only of being exposed, but for her life. Just as you were.'

The sudden impulse to defend Lydia was as strong as it was unexpected. Her voice – that disturbingly familiar contralto – came to mind, as did the sideways glimpses I had had of her in that Ipswich parlour and I was filled with a sensation that I would be hard put to explain.

A sensation of loss.

PART 6: AFTERWARDS

Harry

Our investigation at an end, I felt no urgent need to share what we had discovered and I allowed Mari Thomas's death and burial to come and go before I made public a version of the truth; a version that exonerated Rebecca and named David Thomas as the murderer of both Margaret and his own unborn child. I felt that his guilt should be known, even if he was safe from the hangman's noose in America. Whether I would have been so keen to name him had he still been in Cardiganshire was a question I did not allow myself to dwell on.

I also wrote a letter to Bowen, setting out the whole sorry story and asking for his discretion. As coroner for the Teifi Valley and presiding officer at the inquest into Margaret's death, however reluctant, I felt he had a right to know.

Appropriately enough, a reply arrived from his wife on the day when Margaret's bones – and those of her poor, unwanted child – were given a proper burial in the Treforgan plot. In her letter, Mrs Bowen thanked me for my consideration in writing to her husband and informed me that he had been gratified to receive the information, especially as he was unlikely to act as coroner again.

'Did you know Bowen wasn't well?' I asked my father.

'Anybody setting eyes on the man could see he wasn't well,' was his somewhat tactless response.

A week later, my father received a visitor. Although it was unusual for him to entertain at Glanteifi, I did not think too much about it until my presence was required in the library.

The visitor – introduced by my father as Pomfrey, a fellow magistrate and a friend of Bowen's – greeted me with an over-jovial demeanour that told me my father had made him aware of my failing sight. He managed to restrain himself from assuring me that my other faculties would grow to compensate for my inability to see but I sensed that it was a close-run thing.

'I'll come straight to the point,' Pomfrey said, after neglecting to do so for several minutes. 'Leighton Bowen is unwell – unlikely to recover, poor devil, according to the medical men. Which leaves this part of the world in want of a coroner. Urgently. There's just been an unexplained death over on the coast.' He hesitated. 'Point is, Bowen says we should ask you to do it. Apparently, despite –' I caught a hand waving, presumably in the direction of my deficient eyes, '– you have a talent for weaselling out the truth in these matters. Bowen says you speak perfect Welsh, as well.' From his tone, he might have been suggesting that I was fluent in Hottentot. 'So, will you do it?'

'You're asking me to take up the post of coroner for the Teifi Valley?'

'Well, that's not in the magistrates' gift, obviously. There'll have to be an election, by and by. But, *pro tem,* yes.'

I blinked. 'I presume you've discussed this with my father?'

'Indeed I have not! You're of age. Your being a barrister more than qualifies you for the role, as does Bowen's recommendation. I simply asked your father whether I could trespass on a few moments of your time.'

I inclined my head. 'I beg your pardon. I've become accustomed to being treated as if I'd lost my wits instead of my sight.'

I saw a movement that I assumed was his own bow of forgiveness and the tension in the air fell somewhat.

'I'll do it on one condition,' I said.

'And that is?'

Since the end of my investigation, I had resisted my father's attempts to pull me into the administration of the estate whilst, at the same time, failing to take the necessary steps to fit myself for practice as a solicitor. I had, in short, frittered my days away in frustrated futility. John Davies, on the other hand, had had no choice but to return to clerking and to the inquisitions of an employer whose curiosity must be satisfied without trespassing on confidences. I wondered whether he was as bored as I had been since our association had come to an end.

'It must be understood,' I said, 'that I will appoint my own coroner's officer. You see, Mr Pomfrey, it is essential that I work with somebody who understands that, though I cannot see properly, I am far from blind.'

The Unitarian Manse,
Ipswich

My dear Mr Probert-Lloyd

May I return your wishes for a prosperous and happy new year? Though eighteen hundred and fifty-one is a week old, your letter arrived only yesterday so I hope you will forgive the tardiness of the greeting.

I consider it a great kindness that you should write and give me such a detailed account of the outcome of your investigations. All the more so as I imagine it must be onerous to write using the apparatus you describe, especially as you cannot, then, read what you have written. I must confess that, often, on re-reading something I have composed, I am entirely unsatisfied with it and am forced to begin afresh.

It is kind of you, also, to permit me to ask any questions that I may have concerning your enquiries. However, I prefer not to bring those times to mind if I can help it. What is past is past and we must look to the future if we are not to run mad.

You were perceptive enough to suggest that I might miss the frank interchange that men are accustomed to engage in concerning the issues of the day and I must confess that, since Nathaniel's passing, I do, often, long for such robust conversation. I, therefore, accept your invitation to engage in epistolary exchanges of that nature with great gratitude. Perhaps being physically separated from the author of the views I will express may make them more acceptable to you simply as opinions on the government of our nation and not the opinions of a woman.

As you have been kind enough to suggest the notion, perhaps I can leave it to you to suggest the first topic of conversation?

I must confess, I am a little uneasy as to the reaction of whoever will read my words to you but I must trust that you will choose your lector with care for their opinion of you, not to mention the opinion they may form of your humble correspondent,

Lydia Howell.

The Rebecca Riots in *None So Blind*

In an early chapter of *None So Blind*, Harry balks at trying to explain the Rebecca Riots to Gus and simply allows him to think of them as criminal acts of tollgate destruction. But the causes of the Rebecca movement were a little more complicated than that – so why didn't I get Harry to explain?

I could have persuaded him to talk about the plight of tenant framers – how, after the Napoleonic wars, incomes had fallen while costs rose, leaving many near destitution. I could have allowed him to explain the Byzantine system of tithes, county rates, parish rates and church rates which farmers were subject to and which left little money for basics like tea and soap. But that wouldn't have worked, in terms of narrative, because a) living through the 1840s, Gus would have known the basics already, and b) it's unlikely that he would have been interested in the bits he didn't know.

In West Wales as in London, the assumption held sway that, in matters of the law, those of lower social class would appear as the defendant while it was the right and duty of those higher up the social scale to sit in judgement on them. But, for Welsh farmers, its effect was more corrosive as the presiding magistrate might very well have an interest in the case he was trying and the resulting harsh judgements gave the people of West Wales more to feel aggrieved over than their metropolitan counterparts.

And, as in matters of law, so in religion. Nonconformity was prevalent in west Wales and created tensions along sectarian/class lines. Eighty per cent of the Cardiganshire population attended

Nonconformist chapels but they were, nevertheless, still obliged to contribute to the upkeep of the Anglican church and its ministers via the tithe and the parish rate.

Harry and Gus would have agreed on one thing, however. The much-vaunted electoral reforms of 1832 hadn't changed the lives of tenant farmers as much as the reformers might have hoped. Granted, some of the more successful tenants now qualified for the vote, but they could only vote for the candidates who presented themselves and the political system – certainly in West Wales – was still heavily biased towards the Landed Interest. No wonder the farmers felt that direct action was the only way in which their voices would be heard.

Initially, Gus asks whether the riots were about bread and I could, plausibly, have had Harry reply, 'No, potatoes.' Gus might have accused him of being facetious but, actually, the humble potato was partly responsible for the desperate situation that lay behind the riots. In contrast to contemporary west Wales, which finds itself being stripped of its young people by a combination of poor employment prospects and a shortage of affordable housing, the early nineteenth century saw a steep rise in population. As in Ireland, people resorted to potatoes instead of bread as a staple carbohydrate because a family living on potatoes only needs a quarter of the acreage that it would take to support them if they were relying on grain for bread.

So, the available land could support more people but, inevitably, more people quickly resulted in an increasing pressure on other resources. At one end of the agricultural spectrum, prosperous farmers could take on a second tenancy, depriving another family of a living and forcing young people to wait well into their twenties to marry; while, at the less prosperous end, labourers and their families eked out a meagre living on ever more marginal common land, and an unlucky few were starved into the workhouse. These imbalances caused resentment between neighbours and outraged Rebecca.

What Gus might have asked, if he was the kind of person to scoff less and wonder more, is why tollgates had suddenly become the focus for mass action. It wasn't as if they were new – the turnpike trusts that had made themselves responsible for improving and maintaining west Wales's roads had been in place for decades.

The answer is Thomas Bullin.

Bullin was a 'toll farmer' – a species of person who bought the right to collect tolls on turnpike roads – and had secured collection rights on almost every trust whose gates were attacked by Rebecca. Bullin was a gift from the gods to the gentlemen trustees. He took the burden of day-to-day responsibility from them and did so at very handsome rents as he bid far higher than anybody else for the privilege of separating the farmers and carriage owners of west Wales from their money. But Bullin demanded something from the trustees in return. In order to recoup his initial investment, he persuaded them to let him increase the number of tollgates at key points. It was one of those new gates, at Efailwen in the foothills of Pembrokeshire's Preseli hills, that was Rebecca's first target.

Put in place just as the lime-carting season was about to begin in May 1839, the new Efailwen gate enraged the local farmers and, within a week, it was pulled down to the accompaniment of all the carnivalesque elements that came to define Rebecca: men with their faces blacked, many dressed as women, riding out after dark to the accompaniment of much noise from makeshift instruments and the discharge of guns, to conduct a mock trial of the offending tollgate, followed by its complete, almost ritual, demolition.

Lime carting gets only a passing mention, from John, in *None So Blind* (though it forms a significant strand in the next book in the series) and it requires some explanation.

The soils of Cardiganshire and northern Pembrokeshire tend to be acidic and benefit from treatment with alkaline slaked lime to redress the balance and promote crop growth. Lime was carted northwards from the rim of the Pembrokeshire coalfield and westwards to the coast, where it was shipped to numerous coves with beachside lime kilns which turned raw limestone into quicklime. Farmers would take their carts to the kilns and bring back the quicklime to slake and spread on their fields. And, of course, there was a toll on lime carts; their narrow wheels and heavy load were very damaging to the roads. As John points out, the combined price of lime and tolls meant that the Efailwen farmers were caught in an age-old farmers' bind: penniless now if they did pay out, penniless later if they didn't.

Once the lime cart-catching Efailwen gate had been removed, along with certain others in the immediate vicinity, there were no more actions in 1839 but 'Rebecca' was now irrevocably linked with the destruction of tollgates. According to folklore, the name Rebecca was adopted by a cottager called Thomas Rees. Known locally as Twm Carnabwth, Rees was a Nonconformist lay preacher and a prize fighter who persuaded his neighbours that they need not put up with Thomas Bullin's new gate.

Why Rebecca? The romantic version is that when Twm Carnabwth was looking for a womanly disguise for his nocturnal sorties, the only garment large enough was the nightdress of a big, stout widow called Rebecca. However, historians have examined the parish registers for the period and looked in vain for any woman of that name amongst Twm's neighbours.

Given the nineteenth century farmer's Nonconformist fondness for using the Bible to guide his every step, the more likely explanation, and the one Harry gives Gus, is that the name was suggested by a verse in the book of Genesis: 'And they blessed Rebekah, and said unto her, Thou art our sister, be thou the mother of thousands of millions, and let thy seed possess the gate of those which hate them.'

When the second outbreak of rioting began in November 1842, at St Clears, a dozen miles from Efailwen (also caused by Thomas Bullin's erection of a new gate) the precedent had been set and the name Rebecca was immediately appropriated. And, this time, 'the Lady' as Rebecca was sometimes known, began a campaign that did not stop at the destruction of a local gate or two. Unchecked by an overall leader, the riots quickly spread like a contagion in all directions and, by the time the actions finally came to an end almost a year later, outbreaks had extended all the way from Rhayader in the north, to the Glamorgan coalfield in the south. Rebecca-ism represented a colossal act of civil disobedience – the most significant rebellion on Welsh soil since Owain Glyndwr's uprising more than four hundred years earlier.

And, as Harry points out to Gus, it did not go unnoticed in the halls of Westminster. Fearing that the agitation would be taken up by the miners, iron workers and Chartist agitators in the south Wales valleys (potentially sparking a conflagration that might end in a French-style revolution) the magistrates and the government moved to quell the uprising as swiftly as they could; only to find that they were powerless. Despite drafting in Metropolitan police officers, a troop of the Fourth Light Dragoons, the yeomanry and armed marines, only one Rebeccaite action – a well-advertised daytime gathering in the centre of Carmarthen that turned into an attack on the workhouse – was successfully suppressed. On all other occasions, the rioters had been and gone before the forces ever got word that they were abroad.

The march on Carmarthen is a good illustration of why Harry was unhappy with the label 'tollgate riots'. Of the 530 documented attacks carried out by Rebecca-ites, only about half were on tollgates. And it's the nature of at least some of the remainder that provided me with the idea that lies at the heart of *None So Blind*.

As far as I know, there were no Rebecca bands intent on controlling the behaviour of young women but the prevailing social attitudes at the time mean that it's not an implausible idea. Though many of the non-tollgate attacks were on the property and persons of gentry and clergy (and were related, in one way or another, to the grievances Harry failed to explain to Gus) a good number were perpetrated against the Rebecca rioters' own neighbours. Magistrates' informers were intimidated, just as Harry and John are, and those who spoke out against Rebecca or refused to ride with her were punished, as Williams of Waungilfach finds to his cost. Farmers who bid for second tenancies or mistreated their servants or the cottagers who lived on their farms were visited and advised to desist – again, William Williams gets a taste of this. Minor local issues were blown up into acts worthy of retribution and personal scores were settled under the banner of Rebecca. As Harry says, 'once people unaccustomed to power have felt its potency, they are apt to begin wielding it indiscriminately.'

And it's maybe these other actions that illustrate, more clearly than the tollgate riots themselves, the origins of the Rebecca movement. John, quite rightly, says that, 'Rebecca was the *ceffyl pren* by another name'; so what was the *ceffyl pren*?

Like its English equivalent the 'Skimmington ride' and the Scottish practice of 'riding the stang', the practice of carrying the *ceffyl pren* is a kind of folk justice which has been recorded since early Medieval times. However, in Harry and John's Teifi Valley, it was an article of faith that the *ceffyl pren* had been authorised, if not actually instituted, by Hywel Dda, the tenth-century king and lawmaker of Deheubarth, a kingdom more or less contiguous with modern Ceredigion, Carmarthenshire and Pembrokeshire. As such, it was felt to be the 'law of the land' in a way which parliament's law could never be, imposed on the people, as it was, without their consent.

In the 1830s the *ceffyl pren* was enjoying something of a revival in the Teifi Valley and so it probably felt natural to Twm Carnabwth that he should use it for the entirely novel idea of trying an inanimate object – a tollgate – for its transgressions against local decency. And these roots in the *ceffyl pren* must have conferred on the Rebecca movement a certain kind of folk-legitimacy, bolstering the enthusiasm with which men initially joined the riots.

As keen-eyed readers will have noticed, in *None So Blind*, Harry and John describe slightly different versions of the *ceffyl pren* and there were, in fact, still other variations throughout the region. Those visited by the *ceffyl pren* were sometimes made to ride the pole 'horse' and were paraded around the village. At other times and in other places, an effigy of the offender might be used – and subsequently burned – instead.

For anybody wanting to find out more about the Rebecca Riots, the three most comprehensive works on the subject are:

The Rebecca Riots: A Study In Agrarian Discontent by David Williams

And They Blessed Rebecca: Account of the Welsh Toll Gate Riots, 1939-

44 by Pat Molloy.

Rebecca and Her Daughters, Being a History of the Agrarian Disturbances in Wales Known As 'The Rebecca Riots' by Henry Tobit Evans and G.T. Evans

Questions for Reading Groups

In an early chapter of *None So Blind*, Harry says that 'once people unaccustomed to power have felt its potency, they are apt to begin wielding it indiscriminately.' Do you think that's true?

The tradition of the *ceffyl pren* developed over centuries before it became the highly orchestrated affair described by John. What do you think is the purpose of the rioters' cross-dressing, face-blacking and cacophonous 'rough music'?

What does *None So Blind* say about the position of women in nineteenth-century West Wales? What are the different ways in which women in the novel strive to gain and use power?

'We are a visually acute species and our social intercourse is predicated on that sense.' Do you agree with Harry? How does his experience of blindness confirm or challenge this?

The Rebecca Riots, despite being the most widespread and persistent form of civil disobedience seen in Britain in what was a riotous era, are not much celebrated in the area where they took place. Does *None So Blind* shed any light on why this might be the case?

Lydia tells Harry and John that, 'People see what they want to see.' How does this relate to any or all of the happenings in *None So Blind*?

Did the revelation about Nathaniel Howell make you re-assess his attitude to Harry and leadership of a Rebecca band?

Margaret Jones tells Harry that she has to 'make her own way' in the world. Esme Williams calls her 'a young woman who had her eye on the main chance', while Mari Thomas dismisses her as a girl who was 'always going to come to a bad end.' Does Margaret arouse your pity or your censure?

One of the drivers behind Harry's investigation is his need to know how much responsibility he bears for Margaret Jones's death. What's your verdict?

Is Davy Thomas more his mother's creation or Harry's?

If Davy had still been in Cardiganshire rather than in New York, do you think Harry would have handed him over to the magistrates?

Acknowledgements

I know it's customary to end acknowledgements with thanks to one's nearest and dearest in a 'last but not least' gesture but I'm going to buck the trend. More thanks than I can reasonably convey are due to my partner, Edwina, for all her support, love and understanding. She keeps me sane, allows me acres of space to write, think, and wool-gather and takes me on long walks. This is significant as I have no sense of direction and, left to myself, go on the same two-mile walk every day.

As every author will know, the support of one's family is crucial and I'm hugely grateful to my sons, Sam and Rob for their continuing moral support, sympathy when things in the publishing sphere looked bleak and failure, ever, to ask why I wasn't giving up. Thanks, too, to my parents, to whom this book is dedicated, for teaching me, without words, that if you want something, you have to go after it.

Friends have also offered huge moral and practical support in reading the book and making helpful suggestions. Big thanks go to Viv Kent, Jo Fawcett, Judith Lee, Aliya Whiteley, Tim Stretton and Dee Swift for being my enthusiastic first readers and helpful, honest commenters. Even greater thanks to the wonderful Eliza Graham, a busy and successful author, for heroically volunteering to copy-edit a late draft before I sent it out into the big bad world.

Without research, a historical novelist is nothing and I must thank the Wikipedia Foundation for their tireless and increasingly accurate work. People always sniff at using Wikipedia as a source but, as a point of first contact, I find it invaluable. My other great resource, not simply for this book but for the whole Teifi Valley series, is Dr Pam Fisher of Leicester University whose PhD thesis *The Politics of Sudden Death: The Office and Role of the Coroner in England and Wales, 1726-1888* I have found to be the most amazing treasure trove of information in what is otherwise a desert unless you start spending unfeasible amounts of time in archives. Any errors which have crept into the text, it goes without saying, are mine alone.

I have been tremendously fortunate in my editor. Russel D Maclean writes very different books from my own but this has not stopped him truly understanding what I am trying to do and editing with a light touch so as not to get in the way.

His insight has made me a better editor of my own work and I am truly grateful to be working with him on the series.

Finally – and this really is a case of last but not by any means least – my thanks to David Headley and Rebecca Lloyd at The Dome Press who have been full of enthusiasm for taking the Teifi Valley series on in the wake of the demise of my original publisher. It is a genuine joy to be working with independent publishers of ambition, vision and genuine commitment to their authors.